Steven Pressfield

A
MAN
AT
ARMS

Also by Steven Pressfield

FICTION

The Legend of Bagger Vance

Gates of Fire

Tides of War

Last of the Amazons

The Virtues of War

The Afghan Campaign

Killing Rommel

The Profession

The Knowledge

36 Righteous Men

NONFICTION

The War of Art

Do the Work

The Warrior Ethos

Turning Pro

The Authentic Swing

The Lion's Gate

An American Jew

Nobody Wants to Read Your Sh*t

The Artist's Journey

A
MAN
AT
ARMS

A Novel

Steven Pressfield

W. W. NORTON & COMPANY
Independent Publishers Since 1923

A Man at Arms is a work of historical fiction. Apart from true historical personages, events, and locales that figure in the narrative, all names, characters, places, and incidents are the products of the author's imagination or are used fictitiously. Any resemblance to current events or locales, or to living persons, is entirely coincidental.

For information about permission to reproduce selections from this book, write to Permissions, W. W. Norton & Company, Inc., 500 Fifth Avenue, New York, NY 10110

For information about special discounts for bulk purchases, please contact W. W. Norton Special Sales at specialsales@wwnorton.com or 800-233-4830

Manufacturing by LSC Communications, Harrisonburg
Book design by Ellen Cipriano
Production manager: Anna Oler

Library of Congress Cataloging-in-Publication Data

Names: Pressfield, Steven, author.
Title: A man at arms : a novel / Steven Pressfield.
Description: First edition. | New York : W. W. Norton & Company, [2021]
Identifiers: LCCN 2020028529 | ISBN 9780393540970 (hardcover) |
ISBN 9780393540987 (epub)
Classification: LCC PS3566.R3944 M36 2021 | DDC 813/.54—dc23
LC record available at https://lccn.loc.gov/2020028529

W. W. Norton & Company, Inc., 500 Fifth Avenue, New York, N.Y. 10110
www.wwnorton.com

W. W. Norton & Company Ltd., 15 Carlisle Street, London W1D 3BS

1 2 3 4 5 6 7 8 9 0

For Diana

Though I speak with the tongues of men and of angels,
and have not charity, I am become as sounding brass, or a
tinkling cymbal. And though I have the gift of prophecy, and
understand all mysteries, and all knowledge; and though I
have all faith, so that I could remove mountains, and have not
charity, I am nothing.

1 CORINTHIANS 13:1–2

It is one thing to study war
and another to live the warrior's life.

TELAMON OF ARCADIA,
MERCENARY OF THE PRE- AND
POST-CHRISTIAN ERA

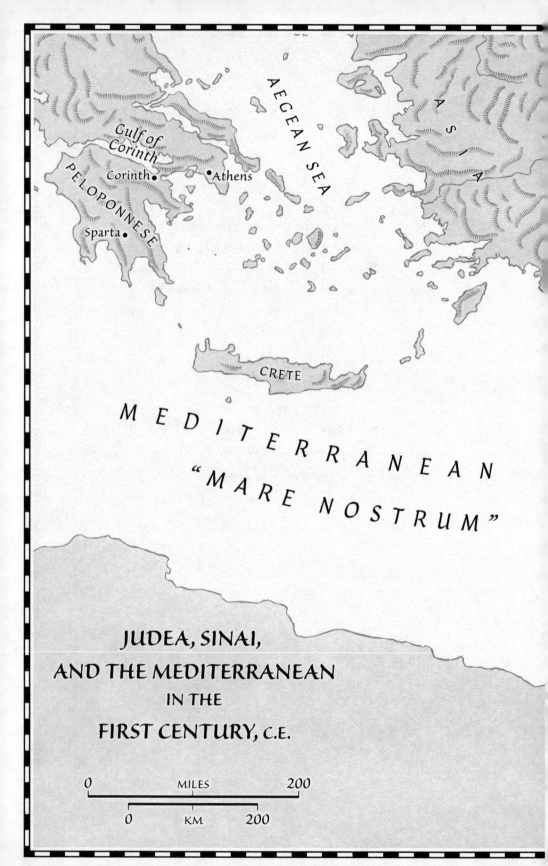

JUDEA, SINAI,

AND THE MEDITERRANEAN

IN THE

FIRST CENTURY, C.E.

0   MILES   200

0   KM   200

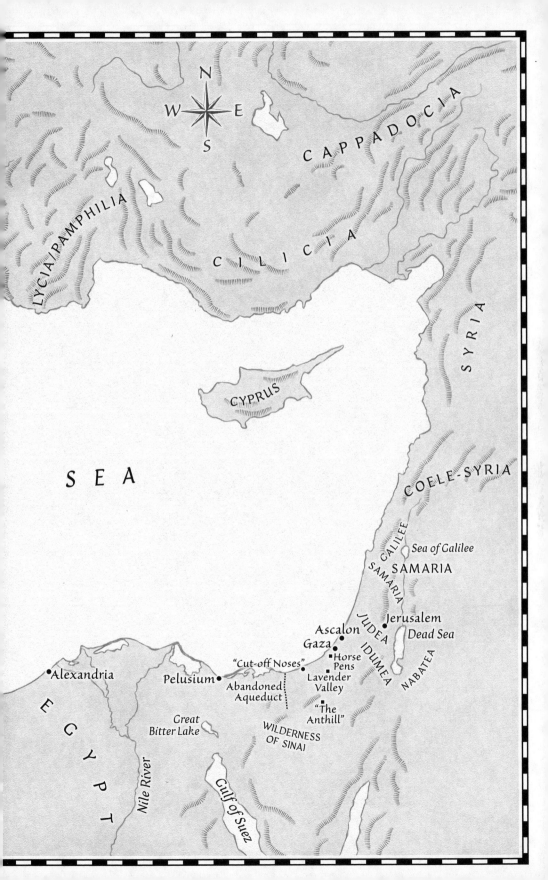

A
MAN
AT
ARMS

BOOK ONE

LEGIO X

– 1 –

A MAN AT ARMS

IN JUDEA, AT MILE EIGHTY-ONE of the Jerusalem-Damascus high-way, is a rising grade so severe and of such protraction that the pace of freight wagons and even travelers afoot grinds to a weary crawl by the time the parties approach the summit.

Here is an ambush site favored by brigands and highwaymen.

For a period during the final years of the reign of the emperor Claudius, imperial Roman cavalry made regular patrols of this point of peril. Travelers would break their journeys at the foot of the grade, awaiting sight of the dust that signalized the mounted legionaries' approach. The *equites legionis* would escort the wayfarers through the zone of danger. But when the Revolt of the Hebrew Zealots began establishing itself in earnest in the months immediately preceding the succession of the new emperor Nero, the Romans no longer ventured so far from their fortress at Jerusalem, nor elected to hazard their skins in service to the subject populace whose insurrectionist sons were murdering their compatriots in the streets.

The bandits came back.

By this time an inn had come to be founded at the foot of the grade. This establishment, constituted at first of tents only, added after a time a palisaded court, which served as a sort of redoubt or bastion. The court held a kitchen under eaves, a saddlery, a wheelwright's, and a stable master's shop, with a communal area for the penning and watering of stock, along with a few common rooms with stone sleeping floors that could be hired for the overnight. The place had not at that time even a name. It was called simply "the Foot of the Grade." It remains in use to this day. Any traveler familiar with the region will know it.

A local youth named David, son of Eli, age fourteen, unlettered but of sturdy limb and abundant ambition, chanced to find himself upon this site on a certain eve in the Hebrew month of Tishrei—the Roman October—in what would come to be called Anno Domini, the Year of Our Lord, 55. David had come out, with two friends of his village, to watch the morning's ambush.

Foregathered in the inn's court upon this evening were some dozen carts and freight wagons, mule- and horse-drawn, along with a number of foot travelers—peddlers, pilgrims, and other itinerants. Two families packing their worldly possibles, one upon a handcart, the other on a laden ass, rounded out the total. Toward midnight a final foot traveler, age about forty, tramped in from Jerusalem, accompanied by his young daughter, a mute whose years appeared to be nine or ten.

The youth David found himself struck by the child's apparition. Feral, dirty, with bare soles and hair so matted it seemed neither comb nor brush could be pulled through it, the girl seemed more a wild animal than a human being. Her father, if indeed that was the relation of the adult traveler who seemed to watch over her, constrained her by means of a leash, as filthy as the child's garment, tied about her waist. Man and girl made no attempt to insinuate themselves into the company within the court but withdrew at once to its most remote corner.

The most striking personage, however, within the enclosure that evening was a man-at-arms, trekking alone, who held himself apart from the main, exchanging speech, or even so much as the nod of a head, with no one. Upon the warrior's right forearm could be descried the faded military tattoo

LEGIO X

of a soldier, or former soldier, of the Roman Tenth Legion. The youth David found himself intrigued by this fellow at once, though hesitant to approach or even to bid the man greeting.

A legionary's enlistment, David knew, was for a term of twenty-five years. A soldier could earn an earlier discharge through being invalided or via an award for valorous service. Those who had completed their term almost always returned to their nations of origin—Spain, say, or Gaul or Germania. Few elected to remain in barren, inhospitable Judea. A colony of former legionaries had established itself at Gaza and another at Caesarea Maritima on the coast farther north, where they had received from the emperor grants of land. To encounter an unaffiliated man-at-arms, however, was extraordinary indeed. How, David wondered, did the fellow support himself? Who would hire a single infantryman? What could a man alone accomplish?

Others within the court had become as curious about the man-at-arms as had David, and in fact after an interval began to approach him, at first tentatively, then with increasing aggressiveness and importunity. The teamsters were organizing the able-bodied into a train for mutual defense, anticipating the morrow's transit of the summit.

Would the man-at-arms participate? Would he assist in confronting the highwaymen?

Would he in fact lead the company?

The man declined.

Taking up his kit, the fellow withdrew to a corner alongside the saddlery, where a cask of drinking water sat upon a bench with a gourd dipper hanging beside it on a cord of rawhide. It chanced that the girl-child crossed with her father toward this pitcher at the same time. The child drew up, plainly fearful of the warrior. But the fellow smiled and held the dipper out to her.

"You first," he spoke in Latin.

The girl, however, withdrew to the protection of her father.

The man-at-arms, reckoning that the child did not speak the occupier's tongue, addressed her a second time, now in Aramaic.

"Don't be afraid. I won't hurt you."

This time the child stepped forward and accepted the dipper. Her eyes, trepidatious yet alive with intelligence, seemed to take in the man-at-arms from sole to crown. For the mercenary's part, he studied the girl with no less penetrating consideration.

When she had drunk, the child returned the gourd to the man-at-arms. He thanked her and asked her name.

The girl made no response.

"Is the child deaf and dumb?" the man-at-arms asked her father.

"She can hear," said the man. "But cannot speak."

The father withdrew with his daughter to the recess within which the pair had originally established themselves.

The man-at-arms' initial refusal of the teamsters' overture had not deterred the company but had in fact prompted them to redouble their efforts to recruit him to their cause. The carters displayed before him their own crude weapons—spears and axes, bludgeons and cudgels—and swore mighty oaths that they would follow the man-at-arms' commands in all actions. They would fight beside him with the zeal of the desperate.

Still the fellow demurred.

It is no trifling business, he declared, to draw arms with the intent to use them. "If I may suggest, gentlemen, why not pay the bandits what they demand? The summit is but a toll station to them. Give them what they wish and pass upon your way."

"You don't understand, brother," said the captain of the teamsters. "We know these blackguards well. They will strip our party raw—and work hell upon us in the process."

The hour was growing late. Torches in hangers lit the court. The yeomen of the train pressed with passion about the man-at-arms. The youth David wriggled through the crush and took up a station in the foremost rank so as better to witness the engagement.

Upon closer inspection, the stranger appeared to be not Roman but Greek. None asked his name, nor did he offer it. His frame was sturdy, indeed muscular; he stood at slightly more than average height. The man-at-arms' years appeared to be between forty and forty-five, though to David's imagination there appeared a quality of indeterminateness to the fellow's age. Hints of gray could be seen in his hair and beard, yet his carriage and aspect were those of a man in the prime of youth. He was clad in the Roman-style *paenula* cloak, scarlet faded to brown, of water-shedding wool, which doubled as a sleeping wrap. He sat at ease upon the floor of the court, legs crossed beneath him, shoulders settled against his assemblage of kit, which itself rested upright against the outer wall of the saddler's establishment.

The man's weaponry was of legionary provenance but adapted in a way that David had never seen before. His throwing weapon was the Roman *pilum,* but cut down to a shorter, five-foot length and stripped of the heavy iron shank at its balance point so that it flew like a javelin and would not bend upon striking, as the legions' pila did intentionally, but would penetrate as deeply as the strength of the throw would allow. The ash shaft of this weapon doubled as a carrying pole, set upright now against the wall of the saddler's shop, from which the man-at-arms on the tramp suspended his rolled tent fly, ration sack, cooking kit, and so forth. Across the fellow's lap, sheathed within a cover of leather lined with sheepskin, lay a Roman *gladius,* the short fighting sword of a legionary foot soldier.

The butts of two throwing daggers could be glimpsed peeking from the braces of the man-at-arms' *caliga* boots. Lashed to his primary bundle, which clearly held all the man possessed, was a bow of extraordinary length, constructed of the Amazon science, glue-laminated of ibex horn and mountain ash, swathed for carry in a wolfskin case that held as well a sheaf of arrows, between a dozen and twenty, whose shafts appeared to be not of the weighty, salvo-range length used by the legionary *sagittarii* but of the lighter, point-blank measure employed by Syrian and Parthian horse archers.

The man-at-arms' cap was of wool with the oil left in, like those favored by seamen for their repelling qualities to rain and sea spray, but topped with the skin of a fox, complete with agate eyes and teeth of marble.

"Will you lead us?" the chief wagoneer demanded again of the man.

"I work for pay," declared the mercenary.

At the teamster's shoulder, a half dozen others of the train pressed forward. Scouts, mainly boys of the district like David, had reconnoitered the ambush site only a few minutes earlier. They reported a force of at least ten bandits barring the road, armed and waiting, clearly purposing to interdict the wagon train when it mounted to the summit in the morning.

"How much?" asked the wagon master.

The mercenary showed ten fingers twice.

"Sesterces?"

"Denarii."

A denarius is worth four sesterces. Twenty denarii is a month's pay for an armored infantryman. The teamster's profit from his entire wagonload would not make half so much.

"I admire your sense of humor, sir," declared the wagon master, though his tone indicated nothing of the sort. "Twenty denarii is twice what the bandits will demand of me."

"But a fifth only," said the mercenary, "of the toll they will exact upon the train entire."

Collective outrage greeted this. Maledictions were cast upon the man-at-arms. Teamsters cursed his arrogance. One man against ten? What warranties would the fellow make against his own flight under fire . . . or even that he would still remain present in the morning?

"A month's wages? Outrageous! I'd rather be robbed by the bandits at the summit than be extorted here by the likes of you."

"As you wish," said the man-at-arms. He tugged his cap down over his brow and settled as if for a nap.

From their corner, the girl-child and her father looked on with keen attention.

The wagon master pressed the man-at-arms one last time. "You must traverse the ambush site yourself if you wish to pass on from here. The brigands will confront you in turn. Would you not rather fight with our armed company at your back?"

The mercenary settled more snugly into his snooze.

At this the wagon master hurled his straw cap to the dirt. "Remain in this place, then! And may you roast in hell! We'll face these sons-of-whores on our own."

And, turning to his comrades, the teamster declaimed in a great voice that the times had reached a pretty pass when men-at-arms lacked the bowels to take on the scum of the highway but instead made sport of their own fellows in need.

2

ORDER

To understand the temper of the historical moment in which the events of this tale took place, one must first acquire an appreciation of the alteration—material, political, and spiritual—wrought by Roman conquest upon the Hebrew inhabitants of Judea.

The people respected the Romans for their military prowess and the ruthlessness with which they applied their power, yet hated and despised them as idolaters and agents of evil. The conquered Jews tolerated the legions and administrators of the empire in the certainty only of these invaders' fixed and inevitable overthrow. The male polity of Judea constituted at that hour, in the vividly recalled triumphs of the Maccabees and the Hasmonean dynasty, a yet-formidable fighting force, armed and seething with insurrectionist spirit, if indeed and of necessity covert.

Recall too that the foundational basis of the Hebrew faith lay in the might and invincibility of their God, the Lord of Hosts, who did not, in their view, look passively upon the affairs of His people but took a fearsome and active part in their protection and defense. Rome the lawless would find herself not merely expelled from the Holy Land but ground to dust beneath the engines of the Almighty, at the hour of His choosing and in a manner that would demonstrate to all the world the majesty of the One God.

How, for their part, did the Romans look upon the Jews? The senior commanders and administrative officers regarded the elite of Judea with a keen and deeply puzzled wariness. They did not understand them—their zeal, their piety, and the depth and passion of their identification with their role as recipients of the Laws of Heaven, of their history of suffering as a people, and their belief in their appointed destiny as purveyors of redemption for all humanity. The procurators and prefects of Rome chose to rule not directly but by proxy, appointing over the subject populace such functionaries of the Jews as could be counted upon to court the favor of the conquerors and to hold their own people in check.

As for the meaner Roman orders, these abhorred and detested the Jews. The degree of Latin arrogance toward the natives of Judea knew few bounds, even those evinced by the *miles gregarius*, the common soldier, serving in what to him was the most remote and forsaken precinct of the empire. The legionaries cursed this hellhole of a posting, peopled by such a pious, refractory, insufferable rabble. To them, the Jews were less than beasts, for at least a wild ass or even a dog could be domesticated to provide service and thus justify what few grains or scraps its earthly overlords deigned to cast before it.

In contrast, the populace of Syria, immediately to the north of Judea, had accommodated itself readily to the ways of the conquerors. The Syrians traded, they collaborated, they blended in.

The Hebrews resisted. Their necks would not bend to the Roman yoke. The Jews rejected every initiative of inclusion and spurned all offers of comity and assimilation.

The Romans, as they had done with unbroken dominion in every quarter of the empire, remade the locals' world in the image of their own.

They constructed dams and erected aqueducts. They rechanneled rivers and dredged out harbors. Roman engineers made fresh water flow to desert places from mountains hundreds of miles away. The conquerors planted strongholds and fortifications; they erected seawalls and carved out ports and anchorages.

Rome built roads. Not the two-rut tracks or caravan traces that had sufficed for centuries in this land, but stone-founded highways broad enough for two wagons to pass abreast. Roman engineers made crooked ways straight and precipitous tracks level. Grades and floodplains that had throttled trade for a thousand years were vanquished now by Roman science and shaped to accept the new throughways.

Before the Romans came, commerce in Judea, Samaria, and Idumaea was limited to what freight could be loaded onto a two-wheel oxcart or laded within a pair of panniers on the back of a camel or an ass—and to those goods that could be shipped without spoiling. Such perishables as fruits and vegetables and even certain wines and oils could be taken to market only locally, lest they waste upon the way.

Then the Romans built their roads. At once the use of heavy freight wagons became practicable. Of a sudden one encountered these every-where, not drawn as before across muck and mire at the dreary pace of oxen, but instead rolling in high form pulled by teams of mules or horses along the newly engineered thoroughfares. Vehicles with iron-rimmed wheels could make not five or six miles a day, as the old caravans, but fifteen and even twenty.

Roman roads were, before all, military highways. Their first custom-ers were the legions. Conquest and the suppression of unrest were these arteries' reason for being. A full legion of fifty-four hundred men, includ-ing cavalry and baggage train, could march from Jerusalem to Jericho in less than a day and from Damascus to Gaza in little over a week.

The Romans dug wells, not randomly across the wilderness (and a day's trek apart) as the Bedouin and the Nabatean Arabs had done for centuries, but in a surveyor's line, one every ten miles, to parallel the new highways. Roman engineers bridged dry riverbeds with spans of stone, making them passable even in the rainy months and rendering any rebel hideout vulnerable to the legions' onslaught. The Romans built cisterns to capture the winter rains. They constructed forts with magazines of sup-plies, weapons, and armaments. They bound the land with strongholds and arteries of military transport as a jailer binds a prisoner with mana-cles and chains.

Then there was Roman administration. To her armies of foot and horse were appended battalions of clerks and functionaries. Roman auditors and magistrates brought order and organization to such affairs as the collection of taxes, the compilation of censuses, and the administration of justice that had resided heretofore in the hands of local princes, religious officials, and outright desperadoes and bandits.

The Romans possessed might beyond measure. They held wealth and skill and knowledge of science and the arts. But before all these they owned order.

In the year of our youth David's birth, a detachment of legionaries was surrounded by Jewish rebels on a waterless crest south of the Jerusalem-Shechem highway. The Zealots held the high ground and were pounding the sons of Rome with salvos of sling bullets and even ten-pound stones hurled by field catapults. The Roman commander dispatched a party of a dozen to break out, fetch water, and return.

They did.

By what means, one might inquire, had this city on the Tiber brought the wide world into subjection? Here is how:

A Roman is given orders and he obeys them.

A rebel party, had it been dispatched from such position of encirclement as that in which the legionaries found themselves, would never have returned. They would have saved themselves.

Such, then, were the alterations that Roman conquest had wrought upon the landscape of Syria and Judea.

But the most revolutionary reordering was neither hewn from stone nor enforced by the sword. It was this:

Mail.

The daily post.

Before the Romans came, the Israelite in Bethlehem or the Syrian in Palmyra lived out his days dissevered from, and in fact in ignorance of, the wider world. His universe ended at the town gate or the communal well. Could he trade? Study? Venture abroad? How, when he could know no more of the world than he could see from his doorstep or make plans for the morrow no farther than the distance he could tramp today?

Rome brought the mail, and the mail brought the world.

At once one knew, even the meanest and most impoverished rustic of the region, not only of Athens and Alexandria, but could send forth missives to such places and, miraculously, hear back from them. The vintner could market his produce beyond the sea, the artisan and the smith purvey their wares wherever Roman roads and Roman couriers could reach.

Rome's motives of course were entirely self-interested. The conquerors believed their highways and waterways and the trade and postal communications that sped along them would bind their subject peoples in such shackles of order and dependence upon their overlords as would render these submissive, compliant, and incapable of rebellion. Yet, as with any world-altering innovation, consequences unintended and unforeseen soon ascended to the fore.

The mail itself, it transpired (or, more accurately, the practicability of the empire-wide transmission of new and seditious ideas), would produce the gravest threat to imperial hegemony, not only in Judea and the East but across the entire compass of Roman dominion. And this peril would proceed neither from hosts nor armies but from the pen of a single man—Saul of Tarsus, who became Paul the Apostle—who, to compound the irony, had himself been among the foremost practitioners of Roman tyranny and oppression.

But let us return for the moment to the bandits on the summit . . . and to the wagon train mounting the grade in the morning, undefended by our man-at-arms, toward its fated and fateful confrontation.

3

A CLASH AT THE NARROWS

D AVID AND HIS FRIENDS HAD climbed to the summit well before dawn. Like theatergoers searching out the choicest seats, they settled upon a rock shelf overlooking the likeliest site of conflict. This was a neck of the summit pass. The pass itself extended between stony slopes for a distance of several hundred yards.

This choke point, called by locals the Narrows, sat at the southern end, the extremity that led down toward Jerusalem.

There the bandits waited. Their numbers had become twelve. Four held horses in a reserve position about fifty feet up the eastern slope. Another six lined the western flank of the pass, hard by the road and about twenty paces above it. They were cooking flatbread loaves for breakfast, with wine and olive oil. The brigands were armed, each after his fashion, with the Damascene-style saber, the shepherd's bow, and the double-headed Syrian lance. Two squatted on their haunches in the roadway itself, laughing over some remark. None betrayed fear or apprehension.

This was a day's work to them.

The boys, David and his friends, recognized by sight several of the brigands. These were goatherds and orchard men of the region, recruited and remunerated on an occasional basis by local villains—hardened cases who had rowed in the galleys or served time in Roman or Jewish prisons.

Now came the wagon train.

The column ascended with such plodding exertion, from the steepness of the grade (and no doubt the dread of what awaited it upon the summit), that the turn of the freight wagons' wheels and the stamping of its draft animals' hooves raised dust barely to the teamsters' ankles. Behind and between the wagons shambled the foot travelers, trekkers, and pilgrims. Before the train and flanking it on both sides scampered another dozen onlookers, children and youths of the nearby villages.

The pair of bandits hunkering on their haunches now stood up. At a sign from one of the flatbread brigands, they advanced several steps toward the approaching train and took up a position blocking the roadway. Three of their upslope fellows likewise descended, though keeping a few feet above the Narrows and to the side. None yet drew their weapons.

The first freight wagon and its two immediate successors crested the grade and advanced onto the flat stretch of the pass at the summit. The wagoneers did not sit on their benches but strode afoot, each at the head of his team and drawing its leader by a halter, upon the left.

"We are unarmed!" called the wagon master toward the two brigands blocking the roadway. "We are prepared to submit!"

One of the flatbread bandits, apparently the leader of the group entire, motioned the pair of haunch-sitters farther forward. These now hefted their pikes and advanced with primary blades elevated. The other brigands, including the horse-holders, had all risen to their feet.

The wagon master advanced with hands held high, palms open and facing forward.

"I see no toll!" called the bandit leader. Apparently, David and other youths reckoned, an envoy of the brigands had made a midnight embassy to the inn and there negotiated terms of passage.

Fifty denarii.

"Come forward! You and the next two!" called the bandit chief. He and his fellow stood now thirty paces before the first freight wagon, which had stopped completely. Behind this vehicle the train and its foot-trekkers also drew up.

The wagon master motioned his number two and three to advance beside him. These scurried forward. Each held up his empty hands. The wagon master displayed one vacant palm. In his other hand he clutched a drawstring purse.

"Deliver!" shouted the chief.

The brigand leader and first three, then five of his cohorts now moved toward the point of juncture, maintaining the advantage of their upslope positions. Clearly they intended to hold the three teamsters at spearpoint until the entire train had passed, lest the wagoneers be plotting treachery.

"We'll come nowhere near you!" shouted the wagon master. He displayed again the drawstring purse.

He slung this pouch toward the highwaymen.

The purse landed with a weighty splat upon the dust of the roadway.

David and his friends glanced to one another. They were having fun.

Now the bandit leader stepped into the road. He carried a heavy shepherd's bow, the kind that stockmen use to protect their flocks from wolves.

"Forward!" he bawled to the wagon master.

No one of the bandits, including the leader, had made a move toward the purse.

"Take your money!" called the wagon master.

"I want you!"

With that, he loosed a bolt that flew screaming past the teamster's ear and struck, with a sound like the crack of a whip, into the front pine facing of the wagon master's box.

"Now!" the bandit repeated. He nocked a second arrow and drew tight.

The wagon master's companions cried to him urgently to obey.

"Take your money and go!" cried the master.

The bandit shot again, this time at the master's lead mule. The bolt struck the beast full in the neck. The animal bawled in the traces and attempted to rear. The poor beast's hooves fouled in the padding affixed to the breastband. It toppled sideways, nearly pulling its three yoke-mates over with it.

"Aieee!" cried the wagon master. His face had turned the color of blood. The arrow may as well have struck him in the guts. He rushed to his wounded animal, clearly the man's favorite, not to say, as the team leader, the mainstay of his very livelihood.

"Forward!" cried the bandit leader, drawing a third shaft. "Or the next one parts your hair."

David felt his friends shinning rearward along the ground. Suddenly the game had stopped being an amusement.

"Go! Go!" shouted the wagon master's two comrades. But the man either wouldn't or couldn't. He clung to his bawling, stamping animal, crying oaths toward heaven.

The bandit leader's bow drew back to full stretch.

"We're coming! We're coming!" cried the second two teamsters, who now, passing the wagon master, scampered forward in terror toward the brigand leader and his confederates.

"I want him!" shouted the highwayman. He had come forward several strides and stood now within twenty paces of the wagon master. The mule in its traces continued braying in agony. Young David felt his own glance turn away, so piteous was the sight. The wagon master, in distress, retreated to the box of his vehicle. David thought, *He's retrieving some salve for his animal or perhaps an instrument to draw out the arrow.*

No.

The man was getting a spear.

With a great cry, the wagon master rushed toward the bandit leader, clearly intending to run upon him with the killing point of the weapon.

The brigand fired.

The bolt struck the wagon master at the nexus where the throat meets the top of the chest, driving powerfully in above the inner point of the right collarbone. The master's momentum carried him forward another three or four strides before he plunged face-first into the road. By the time his torso had hit the dirt, it had been driven through by two flung lances.

"Take them all!" cried the bandit leader.

The horsemen, mounted now and brandishing their lances, charged down the slope. The other bandits strode powerfully forward. Cries of terror rose from the teamsters and pilgrims of the train. These fled in all directions.

At this moment David felt his flesh stand up, responding involuntarily to a sound unlike any he had ever heard.

The man-at-arms appeared upon the slope above the bandits.

No one had seen or heard him approach.

Above his head the man-at-arms wheeled a leather sling, the kind shepherds carry to defend their flocks. David knew the power and range of such a weapon. Every boy did. But never had he heard such a keening cry as that that sounded now from this whirling, shrieking engine of death.

The man-at-arms slung.

David could not see the lead sling bullet, so swiftly did it fly. His glance took in only the nearest of the flatbread bandits as the projectile struck him square in the facing of his forehead and, seemingly simultaneously, the rear of his skull blew apart in a spray of bone and tissue. The man dropped like a sack of stones.

Now came the man-at-arms on a dead run.

His first hurled pilum split the guts of a second flatbread brigand beside the roadway. Before this man could fall, the fellow at his shoulder had been opened from throat to navel by a slash of the man-at-arms' *dolabra* pickaxe.

Now it was the bandits who cried in terror.

David saw two dump their lances and turn heels-on to flee.

The man-at-arms slew one with a two-handed slash of his dolabra that severed the man's spine and opened both his kidneys, and the second with an overhand throw that buried a battleaxe, whirling end-over-end, into the mass of muscle between the shoulder blades as this fellow turned to flee.

The bandit leader had wheeled about now. He drew down, from less than thirty feet, upon the man-at-arms. Clearly the brigand's skill with the bow was such that at this range he could drill an enemy's heart a hundred times out of a hundred.

The fellow loosed his arrow.

To David's eyes, wide now as wagon wheels, the bolt seemed to fly as if time had slowed. The youth could see the blood gutter on the iron warhead, and the feather vanes as they rippled in flight.

He saw the man-at-arms elevate his open left hand and, with exquisite deliberateness, bat this shaft aside, so that its killing point nicked the ear of the fox-skin cap upon his head and passed harmlessly by.

The bandit leader, seeing this, turned now and sprang with the fever of terror onto the back of one of the led horses. David could see the fellow's hips above the saddlecloth and his sandaled heels beating upon the animal's flanks.

Without haste the man-at-arms elevated his Amazon bow.

He nocked an arrow.

He drew.

David could not see the shaft as it flew. He only heard the sound and saw the bandit leader pitch first forward, then recoil wildly back, to spill, limbs unstrung, into the dirt as his mount, riderless now, pounded away past the wagons of the train and down the grade in the direction of the inn.

David stood now in the middle of the road. He had come down the slope from his post of observation though he later could summon no memory of executing this passage. He found himself immediately before the man-at-arms. David detected in the fellow's eyes neither rage nor satisfaction. The man's gaze was clear. He was not even breathing hard.

"Retrieve that arrow," the man-at-arms commanded. His tone was neither harsh nor imperious. "Bring it back to me. Wipe nothing from its shaft or its vanes. Then collect my kit from up the slope."

The warrior strode to the purse in the dirt and picked it up.

David, dashing after the spent arrow, passed in his rush the feral girl-child whom the man-at-arms had greeted beside the water ewer in the forecourt of the inn the night before.

Every other individual of the train, excepting the child's father, had either made away back down the slope or taken up a position of concealment behind the freight wagons or among the clefts that bounded the road.

The girl alone stood forward, barefoot upon the summit track, her gaze fixed upon the man-at-arms.

4

EQUITES LEGIONIS

D AVID HEARD THE ROMAN CAVALRY before he saw them. He had scrambled down the track to the body of the bandit leader and was searching frantically among the folds of the fellow's cloak for the arrow that had slain him, when the thunder of hoof strikes and the cries of the mounted legionaries rolled up the reverse grade of the highway, from the Jerusalem side.

Glancing back, David saw a half score of horsemen dismount, hem in, and overpower the man-at-arms, while their squadron mates, two score in number, with the drilled and practiced skill of all legion soldiers, cut off and enveloped the wagon train, its remaining constituents, and the surviving brigands, seizing control of the ambush site and all it held.

The arrow.

Where in the world had it gone?

David could locate the shaft nowhere, till a female pilgrim of the train, reckoning the object of his search, called out to him and pointed another twenty paces down the slope.

David scrambled to the spot. The arrow lay in the stony space between a mile marker and a nest of prickly pear cactus. David snatched it up.

The warhead shone clean in the sun, as did the shaft, absent all evidence of fluid or bone. But the vanes, the feathered fins at the rear of the shaft . . . these were soaked through with some viscous element that was not blood but tissue and gristle. David noted four shallow notches carved into the arrow shaft, just below the fletching.

David raced with his prize back to the wagon train.

The man-at-arms stood at the center of a ring of cavalry lance points. He was speaking in Latin, of which David possessed only a rudimentary understanding, to the cavalry lieutenant, who remained mounted. David recognized the word for "money." The man-at-arms was holding up the drawstring purse.

He was claiming his due.

Up and down the train the legionaries, dismounted now, were tearing the wagons and their loads apart. They were searching for something. David saw two soldiers strip a pilgrim of the train to his ankles, rending his poor pack and baggage and strewing it into the roadway. Another pair of troopers pressed a dame of sixty years against a cartwheel, hoisted her robe to her shoulders, and began groping her buttocks and breasts.

"Where is it?" the soldiers cried.

Up and down the train this demand echoed.

"Which one of you is hiding it?"

David glimpsed the feral girl-child clinging to the skirts of her father. The Romans indeed were masters of terror. They knew how to rough people up, to overwhelm their will to resist, to drive them like sheep. Furious oaths ascended in Latin and pidgin Aramaic. Cuffs and kicks were delivered with fabulous violence.

David's eyes found those of the man-at-arms. The fellow reckoned the arrow in David's fist and with a flicker of a glance communicated, *Keep it safe, don't let these bastards get their hands on it.*

David felt himself flush with pleasure to be acknowledged by this champion. He vowed silently to die before yielding up this bolt.

The Romans had taken in hand the father, the foot traveler with the feral girl. At once their fury found focus upon him.

"Here is the man," one cried.

The legionaries fell upon him.

"Give it over!"

A violent cuff took the father off his feet. The girl was screaming the choked, strangled gurgle of one void of speech, and clinging to her guardian's thigh. Two Romans seized the fellow by both ankles. They upended him, holding him high like a housedame stripping a pullet. Others beat the fellow's ribs with the staffs of their lances.

The man-at-arms took in this spectacle, himself held at spearpoint by half a dozen.

The foot traveler, the father of the girl, had been stripped to the skin now.

His baggage, such as it was, had been sundered and scattered. One legionary, seizing the poor fellow by the jaw, the way a husbandman grabs a sick lamb or ewe, jammed his fingers down the man's throat, as if seeking something secreted there. Next a pair of soldiers spread-eagled the man, while the third rammed three fingers up his anus. The girl flailed at the soldiers, seeking with impotent rage to defend her father.

Now the legionaries turned on the child.

David felt himself recoil with horror as a pair of soldiers seized the girl and tore her from her father. One prized the child's jaw open and thrust his fingers down her throat. Next this man upended her, tearing her tunic over her head as she screamed in mute terror. Three fingers of the soldier's right hand thrust toward the space between the child's legs.

The man-at-arms' face went black with fury. With a single violent stride the warrior broke from the circle of spearpoints and flung himself upon the legionary.

A blow to the temple sent the Roman sprawling. At once two, then three legionaries fell upon the man-at-arms' back. As their weight drove him to the dirt, the girl squirted free.

The man-at-arms could not be contained. Despite the mass of his assailants' bodies and the blows and cuffs with which they assaulted him, the mercenary rose to his knees, striking again and again with his fist into the face of the first legionary.

The girl had bolted now to her father, who sought with mighty urgency to draw her apart from the fracas. She would not budge, but remained rooted, staring with eyes like embers as the man-at-arms continued to pummel the legionary.

A blow to the skull from a heavy chain dropped the mercenary to the dirt.

"Seize him!" cried the lieutenant.

The Romans pinned the man-at-arms to the earth. Clouts from cudgels and lance shafts rained upon his back. Manacles were wrestled onto his wrists. Leg irons immobilized his feet.

David looked up to see the father spring onto the back of one of the Romans' cavalry mounts, a chestnut gelding with four white stockings, and haul his daughter up behind him. The pair made away at a gallop.

Oaths and curses chased them.

Horsemen spurred in pursuit.

Along the length of the train, pilgrims and foot travelers scattered and ran.

David found himself beside the man-at-arms' kit, with its weapons collected about it. One of the legionaries must have hauled this down from up the slope. As if commanded by some inner voice, the youth picked up the gear and carrying pole and hoisted the whole bundle onto his shoulder.

The man himself, in chains now, was being dragged toward a cage wagon, which had at this moment rumbled up, drawn by four mules, a part of the Roman column. Three other miscreants resided already inside this mobile jail.

David's eyes found those of the man-at-arms. His expression sought to say, *I have your kit and weapons. I will keep them safe.*

The man-at-arms perceived and acknowledged this.

David had taken two strides, seeking to get clear of the affray, when he felt a hand seize him from behind and cuff him violently across the back of the head.

A legionary sergeant hauled the youth about to face him.

"Who in hell's name," the trooper demanded in bad Hebrew, "are you?"

David held fast to the man-at-arms' kit and weapons. He indicated the captive, chained now and being manhandled aboard the prison wagon.

"I'm with him, sir. I'm his apprentice."

5

THE MOST DANGEROUS
MAN IN PALESTINE

IN STRATEGIC TERMS, THE CITY of Jerusalem is a conundrum and a contradiction.

The site commands no port or harbor, bestrides no trade routes or arteries of commerce. Its occupation is necessary neither to secure the country militarily (that chore was accomplished from the governor's seat at Caesarea on the seacoast) nor to interdict an invading force advancing from any direction save the east.

Jerusalem is vulnerable to siege. Despite its walls the city has been stormed and taken more than twenty times. It has been conquered by Jebusites, Philistines, Egyptians. Babylonia sacked it under Nebuchadnezzar. Cyrus the Great captured it for Persia. Alexander took it without a fight. The Jews made it their own ten centuries ago under their great king David but it has been captured and overrun many times since.

The land about Jerusalem is itself vexatious. The city perches high upon a sterile, stony crest. Teamsters grumble that all inbound freight must be trucked *up*. Grain and oil, indeed virtually all the necessities of life, must be brought in overland, as river or sea transport do not exist. The countryside roundabout will not sustain the grazing of livestock sufficient to feed a garrison of even cohort size, nor can it support the cultivation of grains or cereals on any scale beyond that of subsistence. Water cannot be brought to Jerusalem via aqueduct because of its lofty siting. Indeed, even the wealthiest families of the city supply their needs in the manner of their ancestors—via maids of the household drawing from wells and bearing this necessity home in earthen jars balanced atop their heads.

Jerusalem's isolation creates even graver difficulties for the garrison or administrative commander charged with the city's occupation and the subjugation of its restive populace. Supplies and ordnance carted or caravanned in from the coastal plain, Syria, or the Jordan Valley may be transported only at great expense and hazard over highways vulnerable to ambush and attack at innumerable places. Nothing can come from Egypt except by sea, as the wilderness of Sinai intervenes, and even such freight must be transported via vulnerable highways from the ports of Gaza, Jaffa, or Caesarea Maritima.

Yet Jerusalem remains for any conqueror the indispensable city of Judea. Here and nowhere else resides the religious and administrative capital of the Jewish people—the Great Temple of Solomon with its sanctuary, the Holy of Holies containing the Ark of the Covenant. Here and nowhere else may the secular and spiritual chieftains of the Jews be assembled, addressed, and reasoned with. These mulish, disputatious, stubborn fellows congregate in their milling, chattering masses. Their schemes and passions, of this world and the next, are as opaque to their Roman overlords as they are inextinguishable to all and every external influence.

And the Hebrews are multitudinous. At the season of the Passover, the city hosts no fewer than a million celebrants, half the Jewish population not only of Judea but of Syria, Egypt, Crete, Cyprus, and the cities of the eastern Aegean.

This at least was the assessment of the senior tribune Marcus Severus Pertinax, commander of the garrison at Jerusalem, serving under the procurator of Judea, Marcus Antonius Felix, himself headquartered at the provincial capital, Caesarea Maritima.

"Our position in this place," declared this officer to his superior in a letter whose contents became widely circulated among the subject populace, "is like that of a lion seated upon an anthill. We may crush the Jews over and over, yet they remain up our ass and nothing we can do will dislodge them."

Two days had passed since the arrest of the man-at-arms at the ambush site on the Jerusalem-Damascus highway. The mercenary had been transported via prison wagon to the legionary detention facility immediately inside the Essene Gate, also called Sha'ar Ha'ashpot or "Dung Gate" (from which all city garbage was hauled each night outside the walls to be burned), the most downslope of the seven gates in the walled city of Jerusalem. The prisoner was held in this establishment overnight, then transferred the following morning, upon arraignment, to the military lockup of the Antonia Fortress, the Roman administrative center of Judea and the largest stone edifice between Ephesus and Babylon.

Young David, struggling under the sixty-pound weight of the man-at-arms' kit, armor, and weapons, had fallen behind the cavalry's pace and required an additional half day to complete the forty-mile journey from the ambush site. He arrived at Jerusalem tardily, fearful that the man-at-arms had already been scourged and put to death. But a post sergeant outside the Damascus Gate informed the lad (after a half dozen others had sent him packing beneath kicks and cuffs) that the fellow yet lived and in fact had been summoned, only minutes earlier, to an interview with the garrison commander, Severus Pertinax.

"Pray, sir," said David, "can you tell me the man-at-arms' name?"

The sergeant eyed the youth dubiously. "You're his apprentice, you say, yet you don't know the man's name?"

In chagrin David asked the sergeant where such an interview between the garrison commander and the man-at-arms might take place. The sergeant gave directions to a carpentry shop beneath the fortress's northern wall. This establishment, with its high roof and open-air eaves, provided a hint of coolness in the infernal Judean forenoons. The garrison commander regularly took his luncheon there, declared the sergeant, and within its precinct frequently received petitioners and other supplicants.

David thanked the man and, hoisting again his cumbersome load, made to step off.

"Telamon," said the sergeant. "That's your master's name. A mercenary from Arcadia in Greece.

"Follow the smell of pine shavings," he added.

David obeyed, making his way within the city walls to the site of the carpentry works. The building was of mud-brick, washed white, with an open beam roof layered in planks and topped with red-brick tiles. Piles of wood shavings to the height of a man's waist lay against the downslope wall. Local boys collected these as lamp chips and as bedding for livestock stalls. David prowled about the perimeter, feigning collection of this material, seeking to evade the notice of the many legionaries trooping in the lanes or lounging in the shaded porches.

Of a sudden he heard his master's voice—*Telamon*, he told himself, seeking to embed the name into memory—coming from inside the woodworking plant. The carpenters, David had learned from locals, were prisoners, mostly rebel Jews and petty criminals. They wore leg irons as they labored.

David could make out the voices of three other men. The tone of their speech was imperious and accusatory. When Telamon answered, it was in single syllables or inarticulate grunts. The exchanges, or the snatches that David could overhear, were in Latin, so that he could divine even less of their import. He could find no way into the shop. Soldiers and warders of the site barred every entry.

The youth discovered a breach, however, between the top of the stall walls of an adjacent livery and the overhang of the carpentry shop roof. Into this cranny he mounted, yet lugging the man-at-arms' weapons and kit, and, working his way forward in a crouch and then a crawl, managed to reach an elevated vantage directly under the eaves. From this site of concealment the boy could see and hear, such as his understanding of the Roman tongue would permit, the interview being conducted below.

Present were the man-at-arms, still manacled and in leg irons; an officer of tribune rank, apparently the garrison commander Severus; an attending officer of lesser station, which the boy took to be an adjutant or second-in-command; and the cavalry lieutenant who had made the original arrest at the Narrows.

"The soldier whose jaw you shattered, whose teeth you beat out of his head," declared the lieutenant, addressing Telamon, "was a good man, a sergeant of sixteen years with numerous awards for valor. Now he will have to be retired and pensioned off. I must train another to fill his station, at hell only knows what expense, not to mention cover the cost of his repatriation and the education of his children. The toll for this, as you know, comes not from the provincial treasury at Antioch but from our own military budget—"

With a look the garrison commander cut the lieutenant off.

"The penalty for assaulting a Roman soldier is death," he said to Telamon. "What do you say to this?"

"What is the penalty," replied the man-at-arms, "for a Roman soldier assaulting a child?"

"I'll tell you what I say," put in the lieutenant. He indicated Telamon. "The prisoner struck not in the passion of the moment—for why would anyone defend a scrofulous urchin unknown to himself?—but with premeditation and criminal intent, to work harm to Rome. He is a hireling of the Hebrew Zealots," declared this officer, "or if not of them, then of any of a hundred Jewish gangs and rebel confederations."

The garrison commander asked the lieutenant what punishment he proposed.

"Let him ride the pine mare," said the young officer, gesturing to the eastern extremity of the manufactory. David craned to look. Against this wall stood a brace of newly hewn crucifixes.

"I would see him on the third day," said the lieutenant, "when the sinews of his loins sever and his guts sluice out through his anus."

The garrison commander studied the expression on the man-at-arms' face. He observed to his adjutant and to the lieutenant that this fellow had trained himself all his life for such a moment, or worse.

"He will not even cry out. Will you, my friend?"

David, peering from his perch, could pick out the military mark on the commander's forearm.

LEGIO X

"I know this man well," declared Severus Pertinax.

Indeed, David reckoned, an unseen current coursed between the captive and his keeper.

"Still serving only for money, peregrine?" Severus inquired of the man-at-arms.

David could make out little of the next exchange, conducted as it was partly in Latin and partly in legionary's slang. The commander addressed Telamon as "peregrine," the Roman term for a non-citizen who had taken service in various legions and legion auxiliaries.

The commander observed to his adjutant and to the cavalry lieutenant that the man who stood before them now in irons had been accounted only twenty-four months previously the ablest soldier of the acclaimed Tenth Legion—the Tenth Fretensis (as opposed to the Tenth Gemina, based now in Spain), descended of Caesar's original Tenth of Gaul a century past. "But the only eagle this son-of-a-whore would salute was one on the face of a gold coin."

The commander remarked to the lieutenant: "By the way, this fellow is no agent of the Zealots or of any sect of these Hebrews. They can't afford him."

To David's eyes Marcus Severus Pertinax, a knight of the Equestrian Order and senior tribune of the Tenth Fretensis legion, appeared the paragon of an officer of Rome—clean-shaven, of impeccable posture, handsome as a god, and possessed of supreme poise and self-command. The youth crept forward upon his overhead beam, hoping to see and hear better. The commander was addressing his adjutant and the lieutenant in tones of mock instruction, indicating the man-at-arms before them.

"You are acquainted, gentlemen, with the practice by which foreign-born enlistees in the legions put aside their native names and take in their place Roman identities—the three-name structure." Severus indicated and addressed by name the pair of sergeants who stood immediately behind Telamon, securing him in their custody. "As you did, Septimus Justus Antoninus, and you, Gaius Procopis Martialis. Not this one."

Here the commander turned directly to the mercenary.

"He kept his single Greek name, absent even a patronymic. Nor is this all, my friends. This man earned his discharge three years early, for valor, a decoration sash set about his shoulders by the legion legate himself. Any other would display such a citation with pride. You cast yours away, didn't you, peregrine? Or did you sell it for silver? Nor did you claim the Roman citizenship that came with such an honor and in fact had been mandated upon your enlistment. You declined. You turned it down.

"You see, my friends," Severus continued, "this man holds himself above such conceits as love of the emperor or bonds of comradeship with those who serve him. Isn't that right, peregrine? To call oneself a Roman would be in your view . . . what? Philosophically deficient? Wanting in self-autonomy? What is that passage from your credo? 'Only fools fight for a flag or a cause.' Yes, that's it. I remember. He is a philosopher, this fellow. That which other, simpler souls call 'honor,' this man styles 'delusion.' Nay, 'self-delusion.' Do I cite your code aright, prisoner?"

"Close enough," replied Telamon.

Severus smiled.

"I could order you nailed to a cross right now and this garrison to a man would buy tickets to savor the spectacle."

The Roman paused.

His aspect softened.

"But perhaps I have been more influenced by your philosophy than I realize. For it seems an opportunity has arisen by which you, and no other, may prove of service to Rome."

A job, Severus said.

An assignment.

"Don't worry, peregrine. It pays. Will you accept?"

Severus produced a leather pouch. He tossed it onto the joinery table between himself and the man-at-arms.

"Note, my friends, that I proffer to this soldier-for-hire no description of the task I wish him to perform. I display only such reward as its successful completion commands. Why? Because our brother-in-arms here, who is too good to call himself a Roman and too proud to accept citizenship beneath our standard, regards all chores of war as equally worthy or worthless. He asks one thing only: 'How much does it pay?'"

"I accept," said Telamon. "What's the job?"

Inch by inch, the youth David had now crept to a spot upon the overhead beam nearly abreast of that occupied by the man-at-arms. He dared not tug the mercenary's kit and weapons so far out from the wall but kept touch with this bundle, barely, by a rawhide strap around one ankle.

Below David now, the garrison commander nodded to the lieutenant. This officer motioned in turn to the pair of sergeants standing in attendance to the rear. These came forward and, with a mawl and pliers designed for this purpose, unpinned the manacles and leg irons that had bound Telamon.

The commander addressed the mercenary.

"That Hebrew whom your reckless intercession helped to free . . . the fellow who took flight on the back of a legion cavalry mount . . . I want him. I want you to find him and bring him back to me."

Severus declared for Telamon's information that the fugitive had been detained in this very fortress, in the underground dungeon reserved for political prisoners and Messianic insurrectionists. It was at Severus's own direction that he, and the mute girl-child in his care, be released. That was four days ago.

"I was hoping that this villain would lead me to an article I seek. But events, as you well know, have transpired otherwise."

David felt a stirring beneath his left heel. He craned to look. A brown rat the size of a man's fist was working its whiskers over the sole of David's exposed foot. David bit hard into his lower lip to stay himself from crying out. He clung with one hand to the beam beneath him and with the other to the rawhide strap that bound him to the man-at-arms' kit and weapons, straining with every fiber to hold silent.

"Who," Telamon asked Severus, "is this man?"

David thought, *Do I dare kick? No. The rat will tumble and I am discovered.*

Below David's perch, the garrison commander continued:

"There are three types of Jews in this godforsaken country. Temple

Jews, Zealots, and Messianics. The first can be bought off for riches or power, the second can be dealt with by force. The last resist everything. They cannot be suborned, coerced, or reasoned with. They occupy not this world but another. The man you will pursue is one of these."

Severus asked Telamon if he had heard of, or owned acquaintance with, that Jewish subversive calling himself Paul the Apostle.

The mercenary replied that he knew the name but little else.

"He is a Roman citizen," said the commander, "a Cilician Jew and former senior functionary under the Sanhedrin known as Saul of Tarsus—and a merciless persecutor of so-called 'Christians' in that capacity. The story goes that he experienced some sort of miraculous 'conversion,' whereupon he became an adherent of that cult which he had formerly scourged—throwing himself into this new role with the same zeal with which he had pursued the prior. Now, based at Ephesus and styling himself 'Paul the Apostle,' he oversees an operation of empire-wide scope in support of and evangelizing for this new religion."

Telamon absorbed this. "He was the man who escaped at the Narrows?"

"No. But the fugitive is a close associate and in regular communication with this Paul. His name is Michael. He is either carrying a letter from the Apostle or is bound for some location or to some individual who will give him the letter."

Telamon inquired of the contents of the letter. Did Severus know what was in it or to whom it was addressed?

"What's in it is easy. Sedition. Where bound? To the Christian underground community at Corinth in Greece. This city is familiar ground to the Apostle. He himself established the Nazarene sect there."

The commander explained that the epistle to Corinth was no brief love note. Its length was three thousand words or more.

"In a scroll, probably, tightly wound, inscribed in minuscule script. It could be as small as a thumb."

The fugitive called Michael, declared the garrison commander, would not be content to deliver this letter to one community only. Severus knew this, he said, from the oaths of defiance the man had spewed when he was racked, in the fortress, upon the wheel.

From Corinth, the Apostle's words would be copied and disseminated to a hundred other colonies, fomenting rebellion and insurrection.

"Rome cannot permit this. The letter must be stopped."

Severus paused at this point, meeting the mercenary's eyes with an expression that sought to convey the urgency and critical consequence of this assignment.

"I don't know where this Nazarene has hidden the letter or how it will be delivered into his hands. That's your job, peregrine. Bring me the document and bring me the man."

David felt the rat step across his heel and mount onto the back of his bare calf. David's privates hung exposed beneath the hem of his tunic. He could feel the rat's whiskers probing ahead of its passage up the inside of his leg and hear the eager sniffing of the rodent's nostrils. The youth's soundless prayers intensified.

The garrison commander continued to the man-at-arms, "This man, Michael, the one whose escape was made possible by your actions, is the most dangerous man in Palestine."

The commander loosed the drawstring of the pouch he had tossed earlier onto the table. A double handful of coins spilled forth.

"Twelve golden eagles," said Severus. "Four years' pay when you were a serving man. And another dozen when you bring back the Nazarene and the letter."

Telamon whistled.

The rat's whiskers now probed the flesh inside David's thigh. For a moment the boy considered leaping from his perch, even if it meant prison or death. Instead his right hand, the one clutching the roof beam, shot toward the rat, snatching the beast at the nape of its neck and crushing its cervical spine with one quick, violent twist. The men below heard the sound, or thought they did, but, after a moment or two of glancing about and discovering nothing, dismissed the intrusion. David clung to the rodent, wringing its neck further lest it spasm even in the throes and give him away.

He felt a sharp pain and realized he had been bitten.

A pellet of blood tumbled off David's thigh, dropped into space, and landed with a soft splat on the pine floor between the feet of the man-at-arms. The mercenary made no move and offered no reaction. Neither the garrison commander nor the other Romans seemed to notice.

David dared draw a breath.

"And what will be his fate, this Nazarene Michael," the man-at-arms asked, "when I bring him back to you?"

Severus indicated the crucifixes lining the walls of the shop.

"The same as yours if you fail."

The commander slid the purse and coins across to Telamon. The mercenary took them.

The commander offered further intelligence to assist the man-at-arms in his errand. He declared that an informer of the prison had delivered certain particulars to the warders, obtained as confidences from the fugitive Michael.

The man-at-arms asked if he might speak to this fellow.

"The informer is a woman," said the commander. "A sorceress, no less."

Severus employed the Hebrew term *kishshephah*, pronouncing it with amusement, as at the depths of superstition and ignorance that flourished in this god-deranged country, as opposed to the Greek term *magissa*, related to the Farsi *magi*, which took the manipulation of the black arts seriously and treated the field with respect. "The woman claims to fly free of this fortress each night, as a raven, and declares that she can strike a foe fatally by incantation if she but first acquire a clipping of that man's finger-nails or a lock of his hair."

The man-at-arms said he would speak with her.

With a nod to his adjutant, the commander ordered the woman summoned. "You'll need a translator," he said to Telamon. "The witch speaks only Hebrew and Aramaic, or at least refuses to communicate with us in any other tongue."

The man-at-arms declared that no interpreter would be necessary, as he had brought his own.

With that, he wheeled swiftly, snatched a board from the carpentry bench behind him, and, thrusting it powerfully skyward, struck the underside of the overhead plank upon which the youth David had made his perch.

The lad plunged in a welter of limbs and timber. The man-at-arms' kit landed with a great crash, scattering utensils and weapons in all directions. Even the wrung rat tumbled. The Roman officers, and the prisoner-workmen at their benches, fell back in surprise and startlement, before bursting into laughter.

"This is your translator?" asked Severus.

The man-at-arms stood over David, extending his hand to help the boy up.

David could find no words, but sputtered unintelligibly, all the while scrambling to collect the warrior's armor and weapons and to reassemble his kit.

"And has this sprat been eavesdropping in the rafters all the while?"

"And even bled a little onto your workshop floor."

The interview concluded upon this note of amusement. The sorceress being sent for, the man-at-arms took up his gear (or such freight as he himself wished to carry, leaving the remainder for David) and stepped out, escorted by the lieutenant and the two sergeants who had loosed his bonds, onto that stone-founded way called by the Romans Via Papilio and by the Jerusalemites the Street of the Martyrs, that led to the southeast forecourt of the Antonia Fortress, in which his interview with the witch would take place.

As he crossed the floor of the workshop, Telamon's glance took in the stacks of crucifixes waiting to be put to use. These instruments, he seemed to note, came in all sizes—some diminutive enough, it appeared, to serve for women or even children.

"Does it work?" the man-at-arms inquired of the garrison commander.

"For what?"

"To hold the populace by terror."

Severus considered this.

"Not really. But it breaks the tedium."

BOOK TWO

GAZA

6

THE SORCERESS

"SHE IS NO SORCERESS BUT a common root doctor," the youth David declared. "And a cracked-pate one at that."

Man and boy had made two camps out of Jerusalem. The pair had put the province of Judea beneath their heels and trekked now across the coastal plain of Idumaea, the ancient kingdom of Edom, toward the city of Gaza, under Roman rule since the death of Herod the Great. From there— Telamon had replied reluctantly and only after repeated importunities from David—their route would bear them into the territory of the Egyptians, via that crossroads called Rafiah, and from there into the wilderness of Sinai. Their train was two Jericho mules, purchased for a single silver "actium" (eight actiums made one Scythian "coson," also called a Roman "eagle") in the stock market outside the Jaffa Gate.

The interview with the sorceress had taken place immediately following the man-at-arms' release, in the packed-dirt court downslope of the Tedi Gate, the ceremonial entrance to the Antonia Fortress. The woman was led out in chains by a single jailer, not a Roman but a Hebrew trusty of the prison. She took her seat upon neither of the two benches provided, nor in the shade, though such was abundant, cast by the eastern wall of the court, but in direct sun with no headdress or veil to cover her face. Telamon sat cross-legged in the dust across from her. David took a place between the two and to one side to perform his duties of translation. The mercenary offered cool water. The witch would not take it.

"You are the one who would hunt the Nazarene Michael," said the sorceress before Telamon had offered a word. "Not for God but for gold."

David found himself, at once and in his bones, terrified of this female.

He took her at first for a leper, so ravaged appeared her cheeks and jaw and so gnarled the flesh of the backs of her hands. Her hair, which was black and thick with curls, grew about her face in an unruly tangle. The sorceress seemed at first a crone of seventy, though upon closer examination David reckoned her years at little more than two score.

She would tell Telamon nothing, the witch declared straightaway and with passionate defiance—neither the content of her conversations with the prisoner Michael nor how she came to establish herself in his confidence. She would speak neither on the nature of her arrangement with the garrison commander nor reveal upon what charge she had been arrested and was being held.

Telamon put his queries directly. "Did you actually see the letter or only learn of its existence by hearsay? Does Michael have it in his possession now? If not, will it be conveyed to him by a third party at some place along his passage to Corinth? Where? By whom?"

The witch regarded the man-at-arms with hostility and contempt. "I saw it, all right. With these two eyes. The Nazarene had it, then burned or destroyed it."

"How long is the letter?" Telamon asked. "Could it be rolled tight and secreted in some orifice of the body? Who is the little girl? Michael's daughter? Why is a child her age being held by the Romans?"

The mercenary declared—from experience, he said—that Roman prisons were rats' nests of informers. "Who else knows what you told Severus? How did he compensate you? What did you trade for such priceless intelligence?"

The man-at-arms sought to quiz the witch about the immediate destination of the fugitive Michael. Did she have any idea where the man was bound first on his route to Corinth?

"If I did," the sorceress declared, "you'd be the last person I'd spill it to."

The mercenary offered money.

The witch spat in the dirt.

Telamon offered to use his influence with Severus to get the sorceress's sentence commuted or even to obtain her release. The woman only laughed.

When she addressed the man-at-arms, which she did repeatedly, interrupting him in the middle of a question or speaking before he had put one forward, it was with such prodigality as is taken in affairs only by one personally wronged in the most intimate and grievous manner, as a lover spurned or a comrade played false.

"What kind of man works such an errand for money? Have you no fear of heaven?"

David had sought in his translation to moderate the ire of the witch's pronouncements, but the vitriol with which she spewed these could not be dissimulated. As well, the man-at-arms' understanding of the Hebrew tongue (the sorceress disdained to employ the more accessible Aramaic) was not as limited, it seemed, as he had professed.

Throughout the interview, the man-at-arms maintained a bearing of equanimity. Never did he raise his voice or respond in kind to the venom spouted by the sorceress. "Ask only, woman," he said at the end, holding up one of his golden eagles. "I will purchase your freedom."

The witch responded as if acid had been flung in her face. Oaths sprang from her lips. She flew free of the prison every night as a raven, she declared, and could claim her liberty at any hour. Neither Severus nor all the armies of Rome could stop her. The woman indicated the

LEGIO X

tattoo on Telamon's forearm.

"You imagine you interrogate me, peregrine. But it is I who have peered into the blackness of your heart. You can hide nothing from me.

Those letters in ink upon your flesh? They are seared as indelibly into your soul. You will not efface them as easily as you think."

The mercenary assimilated this with no overt reaction. He thanked the sorceress for her time and, setting two copper coins upon a flat stone before her, rose and departed before she could spurn this compensation.

For days after, this interview repeated itself in David's recall. Was he too somehow included in the sorceress's hex?

The youth recollected as well, and with equal foreboding, the final exchange that took place outside the Essene Gate between the man-at-arms and the garrison commander.

David had spent the preceding postnoon purchasing supplies and rigging out the two mules for the coming trek. He slept on the straw of the stalls provided by the Romans within the fortress. Twice during the night, alarms sounded outside in the city. Armed detachments, of cavalry as well as foot troops, responded. David could hear their tread, at the double, hastening to the sites of unrest. He heard cries deep in the city and saw flames in distant quarters.

The next morning Severus, attended by the same lieutenant of cavalry who had taken the man-at-arms into custody at the Narrows, saw Telamon and his apprentice off from the slope beneath the south-facing city wall. The young officer turned out to be Severus's nephew, whom the senior clearly regarded as a protégé and even a confidant.

The lieutenant set into Telamon's hand what his superior identified as an "intelligence packet." This bundle, Severus informed the man-at-arms, held a *lex de captis*, a "license of capture," issued under the tribune's personal seal, which would protect the mercenary at sea and on land from any who would attempt to deprive him of his prisoner, as well as letters of safe passage addressed to the harbormasters of Tyre, Sidon, and Seleucia Pieria. The packet contained in addition a military map of the city of Corinth and its environs with notes indicating the last known locations of the Nazarene underground communities, including a roster with names and physical descriptions of the insurrectionists' principal leaders.

The lieutenant addressed Telamon. "The ringleader of this rabble is a man, surname unknown, age unknown, calling himself 'Simon of the Harbor.' He is said to be the political commander, if such a term may be applied to a Messianic sect, of approximately thirty scattered factions, all secretive, located not only in Corinth but throughout the Peloponnese and as far afield as the island of Corcyra. He has a sister, Miriam, also a chief of these seditionists. The only other name we have is that of Josepha, surname and family name unknown, called Parthenos, 'the Virgin.' She seems to be the mystical leader. Of course, these names may be false or cover identities. One or all may also have moved on or been supplanted by others. The intelligence in this packet is months old and may not be unquestioningly relied upon."

David stole glimpses, when he could do so unobtrusively, of the bundle itself. The scribed lines were so many scratches to him; he flushed despite himself at his own ignorant and unlettered state.

Severus picked up from his nephew, continuing to Telamon. "These three—Simon, Miriam, and Josepha, or whatever identities they may now be traveling under—are the individuals for whom the Apostle's letter is intended. They will be waiting for it. It is they who will propagate its message abroad. They are to be considered enemies of Rome. Their eradication is of the highest priority to the emperor. Regarding the latitude of your assignment, it goes without saying that, failing to intercept, acquire, and destroy the letter or return it to us, if you can eliminate these three individuals or any others of their sect, Rome will look most favorably upon your enterprise."

The morning was hot, and the commander shifted uncomfortably inside his *lorica segmentata* armor. He wore a plumed Gallic helmet, as did the lieutenant, along with caligas and bronze shin guards. Both carried gladii like Telamon's—on baldrics with dagger-belts attached—and were attended by two *decurii*, ten-man detachments of heavy infantry.

Along both sides of the Gaza Road, which led south and west down the slope from the Essene Gate, could be seen fresh lines of crucifixes, upon which hung in excess of a dozen of the seditionists called *sicarii*.

"'Dagger men,'" observed the garrison commander. "A new term for a new kind of warrior, if indeed such a title of honor may be applied. These are the Zealots," he said. "Champions of the Hebrews, who lurk among the crowds of the city to plunge their steel into the backs and throats of soldiers of my legion . . . *your* legion too, peregrine."

The tribune peered down the line of crucifixes. "How am I, or any commander, supposed to combat or control such agents of terror? I cannot permit a man of mine to so much as buy a pear in a Jewish market. Our soldiers may venture outside the fortress only in details of four or more—at arms and in armor. The Jews spit on our shadows as we pass in the street. This country will break out in open insurrection, if not this year, then next. What then? We will have to raze the city entire—and we shall."

The mules could scent the blood and agony of the crucified rebels. Both began to stamp and balk. Severus noted the youth David clamp his own beast by the halter and draw it tight.

"This 'apprentice' you carry . . ." The Roman addressed Telamon but nodded in the direction of David. "He and his countrymen would eat our brothers raw in the night. Wouldn't you, boy?"

He addressed David directly now. "Why can't you Jews accept Roman order and Roman prosperity? What more can we do for you than build roads and bring fresh water and make your merchants and traders rich? Yet you slit the throats of our sons in the street. Do we proscribe the practice of your religion? Does Rome insist that you worship her gods, or even pay notice of them? No! Your temple is the greatest in all the East. Your scholars and priests secure fortunes via the commerce mandated and monopolized under your laws and our arms and protection. By heaven, I command the imperial garrison of Jerusalem, yet I cannot make a decision, so much as where to dispose of my cavalry mounts' shit, without seeking permission of the high priests and the Sanhedrin, may hell take them all. This banquet of blessings Rome sets before you, asking nothing except peace, yet still you hate us!"

Severus turned now to Telamon and, with an expression of rue, proffered this estimation:

"For all our differences, mercenary, you and I have one thing in common: we live in this world. These Jews and Messianics do not. They abide in the next and may be reasoned with no more than a shade or a phantasm!"

The commander drew up, realizing he had given way to a fit of intemperance, and one moreover directed at an illiterate child. He reclaimed his self-command, with a smile to Telamon that was not unlike a grimace.

"See how these Jews drive you crazy? Rome has brought into subjection a hundred peoples, yet none remains so stiff-necked as these. Perhaps you were not so foolhardy, my friend, to take your discharge when you could."

Severus set his palm upon the man-at-arms' shoulder.

"Bring me the letter, brother. Bring the man and the letter, and I will double your bounty out of my own purse."

7

AN APPRENTICE AT ARMS

THUS THE MERCENARY AND HIS apprentice set forth. Each bore his
necessaries upon his back. The mules were laden with such impedimenta as the making of camps required, as well as helmet and armor,
straps, spare footgear and weaponry, and the beasts' own fodder and water,
as much as they could carry without breaking down. The man would not
let the boy ride the animal he led or even mount for a moment onto the
creature's back. Instead the two trekked afoot, each at the head of and to
the left of his mule.

The network of traces and tracks that crisscrossed the Judean hills
from Beit Shemesh to the coastal plain of Philistia had been in use by travelers for hundreds, even thousands of years. Sites congenial to the overnight, possessed of springs or shelter, or simply a location out of the sun
and wind, had long since been cognized and established as encampments
known to, and open to, all. These were protected under Jewish custom so
ancient as to predate even the laws of Moses. Pack trains encamped here,
and dealers driving livestock, as well as pilgrims and traders and religious
celebrants. Wedding parties pitched their tents upon these grounds en
route to their destinations, as did kin groups making for the Great Temple
to celebrate the Passover or to observe other holy occasions. One recognized these layovers by the dirt trails leading to them, stamped hard as

stone by footsteps over the centuries or the brick-rimmed firepits scorched black by blazes dating from the age of Solomon.

The man-at-arms shunned such bivouacs except when they served his purpose, and his purpose he kept to himself alone. This made the youth David anxious and uneasy.

When the boy felt unsettled, he talked. He could not stop himself. The man-at-arms did not answer. In two days the mercenary had initiated one exchange only. This was three hours out of Jerusalem, where the traders' road tacked north toward the Jerusalem-Damascus highway, that thoroughfare upon which the ambush at the Narrows had occurred.

"Your village lies down that road," said the man-at-arms.

"So?"

"Do you not wish to tell your father what course you now strike out upon?"

Beneath the hem of the boy's tunic, still-livid welts could be seen. "Tell him? Why? So he can gift me with a fresh set of stripes?"

The mercenary said nothing, but turned his mule south onto the fork that led toward Gaza and the wilderness of Sinai.

"You're my father now," said the boy.

The man-at-arms only grunted.

The countryside sprawled stony and featureless in its descent to the plain and the sea. Toward day's end, at the Well of Avishag outside the village of Bet Natan, the man addressed the boy again.

"I have taken you on because you've shown spirit. But I am not your father or your brother or your friend. You may watch me and learn what you can. If you should be killed as we fare together, I will bury your bones."

And he gave the lad a copper coin, for his labor thus far.

"I expect pay for my work," said the man. "And I offer it."

Man and boy traversed civilized country now, that region that had been six centuries earlier the kingdom of the Philistines before its conquest by the Babylonians under Nebuchadnezzar and later the Hasmoneans but that fell to the Romans in the time of Caesar and Pompey. Farmsteads and vineyards dotted the landscape. Still the man-at-arms avoided communal grounds. His appearance, David came to reckon, inevitably drew attention. The man found this tedious, not to say improvident. So the party, man and boy, made camp upon such eminences and promontories as appeared unoccupied.

"Why do we trek in this direction?" David asked on the initial night. "Won't the Nazarene be fleeing north? South leads only to desert. Our quarry would seek to cross to Corinth by sea from Seleucia Pieria or one of the northern ports, wouldn't he?"

Telamon permitted a fire this evening, but advised the boy that it would be their last.

"Before your sweat or mine had dried after the fracas at the Narrows, our friend the cavalry lieutenant had sent one of his troopers galloping back to Jerusalem to inform Severus of the man Michael's escape. Twelve hours after that, other dispatch riders had alerted every toll station and constabulary along the entire northern route. The Tenth Legion is at Cyrrhus, the Twelfth Fulminata and the Sixth Ferrata at Raphanaea. Elements of the Third Gallica are based at Antioch. The Eastern Fleet holds Ephesus and Methymna and Mytilene and all the ports of the Aegean. Every imperial unit at land and sea will be hunting for the Nazarene in that direction."

On the fourth day, man and boy entered the province of Gaza. No boundary demarcated this but a road marker so stubby a man might trip over it, and that was so abraded by sand and wind that its inscription

ASCALON|GAZA

could barely be distinguished.

The youth sought earnestly to portray his understanding of this scription. The mercenary made no remark, but David could see that he had discerned that the boy could not read.

"We are entering the province of bandits and brigands," declared the man-at-arms. "From this point, you and I will conduct ourselves as if at war."

Telamon set into the youth's hand from his own kit the legion-issue dolabra—the pickaxe-shaped entrenching tool with which he, the mercenary, had disemboweled the second bandit at the Narrows.

"From this hour, you and I take no action without a weapon at our side. We don't eat, we don't sleep, we don't heed nature's call empty-handed. No moment shall pass between now and the accomplishment of our mission in which both of us slumber at the same time. One will always be awake and on guard. If I catch you sleeping, you will never wake again."

They camped that night on a promontory, with no flame.

For the first time David discovered himself experiencing fear.

He thought of his father's house, and of the cramped cubby that he and his two younger brothers shared. He thought of his mother and his three sisters.

He thought of Jerusalem. David had visited the place only once before—with his family, for a Passover seder, when he was too small to appreciate either the city or the political situation in which it was entangled. It was not until this occasion, traveling with the man-at-arms, that he perceived the metropolis for the first time with grown-up, or nearly grown-up, eyes.

There, David now recalled, above the warren of lanes and alleys that comprised the walled city, rose the plateau of Mount Moriah, where Abraham had bound Isaac, when an angel stayed that pitiless blade. The youth saw the Tower of David and the City of David, the original gated Jerusalem, a thousand years old. He trekked to Skull Hill, upon which Jesus of Nazareth, the rabbi proclaimed as messiah by the common and the unlettered, was crucified. And the lane called now by these the Via Dolorosa, over whose stones the martyr bore the cross upon which he would meet his end.

David in his chores of provisioning had passed the Garden of Gethsemane and stood atop the Mount of Olives, looking down upon the Kidron Valley. He saw the field of graves of generations of Jews awaiting the true messiah. In the forecourt of the Temple he observed the money changers at their stalls and tables, amid the clamorous importunities of pilgrims who had trekked across leagues to pray and offer sacrifice. One may not procure an offering of devotion—a kid, say, or even a dove or an unblemished pigeon—with secular coin. Such would pollute the offering and render it unholy in the sight of heaven. A pilgrim's drachmae or sesterces must be exchanged here for temple coinage. This was the site, so David had heard, upon which Jesus of Nazareth had driven these men out and overturned their tables with a violent rush. Could such a lawless fellow truly be the savior for whom Jews had waited for twenty centuries? The idea seemed preposterous. Yet David knew that thousands, even tens of thousands believed. And more every day.

On the Temple Mount David had watched the processions of Sadducees and their rivals the Pharisees, whom the followers of the Nazarene despised as toadies to the Romans. Were they? David noted the Pharisees' worn soles and threadbare hems as they shambled in single file to worship within the court beyond which lay the Holy of Holies, singing psalms penned by King David himself. These were good men, God-fearing, impoverished by choice, who carried on the traditions of scholarship and devotion in the face of Roman conquest, who studied the Books of Moses so late beneath the lamp that their sight went bad and their shoulders became permanently stooped. These acolytes had dedicated their lives to preserving the living lore of the nation of Israel. The line of their fathers stretched back to those who had trekked with Moses, who had been carried off to captivity by the Babylonians, who had returned and with Ezra and Nehemiah had rebuilt the Temple razed by the armies of Nebuchadnezzar.

These men of God, the lofty Sadduccees as well as the humbler Pharisees, existed in David's eyes upon a plane to which a boy like himself could never even dream to aspire. They dwelt, David could see, on a level apart from those who tended flocks or cultivated the land. They could read and write; they understood the Mysteries; they communed with the Almighty. They knew how to address Him, how to hear and comprehend Him; they divined His will. How, David thought, could a boy like himself not respect these learned men, who defended the barricades of the Lord against the folly of the good-hearted but ignorant and illiterate masses?

The Nazarene Michael stood not with these learned masters, David reckoned, but with the rustics and bumpkins. His "religion," if you could call it that, was the faith of the street and of the barnyard, that is to say superstition and humbug, sacrilege indeed, spawned of the laying on of hands and the performance of so-called "miracles," which were often,

David had heard, no more than tricks and sleights of hand, staged "heal-ings" and "restorations," or else hysterical conversions brought about by the massed formation of the wretched and their collective desperation for surcease from sorrow.

And yet—David heard his own voice inside his head—*who am I to judge? What do I know? A boy from a village without even a name, who can neither read nor write and never will.*

Indeed, David thought, though he could recite the Books of Moses by heart, by what means had he learned these? Through the ministra-tions only of his equally unlettered father, an ignorant man who beat his boys habitually yet abased himself before the meanest private soldier of Rome or the lowliest cleric of the Sanhedrin. *Yet how could he blame his father?* David thought. *What abuse has he worked upon me and my brothers that the God of our fathers has not visited a hundredfold on the children of Israel, century upon century, and which continues to this day? King of the universe? Then drive these bastard Romans out! Rout them as the Five Books say You did the Hittites and the Canaanities, Jebusites and Amorites. Where is our Joshua? Where may we find Saul or David and Jonathan? Where is Judah Maccabee?*

The Zealots, David knew, bore the sword for Israel in this day. Their blades skewered the livers of Roman soldiers in the street, as the tribune Severus had declared. These were good men too, David knew. Indeed the boy had lain awake many nights scheming to enlist in their ranks.

Whom to follow? Which way was right?

Does God know all? Does He see the suffering of his people?

How can the Creator of the universe remain silent and remote as those who worship Him are debased and degraded, murdered even in their hun-dreds by the war engines of Rome?

David had no answer to such questions—until that evening at the inn called the Foot of the Grade, when first he set eyes upon the man-at-arms, Telamon of Arcadia.

The youth's conversion took less than an instant.

At once, and to the core of his being, David knew that this was what he wanted, this was who he wished to be.

Here, the youth thought, *stands a man whose feet are planted in the real world, not the sphere of dreams or delusion. Here is a man who fears death, as all do, and perhaps due to his vast experience of war reckons even more keenly the mysteries of fate and chance and destiny, yet who faces these down every day and bears the scars to prove it.*

This man seeks not some sphere beyond the mortal or the mundane but instead dwells in this world of dust and strife, without illusion or self-delusion.

David knew at once that he would follow this man. What he taught, David would learn. What he commanded, David would perform.

He, the youth, would enroll himself in the academy of the highway and the school of conflict. Such secrets as the man-at-arms might impart, David knew, would have to be prized from him one lesson at a time, one action, one word. David did not care. Whatever the price, he would pay it.

Why this one? David asked himself now, as he trekked in the train of this solitary mercenary. Why him and not one of the thousands of pike-men and archers and cavalry riders, Jew and Gentile, whom David had encountered over his short but keenly observed span of years?

David sensed something about this individual. He could not have articulated its essence, even in part, even to himself. Yet the boy felt in this man something deeper and more profound than simply "strength" or "skill" or even *andreia*, "manly virtue" in the Greek sense.

This man-at-arms had a religion too. It was not a faith of the lamp or of the blessed by-and-by. It was not a soldier's code or a code of honor. It was sterner and more solitary, a doctrine shorn of pity even for oneself but which touched somehow, David sensed, upon a truth as immutable as death and as primal as creation.

David resolved that he would give all he had, and all he ever would have, to acquire that which this man-at-arms possessed—this wisdom, this understanding, the knowledge of these mysteries. He would die to be and to become, himself, like this man.

BOOK THREE

THE LITTLE DESERT

8

THE STOCK PENS

DAVID TURNED THE CORNER TO the stock pens, and there was the horse—the stolen cavalry mount upon which the Nazarene Michael had made his escape. The animal was a chestnut gelding with a white blaze and four white stockings. It was missing its saddle and all equipment of war. It wore a halter but no bridle.

Telamon saw the horse in the same moment. If his expression altered in any degree, David could not detect it.

Yet clearly the mercenary had led them to this location expecting to find exactly this.

The place was a mixed Judean, Samaritan, and Egyptian settlement, a trading establishment sited at a highway junction called by the Israelites Anthedon and Bardawill by the sons of the Nile. It sat within sight of the Great Sea—Mare Nostrum, as the Romans named it.

Hot.

The place sizzled in the forenoon, pungent with horse, camel, and mule droppings, not to mention the pellets of sheep and goats hemmed in cactus-fenced pens baking in the sun.

The night before, David had suffered a second bout of irrational terror.

He had made up his mind to quit Telamon. He would go home. Better to face the wrath of his father than another day of trekking in silence, waiting for this strange, hard man to acknowledge his presence, let alone care about it. But in the morning, the youth could smell the breeze off the sea. He realized he was not as frightened at the prospect of venturing into the wilderness as he had been the night before. He upbraided himself silently for yielding to such phantoms as spawn in the dark.

The man-at-arms' appearance at the stock pens created its expected stir. The pen boys and stock wranglers, the local farmers bringing their rams and ewes to market . . . none failed to note the LEGIO X tattoo on the mercenary's forearm, or the quality of his weaponry, or the burnt-leather cast of his face. David had to admit to himself that he enjoyed the notoriety of being associated with this man.

"How did he come into your hands?"

This was Telamon, addressing the stock master. The pair stood in the sun-dazzle beside the third of some half dozen rings. In this country where wood was scarce, the stock pens were compassed in stone intermixed with prickly pear cactus in stands as high as a man's chest, with pole gates at intervals. Boys and stock handlers leaned against or perched atop these rails, eyeing the horse. A rope enclosure of its own had been rigged for the animal.

"Blind luck," said the master. "Though such good fortune could cost a man his neck."

David noted the military mark on the stock master's right forearm:

LEGIO VI

This settlement, the youth reckoned, must be a "grant hold"—*conlocationem*, in the Roman tongue—that is, land given to retired legionaries as a mustering-out reward for service.

The stock master himself was a salt of some fifty years, bald as a turnip, with gray in his beard, a sawed-off left ear, and four front teeth made of ivory. Beneath the hem of his tunic could be seen ancient but still-lurid burn scars down the backs of both legs. David saw the man take notice of the soldier's mark on Telamon's forearm, as the mercenary noticed that of his new comrade.

Neither proffered a word in acknowledgment of this, but the tone of each altered when now they bespoke one another. At a nod from the master, a stock boy brought cool water in an earthen crock with a gourd skimmer. Telamon thanked his new mate. He accorded the first refreshment to David. Only then did he drink himself.

The horse, it fell out in conversation over the succeeding minutes, had been discovered running free in the dunes northeast of a place called Rafiah, which site was apparently within several miles of these stock pens. The animal was parched and famished but still needed two teams of riders to be brought to hand. The men recognized the beast at once from the brand on its hindquarters—the **X** of the Tenth Legion—as a runaway or stolen stock. To be caught by the army with this prize in one's possession was death on a Roman cross.

"What d'you think of this specimen of horseflesh, lad?" said the master to David, clapping a hand upon the boy's shoulder. "His worth is more than the likes of you and me will earn in a lifetime. Ten years' schooling went into this bastard—and better care and feed than any road-slapper beneath the rank of file-sergeant. He can charge boot to boot, execute a Laconian counter-march at the full gallop, and hold a surveyor's line amid the trumpets. Smart? This fellow can do everything but stand on his hind legs and talk."

David's glance swung to Telamon. That this horse was free meant two things for certain:

Telamon had been right about the direction in which the Nazarene Michael had fled.

And the fugitive was now on foot.

"See this hobble?" said the stock master to Telamon. He held out a stout leather wrapping, like a man's belt, lined with lamb's wool and meant to be cinched about a horse's forelegs, below the fetlock, to hold the animal in place for grazing or an overnight camp. The binder between the buckles had been chewed through.

"This animal had been secured in such a manner every night since he was a colt and never gave a thought to so much as a nibble. But the first night the thieves hobbled him so, he waited till they corked off, then 'chomp-chomp' and away he goes!"

"No saddle or bridle?"

"You'll find 'em where the runaways last made camp, I'll wager. Burned now, or buried so deep no one will ever find them."

"Where," Telamon asked, "would you guess that camp would be?"

The stock master smiled. "Exactly where you're going."

As Telamon and the master yarned, a camel-and-horse train appeared from the south, emerging from the mirage upon the track that arose out of the wilderness of Sinai.

The caravan entered the pens by a hinter trace screened by a line of tamarisks—an entrance intended, it seemed, to obscure the train's apparition from observation from the main road.

David noted the stock master hailing the leader in welcome by name, while whistling up the stable boys, who came scurrying to take charge of the stock, to water and feed them, see to their tack and pack rigs, and to offer food and drink to the men of the caravan. David found himself glancing to Telamon. The man-at-arms observed these new arrivals closely.

What struck David about the company, aside from the thick and heavy coating of dust and loess—the talc-like grit of the desert that seemed to adhere to every surface of flesh or fabric—was that, though the freight their beasts bore was of extremely modest dimensions (only five camels, with panniers that lay almost flat against their flanks), yet the detachment was protected by no fewer than a dozen riders—black-hooded, with their faces masked—all Jews of the orthodox sect of Sadducees, identified by their balloon trousers and nine-foot lances, mounted on the swift, hardy runt ponies of the peninsula, and all armed to the teeth.

"A train out of Alexandria," the stock master remarked, observing David's puzzled expression. "Twelve days these have made, across the full desolation of the wilderness." The freight borne by this train was bound, the master said, for the Great Temple in Jerusalem. It would return in twenty days and make the run again.

"What's in the bags?" David asked.

"That which," said the stock master, "no Roman tax collector will ever see."

David noted that the mounted warriors took especial notice of

Telamon and the legion-derived aspects of his kit, before concluding apparently that he was neither spy nor serving soldier but a solitary man-at-arms on the tramp.

The caravan riders handed their animals into the care of the stable boys. They themselves, dismounted now yet retaining their arms, made their way to the shade of the outdoor kitchen. Four of the warriors detached themselves from their fellows. These remained beside the laden camels. They took at this time neither food nor drink.

The stock master turned again to Telamon.

"He'll be going for the Anthill," the fellow said.

"Who?"

"The man you're after."

David's ears perked up at this. The youth had heard tales of this place, an outlaw refuge so deep into the desert that not even the Romans dared venture there.

The Anthill, so the stories said, was a city entirely underground, populated by three wildly disparate communities—ascetics and anchorites seeking ecstatic visions in the wilderness; political refugees hunted by the Romans; and outlaws and slave traders, bandits and freebooters of the native tribes whose raiding territories encompassed all Sinai. These abided communally within the Anthill under a truce ancient as Adam. "But you reckoned that," said the stock master to Telamon, "before you came."

David studied the cagey old fellow. Roman cavalry, he thought, had surely come through these pens in the past few days, seeking the stolen horse and the man and child who made off with it. They would keep no secrets in such a place and with such a mate.

Telamon seemed to be thinking the same thing.

"This man I'm after," said he to the master. "Would he have tarried here in his flight?"

"Ah, such a fellow would be far too canny for that."

Telamon laughed and set a silver "Antony"—the old-time denarius minted in the wars against Octavian and still in use—into the master's palm. The mercenary paid to have his own mules looked to. He desired especially, he told the stock master, that their hooves be examined by one possessed of veterinary competence, particularly the inner-sole "frogs," which must be sound and clean of all stones or spines.

The master regarded him.

"This man you're after? May I ask, is it he alone you seek, or some item of value that he carries?"

Telamon made no reply. He requested of the master that he have his stable attendants shave the backs of both mules and that he suffer the youth David to look on and learn. The coarse hairs along the beasts' spines, sweated and matted beneath the weight of the pack frame and panniers, inevitably twisted themselves into knots that dug into the animals' flesh like burrs under a saddle. Shaving cleared these irritants away.

The master said he would see to this at once.

"Him for whom you work this assignment . . . he resides in the Antonia Fortress at Jerusalem, does he not?" The stock master indicated the wilderness to the south. "So you would, in this officer's service, venture out and back?"

The master cried up his boys, who came on the run to take hold of Telamon's beasts and look to their needs.

"The desert is a gantlet of outlaws and desperadoes," said the master to the mercenary. "Its way of life is banditry. If you own good sense, and I believe you do, you'll not double your track and the jeopardy in which such a course would place you, but instead keep making west."

The stock master took Telamon by the elbow and drew him close.

"And I will tell you something more, my friend. If this 'item of value' is what I think it is, you will upon acquiring it neither sleep nor eat until you stand within the court of the *prefectus augustalis* in Alexandria in Egypt. To him and not to Jerusalem will you render this prize. For Alexandria, a mighty city dear to Rome, may draw on the imperial treasury to reward those it favors, while Judea must rely upon the straitened coffers of its military establishment."

David attended upon the stable boys while they looked to the mules' hooves and backs and helped pad and re-rig the animals' pack frames. When the youth sought to interrogate these lads about the contents of the Black Hoods' camel packs, the boys giggled and glanced furtively about.

They were Idumaeans, rude fellows of the frontier villages, who spoke a dialect David's ear could barely penetrate.

From the barn the youth could see Telamon outside with the stock master. The pair knelt together. The master was drawing something with a stick in the dirt. Telamon put forward questions, indicating certain points in the scribble. David could see the stock master answer these.

After several minutes, the master and the mercenary moved together to a bench beneath the sunshade of the outdoor kitchen. There they shared a meal of alphita bread, boiled eggs, salt, and olive oil. At repast's end the master made to make this meal a gift. Telamon declined with emphasis. David could see him set two copper coins beside the dishes and hand another to the kitchen urchins who had served them.

At the gate the stock master strode forth to see Telamon and David on their way. To the youth he passed a parcel wrapped in a frond of areca palm—a dinner of bread, eggs, salt, and oil, as he and the man-at-arms had just shared. David thanked him. The boy's glance kept returning to the covered stockades, to the Black Hoods and their weapons and wares. "*Shomrim*," said the master, employing the Hebrew term for "guardians," as of the people and the faith.

"An army-in-waiting," he observed to Telamon. "For that day when their God commands them to cast off the Roman yoke."

Telamon and David took in hand the leads of their mules' halters and turned the beasts toward the southwest, the direction of the wilderness of Sinai. The stock master pointed to a range of basalt ridges receding into the deep distance. He suggested that Telamon make his first camp at the westernmost shoulder of this formation, a place called the Lavender Valley, on the trace to Wadi Alnahl. A man there named Timothy would have observed and acquired intelligence of every party entering the wilderness by this route.

"You'll need a *dolet*," said the master. He used the Hebrew word for "gift," as in that offering of respect that a guest donates to his host in return for haven and hospitality. The veteran indicated a row of clay vessels squatting in the sun. "Help yourself to as many as you like. A good wine jar is always welcome."

At a nod from Telamon, David collected several. He secured them with scrupulous care among the mules' loads, in such a manner as to keep them from jostling against one another. The stock master looked on with an expression of amusement.

"And can it be, my lad, that you own no trepidation about venturing into this cruelest of wildernesses, populated by the half mad and the wholly iniquitous?"

"I follow my master," David declared. "And, reverencing heaven, seek no further surety."

9

THE LITTLE DESERT

THE DESERT DID NOT BECOME desert all at once.

Man and boy came first to a village called Abusan al-Kabir, so destitute it had not even a market but one bought *lupa* melons on the roadside from barefoot waifs and toothless housedames; then a slightly larger village called Wadi Kabrit. David could smell the sea from both places and, at a third site, whose name he forgot, could glimpse palm trees above the shore, though he could not actually see the water.

A good Roman road, the Via Solitudia, stone-founded and two wagon-widths broad, ran along the coast. Telamon, however, kept clear of this.

"Him we pursue will not risk this track."

Rather, the mercenary took the camel trace used by Bedouin and other nomadic grazers of stock, which followed the great circle route from Petra in Arabia Nabatea to Beersheba, and from there across Sinai to the Great Bitter Lake and Egyptian Pelusium and the easternmost mouth of the Nile.

Signs of civilization remained abundant in this region of pre-desert. Migrating birds passed in numbers. Droppings of sheep and goats littered each site against a cliffside or wadi wall beneath which animals could be temporarily penned or rested. Caravans passed. One spied renunciants, sometimes alone, other times in colonies, camped in cave pockets or tucked under stone shelves scoured from the faces of escarpments.

David had imagined that the wilderness would be untenanted, a land-scape void of life and traffic. To his surprise the place bustled with activity, of men and beasts and even of vegetation. Early in the postnoon he and Telamon entered a depression between ranges of hills. Ahead David could make out a landscape of bushes, which he took to be tamarisk or perhaps acacia. Approaching these, he realized they were people—women harvest-ing desert plants.

The females were swathed head to foot in brightly colored muslin, with only a slit for eyes and nose. Each carried a skin of drinking water and, trailed behind her upon the earth, tied by a tether about her waist, a great billowing sack of linen.

Telamon hailed the most proximate of these harvesters as he and David came up. "What do you reap, sisters?"

The dame held up a withered sprig. She wore mittens of rawhide and took care not to let the plant near her nose or mouth or to breathe its vapors.

"*Haban, ashkar,* Sodom's apple." She indicated a smaller, second sack about her waist. "And devil's trumpet."

"Are you witches?" Telamon asked.

The woman laughed. "Slaves."

David noticed, then, warders among the foragers, in muffled garb as well, armed with bows, slings, and lances.

Man and boy sat out the heat of the later postnoon at a spring beneath an outcrop. A father and son had taken shelter in this shade as well. The pair led an ass so small that David thought at first it was a dog, yet laden with a load as weighty as that borne by Telamon's broad-backed Jericho mule.

"What are you doing out here?" David asked the boy.

The lad lifted the flap on one of the sacks on the ass's back. The bag writhed with live scorpions.

"We milk them," he said, "for the poison."

The venom would be processed into an elixir called an *almahlusat,* "vision maker," the father explained. This stuff was much prized in Alexandria and even in Rome. "Priests use it too," he said.

"What for?" David asked.

"To see God."

"The desert is a *froomah,* my boy!" declared the father, using the Nabatean word for "pharmacy." "Whatever ails a man, God has here planted its antidote. And free of all imposts!"

One traversed this pre-wilderness, David came to understand, from inhabited place to inhabited place, or more exactly from well to well. Encountering a fellow upon the trail, a traveler proffered news of the country through which he had passed and received the same from him he hailed.

Out here, when you asked how far it was from point to point, the answer was given in wells. "To Wadi Alnahl, four wells." "Alexandria, thirty."

David dared not ask Telamon where the Big Desert began, or when they would come upon it. The mercenary, he knew, would only cede him a stern look.

Man and boy came late in the day to a sere valley so devoid of life that neither could pick out a tree or even a bush. David was tramping in a semi-stupor, brought about by the double oppression of the late sun glaring into his eyes and the waves of fire yet ascending through his soles from the still-scorching desert floor. He had fallen twenty paces behind Telamon.

David noticed a bee land on the back of his right hand.

How odd, he thought, *here where there are neither blooms nor flowers.* A second touched down, then a third and a fourth. David heard a fierce buzzing, then felt a shadow, like that cast by a cloud, hissing directly above. A bee flew up one of his mule's nostrils. The beast balked and squalled.

Before David could reckon or react, a swarm of thousands filled the air about his eyes and ears. Ahead, he saw Telamon enveloped by the same assault. David's mule bawled and kicked; the boy had to seize the halter rope with both hands.

"Master!" he heard his voice cry. He scurried forward, fleeing this onslaught, which followed, emitting a keening thrum that seemed to drown utterly David's cries.

Through the furious cloud about his head, the boy spotted an upright post, or perhaps it was a stump, standing beside the mercenary. Telamon was speaking to this.

David realized the post was a man.

The man's flesh was covered in a carpet of bees.

David hastened up.

Bees fashioned a beard upon the fellow's face and a helmet atop his brow. The swarm made him as well a coat and trousers, and even ankle-boots about his feet.

"Hold still," the fellow commanded. "Do not swat. And whatever you do, show no fear."

Bees in myriads enveloped Telamon and David. But no mass settled upon either's flesh as they did upon the man made of bees. Instead the bees swarmed in a cloud about their heads.

"Remain calm," said the man. "These will wing away in a moment."

Sure enough, after a few seconds the swarm took flight. By the count of twenty the host had vanished entirely, except those settled upon the man made of bees. These seemed utterly at ease and void of agitation. They neither buzzed nor hummed.

"Welcome to the Valley of Lavender," said the fellow. He gestured around the shoulder of the ridge. There, extending for miles within a sheltering cove, spread a carpet of bloom, in vivid blue, pink, rose, purple, and violet. "You are free to pass through."

David stared at the man in astonishment. Bees filled the pockets of his ears and the voids of his nostrils. They trod even upon the lashes of his eyes.

"Are you all right, sir? Does this swarm remain upon you night and day?"

The man laughed and indicated that he felt no distress.

"But," said David, "don't they sting you?"

The man smiled with lips made of bees. "I am all stings," he said.

Telamon's glance to David said, *Uncover the panniers.*

The youth obeyed.

"If I may ask," the mercenary addressed his host, "are you called Timothy?"

"I am."

The mercenary introduced himself and David. He said nothing about the errand he ran or whom he ran it for. He indicated the load of clay jars that he and the boy had carried on their mules from the stock pens. "We have brought you a dolet."

The man made of bees thanked Telamon and directed him and the boy to follow.

Telamon and David were not permitted to enter the Valley of Lavender. They were led by their host a quarter mile beyond the shoulder of the ridge. From this vantage they were directed to a bivouac among tamarisks at the southern terminus of the vale.

"Leave the jars there," said the man. "I will send a boy for them later. There is a spring with a pool, at which you may refresh yourselves. Stay just the night. You are the only travelers at the moment. You will be alone and safe."

The pockets of the man's eyes cleared themselves now of bees, as did his nose and upper lip. David found that he was already becoming accustomed to this odd apparition.

"We were told at the stock pens in Gaza," said Telamon to Timothy, "that you might possess intelligence of any who had passed this way."

The mercenary reached for his purse.

Timothy's raised hand made clear that the offer of remuneration was unnecessary.

Telamon apologized at once. He begged the man's pardon if he had inadvertently offered offense.

"In the wilderness," said Timothy, "all in need are aided, as each himself may one day be in need of aid."

The man made of bees straightened and glanced about. Clearly he was readying to take his leave. No other human or animal stood visible as far as sight could carry.

"He whom you seek," said Timothy, "passed this way three nights ago."

The fellow unslung an article from his shoulder. David realized that the man was carrying some kind of rucksack. From its folds the fellow withdrew a clay jar the size of a small melon. The jar was sealed across its mouth with wax and tied with twine.

"Honey," said the man made of bees.

He handed the jar to Telamon.

"This will be your dolet for the Anthill."

The man turned and began to step away, still enshrouded.

"Sir!" Telamon hailed the fellow to turn about. The mercenary thanked him for the honey and for access to the spring and camping ground. "How did you know that we sought someone? Or that we were bound for the Anthill?"

"Only a fool or a madman ventures into this wilderness unless he seeks an item of value. I possess acquaintance of the man who passed by three nights ago. He told me you would be following."

David wished urgently to ask, *Did the man mean us specifically? Or just any party who might be in his pursuit? And did he give you permission to direct us upon his trail?*

The boy bit his tongue, however, seeing Telamon refrain from seeking this intelligence.

The man made of bees stood now directly before the mercenary. His face had momentarily cleared of the swarm. He was an individual of middle years, David saw, with kindly eyes etched by what the boy could reckon only as sorrow.

"If I may ask, sir," said Telamon. "How did you come to be in this place? Were you born here?"

"I was born in Jerusalem," the man said. He displayed his palms, void now of their sheathing of bees. In the pit of each stood a deep lurid scar, the produce of such a puncture as could be inflicted by no instrument other than an iron spike.

Again David curbed his tongue.

"Enemies of the empire preserved me," said the man made of bees. "They brought me to safety here. These healed me." He indicated the swarm still buzzing about his arms and shoulders. "I serve them now," he said. "And all who pass by."

Telamon again thanked the man for his hospitality and for the intelligence he proffered. The mercenary's glance to David instructed the youth to take up his mule's halter and to follow to the camping ground at the terminus of the ridge. As David did so, he saw Telamon turn back and again hail the man made of bees.

"May I trouble you with one last question, my friend?"

The man faced about.

"If others," said Telamon, "should pass this way and inquire if the boy and I have come through here, will you tell them?"

The man indicated the swarm now re-enveloping him. "That," he said, "will be up to these."

10

THE FIVE-MILE PAN

DAVID COULD NOT GOVERN HIS restless mind and tongue.

"Why do we lead these mules?" He spoke up on the postnoon beyond the Lavender Valley. Telamon had terminated the day's trek and set about to make camp. The mercenary did this always hours before last light, selecting a site that could not easily be gotten above by enemies. He would prepare bread in a ground oven, a flat loaf that he tore in two and which he and David devoured with olive oil and raw onions. The mercenary's drink was *posca*, a Roman brew of vinegar and wine that David found repulsive.

At camp the man-at-arms saw to the animals first. Only after the beasts' needs had been attended to did Telamon permit himself and David to take food or even to sit. The mercenary performed next his calisthenics, a chore of half an hour. Man and boy then repacked such kit as they had made use of in preparing camp, reloaded the mules, and moved camp to what, to David's eyes, invariably appeared the most remote, inhospitable site imaginable.

"Sleep," Telamon would say. "I'll take the first watch." But David could not sleep—until it was his turn to stand sentinel, when he struggled so mightily against slumber that he took to slapping himself across the face and even pricking his flesh with camel thorn to keep from dozing.

Telamon enacted the identical protocol the following day, from trek to early camp to sleeping camp. David held silent throughout. As man and boy off-loaded the mules for the second time, however, the youth could maintain this posture no longer.

"Why must we pitch camp twice each day? I thought we were in haste pursuing the Nazarene Michael. And why won't you let us ride these beasts? Don't we wish to make speed? Why didn't we take horses? Why must we tarry at the pace of these glue-footed creatures? And why not at least let them bear our personal kit? You make us carry all our gear ourselves. All these animals pack is water and fodder for themselves and a few spear shafts that we'll never use and a couple of pots and a hand mill. And why must we pitch camp so far up these stupid slopes? It takes us two hours of trekking to get to these sites. What for? We only descend again in the morning, wasting even more time! I thought the reason for Roman training was so the legions could cover long distances fast. Yet we amble and dawdle, making camp in the middle of the afternoon letting hours of daylight go to waste, only to pack up and make camp again!"

Telamon said nothing.

"And why do you never answer my questions? How will I learn to be a warrior if you will not teach me?"

The next morning, an hour into the day's trek, the mercenary drew up on a ridge overlooking a basin between two basalt ranges. Spines of rocky hills flanked this pan, extending ahead as far as the eye could see.

"By what route," Telamon asked the boy, "would you cross this flat?"

David pointed to a camel trace running down the center.

Telamon said nothing.

Two hours later, as man and boy stumbled, leading the mules, along the talus line of the northernmost of the ridges, slipping upon jagged scree and laboring with painful effort across broken ground, David cursed himself for even venturing a query.

Several hours on, they halted. Telamon lifted the pack frame and panniers from his mule to let the beast rest. David did likewise, though he thought it ridiculous to favor the animals so.

"We never cross a valley or any stretch of open ground by a road or trail," the mercenary said, "but always from ambush site to ambush site. This is called highlining."

He indicated the stony trace beneath their feet. "This track is called the talus line. You have been a shepherd. What do you see now before you? A trail made by wild goats and harts and mountain asses. These shy animals will be our guides. From this trail we can see any enemy crossing the pan below, yet he cannot see us unless we choose to show ourselves. If we were a legion, indeed we would cross by the valley floor. We'd have no choice, trekking with a baggage train and camp followers as numerous as our soldiery. But we are only two. Upon this ground we are the equal of a legion."

A few hours farther, making camp, Telamon spoke again.

"We travel with mules because horses' legs will break in these mountains. A mule descending a slope in darkness will never step false. In extremity a mule will lead us to water, while a horse will wander in circles and die. We can sell these beasts if we need cash, or trade them, or eat them should we become desperate. And they're good company. See how attached these two have become to us already? You lead yours by its halter no longer, nor do I. We have stopped hobbling them at night. They will not abandon us, believe me, even under fire."

David was so relieved that Telamon had spoken that he found himself actually smiling.

"Should we give the animals names, then?"

"No," said Telamon at once. "I'm sorry I know even yours."

Night fell. Man and boy had moved to even higher ground, having dispersed their "bread camp" so that no sign of it remained. The mercenary bedded down the mules in a hollow. He himself took up a position—hatless, cross-legged, with his gladius sword in its sheath across his knees and two pila javelins at his side—upon a stony eminence looking back over the pan they had been crossing all day.

"Sit," he said, indicating a spot next to him.

David obeyed. He too set weapons to hand—the dolabra Telamon had given him and a dagger of his own possession—and faced back, like the mercenary, out over the plain.

"What are we doing?" David asked.

"Watch."

"Watch what?"

Telamon offered no answer.

An hour later the man-at-arms had not moved. He had not risen or even stretched. The sun had vanished; night's chill was coming down hard.

The boy shivered. His teeth chattered. His mind balked like an unruly colt. He chafed; he scratched; his joints screamed. At two hours he shifted as if to rise. Telamon's hand caught his thigh. The man pressed the boy back into his sitting posture.

"I have to piss!"

"Then piss."

Again the boy sought to stand. Again the man held him down.

"Make water where you are."

The moon crawled across the frozen sky. David counted silently to a thousand. When he glanced again, the moon had barely budged. Twice he checked and was sure the orb was moving backward.

Six hours in, the youth was certain he was losing his mind. Thoughts of terror and dislocation ricocheted inside his skull. He saw jackals. He saw wolves. Scorpions tiptoed across his ankles. He saw the devil. He saw God. He saw his mother and his sisters.

He realized at one point that he was urinating through his tunic into the dirt.

"Sir, I'm freezing."

Hour eight. The youth again shifted to rise. The man's hand held him down. He would not let the boy move.

Twice in the night the boy dozed. Both times he awoke with a start, feeling the sharpened apex of the man-at-arms' sword, tucked under the flesh of his tottering chin.

Dawn approached. The boy's knees felt as if they had turned to stone. Rigor mortis seemed to have set into his jaw. He could not feel his extremities.

His solitary vow was to terminate this self-imposed indenture.

He had been a fool to undertake this enterprise.

Hell itself could not be more excruciating.

The boy blinked and rubbed his eyes.

The five-mile pan beneath him had turned a pallid pink with the first glimmer of dawn. The air yet crackled with the night's chill.

Telamon's posture remained upright. He had neither risen nor spoken nor moved all night.

"Still here?" the man-at-arms said.

The boy was struggling in his mind to frame the words that would emancipate him from this folly.

"Tell me what you saw," said the man.

"You mean in my head?"

"I mean out there."

Telamon indicated the five-mile pan beneath them.

"Did you see that column of horse? Do you see it now?"

The boy blinked and strained.

"There," said the man. "See the dawn light reflecting off their armor?"

David's eyes refused to focus. Both cheeks reddened. His bones rattled inside their sheaths.

Telamon pointed again across the plain.

David saw the column now.

"Romans," said Telamon. "They've been visible for the past hour, tracking along the exact course they expect us to be taking."

The boy felt his whole body flush with shame.

Sit.

Watch.

How would he ever become a warrior if he could not accomplish even these?

Telamon indicated the equites legionis advancing in column of twos, at a walk, across the basin below.

"Why," he said, "do you think those cavalrymen have come out here?"

The youth hesitated. "The garrison commander sent them."

For the first time, the man-at-arms' expression indicated approval.

"When we have got the Nazarene Michael and the letter," he said, "these troopers will run us down and kill us."

11

THE PASTEL CANYON

B Y MIDMORNING MAN AND BOY had passed on to a broad, stony plain with limestone ridges ascending on each side. They crossed this briskly, afoot beside their mules. Nearing noon Telamon inclined the train toward a spiny patch of tamarisk that appeared to offer shade. The man had not spoken all morning.

David was thinking, *Soon he will stop to off-load the mules and let them rest.* The boy anticipated this with pleasure, as it meant, for him, a gulp or two from the water skin.

Instead Telamon slowed and permitted David to pull up beside him. "What do you make," the mercenary said, "of the solitary rider trailing us?"

David again experienced a flush of mortification. He was too ashamed even to turn and look.

"You mean the Romans, sir?"

A stern glance answered this.

"Whoever he is, he's been tracking us since the Lavender Valley. Should we let him overhaul us?"

"Let me kill him, sir!" These words sprang with passion from David's lips, seemingly unbidden.

Telamon smiled.

"I will!" said the boy. "Lead us to a straitened place. By heaven, I'll show you!"

Man and boy continued across the stony pan. David peered again and again into the desert behind them. He could see nothing.

Kites and ravens soared overhead.

Had you flown among them, high above the wilderness floor, you would have seen the man-at-arms halt the train within a copse of terebinth and acacia, at the foot of a granite ridge.

A well.

From your vantage soaring above, your gaze would have taken in a practiced drill performed in silence by the man and boy. The mules were halted first and hobbled at a distance from the water. Youth and man off-loaded the panniers from the beasts' backs, then the pack frames. Next they rubbed and dried the animals' chafed and sweated hides. The beasts bawled now, smelling the water.

At a sign from the man, the boy crossed to the well and, plunging the water skin by its plaited leather thong, awaited the splash at the bottom and the feeling of the skin filling through its open mouth. He hauled this vessel hand over hand back up into the sun. By then the man had rigged the three-pole stand with its basin of oiled calfskin that made a drinking trough for the mules. The man spoke quietly to the animals as the boy crossed back, bearing the glistening, dripping skin.

The boy filled the basin.

The animals were permitted to water.

The boy trotted now to the eastern edge of the oasis. He peered back into the noon haze, seeking sign of the rider following. He could spy nothing.

The boy returned, feeling Telamon's eyes upon him.

This next you would have witnessed, had you been sailing overhead with the ravens and kites.

The man now stripped his robe and strode to a patch of shade within the grove. There he commenced his exercises at arms.

First he faced the bole of a stout acacia. Using this in the stead of a Roman-style "post," he moved through a series of evolutions, first hurling the pilum from a distance, then working the gladius from close range. The man-at-arms moved without haste and without sound. Thrust, parry, turn, strike. Advance to a pass, wheel about, thrust, withdraw, thrust again. The boy heeded with fierce attention.

The man offered no instruction. He did not speak a word. Finishing his exercises at the post, he stepped to an open space upon the hardpan. Planting his feet wide and at an acute angle one to the other, the warrior moved with exquisite intention and concentration through a second series of evolutions, first freehand, then with the gladius. These calisthenics rehearsed actions prescribed for combat—certain thrusts and parries, advances and retreats, turns and wheel-abouts.

Again the man-at-arms proffered no verbal direction.

At one point the man struck a certain stance. He motioned to the boy, instructing him to approach. The man directed the youth to take up the twelve-pound iron shield that rested now among the mules' unloaded gear and to secure this device as firmly as he could upon his own left forearm, planting his left shoulder within the upper rim of the bowl.

Rush upon me, commanded the man-at-arms.

Hit me.

The boy hesitated.

The man insisted.

Don't come at half speed.

All-out.

Hard as you can.

The boy obeyed.

The bowl of the shield rang like a bell as the youth slammed at a flat-out sprint into the man-at-arm's shoulder. The man's stance did not budge even half a handsbreadth. The boy sprawled, dazed, upon the ground.

Again.

Again, harder.

Harder still.

The youth collided, each time, as if into a wall of stone.

The boy's brow, left ear, and both hands were bleeding from sustaining the impact of the iron shield upon the fixed, immovable target.

The man indicated that the boy could stop. He assumed again the stance he had employed throughout.

"This," he said, "is called 'castling'."

He gestured for the boy to attack again.

This time, a split interval before the fatal instant, the man peeled to the side, out of the path of the youth's onrush. The boy sailed wildly past, touching nothing. Amid the lad's plunge, the man caught him by one ankle and upended him bodily, employing a gesture so compact it seemed he had barely moved, flipping the youth with powerful violence into the dirt. All breath shot from the lad's lungs. The boy peered up, stunned and breathless. The claw of the man's left fist clutched him by the privates, the talons of his right seized him around the throat.

"That turn," the man said, "is called 'beetling'."

He helped the boy up.

All defensive actions in combat, Telamon told the lad, were variations on castling and beetling.

Man and boy took their lunch of parched barley mixed with oil. The man drained a bowl of posca. The boy took water.

"If I may ask, master." The youth summoned courage to speak. "What was the nature of your acquaintance with the tribune Severus?"

The man-at-arms drew up at this. For a moment his brow darkened, as if he took offense at the presumption of the youth's query. Then his countenance relented. He seemed, in his way, to approve of his apprentice's temerity.

"These arts of combat I teach you now," the mercenary said, "I taught to him."

The train, repacked, pressed on westward toward the true beginnings of the desert.

The mirage began to clear with the postnoon.

At one point, at a distance to the flank, David sighted what appeared to be a column of smoke. Telamon with reluctance inclined the train to investigate.

The smoke was a man—naked and solitary, with no sign of a camp or of any baggage.

"Who is he?" said David.

"An anchorite. A hermit seeking God."

The fellow danced barefoot across the fiery floor, chanting some ditty comprehensible only to himself.

"Leave him be," said Telamon.

Man and boy passed on.

An hour farther, the noon mirage cleared completely. For the first time, David could see the dust of the rider trailing them.

He glanced to Telamon.

Telamon saw this too.

Deeper into the postnoon, man and boy entered a region of narrow, wind-sculpted canyons, whose walls rose high above them and whose smooth, pastel-hued flanks pressed so tightly about their lane of passage that they had to lead their animals from directly in front.

"The rider trailing us," said the boy, "can pass no way but through this canyon if he follows our tracks." The lad's right hand clutched his dagger. "Let me leap upon him, sir."

The mercenary smiled. "And what will you do with that chicken-sticker?"

"Teach him manners."

The man laughed and trekked on.

The boy followed, sullen and grumbling.

The pair came minutes later to a singularly straitened passage, with rock shelves above the height of a mounted man on both sides.

"I can take him here from above. Please, sir. Let me!"

"And what if our pursuer is an innocent? Perhaps another holy man, as we encountered earlier."

"This son-of-a-whore is no innocent."

"He's a whore's son now, is he?"

The boy would wait no longer, but springing onto his mule's back and launching himself from this platform, he scampered up the canyon wall to a ledge upon which he could remain hidden from any rider approaching along the canyon lane and from which he could with ease leap upon the intruder.

Telamon said nothing, only stretched his arm back from his position in the lead and took the halter rope belonging to the boy's mule.

"Thank you, master. I shall not fail."

Telamon hiked on for another half furlong, until the passage widened to a room-sized clearing. Here he hobbled the mules, set their nosebags with a portion of parched oats, and, taking a javelin and his sword, scampered soundlessly back along the sand floor till he came to a shelf across from the boy's and some half dozen steps above it.

Minutes passed.

Man and boy strained their ears, seeking the clinking sound of a harness and buckle, or the snuffling nicker of an approaching horse.

Once the boy farted.

The man had to bite his lip, so comical appeared the expression on the lad's face.

All at once here came the rider.

The pursuer rode hooded and muffled. His gaze appeared centered only upon the hoofprints in the sand before him.

With a cry, the boy launched himself.

He missed.

The youth had leapt with too much enthusiasm. His left shoulder first, then his skull above the ear crashed into the far wall of the canyon.

"Auggh!" the rider cried, struck sidelong by this unexpected projectile. His mount reared. The man was thrown.

David, burning with mortification, leapt upon the fellow, who swung his elbow wildly in self-defense. Telamon saw David's dagger sail from the boy's grip.

The rider fled afoot.

David tackled him.

But now each had become entangled in the other's robes.

David punched and kicked at the interloper. He seized the fellow's cowl and tore it back to reveal his face.

The rider was a woman.

The sorceress.

The female's rat's nest of curls spilled forth from beneath her hood.

She rose and clawed at David's eyes with her filthy talons. A furious kick struck the youth squarely in the testicles.

The witch was shrieking now, in Hebrew, calling down curses upon the lad, who, recognizing her (not to say being doubled over from her assault upon him), broke off his attack and toppled backward against the canyon wall.

The sorceress loomed over the boy with both fists clenched, hissing and spitting like a hellcat.

Telamon, laughing from his belly, looked on from his shelf above.

BOOK FOUR

THE ANTHILL

12

JUICE OF THE ELAH

THE NIGHT AND THE MORNING passed. The party of Telamon and David had cleared, now, the region of canyons. They trekked a plain of gravel *serir*. To their rear, so far behind that only the dust of her tread could be glimpsed, trudged the sorceress.

David, addressing Telamon, gestured toward this trailing wisp.

"Sir, might we, without producing hazard to ourselves or our mission, display some measure of pity for the poor woman?"

"It was you who begged me to let you kill her."

The witch, once she had affirmed her victory over David in the canyon, had collapsed to her knees, unstrung by exhaustion and desiccation. Her pony appeared in equivalent straits. Telamon collected the beast. He stripped the woman naked and confiscated her weapons, of which she bore three—a *sica* dagger; a sling with twelve lead bullets; and a weighted dart concealed in her waistband. The man-at-arms donated enough water to bring the sorceress's animal to lifting its head again. He would give none to the woman.

"I am not following you," the witch swore. "I escaped from the prison. I make now for the Anthill, as do all fugitives fleeing the armies of Rome." The sorceress beseeched Telamon's mercy, citing her own aid of him during the jailhouse interview.

"You told me nothing," said Telamon. "You are sent now by Severus, with treachery alone in mind."

The first night fell. The man-at-arms would not permit the female to make camp within a hundred paces. He gave David leave to look to her horse but refused all accommodation to the woman herself. Setting the first night's watch, he bound the witch at the wrists and the ankles and staked her to the earth. He directed David to kindle a lamp-fire beside her and to keep this alight throughout his turn on watch. If the female managed to free so much as one limb, the boy was to kill her.

The woman swore a mighty oath that she bore no confederacy with Severus or any entity of Rome. She had broken free of the Antonia Fortress by means of the black arts, she declared, and trooped now upon this trace only because it was the most direct route to the Anthill.

Telamon inquired of the woman how she got past Timothy at the Lavender Valley.

"That fool? You think I let him see me? I soared past as a raven, black in the night!"

Telamon smiled. "You and your pony?" The man-at-arms indicated areas of swollen flesh about the witch's limbs. "But other sentries spotted you, didn't they? Those are bee stings on your hands, arms, and face."

The sorceress snarled.

Telamon instructed David in how he was to make an end of her.

"You have slaughtered sheep and goats?"

The boy nodded, grimly and reluctantly.

"One strong blow here," said the man-at-arms, "between the eyes, to stun her. Drop her into the dirt facedown. Set your knee between her shoulders with all the weight of your body holding her in place. Set your blade in your right hand beneath her jaw. Press your left palm against the back of her head. Jerk up hard with your right hand, making sure you open the windpipe as well as the artery. She'll bleed out quicker than a goose."

The boy protested that he could not do this.

Telamon regarded him.

"That sica in her kit. Whose liver do you think she aims to pierce with it? After she pierces mine?"

Hearing this, the woman cried, in Hebrew, for David's ear, that Telamon was a brute and an enemy of heaven and that he, the youth, would find his soul accursed forever if he acted in such a monster's abettance.

The youth turned toward Telamon to translate.

"I understood," he said.

The man-at-arms declared that the witch was his, David's, responsibility. "Kill her now or kill her later. You will have to do one or the other."

The boy could not.

The man-at-arms turned away toward the camp.

Morning came. Man and boy, now leading three animals, passed out of the region of canyons and emerged onto a broad stony plain cut by numerous dry riverbeds.

They made their early camp in the shade of a shallow ridge. Telamon looked to the animals' needs, performed his calisthenics, then prepared a ground oven for baking the day's loaf.

Out on the wasteland, the sorceress staggered into view, afoot.

David watched her.

After an excruciating interval the woman managed to stumble into such proximity of the camp as to make her voice heard.

"I will not beg," she cried.

Telamon was standing, facing her. The witch's state had clearly become extreme.

"May I come out of the sun with you?"

"Remain where you are."

"May I make a collection?"

The sorceress meant would Telamon permit her to gather roots and herbs.

"You may not," he said.

"Will you spare me at least enough water to make a tea?"

"I will give you nothing," said Telamon. And, setting a hand upon the hilt of his sword, he advanced upon her.

The witch withdrew.

Telamon caught his mule's halter and turned to David. "We will move to make our night camp now."

The man started off.

The boy resisted.

"Sir," said he, "we cannot leave the woman in this state."

"Why not?"

"Do you see her ankles?" Suppurating sores ran along the flesh of both the sorceress's legs. "Leprosy devours her!"

"Those are sores from prison irons," said Telamon. "Either way, her broths and poultices will do nothing to allay the affliction. She'll be dead before two more dawns."

David bore over his shoulder one of the party's three water skins. Defying his master, he strode back to the woman. He splashed the liquid into her cupped palms. The witch gulped greedily. Among her kit David spied a small bronze basin. He filled this as well and left it with her.

The boy marched back to Telamon.

"Your heart is too kind," pronounced the man-at-arms.

But he did nothing to overturn David's intercession.

The pair moved on, establishing their night camp upon an elevated promontory about a mile farther west.

With dawn they moved out again, leading their two mules and the pony they had taken from the sorceress. They glimpsed wolves in the half-light, and a herd of a hundred gazelles, so shy they bolted at thrice the distance of a bowshot.

"Sir!" David exclaimed of a sudden, pointing rearward. "Do you see?"

The sorceress could be descried in the distance, hobbling toward them upon a crooked staff. "She must have been tramping all night," David declared. The youth begged his master to help. "Sir, the wolves! They will scent her!"

With a gesture Telamon silenced the boy. He signed his permission to bring help to the woman. David seized a water skin. He grabbed the pony by its halter and bolted at once to the witch's aid.

Telamon looked on, unmoving.

As the youth assisted the sorceress in her painful passage, the man-at-arms stepped away toward a stand of *elah* trees, called by the Arabs *butm*. The mercenary cut several green branches, carved slits in them lengthwise, and laid them out in the warmth of the fast-ascending sun.

David and the woman came up.

Telamon permitted the witch to take water. He allowed David to tear for her a few scraps of last night's bread.

Clearly the sorceress was suffering terribly.

The man-at-arms rearranged the branches of elah, apparently drying them in the sun. He tested them for some quality known only to him. He still had not spoken. Neither had the witch. She lay now in a scrap of shade beneath the bellies of the mules.

Again without a word Telamon kindled a hasty fire. Laying the stalks of elah across the flame, he succeeded in extracting a quarter-cupful of the bitter, stinking sap. He mixed this with vinegar and reduced it over the blaze until it clotted into a rank, viscous paste.

"Bring the woman."

David obeyed.

"What is that?" The witch eyed the extract dubiously. Telamon commanded her to sit upright and extend her bare, lesion-ravaged calves before her in the sand.

Telamon instructed David to seize the woman by both elbows and hold her fast. He himself sat full weight, straddling her knees, facing toward her soles.

"Turpentine," he said.

He applied the paste to both the woman's ankles, directly upon her sores.

The witch shrieked and struggled to break free.

After moments the pain seemed to abate slightly.

The woman remained yet sobbing when Telamon plucked a glowing twig from the fire. With a sudden motion he touched this brand to one ankle, then the other. The turpentine flared into flame.

The woman's eyes ignited in agony, then rolled back into their sockets. She collapsed rearward, deadweight upon the sand.

David had sprung to his feet as if scalded. He stared at his mentor with wild eyes.

"That should do it," Telamon said.

The mercenary stood. He collected his mule, ready to move out, and signed to David to collect his and the witch's pony as well.

"If she doesn't die tonight, she'll be walking by the day after tomorrow."

13

FIRE FROM THE UNDERWORLD

D AVID COULD SEE THE SMOKE from ten miles and smell it from five. The youth and his mentor came over the final ridge. The Anthill lay before them at a distance of two thousand paces. Figures, too far away to identify as afoot or mounted, scurried in all directions. Dense plumes billowed from multiple clefts in the earth.

"Hell is upon them!" the boy exclaimed.

David began stripping the panniers from his mule, clearly intending to leap upon the beast's back and rush to the aid of the burning colony. Telamon seized the boy by the shoulder.

"How," the mercenary spoke in a voice devoid of haste, "does a warrior cross an open plain?"

David turned to his master with eyes frantic with distress. "Sir! People are dying down there!"

The man-at-arms' expression did not alter. "How does a warrior cross an open plain?"

David's jaw clenched. The veins pulsed upon his temples.

With effort the youth brought himself under control.

"A warrior crosses an open plain at arms," he said. "And approaches in stealth from the flank or rear."

"Good," said Telamon.

He released the boy.

Forty-eight hours had passed since Telamon had dosed the witch's wounds with the resin of the elah tree and abandoned her upon the gravel plain.

The woman had indeed regained to capacity to walk, but haltingly and with near-crippling pain. As before, she set out upon the trail of the man and boy. She too saw the smoke of the Anthill. She struggled forward, making such haste as she was capable of.

She mounted the final ridge with pain that nearly dropped her faint.

The smoking colony lay before her. For moments the sorceress could not catch her breath. She could see now, far in the distance, the man and boy. The pair was crossing, leading their animals, wide to the north of the inferno that was the Anthill.

When the mercenary and his apprentice came abreast of the blaze's north-south axis, still nearly a thousand paces out from the northernmost extremity, they turned by the flank and began to transit back toward the colony. Telamon led. Man and boy maintained a lateral interval of fifty paces and the same margin fore-to-aft. Both bore weapons at the ready.

The sorceress had started down the ridge now, advancing straight toward the Anthill. She was still too far away to make out details. She lost sight of Telamon and the boy as they entered the precinct of the conflagration and their passage became obscured by the dense, billowing smoke.

The woman pressed forward with all her strength. She could see now individuals and groupings of half dozens, some rushing about, others collected in companies in postures of shock and horror. The emergency clearly had not expired. Peering through the murk, the witch espied a figure spilling forth from one smoking portal, clutching a bundle that appeared to be the size of an infant. Other figures dashed forward. The man delivered the babe into the arms of these, then himself collapsed upon the earth. About the infant, women first crooned and goggled, then gave themselves over to shrieks of woe.

The sorceress had reached the margins of the calamity now. She did not need to ask what had wrought this fiasco. A course of horse and camel tracks, made by scores of men, led away to the north from the site of the holocaust.

Marauders.

Upon both flanks of this highway could be seen figures of the dead and dying—denizens of the Anthill—some shot with arrows, other speared through by belly- and back-thrusts of lances. Numbers more sprawled in postures of extremity with the rags of their garments smoldering.

The woman caught sight of Telamon and the boy now.

The mercenary strode through the swell with furious purpose, calling the name "Michael" and peering intensely into the faces of the wraiths kneeling, squatting, and staggering about.

"Michael!" the man-at-arms continued to cry.

The boy called the name as well but in a voice muted by horror. His glance, void and hollow, took in the chaos on all sides as if unable to assimilate its reality.

The sorceress had now fully entered the precinct of catastrophe. Distraught figures approached her. All were out of their minds with grief and woe. When these remarked the witch's ravaged lower extremities, they took her for one afflicted in the conflagration. They helped her. From these sufferers—women and girls of the Betar Yazidi, boys whose bloused trousers showed them to be bustard hunters of the Tamarizda, even elder dames bearing the cheek and brow tattoos of the Cicatricea—the sorceress gleaned a sketchy chronicle of the calamity.

The blaze had begun underground. Raiders of the Idumaeans, riding out of the Negev, or perhaps Nabatean Arabs marauding via Beersheba—none could say for certain amid the bedlam—had set fire to stores of dried fodder in the subterranean stock pens used to hold sheep and goats. The brigands' aim had been to sow panic by the volume of smoke and thus to drive the inhabitants of the colony up into the open. In the event, however, numbers of sheep caught fire themselves. A stampede ensued. The animals, mad with terror, broke through all barriers. They entered the below-ground market area of the Anthill, overturning stalls and setting further shops and passages alight.

It chanced as well that on this date a gathering of Mithraic Yazdani

tribesmen had assembled at the colony to celebrate the birth of their arch-
angel, Tawusi Melek, who took form, the pious believed, as a peacock. The
Yazdani in their pilgrimage had brought with them, or purchased from
shopkeepers who had in advance laid in a stock for this purpose, a number of live peacocks and peahens. These creatures are notoriously vicious
when cornered and are possessed as well of no mean strength. By scores
they too stampeded, causing even greater injury and confusion than had
already existed. How many inhabitants of the underground city were
trampled in the populace's rush to escape, no one could yet reckon.

"Michael! Michael!"

The sorceress could hear Telamon crying the Nazarene's name. She
saw him interdict and interrogate one individual of the colony, then
another and another. The woman could not make out the mercenary's spe-
cific speech—he was too far away—but she could tell by the manner of his
inquisition that he was describing the Nazarene and soliciting intelligence
of his fate or whereabouts.

Now an ominous evolution began to take place.

As the witch advanced among the multitude, she remarked men of
the colony taking notice of the mercenary and pointing him out to others. Their manner indicated suspicion and hostility. One fellow whom
Telamon had attempted to interrogate dashed away to a knot of others,
addressing them urgently while gesticulating toward Telamon.

This group now made off, rallying others.

The sorceress noted several of these taking arms, while more called
for weapons of their own, which were brought straightaway by boys and
women. This company, now numbering upward of a dozen, began tracking and closing upon the man-at-arms.

Telamon saw this.

The sorceress saw the mercenary instructing David to get clear and in
fact physically propelling the youth apart from himself.

She could see the boy resist.

At once the armed men surrounded Telamon.

The witch saw swords and spears. She heard angry voices. Others of
the colony, even women and children, swelled toward this confrontation.

The sorceress pushed and shoved her way forward.

When at last she broke through the crush, she saw Telamon, gladius in one hand, pilum in the other, braced in the center of a ring of hostiles. David, clutching his dolabra in both fists, took up a stand at the mercenary's shoulder.

An elder with great red mustaches had stepped forth from the circle. He demanded of Telamon his name and enterprise.

"I declare my business to no one," the mercenary replied, "who confronts me at arms."

More men hastened up. At a sign from the mustached leader, three stepped forward with bows drawn and shafts aimed at the center of Telamon's chest.

"Explain that on your arm!" the chief demanded.

Every eye held upon the mercenary's military tattoo:

LEGIO X

The witch's gaze darted from the bowmen to Telamon. The archers advanced with clearly murderous intent, leveling their shafts at nearly point-blank range. The mercenary's soles gripped the earth. He seemed upon the instant of rushing his antagonists.

At this moment a form burst from the margins of the circle.

A child.

A girl.

The sorceress recognized this figure at once.

It was the mute, the feral daughter of the Nazarene Michael.

The child dashed straight to Telamon. She flung herself upon his waist, throwing both arms about him and burying her face in the wool of his cloak.

The child's garments were singed and charred. Her face and arms bore signs of burns. Even her tangled hair appeared scorched about the edges.

At once matrons and dames among the throng, and no few men, began clamoring, demanding that the man-at-arms release the child to their care.

The girl clung to Telamon as to a crag in a storm. She would not let go.

Sputtering the crude cries of one without speech, the urchin by signs seemed to plead with the man-at-arms to protect her and to act as her champion. She pointed desperately along the track left by the fleeing raiders, as if to implore the mercenary to follow in that direction—and, apparently, to take her with him.

"What?" said Telamon. "The brigands took your father?"

The child gestured again, even more frantically, to the trace taken by the retreating bandits.

Yes! she communicated by sign. *We must pursue them now!*

The mercenary himself appeared surprised, even bewildered, by the girl's embrace and by her desperate adherence to his side. With one hand he tugged the child behind him, simultaneously keeping her close and shielding her with his body from the half circle of men who surrounded him.

Telamon confronted his accusers. "What do you want? What have I done to call forth such fury?"

The answer broke from a dozen voices at once.

A day before the catastrophe, a detachment of imperial cavalry, all bearing the **X** mark of the Tenth Legion, had appeared at the colony. They demanded that the inhabitants hand over a fugitive—a Nazarene named Michael, who had fled to this sanctuary from a Roman prison in Jerusalem.

The people en masse refused.

The equites legionis, outnumbered, rode off.

Twenty-four hours later the raiders came.

"You see," the leader said, "what they have done."

Men of the Anthill pressed even more proximately about Telamon.

"He is a spy sent by Rome!" bawled one man.

"Kill him!" cried another.

The elder with the mustaches held his comrades back. He confronted Telamon. "The Romans and the Arabs wanted this man Michael. Why?"

Telamon would not answer.

"You pursue him too. To what purpose?"

The man-at-arms refused to respond.

"Curse you, then!" cried the elder. "Your greed has destroyed our world!"

Weapons of murder were poised to eviscerate Telamon.

"Wait!"

The sorceress now burst forth.

All eyes turned to this wild-haired, half-crippled apparition.

Men of the colony drew back in startlement.

The witch scuttled to the mule that David had led.

"We have brought you a dolet!"

And she produced the clay pot of honey given to Telamon by the man made of bees.

The mercenary glared at the witch in shock and surprise. "You! Get away from that!"

The woman stumbled toward the elder, bearing the pot.

"What hag is this?" one onlooker bawled.

Another snatched the vessel from the sorceress' grip.

The jar shattered upon the earth.

Men now seized the witch as well.

"Kill them all!"

"Send them to hell!"

Again the mob rallied with fatal intent.

Suddenly the girl-child broke from Telamon. She dashed into the center of the circle. Bending to the earth, the girl seized one of the shards from the jar. She snatched up a flake of charcoal.

Stepping before the elder, she scrawled upon the clay in Greek:

PHILOS

The child displayed this to the chief, then held the shard high for all to see.

Philos.

"Friend."

Again she clung to Telamon.

Voices in the crowd identified the child.

Numbers confirmed that they had seen her about the colony. She was the daughter of the Nazarene Michael—the fugitive the Romans hunted, the man the Nabateans made off with.

Now here she stood, attesting with furious vehemence that this man-at-arms, who also sought Michael, was her friend.

The passion of the colonists abated.

Faces turned to the leader.

"Who is this child?" he demanded of Telamon. "Who is this crone?"

"Keep the witch. She is not with us."

"Us? Who are you? What evil fate has brought you among us?"

Clearly none among the throng, even this elder, comprehended the scheme that had wrought the devastation of their home or the place of these strangers within it.

God's wrath?

Some sin or failing of the community?

Or just chance? Bad luck?

The leader turned at last to Telamon.

"Go!" he said. "Get quit of this place, all of you, before the Almighty thinks better of the clemency He has shown you."

BOOK FIVE

CUT-OFF NOSES

14

THE WILDERNESS OF SALT

THE RAIDERS' TRAIL WAS NOT hard to follow. The marauders had made no attempt to conceal their passage. They rode, it seemed, in a state of heedlessness.

Telamon's eye, and even David's, could with ease identify intervals where sub-parties had galloped off from the central trace, perhaps chasing game—gazelles or ibexes or the wild asses the Arabs call *ariama*. Or perhaps youths among the freebooters were chasing each other for sport or from the exuberance of hope for fortune. Even the raiders' camps were left like dumps, with refuse blowing in the ground-scouring gale that arose each evening the closer one got to the sea.

The earth across which the man-at-arms' party pursued was salt—crusty and acrid. Saline flats threw up shrouds of bitter ash that whirled and gyrated on the wind. Telamon trekked with a scarf wound to cover his nose and mouth, as did the others.

The mercenary would let no one ride save the child, whose burns were more severe than the man-at-arms had at first reckoned and more debilitating than the girl would admit. Telamon compelled the sorceress, who yet straggled in the party's train, to collect such medicinal herbs as she could to make poultices and salves. The witch exploited this opportunity to insinuate herself, by the balms she produced, into the man-at-arms' graces, or at least to hold him off, day by day, hour by hour, from abandoning her.

"The Nazarene will need my help even more than the girl," she declared, "if indeed we find and free him."

In truth the sorceress's medicaments worked to remarkable effect, not only in easing the child's torment, but in fortifying the entire company upon the march. The witch produced a tea of tansy and desert hawthorn that kept the watch alert at night and a chewable resin of *samwa* leaf and horsemint that worked wonders to mitigate thirst on the tramp. She even manufactured a cud of *baatharan* and *eilejaan*—"cure" in the Bedouin tongue—whose effect upon the animals was to calm them amid the sudden squalls and whirlwinds of the wilderness and to temper their impulses to spook at the smells and sounds of wild animals prowling outside the camp at night.

The witch, emboldened by Telamon's momentary sufferance of her presence, began to afflict David. "How many days till we reach the sea?" she inquired of the youth late in the first postnoon out of the Anthill.

The boy did not know.

"Ask him," said the sorceress, indicating the man-at-arms, who tramped ahead across the crusty, sun-dazzling flat.

David demurred.

"You fear to approach him," declared the witch in mockery.

She called David "my little warrior" and made sport of him out of earshot of the others.

"Why do you serve this man so slavishly? He will abandon you the moment you become a burden. You are a Jew. You should be true to your people. Why bow to this servitor of Rome?"

David made no answer, only lengthened stride to free himself of the woman's tongue. The witch matched him, however.

"You remain above the earth only by the incantations I have cast to protect you, though you are ignorant of them."

David fled again.

"Stop plaguing me! Why did you track us from Jerusalem in the first place? My master believes you work treachery for Severus. Do you think he doesn't remark you making your 'collections'? He sees you loiter. You are leaving signs, marking our trail."

The sorceress mocked David even more boldly. "Think I work perfidy, boy? Do something, then. Kill me, if you dare!"

The mercenary and the girl turned back at this, drawn by the altercation.

The sorceress took note of their attendance.

"You dare not, do you?" the witch addressed David, but with such force as to be heard by the man-at-arms and the child. "Because you know I will strike you blind or render you a leper!"

The girl, watching, hooted in scorn.

The witch spun toward her. "What are you looking at, you feral rat?"

The child assumed a posture of derision, scowling exactly like the sorceress, with snarling lip and crooked, accusatory finger.

The witch snatched up a stone and hurled it at the girl.

The child laughed and trotted away, on the woman's pony, which had by default become her own.

In camp that night, the witch made a point of laying her bedding beside the girl's. When Telamon had moved apart on watch, the sorceress spoke to the child alone.

"Your father has the Apostle's letter now, doesn't he? He met up with a confederate at the Anthill. That was the scheme, wasn't it? It was why you went there."

The girl spat and moved her blanket away, toward the spot where the man-at arms had taken up his post.

The witch cackled. "Think this man is your savior, girl? He serves Rome, this villain—to overhaul your father and bring him back in chains. He will not preserve him, you boob, but turn him in for gold."

The second morning the sorceress fell in beside Telamon as they marched. David, who had held that station, edged apart.

"He has the letter now, the Nazarene," the witch declared. "Someone brought it for him at the Anthill. That filthy urchin virtually confirmed it last night."

Telamon regarded the woman skeptically.

"Tucked in his guts," said the sorceress. "Or wedged up his ass, if the Arabs haven't pried it out of him yet."

The woman adopted with the man-at-arms a more conciliatory tone than she had taken with the youth or the girl. It seemed that she had miraculously acquired a speaking knowledge not only of Greek but of Latin as well—with a Judean accent.

The sorceress observed to Telamon that the tradition of accord at the Anthill was of such antiquity, not to mention that its effect—a haven free of fear for all—was so critical to the survival of the contending clans, tribes, and kin groups who took refuge at the colony, that something of great moment must have intervened to incite the Nabatean raiders to commit the irrevocable breach of violating the truce.

"What can this be but Roman treasure? A bounty on the Nazarene! No longer are you the only one, mercenary, who vies for this reward—if indeed you ever were."

Telamon interrogated the sorceress, as he had at Jerusalem, as to what she knew about the letter of the Apostle. "You were the one who gave up the Nazarene in prison. How did you get him to confide in you?"

"If that pirate proffered a truthful word to me," declared the witch, "it was for his purposes alone. Not I, nor any other, could extract from him a single syllable that he did not wish to render. If you don't believe me, ask Severus, who racked the man for two days and nights to no avail. It was the Christian who used me, not I him."

The sorceress claimed to know nothing of the letter itself, save that it would be long—five thousand words at least—and that its contents would be compelling.

"He who composed it, the so-called Apostle Paul, is a poet. Give him that. The man is a genius. Whatever is in that epistle, it will ignite a conflagration among all who receive it. The Romans fear these verses, sight unseen, more than all the daggers of the Zealot sicarii, more indeed than a revolt in full strength by all the sons of Israel."

Past noon of the third day, Telamon drew up at the bones of a Nabatean camp. Hoof tracks of a dozen veered off to the northeast, those of another double handful to the northwest. A lesser trace, of perhaps six or seven, continued directly to the sea.

"Which do we follow?" asked David.

"The Arabs will not call them by this name," said Telamon, indicating the tracks leading east and west, "but they who left these prints are security elements, sent ahead to the sea to protect the main party's flanks."

Telamon turned to the girl.

"Your father will be with this middle trace. These half dozen will be the ones holding him."

That evening the man-at-arms' party came upon a rock quarry, hollowed from a spine of limestone hills. The excavated void was the size of a small city and deep enough, in cubic volume, to swallow such a municipality whole.

All day the company had been passing the remains of stonecutters' camps, with great mounds of ashlars and masonry blocks stacked in ranks like catapult ammunition.

"I labored here," the mercenary said.

He indicated a surveyor's trace, visible at intervals beneath the windscoured sand. The line, chiseled into the stone where it peeked forth above the earth, ran straight from the horizon in the north into the wilderness to the south.

"This would be a highway," the man-at-arms said. "Eight meters across, of cut stone, over a foundation two meters deep." He pointed west, toward a ridge of basalt. "There, an aqueduct."

David peered. The witch and the girl did too. They could see, two miles distant, half-constructed pilings tracking a course from the peaks to the south.

"Legions erect such wonders. Mine, the Tenth Fretensis, worked the track from the seacoast to here for two and a half years. It was punishment duty," he said. "To restore a force gone sour and ready it for the next campaign."

Telamon pointed west to the aqueduct line. "The Sixth Ferrata cut that pass, four miles long, through solid granite."

That night the mercenary permitted a fire.

"The deities of Rome," he said, speaking to no one in particular, "are Order and Conquest. The legions labor to remake the world in the service of these gods. The Anthill? That would become a Roman city— Claudianopolis. I have held the plans in my hands. This highway would link it to the sea. That aqueduct would make a garden of the desert around it."

The mercenary stood then. The girl's eyes tracked him intently, as did David's. Whatever thought hung upon the man's tongue remained unuttered. "I'll take first and last," he said, meaning the watches he would stand this night.

David drew a breath. "Sir, if I may ask . . . why did you quit the legions?"

For a moment the man-at-arms regarded the youth as if surprised, even gratified, at the temerity of the query.

"I was in the legions. I was never of them."

The sorceress too had turned toward Telamon, attending keenly.

"Two laws only govern the cohorts of Rome," said the mercenary. "Stay in ranks and never abandon the eagle. But what does this standard represent, save the vanity of the empire and the vainglory of her commanders? I fought once for pride and honor. No more."

David summoned his courage again. "Why then did you fight, sir?"

"He fights for money," declared the sorceress. "One side is the same as another for him. He serves gold and nothing more."

The girl-child's gaze held fixed upon the mercenary. He seemed to feel it.

"I do not serve money. I make money serve me. At campaign's end, I care for neither praise nor blame. I want cash. I want to be paid. In that way, war is work—nothing more. To serve for money detaches the warrior from the object of his commander's desire. I serve for the serving only, fight for the fighting only, tramp for the tramping only."

The mercenary turned away to mount toward a rock shelf that overlooked the camp.

"Scatter the fire. Get your heads down."

By midmorning the next day they could smell the sea.

Telamon drew the party up in a dry wash within sight of the coast highway.

"The town ahead is called Rhinococura, 'Cut-Off Noses.' It will be a port one day, when Roman engineers at last realize their design. Now it's barely an anchorage."

He paused to make sure he held his charges' attention.

"The raiders will be down there somewhere. Tomorrow morning they will take the highway either east to Jerusalem or west to Alexandria, to whichever establishment they believe will pay more for the Nazarene."

He declared of the bandits that they would be in their cups tonight, celebrating their sudden prospects.

"We'll go in past midnight," the man-at-arms said, "and kill them all."

15

CUT-OFF NOSES

THE PORT CITY OF RHINOCOCURA was, as Telamon had character-ized it, neither a port nor a city, but a ragged jumble of mud-brick huts and disused construction engines set up along the gale-scoured strand. To the east, inland but paralleling the coast, ran the thirteen-mile pass called by the Romans Tosta Caesio and by the Arabs Ji'radi.

There was no harbor yet. The Romans were building one. A crude wharf called the Spatha, "Longsword," ran out into a shallow anchorage. The Romans, Telamon declared, had been dredging this with weight-powered cranes mounted on barges and with mule-drawn towlines. The enterprise had been abandoned, however, when the assigned legion, the Sixth Ferrata, was called away to Judea to reinforce the Tenth Fretensis and elements of the Twelfth Fulminata in containing the rising unrest spurred by the pop-ular ascension of the Hebrew Zealots and other insurrectionist factions.

At the hour midway between noon and sunset Telamon moved the company to a wadi immediately south of the abandoned construction site from whose northern terminus he, lying prone within the concealment of a line of tamarisk, could observe the road that approached from the east. He could not see the sea but could hear on the wind the gentle slap of its waves. He sent David ahead on foot, robed and barefoot like a shepherd boy, to undertake a preliminary reconnaissance.

The boy returned several hours later. He had not found the fugitive Michael, he declared, but had succeeded in locating a tented camp upon the strand, where a party of Nabatean slavers had taken up quarters. Their numbers were eight. David counted six horses within the camp, secured to a rope line, and five camels, two with riding saddles beside them in the sand, the others apparently used as beasts of burden.

Telamon approved the boy's report.

The man-at-arms next reconnoitered the town himself. Garbed in a hooded robe and armed only with a dagger and a quarterstaff, the mercenary made his way to the site described by David. He located and made a reconnaissance of the slavers' camp from a distance but dared not approach at close hand, as, even disguised as he was, his stature and bearing attracted attention.

The town, Telamon confirmed from observation and converse with several locals, supported a desultory trade in slaves captured either from coasting vessels or brought out of the desert by nomadic brigands. The market fronting the strand, he was told, served as an auction site on alternate sessions for livestock and humans. The settlement's primary industry was fishing. A lamentable-looking fleet, careened this day for lack of wind, harvested sprats, shrimp, and a type of mussel called by the Romans *gallus*, "rooster," that was a delicacy prized in the harbor markets at Gaza, Pelusium, and Alexandria. This much Telamon gleaned from encounters with fishermen and other natives of the town.

But he could confirm Michael's whereabouts neither by sight nor by reliable intelligence. He could not determine with certainty even if the Nazarene had been brought to this place.

"I will find him," said the sorceress when Telamon returned to the wadi.

"Go with her," said Telamon to David. The sun had begun its plunge to the horizon.

Telamon passed the interval approaching twilight alone with the girl at their encampment.

The man-at-arms performed his calisthenics. He whetted the edges of his weapons. He repacked the mules' side bags and panniers, making them ready upon sudden notice. He set these rigs beside each animal but did yet load their weight onto the beasts' backs.

The girl observed every move the mercenary made. She studied with particular keenness his weapons drills. When Telamon practiced the stance called "castling," the girl planted her own feet exactly as he did and struck the pose with identical scrupulousness. Rehearsing the tumbling motion called "beetling," the mercenary looked up to see the child mimicking his moves with uncanny exactitude.

At intervals the girl approached the mercenary, making urgent sounds and gestures to the effect—or so the man-at-arms presumed—that the rescuers, meaning Telamon and David, must not delay but strike at once against the raiders, before her father Michael had been tortured or killed.

Telamon sought to communicate with the child, but the signs by which she attempted to express herself left him confounded. He could not tell if she was simpleminded or merely unnerved, as any child might be in such circumstances.

The girl, discerning Telamon's scrutiny of her, glowered back with knuckles on hips and a glare of indignation. Her stance seemed to proclaim, *Because I am dumb does not mean I am stupid.*

"How old are you?" Telamon asked.

The child shrugged.

"Where from? Where were you born?"

Another shrug.

"Could you ever speak?"

The girl shook her head.

Telamon studied her.

"How does a sprat like you know how to write? Who taught you? Can you make more than the one word you scribbled at the Anthill?"

The girl scrawled in the sand.

MITERA

"Your mother taught you?"

The child confirmed this.

"Where is she now?"

The child faced Telamon defiantly.

"Dead? How long?"

Two fingers.

The mercenary absorbed this.

"When we go in tonight after your father, you'll stay here with the mules."

The girl stamped and shook her head vehemently.

"Someone must watch the animals. They must be ready when we flee."

The child mimed the posture of the sorceress. So perfectly did she catch this attitude that Telamon could not hold back a laugh.

"Not her," he said. "You."

The girl stomped again and scowled. Again she struck a likeness of the witch. This time she pointed forcefully to Telamon's gladius. She drew her hand across her throat.

"Don't trust her, do you?"

The child's motion again urged, *Kill her! Why,* the girl's expression seemed to demand, *do you permit this evil woman to remain?*

Telamon again studied the child. He seemed unable to decide if she was a crude little brute or a cunning and keen observer of the issues of war.

"Does the name Caesar mean anything to you? I mean the original Caesar, who commanded my legion, the Tenth, a century past, in Gaul?"

The child's look answered yes.

Telamon was not sure he believed her. But his posture seemed to soften somewhat. The man-at-arms had been standing. He had loomed over the girl at his full height. Now he bent at the knee and knelt, so that his eyes descended to the same level as hers.

"In Gaul, a great enemy of Caesar's, named Vercingetorix, once sent scouts on horseback to dog the legions' column. Keen young officers of the Romans urged their commander, 'Let us ride out and kill these barbarians.' But Caesar would not permit this. 'The foe sending scouts believes he spies upon us. But it is we who spy upon him,' Caesar explained to his officers. 'I fear the enemy only when I cannot see him. So long as he remains close, I rest at ease.'"

The child absorbed this.

Does she understand? Telamon's expression seemed to wonder.

The girl straightened and gestured in the direction of the slavers' camp. She struck her chest with the flat of her palm.

Take me! Tonight take me!

Telamon shook his head.

"There will be armed men in that camp. Eight at least, maybe more."

The girl's jaw worked. She had a fistful of stones and now hurled these one after another, hard, against the wall of the wadi. She did not throw like a girl.

Night fell.

The sorceress and David had not returned.

The girl had become so agitated that Telamon was not certain he could constrain her.

"Will your father give up the letter to the Arabs?"

The child's glance flared.

"If they torture him? Do you think he has given it up already?"

Never, declared the girl's expression.

"Why does he care so much? Why do you? What is the letter to you? What good do you imagine it will do?"

The girl stood to her full height, jaw jutting.

A rustle came from the seaward approach. Footfalls could be heard and then David and the sorceress materialized from the dark.

"The man you seek, called Michael, is bound and muffled upon the strand," said the witch. "The slavers are scourging him with the knotted rope and with fire."

16

THE SLAVERS' CAMP

DAVID COULD SEE MICHAEL NOW. The Nazarene hung limp, lashed by his wrists to the flank of a beached sardine boat. A fire of mounded coals glowed in the sand at his feet.

The raiders' camp squatted among careened fishing vessels on the strand of the disused anchorage. A pair of sentinel fires flanked the site with a space of about fifty paces between them. The Great Bear had reached its nadir; the blazes had begun to burn down. Time was the Roman third watch, past midnight but not yet into the Hour of Embers, when watch fires must be restoked and banked to last till dawn.

Telamon had left the sorceress in the wadi with the mules and the horse. The girl-child had pleaded desperately in her wordless tongue to be permitted to go with Telamon and David. Instead the mercenary had left her to stand sentry over the witch. Into the child's hands he set David's dolabra, the whetted entrenching tool with which he, Telamon, had slain two of the bandits in the original clash at the Narrows. He instructed the child, for the sorceress to hear: "If this woman attempts treachery, split her guts."

Telamon took only the boy with him, arming himself with the gladius and a length of rope. He strapped two throwing daggers to his ankles. David he outfitted with a single javelin. The youth carried a dagger of his own.

Man and boy entered the sea a quarter mile east of the slavers' camp, slithering out beyond the flare of the bonfires. The water was so shallow here—reaching barely to a standing man's calf—that the mercenary and the youth could not swim or even dog-paddle but must, lying prone upon the gravelly bottom, propel themselves like crayfish, by fingers and toes, while their heads and the upper portions of their shoulders and backs peeked visibly above the surface.

There were no real tides in this part of the Roman Sea. Wavelets lapped upon the strand with a slapping sound that rose to an audible thump only when multiple waves broke at or near the same time. The water was warm and so briny that it stung the eyes like vinegar.

It took nearly two hours for the man and boy to work their way laterally from their point of entry to a position opposite the slavers' camp.

Two factions among the brigands wrangled over Michael throughout this interval.

The first wished to murder the Nazarene outright and cut his belly open in search of the letter. At least that was what David reckoned from their gesticulations, as he understood few phrases of the Arab dialect. The second contingent argued with equal passion—and backed their case with no few blows and cuffs exchanged with their confederates—that the captive must be kept alive for delivery to the Romans, so these could interrogate him. "Even if we cut him up and find the letter, he is worth more alive than dead!" That at least was what David imagined this caucus contended.

At length the slavers tired of their sport. First one, then another settled onto the sand beside the fire. They dozed. Three or four others, who had been carousing with women beside a stand of three careened vessels at the eastern terminus of the camp, found berths to lounge in as well.

The Nazarene hung like a gutted sheep. His outspanned arms, lashed at the wrists, pended from two cleats on the gunwale of the westernmost careened vessel.

"Is he dead?" David whispered.

The boy felt a hand on his shoulder. Telamon nodded toward the strand. His expression said, *Take this.*

Into David's hand the mercenary set his own gladius. He himself took the boy's javelin.

"Cut the Nazarene down. He will drop dead weight when you slice the first rope. Catch him. Hold him up. Do not let him cry out."

"What will you do?"

"I'll take the two snoozers."

The pommel of the sword, when he set it against the heel of his hand, felt to David like a living thing. Terror gripped him. He urinated into the tepid water. He experienced an overwhelming urge to void his bowels.

"You can do it." Telamon spoke quietly. "I'll be beside you before you finish the first cut."

David wanted to say, *When?* But he could not make his lips move.

"Now," said Telamon.

The mercenary stood to his full height and started forward.

David tried to rise.

His knees would not obey him.

Telamon hauled the youth upright.

"Go!"

With powerful strides the man-at-arms started in.

At that instant an Arab on the strand—one concealed by shadow, whom David had not noticed—cried out and pointed excitedly toward the sea.

For a terrifying instant David thought the bandit had spotted him and Telamon. *Indeed*, the boy thought, *how could he fail to see us?*

But the fellow was gesturing past them, out to sea.

David heard voices hallooing from offshore. He turned to the rear and saw a military vessel—a single-banker, thirty-oared . . . nay, *two* such craft—emerging from the dark, making straight for the strand.

Voices onboard hailed the shore.

Brigands on the beaching ground responded, waving the vessels in.

The bandits had not yet seen David and Telamon.

Man and boy had reached the sand now. David sprinted toward the bound Nazarene.

To his left the youth saw Telamon fall upon the two raiders who had dozed beside the fire. One was rising. The mercenary drove him through with the first pilum. David saw Telamon snatch the curved sword from this fellow's grip. The boy heard a whooshing sound. The second bandit's head, lopped from its shoulders, rolled like a melon a few feet across the sand, then stopped and rocked, eyes still wide with terror, bearded jaw working.

The gladius spilled from David's hand. He dropped to his knees. Everything he had eaten in the past three days came retching from his guts.

The boy felt Telamon above him. The man-at-arms flung the first bandit's sword away. He snatched up his own gladius. With this he cut the Nazarene down. He lifted Michael, full weight, to carry him across his left shoulder. "Grab the pilum!" the mercenary shouted to David, pointing to the iron lance buried in the first brigand's belly.

The slavers' camp had come vividly, violently alive. Armed men raced everywhere.

The two military boats were beaching.

They were fast corvettes—dispatch vessels, called in the Roman tongue *naves actuariae.* David recognized them by their outriggers and their double rudders, one fore and one aft. These were the fastest ships in the imperial navy—coasters that could be run up onshore in either direction, deliver their messages or drop their cargo, and get off as swiftly as they had landed.

"Get the pilum!"

The boy was still on his knees.

Bandits rushed at Telamon from three directions. David saw the mercenary impale one with an uppercut so violent it lifted the man completely off his feet. The man-at-arms cut down two more in quick succession, all while bearing the weight of the Nazarene Michael on his back.

The boy came to himself beside the coals that the Arabs had used to heat the irons they used to torture Michael. Before him in the sand, on his back, sprawled the first speared slaver.

Men were sprinting toward David and Telamon from the first of the Roman boats. The boy saw swords and torches. He saw shod feet and drawn bows.

David had grasped the pilum now. He had it by the throwing shaft. He peered down at the man in the sand.

The brigand was still alive.

He was on his back, beside the coals.

The man clutched the spear in his belly with both hands. He would not let go.

"Use your foot!" Telamon shouted.

A tug-of-war began between David and the impaled marauder.

The first onrushing Romans were now less than fifty feet away.

David could hear their shouting voices.

"Your foot!" the mercenary bawled to David. "That thing at the end of your leg!"

David set his heel onto the chest of the speared desperado.

"Pull!"

David did.

A form burst from the darkness directly before the boy.

The young lieutenant.

The cavalry officer—Severus' nephew and protégé—from Jerusalem!

For long moments David did not recognize him.

The lieutenant had no such trouble. "You!" he cried. "How are you here? Where is your master?"

In the darkness and confusion, the officer had somehow not seen Telamon.

David knew him now. The youth goggled in disbelief. Why had the Roman sailed here? For Telamon? How could he know . . .

The officer raised both arms. He bawled to his men to hold off—and to compel the Arabs to do likewise.

At this instant Telamon strode into the firelight.

The lieutenant hesitated only a moment. "Outstanding work, peregrine! Have you got the letter? Where is the girl?"

Telamon stared at the Roman. He seemed, on the instant, as taken aback as David.

"The Arabs sent a rider from the Anthill," declared the lieutenant. "I sailed from Gaza last night under Severus's orders. The oarsmen have been rowing for twenty hours straight."

The cavalryman's eye fell upon the body slung over Telamon's shoulder. He seemed to notice it for the first time.

"Is this him? Is this the Nazarene?"

The lieutenant was clad in caligas and a white woolen tunic, over which he wore a segmented breastplate and a scarlet paenula, the legion officer's winter cloak.

Telamon still had not spoken.

"I have brought your gold," declared the young officer. "Do you have the letter? Give it to me!"

David sensed rather than saw a form hurtling from the darkness. An Arab clutching a two-hand Damascene scimitar sprinted directly at Telamon. The curved blade flashed in the firelight. David heard the bandit's war cry. He saw the man elevate his sword to strike . . .

The boy, seeking to recall his own actions later, could not state for certain where he had stood or precisely what motion he had executed. He felt the onrushing Arab's weight slam into his own right hip, then bound and sail over him, upending in midair. The brigand crashed onto his back into the sand.

David heard the terrible sound of sinew and bone being punctured by thrusting steel. He turned to see Telamon hauling his gladius, its blade nearly hilt-deep, from beneath the sternum of the falling bandit.

The boy remembered little after that.

He recalled the lieutenant standing across from Telamon, confronting him with teeth bared and gladius in hand. Both men's faces were lit by the embers of the bonfire. The Roman was shouting at the mercenary to give up the Nazarene.

Telamon would not.

The officer bawled at him in fury.

Blows were struck.

Legionaries piled into the fracas.

Telamon slew one with a thrust of the pilum David had taken from the impaled brigand.

The lieutenant thrust with his sword at Telamon. The mercenary parried and struck back. David saw a gash open on the young officer's forearm.

Somehow horses appeared.

The sorceress.

The girl.

Cries flooded the darkness. David lost all sense of orientation within a fire-flickering vortex of limbs and faces, blows and hooves and slashing blades.

The boy found himself helping Telamon haul the Nazarene, who was conscious and struggling to speak, up onto a horse's back, behind the mercenary. Then they were all on the mules and on horses snatched from the raiders and galloping away down the wadi into the dark.

17

THE INNER DESERT

MICHAEL COULD NO LONGER RIDE. Half an hour into the desert, Telamon had to halt the party's flight.

He cut branches from a terebinth tree to make a drag litter. The Nazarene was laid upon this, swathed in the mercenary's sleeping robe.

Telamon commanded the sorceress despite the dark to make a collection. This she did, producing from various aloes an astringent poultice and a binding salve. These were applied to the Nazarene's burns and to the many broken places upon his flesh. The Arabs had taken his left eye as well, burning it out with a point of iron.

The witch of her own contrived an anodyne of wild licorice and *Ephedra arabica* that she claimed was as potent a painkiller as Mesopotamian opium. She administered this to the Nazarene as a tea, which he must take down scalding hot. Michael was awake through all this. He could neither speak nor sign.

In such condition the Nazarene was hauled all that night and all through the next day by the stronger of the two mules. The girl rode at her father's side the while, beside herself with anguish and distress.

Both horses carried off from the raiders failed. One bolted in terror, descending a slope the first night, and plunged to its death; the second snapped a foreleg treading into an animal burrow in the dark.

Telamon hoodwinked the poor beast with his cloak over its eyes, then dispatched it as mercifully as he could. The mercenary did not fail, however, to carve substantial chunks of the animal's haunches for tomorrow's feed, wrapping them in a bladder cut from the beast's entrails and flushed clean with its own blood. As well, Telamon cut out both liver and heart and, slicing these into strips the length of a man's finger, compelled each member of the party at the next hurry-camp to choke these down raw (he would not risk a fire) for the strength of their vitals. He himself devoured every ounce that the others would not endure.

The party trekked raw desert now, void of roads or trails. What camel traces appeared the mercenary would not trust, fearing that they might lead into camps of other freebooters. He moved south and west, taking his bearings from the pointer stars of the Great Bear and from Polaris in Ursa Minor. The party fled away from the sea and into the inner desert.

All through the first day and the second forenoon, the fugitives could see the dust of their pursuers. The clouds were two, advancing in parallel several miles apart. They seemed to trade leads as they rode.

"The Romans intend to beat the Arabs to the prize," Telamon speculated. "The Arabs feel the same."

Toward evening a third and fourth column could be descried, one advancing out of the east, the other from the west. The man-at-arms guessed these were the slavers' security parties, the ones that had split off earlier from the main raiding element. "That," he said, "or other tribesmen seeking a Roman bounty."

The sorceress still hobbled from her wounds. When Telamon refused her entreaties to share the girl's pony—"I'll tell you," he said, "when you've earned that privilege"—she cursed him furiously.

The witch's ire soon found a secondary object in the child herself. She tramped beside her, between the girl and the mule dragging Michael's litter.

"Think this man is helping you?" The sorceress thrust a bony claw in Telamon's direction. "Because he didn't hand your father over to the Romans back at the anchorage? Don't be a fool! He didn't do it because he doesn't have the letter yet, you imbecile!"

David upbraided the sorceress for this malice. The witch spat and turned away.

She addressed Telamon now, indicating Michael.

"How do you plan to get the letter, peregrine? He's got it sewn into his guts. That, or wedged up his ass. Cut him open and save us all from this suffering. I'll do it for you if you lack the bowels!"

David hurled a clod at the woman, commanding her again to hold her tongue.

"And you?" The witch confronted the boy. "You're a more ignorant rube than this voiceless guttersnipe! What do you think your master will do when he gets the letter? He'll take it not to Jerusalem—how can he now, after he nearly decapitated the garrison commander's nephew?—but to the Roman governor in Alexandria." She pointed west toward Egypt, the direction in which the party was indeed trending. "Egypt's master has more money to pay, doesn't he, mercenary? And he'd love to reap the glory in the eyes of Rome. That's your plan, isn't it?"

Telamon let the witch ride just to shut her up.

The Nazarene's suffering had become acute from the pounding his litter took over the rocky and uneven ground. Not even the sorceress's analgesics could relieve it. The void of Michael's left eye wept blood and a whitish yellow fluid that Telamon said the legions called *pus*.

At the mercenary's direction, the witch packed Michael's socket with pulp extracted from the disks of prickly pear cactus, changing this crude dressing every half hour. *Give the woman credit*, David thought. Despite her ceaseless provocation and fulmination, she had assumed after her fashion the role of nurse and caregiver. Dismounting at intervals, she hobbled alongside the Nazarene, chanting such ditties as she thought might offer succor. Michael himself seemed beyond awareness. Could he hear? Did he know where he was? The child tended him at every halt, of which Telamon would permit few.

Twice during the second night Michael arose from his delirium into intervals of lucidity. In the first he spoke urgently and for no small duration to his daughter, taking pains that his speech be overheard by none other. The child for her part made fervent report to her father, apparently about events at the Anthill and afterward, communicating via sign and an idiom of grunts and bleats that served as a language between the two.

The Nazarene's primary preoccupation, judging by his gestures and the attendance he displayed by means of observation, appeared to be to assess the character and aims of the man within whose captivity he now found himself. His queries to the girl seemed to be, before all else, about Telamon.

At the second instance of clarity, the Nazarene found the strength to address the mercenary directly. Telamon had crossed to the wounded man's side. He knelt beside his litter. Michael pleaded with the man-at-arms to leave him to die. "Only take the child," he implored. The Nazarene declared himself a burden, whose care slowed the company and made it vulnerable to being overtaken.

Telamon refused to hear this.

Michael continued. "You are the man Severus Pertinax sent after me from Jerusalem, yes? Why you, when he has dispatched cavalry and published bounties as well? Who are you? What are your instructions?"

Telamon silenced the Nazarene with a hand. "Save your strength," he said. "Your job now is to survive."

Michael studied the mercenary. "Why are you helping me? I will die before giving up the letter to you. You know that."

Telamon made no answer. He wrapped the Nazarene for warmth in his own cloak and pillowed the man's broken body with his own sleeping fleece. Only later, when the Christian at last fell into a merciful drowse, did he, the man-at-arms, break his silence, addressing the girl-child, though in the hearing of David and the witch.

"The Romans could not break your father on the wheel, and neither could those bastards with the rope or with fire."

Telamon's gaze turned to the slumbering Nazarene.

"Here is a man," he said.

At dawn the mercenary sighted a squall line to the southwest. He drove the company toward it. A great windstorm arose with the evening. Telamon pushed the others through this. He would not let them stop. The gale effaced the party's trail, even the deep tracks of the laden mules.

Finally, at the third dawn, the fugitives scoured the horizon to their rear and saw nothing.

They were deep into the inner desert now, beyond maps or experiential knowledge.

A basalt ridge ascended a mile to the west. Telamon led the party up this face, carrying Michael in his arms when the big mule balked from fatigue. A cut in the rock would serve to conceal the company. The mercenary himself, with David, sought and found an overlook, a shallow shelf with a ten-mile vantage back across the series of ridges they had spent the past two days crossing.

"Sit."

Man and boy took up postures exactly as they had on the second evening into Sinai. The hour was dusk. As they peered east, their vantage extended unbroken, lit dramatically by the sun sinking behind them.

Over his shoulder, Telamon could hear Michael's voice, coming from the rock-face cut. The Nazarene could make speech more comfortably now. His straits remained extreme, but his spirit refused to yield. He was speaking, in Greek, quietly and purposefully, to the girl.

The mercenary could feel David, seated upon his left, struggling to banish the exhaustion that racked his bones. The youth fought to bring his mind to focus upon what he must do now, to be still and to look out.

"David," said Telamon.

The boy straightened with a start. This was the first time he had heard his mentor address him by name.

"Yes, sir?"

"Back there on the strand . . ."

"Sir?"

"You did well."

The man could feel the boy flush with pleasure and summon fresh resolve.

Telamon felt a figure approach from behind on his right.

The girl.

The child had come forward from the rock camp. Telamon did not turn toward her. He spoke no word, nor proffered any indication that he had become aware of her, yet his senses held keenly attuned to every aspect of her posture and intention.

The child remained stationary for several moments observing the mercenary and the boy in their seated stations.

She sat too now, upon Telamon's immediate right.

She assumed an attitude identical to his.

As the mercenary's gaze faced east over the desert, so did the girl's.

Telamon said nothing.

He listened to the child breathing.

The girl was matching her inhale and exhale to his.

Her eyes scanned the desert exactly as his did.

Telamon could feel David fidgeting on his left.

The girl had settled, still as a stone.

When darkness fell and a hard chill came down, she did not move.

Her breathing had composed itself into a steady, soundless rhythm.

Once, after several hours, Telamon rose. He returned with bread and oil, on a flat stone, and a half bowl of posca. He gave some to David and some to the girl.

He reported to the girl that Michael was resting comfortably. The sorceress, he said, sat up beside him.

Past midnight Telamon thought he spied a flicker, miles out, on the pan to the east.

Flame?

He blinked and rubbed his eyes.

Could the pursuers be advancing under torchlight?

The mercenary felt a sharp rap on his right shoulder. The girl. She had shifted from her perch and moved flush to Telamon's side.

She pointed out across the desert.

"I see it," said Telamon.

David had come alert as well. He too peered into the distance.

The girl shook her head adamantly.

She held up two fingers.

Again she pointed east.

Telamon's eyes strained.

He saw only one glimmer.

The girl rapped his shoulder again. Again she held up two fingers.

She thrust this sign emphatically before Telamon's gaze and pointed with fiery intensity to the south of the first glimmer, the one Telamon's glance had fixed upon.

Telamon saw the second column now.

The girl was right.

"Torches?"

The child nodded vigorously.

David strained but could make out neither the first glimmer nor the second.

What he did note, turning back toward his master, was a flare in the mercenary's eye—the faintest flicker only, appearing for an instant and then vanishing.

This look was for the child, and it was unmistakable.

It was a glance of respect.

18

KNOWLEDGE OF TERRAIN

T HE SUN WAS UP AND the party was moving fast to the west, or as fast is it could, burdened as it was. Telamon wanted the rising sun behind him. He wanted to see as many miles ahead as possible.

"We're in trouble," he said.

He tramped beside Michael. The Nazarene could lift his head now, at least a little, from his berth upon the litter. The sorceress strode a few steps ahead, leading the smaller mule. Telamon addressed them both.

"There's a term in the legions—*locorum notitia*. 'Knowledge of terrain.'"

David and the girl trekked alongside, edging closer to hear.

"We don't know this desert. The Arabs chasing us do. They are leading the Romans and the Romans are following willingly. Why have they split their party into two columns? They're herding us. They're driving us where they want us to go."

He told Michael and the sorceress about the sighting last night.

"Why do they ride with torches? Not to help them see. They can do that easily by the light in the sky. The torches were for us. To show us how near our pursuers are and how fast they're closing on us."

Michael again pleaded with Telamon to leave him behind. "Take the child and flee. You have a chance without me slowing you down."

Telamon ignored this.

"Severus's own lieutenant was on the strand at Cut-Off Noses," he said. "Why? The officer the tribune trusts before all others. Dispatched by thirty-oared cutter *after* the initial column of cavalry pursuing us. Why?"

The man-at-arms confronted the sorceress.

"Something changed, didn't it? What? You were there in the prison. Severus cut you loose and put you on a horse. What did he tell you?"

The man-at-arms glanced, for the briefest of moments, to the girl-child. His look said, *This is why I have kept the witch.*

The sorceress insisted, in the most emphatic terms, that she knew nothing.

"What do you imagine," said Telamon, "that the Romans will do with you when they overhaul us? They will hand you over to the Arabs for their pleasure. Tell us what you know, and we have a chance."

"Nothing," the sorceress declared. "I know nothing!"

Telamon indicated the wilderness ahead. The landscape was constituted of flat featureless desert cut by a series of dolomite ranges, some as high as two thousand feet.

"We don't dare enter those mountains. They're full of dead ends and blind canyons. But we can't remain here on the flat. The Arabs and Romans will run us down in a another day, maybe sooner."

The fugitives glanced behind them to the east. The twin columns of their pursuers' dust could be seen maneuvering exactly as Telamon had pronounced, each advancing at the oblique, to contain and direct the party in its flight.

Telamon drove the company on.

Past noon they rounded the base of a ridge and, trooping along it for a quarter hour, found themselves walled off by a sheer face with no passage around or through. Fortune alone preserved them, at the ultimate instant, when an alley presented itself.

Behind them the raiders and Romans, both columns, had entered this runway. They were close enough now that the sun's reflection off their elevated lance points could be glimpsed within the dust that obscured their actual mass.

Both mules were now lathered and flagging. The pony could no longer elevate its head. Telamon ordered it abandoned. He took its load onto his own back.

Twice Michael attempted to rise from the litter and walk on his own. Each time he faltered. Each time the girl helped him back onto the carrier.

The party had mounted now to an escarpment, a stony plateau of dolomite and schist without brush or cover.

The rising surface of the scarp seemed to extend to infinity.

The mule dragging Michael began to founder. Telamon put off the baggage he was carrying. He abandoned it. He took the Nazarene upon his shoulder. David dragged both mules. The girl bolted ahead in dashes, scouting the trail, then scurrying back. Behind them now they could see the twin columns clearly.

At Telamon's orders the party dumped every item of kit that wasn't essential. "It's loot," he said. "It'll slow these sons-of-whores down."

Indeed this proved true. The pursuers diverted, snatching up Telamon's targeteer shield and pack blankets, and a single pilum that the mercenary had discarded. David peered behind. For an interval—how brief the boy could not say, so exhausted was he—he permitted himself to believe that they in flight had put additional daylight between themselves and their pursuers.

Then the girl came sprinting back from ahead.

David saw her eyes.

"What?" Telamon demanded.

The child was pointing up the trail and gesticulating in distress.

Telamon set Michael down. He dashed forward, trailing the girl.

David followed.

The escarpment ended.

A cliff fell off before them.

The plateau continued for miles ahead. They could see it. The same scaly dolomite, the same level schist, the same featureless pan.

Except a thirty-foot-wide chasm separated the plain they stood upon from its continuation of the far side.

Telamon peered down.

The rift plunged hundreds of feet.

David had hurried up now. So had the witch.

"There must be a way down," Telamon said. He sent the woman and the boy over the edge to scout for trails. "Look for a path. An animal track. Anything we can use to get off this summit."

He himself hastened back to retrieve Michael.

When he returned, the sorceress had found a goat trace.

Dragging the mules bawling and skittering, the party succeeded in descending fifty feet, more or less, by switchbacks so narrow that one person only could proceed and so precipitous that that solitary individual must advance only by clinging to hand-cracks in the sheer face.

The trail ended.

The mules refused to budge.

The party collected on a shelf barely broad enough to hold its number.

Telamon sent David back up the path to report on the raiders' approach. "Don't let them see you. There's a chance they'll miss our track down this face."

Telamon set Michael down.

"You're an optimist," the Nazarene croaked hoarsely.

The girl stepped to her father. Taking his weight, she helped settle him into a cranny against the escarpment wall.

Telamon scanned the far cliff face.

So close!

His glance picked out a rock formation directly across—a stone tower with a tapered peak, perhaps a dozen feet high. Strong. As big around as a stone chimney.

"Get my bow," Telamon commanded the sorceress, indicating one of the panniers on the stronger mule's back. "My bow and a rope."

"To do what?"

"Just get it."

The witch obeyed.

From above, David called, "The raiders are coming straight at us! A thousand yards."

Telamon rigged the rope to an arrow so that its first few feet formed a loop, like a lasso one might use to catch a horse.

Drawing his bow to its fullest stretch, he shot the bolt across the chasm toward the chimney outcrop on the far side.

"Are you mad?" cried the sorceress.

The others stared, equally incredulous.

The witch bawled. "If you want to shoot, shoot at the Arabs!"

Telamon was trying to lob the looped rope across the crevasse, to lasso the chimney outcrop on the far side.

The first shot fell far short. The weight of the rope was too great. Arrow and rope plunged away into the chasm.

"Have you lost your wits?" cried the sorceress. "The rope is too heavy. You can't reach across this void, and even if you could . . ."

Telamon reeled the rope and arrow back.

He shot again.

Again.

Each time the heavy line fell short.

"Seven hundred yards!" David called.

"Give us weapons!" howled the witch. "Let us fight!"

Telamon tried again with the bow. His mightiest pull yet. Arrow and rope sailed with spectacular power across the chasm.

Still short.

Telamon hauled the line back, hand over hand, to try again.

Suddenly the girl-child appeared before him.

She tugged upon his arm.

Telamon ignored her. He continued hauling in the heavy line.

The girl prodded him again, harder. This time he looked.

The girl held out a lighter rope. She gestured emphatically.

"No use," Telamon said. "It won't hold my weight."

He continued reeling in the original line.

The girl poked him again.

She pointed to herself.

Again the child held out the lighter rope.

For the second time she indicated herself.

"You?"

The girl struck her chest, hard, with the flat of her palm.

For the first time, the man's eyes and the child's truly met.

"All right," he said. "Make yourself ready."

19

THE CHASM

TELAMON UNSTRUNG THE HEAVY ROPE. The girl handed him the lighter line. The mercenary fashioned a noose. He rigged it as he had the other—to the tail of his arrow, the final inch before the vanes.

"This is how you aim to save us?" the witch wailed. "Sending that monkey across?"

Telamon glanced briefly to Michael, as if for permission. The child's father seemed to nod.

Telamon drew the bow to full stretch.

He shot.

The arrow, tugging the lighter line, sailed with easy power. Its loop opened wide. It caught the chimney!

Telamon reset his feet to a secure purchase. With his right arm he whipped the line to send a wave along its length. Across the chasm, the loop settled round the outcrop, like a sailor's bowline over a bollard.

"Five hundred yards!" cried David from above.

Telamon hauled the line taut.

The girl was already lashing the length of heavy line about her waist.

The mercenary strung the near end of the light rope round a strong outcrop, looped the excess about his own waist, and tugged the line tight.

The girl stepped to Telamon at the brink. The mercenary checked and rechecked the line until he had satisfied himself it was secure. He reached to his right boot and tugged a throwing dagger from its sheath. He tucked this into the girl's waistband.

"If the Arabs get to us on this side, cut the rope and run."

The girl glanced down at the dagger. David stared curiously too. Into the butt end of the haft was carved an **X**—apparently representing the Tenth Legion. The child secured the knife. She stood now directly before Telamon.

"Your hands," said the man-at-arms. "You'll need something to—"

The child held out her palms.

Both were thick with calluses.

"This will be our finish," declared the witch. She turned away, as if unable to watch.

The girl was already gone.

On the rope.

Over the chasm.

Telamon clutched the near line, steadying it with all his strength.

Michael glanced from the girl to the chasm below.

The child, nimble as an acrobat, crossed hand over hand along the line.

"Four hundred yards!" David shouted. Telamon called him to return. The boy scampered back down the trail to the shelf.

Telamon: "Pull two iron rings off the mules' harness."

David obeyed.

"Bring me the packs."

The sorceress cried in distress. "You think to send the rest of us? How? Swinging like apes upon this laundry line?"

The child was three-quarters of the way across now.

One of her hands slipped.

Michael gasped.

Telamon hauled harder on the rope to steady it.

The girl recovered.

"Swing a leg up!" Telamon shouted. "Get a knee over the rope!"

The girl did.

Fist over fist, she pulled herself the last few feet.

The child alighted in the dust on the far side. Immediately she untied the heavier line from around her waist. This she rigged into a loop. She bound it around the chimney outcrop.

The sorceress stared. "Does she know how to tie a knot?"

Telamon: "We're about to find out."

Over the near, loose end of the heavy line, Telamon slipped two iron O-rings from the mules' harnesses. To these he secured a pack containing a cut-down version of the party's indispensables—weapons, water, medical kit. He hauled the light line back from the far side of the chasm. He lashed one end of this to the pack and wrapped the other around his waist. Then he looped the near end of the heavy rope about the same stout outcrop to which he had originally lashed the lighter line.

Telamon tugged David forward.

"You're next."

He himself readied his bow and a brace of arrows. He glanced above, to the summit track upon which the raiders would likely appear.

David grasped the heavy line. It gave—one foot, two—under his weight, even before he had stepped off over the void. "Work down the rock face," commanded Telamon.

The youth, teetering on toeholds, lowered himself below the shelf as far as he could before swinging out over the chasm. "Go!" Telamon cried.

David stepped off. His weight made him plummet violently the length of his own height before the rope stretched taut and, after several wild rebounds, began, swing by swing, to stabilize.

Across the chasm, the girl was hopping and pointing excitedly at the summit above the party.

David heard men's voices. He looked back toward the shelf. The sorceress was assailing Telamon. "You're not sending the rest of us over? The sick man too? How will I cross?"

"You're a witch," said the mercenary. "Fly."

David worked himself, hand over hand toward the far side.

Across the chasm, the girl tugged with all her strength on the rope, trying to stabilize it from swinging.

Telamon called Michael to him. He lashed the Nazarene to his own back. "This is madness!" cried the sorceress.

Telamon turned for the briefest moment toward the mules, who looked on forlornly. "Sorry, girls. I'd take you if I could."

With Michael hanging off his back, the mercenary lowered himself as David had done before him—down the face of the precipice, one hand clinging to the rope, the other, along with the foremost hobnails of his caligas, clutching the last hand- and toeholds upon the rock. David himself clung to his own portion of the line, yet swinging over empty air. "Hang on!"

The mercenary, with the Nazarene on his back, swung out over the void.

On the far side, the girl jigged with alarm as the rope began to swing violently and to plunge from the sudden addition of the weight of Telamon and Michael.

The raiders had now appeared in force on the summit—Romans and Nabateans intermingled, mounted and afoot. For moments, all peered blankly across the void. They had not yet discovered Telamon and the others below them.

David dangled still, five feet that seemed to him like five hundred from the safety of the far side, on the wildly swaying and rebounding rope. He could see the immediate shelf of rock, so close it seemed he could touch it, on whose slippery surface the girl braced her unshod feet and hauled with all her strength against the swaying, swinging rope. Her eyes frantically urged the youth to keep going. David had hooked both legs over the rope, first by the knees, then, as his strength began to fail, by the ankles.

Telamon, carrying Michael, had reached the one-third point of the crossing now. Lashed about his waist was the light line, which he had fastened to the pack that held the party's gear and weapons. This parcel, linked to the heavy line by straps and the pair of iron rings, squatted now on the shelf at the feet of the sorceress.

Later David would remember peering back from a point nine-tenths of the way across the chasm. He could see Michael, lashed to Telamon's back and clinging to the mercenary's neck with both arms while his feet dangled wildly beneath him. Beyond Telamon and the Nazarene, David could see the witch, hopping with fright and fury upon the final outcrop. The boy could hear her curses, even over the hammering of his own heart and the pounding of his blood in his ears. "You would abandon me, you blackguard!" she was shouting at Telamon, appending curses of eternal damnation in Latin, Arabic, and Aramaic.

Telamon was shouting to David to get clear, so he could haul the gear bag from the outcrop. The youth summoned his spirit. His feet touched the far cliff. The girl caught him. Somehow the boy managed to claw aboard the shelf.

"I'm over!" he shouted to Telamon.

David saw the mercenary tug the second rope, the one yoked to the baggage. The sack dragged heavily across the last foot of the shelf, then swung clear and plunged into the void. The iron rings caught. The rope stretched like a bowstring, shooting violently down, up, then down and up again. David heard himself cry out. For moments it seemed that the initial rope, stout as it was, could not possibly stand the shock of the fall, that the ties would come undone or the line itself snap. But the apparatus held. Telamon clung to the rope with impossible strength. He resumed inching across the cleft.

At this moment the raiders spotted their prey. David could see them pointing down the cliff face. He could hear their cries to one another.

The marauders grasped now what lay before them. David could see them loosing their bows, snatching fistfuls of arrows, and scampering on foot down the rock face to the final outcrop.

At this moment the sorceress leapt full-out onto the swinging pack.

The rope sang. David watched with horror as the line strained so taut he could hear fibers snap along its entire length. The witch had flung herself like a diver from the brink of the outcrop onto the now-bounding pack. She clung to this with both hands and both feet.

David saw Telamon's left hand tear loose of the rope. Michael's weight jerked the mercenary down. Meanwhile the heft of the packs, doubled by the witch's weight, pulled the rope into an acute angle like the Roman numeral V.

David now joined the girl, hauling on their end of the line, trying to stay its unrestrained swinging.

The raiders scrambled down the narrow, precipitous track, seeking the final shelf. David could hear them crying in their tongues, "Cut the rope!"

It seemed nothing could prevent them from achieving this. Then the mules bolted. In terror of the shouting, down-scrambling brigands, the pair of jennies, one behind the other, stampeded up the path toward the summit. As Telamon had said earlier, no beast short of a mountain goat can tread steep slopes as nimbly as a mule.

Past the raiders the beasts charged. Boulders and great stones bounded everywhere. The pursuers clung in terror to the cliff face.

Telamon had somehow found the strength to re-grasp the rope. He had two hands on it.

Now the raiders' arrows flew.

David saw two drill the rear of the gear pack and a third slice through the sorceress's skirts. Now she was cursing *them*.

The Roman lieutenant had reached the shelf. He was crying to the Nabateans in pidgin, "Stop shooting!" and slapping with both hands at the raiders' bows.

The Arabs jeered and rebelled.

Telamon reached the far side.

David and the girl hauled him and Michael aboard. In moments Telamon had pulled in the sorceress and the baggage.

"Peregrine!" the lieutenant shouted across. The distance from one side of the chasm to the other was slender enough that a stone could be cast with ease from one face to its opposite. The young officer could be heard clearly, despite the jibbering and hooting of the brigands about him.

In a mad pileup, Telamon's party plunged for cover behind the boulders of the outcrop. Across the cleft, the lieutenant at last succeeded in quelling the Nabateans' volley after volley upon them.

The lieutenant stood at the very brink of the far shelf. He removed his helmet and called with firm purpose across the chasm:

"Peregrine! I am Quintus Flavius Publicus. You know me. I am the officer who took you captive at the Narrows. I stood present when you met with my superior, Marcus Severus Pertinax, in the carpentry shop at the Antonia Fortress in Jerusalem. And it was I with whom you clashed hand-to-hand three days ago on the strand at Cut-off Noses."

Telamon stepped forth from shelter back onto the outcrop.

"How may I be of service to you, Quintus Flavius Publicus?"

Indeed the mercenary possessed acquaintance of this officer. The ambitious sons of the noble families of Rome must by law serve in the legions. This was how they made their names and acquired experience of command. Quintus Flavius was one of these. If he proved of stout mettle and noble ambition he would advance from his current command as a junior "thin-stripe" tribune to that of senior "broad-striper," then legate, commanding a legion, and finally to senatorial rank.

"We are men of reason, you and I," declared the lieutenant. He proffered apologies for the melee on the strand at Cut-Off Noses. It was a misunderstanding, he swore, compounded by the dark and the jumble of languages. He intended here and now to set this aright. "Give us the letter. I will triple your bounty and guarantee safe passage for you anywhere in the empire."

"Where is Severus?"

"Coming by sea. I have sent for him."

"I will deal with him and him only," declared the mercenary.

"If you so wish," the lieutenant responded. "But place yourself beneath my protection now. Only I can preserve you from these savages . . ."

The raiders catcalled and jeered at this. Arabic is a language rich in invective and imprecation, and no dialect possesses a more abundant lexicon of this than the Nabatean. Salvos of insult flew across the canyon. The lieutenant sought to contain this. The marauders ignored him. Their oaths and execrations redoubled.

"Hear me, peregrine! You see these barbarians. Can you imagine what they will do to you, should they take you captive?

"You cannot escape," the officer called across. "You are on foot. We and these Arabs are mounted. Word of you and your captive has been published abroad from Gaza to Alexandria. I know of three parties of tribesmen who pursue you now out of the east, each more ungovernable than the next, and have heard rumor of four more, advancing from the west, from Egypt, to intercept you from the direction in which you flee. See sense, brother. Give up the letter!"

"I do not have it, Quintus Flavius. I have not found it. You will not get it from this man," said Telamon, indicating Michael. "So far, I have failed as well."

"Leave him to us, then. I will deliver your full emolument. I give you my word as an officer."

Telamon seemed to consider this. The girl-child, reckoning this, burst from behind the outcrop and dashed to his side. With both hands she seized the mercenary at the wrist and tugged upon him violently.

"By our bond as soldiers," called the lieutenant, "and by the gods of my ancestors, I swear no harm will come to you or to those, other than the Nazarene, whom you protect."

Telamon gave no answer. The girl, clearly in distress for her father, heaved yet more fervently upon the mercenary's arm.

"Why do you hesitate, peregrine? Are you thinking of delivering your prisoner to Alexandria instead of Jerusalem? Be assured, you will get no more from the governor there. Two fast corvettes sent from Gaza will reach his city tomorrow or the day after with orders not to engage you. Your luck has run out. Act with reason! Give us what you promised and make yourself a rich man!"

Telamon's eyes now lowered to the girl's. The child had ceased pulling upon his arm. She simply met his gaze.

The lieutenant called again. "You fear for the child, my friend. I understand. Deliver her then into Rome's safekeeping! Simply leave her with the Nazarene. On my honor, no harm will come to her."

The child's eyes continued to hold Telamon's.

"Hand the girl over to our care," called the lieutenant. "Do not suffer an innocent to perish in this wilderness. Let us return her to civilization and safety. She is but a child!"

Telamon faced across the chasm toward the officer. With the blade of his gladius, he cut the heavy line that had been wound around the rock chimney. The rope's end plunged into the chasm.

"There are no children in this company," he said.

BOOK SIX

INTO THE STORM

20

THE STORM

B OLTS SPLIT THE HEAVENS.
Lightning rattled across the horizon. Winter's first storm had broken, half a league to the west. Telamon made straight for this. He carried Michael now, with an arm about the Nazarene's waist and the man's elbow across his shoulder. The fellow pleaded yet to be left behind. Telamon would not hear this. Michael hung from him, seeking with what little strength he owned to hop or tread or take at least some weight off the mercenary's shoulder.

The man-at-arms had confiscated from the girl-child the dagger he had set in her hand before the chasm crossing. Michael's person and garments he had searched again, satisfying himself that the Nazarene bore no weapon or any tool or article that would serve as such.

David plodded in Telamon's train. He could make no sense of the man-at-arms' actions. The mercenary offered no explanation. He simply marched. All in the company reckoned their peril. Each understood that the storm was their hope. They must reach it and its sheltering deluge before their pursuers overtook them.

The party found a track and descended from the scarp.

Hazard now redoubled, as the mounted detachments in pursuit were, or must be soon, upon this same flat.

Telamon would not let the company rest. They slogged for an hour, then another, beneath a leaden sky that seemed to have lowered so closely above them that they could touch it simply by reaching up a hand. The day had gone frigid. For a further hour the mercenary bore Michael. The man-at-arms succored even the sorceress, permitting her to cling to his free shoulder.

At last the heavens opened. Rain descended in volumes unimaginable, turning the surface of the basin across which the party trekked first slick with ocher-colored runoff, then into a mucky, treacherous wilderness, sluicing with debris flows and rockslides as the downpour turned every runnel and dry riverbed into a torrent.

Telamon pressed the party harder. The mercenary herded his charges before him, driving them to make all the speed they could against the elements and their own infirmities.

Night came down, raw and howling.

The deluge intensified.

David pressed alongside his mentor, taking a portion of the burden of the Nazarene. "Sir! I must hear this from you: What do you intend toward this man and the child?"

Telamon only pushed on into the storm.

"Are they our captives? Is it our object, as the lieutenant declared, to bear them to Alexandria and sell them there to the Roman governor?"

"We have taken on a job," said Telamon. "We will finish it."

"Because if that is our aim, sir, I wish no part of it. Such an act would be infamous. I will not participate in it."

The sorceress cackled at this. She and the girl had borne in closer to hear the mercenary's response.

"This was your part from the beginning," the man-at-arms addressed his apprentice. "You knew it as well as I."

A floodwater stream interdicted the party's progress. The mercenary drew up, scanning for a crossing.

David took up a position defying him.

The boy, apparently, meant what he said.

Telamon shook his head.

He was still carrying Michael.

"The lieutenant spoke true when he said his men and the Arabs would get back down off that scarp and around it almost as fast as we could descend it. They're mounted. We're afoot. We must push our pace while the storm effaces our tracks." The man-at-arms indicated the wilderness to the west, the direction in which he led the company. "And since you have hearkened so attentively to the counsel of our friend Quintus Flavius Publicus, you heard him cite additional parties hunting us, perhaps coming from ahead, from Egypt, from Alexandria."

The mercenary's eyes had gone dark with exhaustion and strain. He continued to David, but loud enough for the others to hear.

"Do you imagine the bounties offered by Rome apply only to the Nazarene? Your neck and mine are worth fortunes to these sons-of-whores." Lightning carved the heavens. The deluge sluiced in sheets across David's brow. "Or is it your wish," said Telamon to the youth, "to tarry here and debate these niceties with the sons of Rome and Nabatea?"

The party crossed the flood with what felt like the last of their strength. An hour farther on, they came opposite a basalt bluff. The sorceress indicated a colony of caves, visible along the face. She pleaded with Telamon to let the company mount to these, if only for a few minutes, to get out of the storm.

The mercenary rejected this. "A few minutes become an hour, then two, then all night. We'll wake to sword blades at our throats."

The party pushed on to exhaustion and beyond. The witch stumbled at David's shoulder, hobbling on her yet-unsound calves and ankles.

Twice the woman fell behind, then a third time and a fourth.

Each time David trekked back for her.

The final time, bearing her forward, the youth saw Telamon approach out of the gloom. "Drop her," he commanded.

David would not.

"What meager truth she might have given up," the man-at-arms declared, "she has already. She is worthless to us now."

Recalling this night later, the youth could not say what impulse impelled him to defy the man he had chosen as his master. Perhaps it was anguish at their mutual errand and his own complicity in it. Maybe the cause was despair, or fatigue, or simply terror.

David saw Telamon draw his sword. "Either you do it," the man-at-arms said, "or I will."

And he advanced upon the sorceress.

"She's trying!" cried David. "I'll bear her! We won't fall behind. For God's sake, what do you intend?"

The mercenary stepped past the boy. He seized the witch by the hair and wrenched her to expose her throat.

At this instant the girl-child materialized from the murk. With both hands she seized Telamon by the wrist. The child clung to the mercenary with such vehemence that when he raised his sword arm to strike, she came with it bodily—bare soles, sodden garments, storm-plastered mane, and all.

Telamon's arm lowered.

He stared at the girl.

"Who *are* you?"

He turned from the child to David and to the witch.

"Who are *all* of you?" the man-at-arms cried. "And how, by the sunless track to hell, has my life become so entangled with yours?"

21

THE WADI

THE PARTY WAS CROSSING A torrent when they heard horses. David spun and saw a dozen black-hooded phantoms at the gallop, pounding across a mudflat toward the roaring watercourse.

Telamon's company had been checked for a quarter hour by this flooded riverbed. They had roped it to fashion a crossing. The mercenary had waded over first, securing a line above the far bank. He had next carried Michael, then with David's aid had gotten the sorceress and the girl over. The child was mounting the bank immediately above the youth. David could see her bare toes digging for purchase into the mud. The witch had climbed out before the girl. She scrambled, now, over the top of the cut. Michael knelt above her on the summit, extending a hand to help her up.

At this instant a black arrow buried itself to the vanes in the muck beside David's cheek. Another followed, screaming past his opposite ear.

In the fight at the Narrows, time had seemed to slow. David recalled arrow shafts passing before him in their flight as if they were floating; his eye could make out every detail of shaft and fletching; he could even see the bolt flex and rotate as it flew.

This now was the opposite.

All action quickened. Minutes became seconds. Seconds compressed to instants.

David saw the leading pair of riders plunge at the full gallop into the torrent. He saw the horses' knees churn into the mud-colored flow. He saw Telamon, calf-deep in the stream, take up that station he called "castling."

The man-at-arms unhorsed one rider with a slash of his entrenching tool. The blow severed the man's rein arm at the elbow.

Another swing took down the second man.

David clawed with all his strength up the bank. He clutched in his right fist the remaining pilum, the five-footer that Telamon had not jettisoned. The youth thought, *I will "castle" at the peak. I will make my stand there.*

In the stream Telamon had fallen upon one of the raiders he had unhorsed. From this man's grip he wrested a Parthian-style composite bow. He stripped this same attacker of a *xiphos*, a Lakedaemonian-style shortsword.

The marauders galloped wide around Telamon, two on the downstream side, three on the upper.

The mercenary bawled to David, "Face toward the foe! Don't let him see your back!"

The youth glanced for an instant only to the bank summit at his rear. He saw the witch snatching stones from the ground, bracing to hurl them. The girl too armed herself with rocks for throwing. Michael, for all his wounds, made his way to the child's side, empty-handed, seeking to defend her with his flesh alone.

One of the black-garbed specters spilled from his mount when the beast balked at the wadi wall. David saw the rider leap powerfully free and mount to the crest on foot, sleeves billowing, a curved slashing sword in his right hand.

This demon rushed straight at David.

The youth planted both feet in the muck and braced to receive the fellow's onrush.

The man hurtled past David.

He made for the girl.

The Nazarene defended his daughter.

Stepping into the path of the assailant, Michael received the brunt of the man's onslaught. The pair fell and tumbled. The girl vaulted into the fray, clawing with bare hands at the attacker. The pirate sprang to his feet.

Again he flung the Nazarene aside.

Again he went after the child.

David could hear himself screaming. He felt in the flat of his palms only the buck and shiver of the pilum's shaft as he drove the warhead with all his strength into the meat between the attacker's shoulder blades. The iron deflected as it made contact with the fellow's dorsal spine. David could feel its nose deviate downward and to the right as it entered the lung. The youth hurled all his weight into the thrust.

The pilum snapped at the joint where the iron met the ash.

David did not see the next two attackers. This pair too, dismissing every other of the fugitive party, rushed past seeking only the child.

The boy did not see Telamon hamstring the first of these as the man hurtled across the summit flat, then pierce the fellow's liver from behind with a thrust of the xiphos he had taken from the first attacker in the torrent.

David did not see, across on the flat, the second black-hooded banshee stalk with furious strides upon the girl, clutching a sica dagger and bawling some unintelligible war cry. He did not see Telamon let fly two arrows in such immediate succession that the iron head of the second seemed to fly from the bowstring before the vanes of the first had cleared the horn-and-sinew of the grip.

Two more attackers fell.

Telamon mounted before David now, clambering up the bank from the torrent. The first black-robed assassin yet writhed beneath the boy, struggling to rise against the youth's weight and the lance head of the shiv-ered pilum. The mercenary, with two furious back-handed slashes, lopped the attacker off at the neck. David felt his pike plummet, dragged down by the weight of the collapsing foe; then Telamon's right hand wrested him under the arm and hauled him upright.

At once David's sight and sense returned.

He saw a sixth attacker, afoot as well, stalk directly upon the girl. The child's father, hobbling upon limbs that could barely support his stationary weight, flung himself into the path of this man. The assassin beat Michael down with a blow of his fist. He seized the child by the scruff of her robe and lifted her before his eyes, crying some demand that was lost in the din of the torrent.

The girl spat in the killer's face.

The man raised his blade.

Telamon stood directly behind David. The boy could hear the man-at-arms' bowstring draw. The shaft hurtled past David's ear, so close the boy seemed to feel the vanes themselves flick his skin. The warhead struck the black-garbed man-killer's upper right arm, which clutched the dagger meant to open the child's throat, and drove through its muscle and sinew into the bone of the attacker's cheek. This it pierced as well, entering the well of the skull with a sound like a maul hammering a spike. David saw the attacker rock and shudder, then pitch sideways as his knees and shins collapsed beneath him.

Before David could command his own limbs to move, Telamon had crossed to the girl's side. With a sweep of his right leg, he drew the child behind him, shielding her with his belly, thighs, and calves. Simultaneously his upper body, head, and eyes swung to scan the field of conflict, seeking any attacker who might still pose peril.

"Search among these!" Telamon commanded David and the others. "Find me one yet breathing."

The mercenary lingered an instant only over Michael, enough to reckon that the Nazarene stood in no immediate hazard.

A glance to the child determined the same of her.

Telamon stood now to his full height. His chest, neck, and face were black with blood and tissue. The veins of his temples stood out like ropes. He spat, once and again, and wiped his face of mud, blood, and sand.

David felt all breath leave his lungs. Could every attacker indeed be fallen? For moments the boy could not believe the clash was over so quickly and with such finality. But Telamon's sense, as with all matters concerning mortal strife, remained infallible. Nine black-hooded figures sprawled motionless—four in the river, two on the bank, two at the summit, with the final dagger man yet tangled limb upon limb before the trembling, wide-eyed child.

"Who are these?" David heard his own voice cry. "Are they Nabateans?"

Telamon strode swiftly among the bodies, seeking one yet living to interrogate. He tugged up one corpse, then another, dumping each in turn as he reckoned their life-fled state.

"These aren't Arabs," he said. "They're Jews."

22

ZELOTOI

I T TOOK NEARLY TWO HOURS, scrambling in the dawn with a great length of rope seized from the attackers' kit and borne between them as a herding device, to corral four of the assailants' animals—two saddle mounts and a pair of pack mules. Telamon called off pursuit of the others. The beasts were too shy and too canny to let themselves be caught. Nor could the party tarry, he declared, as other bands of pursuers, foremost among them the Romans and Nabateans from Cut-off Noses, must surely be closing in as well.

A murk-shrouded sun had mounted clear of the ridgeline when the four leading the animals—Telamon, David, the girl, and the sorceress—arrived back at the riverbed, which ran now at barely ankle depth and whose force was diminishing perceptibly with every moment. The party discovered Michael in the posture it had left him—sitting upright, utterly depleted, with his back against a barrow of sand, while the corpses of the attackers sprawled in various postures of mortality in the muck at his feet.

"Had enough yet, Nazarene?" spat the sorceress, crossing to stand above him. "Ready to cough up that prize you hoard with such devotion?" She indicated the carpet of carnage. "Or must we all die to surfeit your fanaticism?"

"Leave him alone," said David. "He doesn't have the letter. If he did, he'd have—"

"Oh, he's got it. He's got it in his belly! Inside him in a lamb's-gut pouch, or some such device. Do you disbelieve me? Remark how delicately he steps when he heeds nature's call. He shits the parcel out, rinses it, and swallows it again. That, or he's got it so far up his ass you'd have to put your arm in to the elbow. Cut him open! You'll find the letter."

Telamon had crossed before the witch now. To David he handed the halter of the mount he was leading and instructed the youth to see that the animals, all of them, got clean water and whatever feed could be found in the attackers' packs.

The mercenary drew his gladius.

With its blade he indicated the bodies strewn about the site.

"Who were these Jews?" the man-at-arms demanded of the sorceress. "I've seen others garbed in the same black hoods."

The witch ignored this. Her bony claw thrust again at Michael.

"He had the letter in prison. I saw it. I saw him with it. And, by all that's holy, he packs it still!"

"These are Zealots." Telamon addressed the witch. "And you brought them upon us."

The man-at-arms seized the woman by the garment about her neck. He drew her upright, twisting till she cried out. The point of his sword pressed against the flesh of her throat.

"You've been leaving a trail for them from the first. They, not the Romans, were the ones who bought you out of prison. Who are you to them?"

Michael, despite his wounds and his state of debilitation, had gotten to his feet. David drew up as well, breaking off from his chore of tending the horses. The girl too crossed before the sorceress.

The witch turned to confront each in turn.

"*Zelotoi*," she spoke, employing the Greek term, with its connotations of madness and unquenchable hatred.

Telamon held the woman fast. "You are one of them."

The witch's eyes answered for her.

"Their whore?"

"Their queen."

"That," said the man-at-arms, "is the first thing you've said that I believe."

Telamon released the woman.

She dropped to her knees in the muck.

David searched the witch's eyes. "A Zealot? You have dogged us for them and not Rome?"

"Rome? This I got from Rome!" The sorceress displayed the yet-lurid lesions upon her legs. "And this!" She craned her neck to reveal scars of the dungeon's rope and the rawhide choke-binder.

The others circled around her. The sorceress regarded them, each and every, with disdain mounting to detestation. But beyond all she fixed her scorn upon the youth David.

"Have you any notion what 'zeal' means, boy? *Kana'ut* in our tongue. It means love of God. It means passion for the right. *Kana'ut* is soul! It is that without which a man is nothing.

"You are a Jew!" The witch bayed at David in a cadence of censure and contempt. "Yet you worship this man-killer of Rome and trail after him like a hound. Who is he but the engine of your oppression and that of all our people? You are sheep—all who have not zeal!"

The sorceress rose to her feet before Telamon. She gestured to the bodies spread about him in the mire.

"And you, peregrine. Do you dream you have outrun the Black Hoods because you have slain this handful? Two more parties of shomrim left Jerusalem on the heels of the equites tracking you—I saw them—the first of the Sanhedrin, forty on horseback and camel; the second of the Pharisaical Guard, in numbers even greater. These dead at your feet were caravan riders, sent from the Council of Ten in Alexandria. Yes, ahead of you! West! From the place to which you flee!"

The sorceress saw that her words had hit their mark. She stepped now with even more brazenness before the man-at-arms.

"You will never cross the Nile alive. Every port from Pelusium to Alexandria is barred to you. A hundred tribes and bands hunt you. Flee back to the Anthill? Two cohorts of your own legion are there already, dispatched by Severus Pertinax with a pledge of twenty golden eagles to him who brings in your head."

Telamon's fist tightened upon his sword.

"Go ahead, murder me," the witch spat. "Open my throat, you villain. But before you do I will school you in how the conquered and the vanquished fare beneath your heel.

"What is 'zeal,' mercenary? It is that alone which stands up to the legions in this land. Shall I recite their names and stations? Every Jew knows them. The Third Cyrenaica and the Fifteenth Apollinaris at Alexandria, the Third Gallica at Antioch. The Sixth Ferrata—stop me if I recite awry—at Raphanaea and at Cyrrhus the Tenth Fretensis, in which you have served, may God damn your soul. Wait! I have left out the Fourth Scythica at Zeugma . . . and the Twelfth Fulminata with the 'Iron Legion' at Raphanaea. Zeal and zeal alone checks these engines of war from grinding Israel into dust."

"So," said Telamon. "You know the legions."

"I know Caesar took Gaul with only four. Tiberius subdued all Germania with six. Yet now your master Claudius Nero marshals seven and threatens to dispatch more to hold down my people in this land, which is worth nothing to Rome except as another emblem of conquest. What is the empire? She is the devil! The she-bitch of the world! All that is barbarous and unholy arises from her, and yet . . ."

The witch turned now, with even more furious impetus, to Michael.

" . . . and yet greater wickedness besets the children of this land. From what quarter? Our own sons! Our brothers! You!"

The woman's forefinger thrust to the center of the Nazarene's chest.

"You who would sever Jew from Jew. You who would subvert the soul of Israel with your madness of 'the kingdom of God' and your rejection of all that the prophets have given us down three thousand years of exile and suffering. What is Israel? It is that lore, those agonies, that history. You would replace it with what? Your make-believe 'messiah' and his teachings of the barnyard?"

The Nazarene made to shove the witch away. She pressed with even greater vigor upon him. David sprang to the man's side, drawing his dagger to defend him.

The witch belted the youth across the face.

Before any could react, the woman had snatched the dagger. With the speed of a striking snake, she leapt at Michael. In an instant the woman had torn the Nazarene's robes open and thrust her blade toward his exposed belly.

"Yes!" cried the witch. "This is zeal!"

Telamon advanced upon her, gladius drawn.

"Back!" barked the woman. "Or I'll gut him this instant."

The sorceress's blade poised fractions apart from Michael's loins.

"We will see the letter now! I will carve it out of him!"

Telamon's glance swung to David, then to the child. The girl's eyes were molten with anguish. She seemed upon the instant of flinging her own flesh onto the witch's blade to spare her father.

Michael saw this. "Hold, child! I am ready to die."

The moment hung, terrible with dread. The witch, it was clear, was ablaze with passion to eviscerate the Nazarene. At the same time Telamon's sword loomed, an instant apart from taking her off at the neck.

The mercenary's voice broke the standoff.

"Go ahead, split the man's guts," he said. "But you won't find the letter."

The man-at-arms relaxed his sword hand, just slightly.

He took half a step back.

"Your friends the Zealots knew where the letter was. You saw how they struck, deliberately and with unified intent."

"What are you talking about?"

"But they didn't go after the Nazarene, did they?"

The sorceress's glance shot to Telamon. *What is this?* her eyes seemed to say. *Some kind of trick?*

With his blade Telamon indicated the nearest of the slain Zealots. "This one could have cut Michael down right here. But he sprinted past without attempting a blow, didn't he?"

The mercenary gestured to the corpse of a second attacker.

"This one never even glanced at the Nazarene. That pair, the same. They went after the girl. They all did. Why? Because they knew something we don't. From where or whom, I have no idea. Some source in Alexandria? The Sanhedrin? An informer attached to the Apostle?"

The sorceress seized Michael even more forcefully with her free hand. She thrust her blade a hairbreadth into the Nazarene's flesh, enough to draw blood and make the man jerk back involuntarily.

From the folds of his robe Telamon withdrew a clay pot shard—the one upon which, back at the Anthill, the child had scrawled a word.

Telamon tossed this onto the ground between the witch and Michael.

PHILOS

"What are you saying, peregrine? That this urchin carries the letter?"

The mercenary's glance swung first to the child, then to the Nazarene.

"A girl who cannot speak," he said, "and a man who will not. What better pair to conceal an earthshaking secret from an empire?"

The witch's blade withdrew, just a little, from Michael's belly.

Telamon advanced a half step toward her.

"You saw the letter in prison," he said. "You told me you saw it in the child's hands."

The sorceress's expression confirmed this.

"The girl can read. She read the letter and committed it to memory. Then she, or her father, destroyed it."

The witch's eyes swung to the child. "This guttersnipe? This feral rat?"

"She carries the letter now. Here. Between her ears." Telamon tapped his skull. "When she reaches the community at Corinth, if she does, she'll scribe it out word for word."

Telamon again indicated the bodies of the Zealot attackers. "Somehow your Zealot friends knew this or guessed it. The Roman lieutenant did too, at the chasm, when he tried to get us to hand over the child."

The sorceress turned to Michael, then to the girl.

The pair's expressions, despite themselves, confirmed Telamon's supposition.

The man-at-arms took the final step toward the sorceress.

He held out his hand.

Into this the witch set the hilt of the dagger.

"There is no letter," said Telamon. "The girl is the letter."

BOOK SEVEN

TO THE NILE

− 23 −

IN A BOTTLE

"WHEN DID YOU KNOW?"

This from Michael, addressing Telamon. The hour was the Roman third watch, lacking two hours till dawn. The man-at-arms had set the Nazarene upon the back of the stronger of the two mules. The mercenary, trekking afoot, led this beast into the teeth of a gale against which he and the others advanced with strenuous difficulty, muffled to the eyeballs.

"You knew before the Zealot attack, didn't you?"

Telamon refused to engage Michael in such converse. He insisted only that the Nazarene confirm himself fit to ride. The mercenary pointed north to a jagged ridge a few miles ahead. "Can you carry on? We must reach the summit before sunrise."

"You knew before then, even," said Michael. "At the chasm. No, earlier still . . . the Anthill. You knew when the child scribed a word upon the pot shard."

The party had tramped two days from the site of the attack of the Zelotoi. Its configuration had altered however. The girl rode now, beside Michael and the man-at-arms, on the fastest of the mounts recovered of the Zealots. She was armed, with the **x** dagger Telamon had given her at the chasm and then taken back. The mercenary has set this weapon into her hand at the same time he boosted her into the saddle of the lead Zealot's horse.

The sorceress now straggled at the rear of the column, afoot, wrists bound, being pulled behind the last pony. The mercenary staked her to the earth again each night, after her collection mandated by him to sustain and accelerate the Nazarene's recovery. A watch was set over the woman throughout each night, manned in addition to Telamon and David by the child.

The witch had lost none of her fervor for invective. "So now I am the one you imprison! To what end, mercenary? Do you imagine the next company of pursuers will spare you because you hold me? Never! The Almighty will not let them, and neither will I!"

Telamon drove the party on. A fierce windstorm had gotten up in the after course of the downpour and had not abated, save for fleeting lulls in all those hours. This scourge was aggravated by a fresh affliction. Great tumbling diaspores, called by the Arabs *spina* and by the Romans *anastatica,* came barreling upon the company at ground level, driven before the gale in numbers uncountable. The animals, struck with panic by this assault of nature, bawled and brayed and could not be quieted.

"Merciful God!" cried the sorceress. "What *are* these things?"

The siege of diaspores arose without warning. In moments their tumbling mass had blanketed the basin as far as sight could carry. No remedy obtained except to swathe oneself within robes and beat forward into the onslaught.

The tribes of the peninsula call these diaspores "wind rollers," and they name such infestations, when they strike on such a scale, "heaven's harrowing." The plants grow wild, in colonies miles in breadth, across the northern rim of the desert. They are spherical in conformation and stand as tall as a man's waist. In a gale they snap free of their single stems. They roll and tumble. Nothing can stop them. Their form is spiny and desiccated. They cannot be handled, even when stationary, except with wrapped arms and heavy gloves.

Minutes from the assault's onset, the entire plain had become carpeted with these spiny invaders. The party found itself trapped. The horses and mules would not take the first step into this spiky mass. David and the girl tried afoot, but both recoiled at once, pricked even through their woolen robes by the spines of the rollers.

"Burn the stuff," said the witch. "These things are dry as tinder."

Telamon would not permit even a spark, cautious that flame, or even the merest smoke, would give their location away.

When the moon had set and the gale had at last abated and even, in diminished strength, reversed direction dispersing the diaspores, Telamon ordered the party to form up again in a mounted column, with himself in the lead.

"Know this for a fact," he instructed his charges. "The Romans and Nabateans—that company that overhauled us at the chasm—has reached the site of the Zealot attack. Others of the native tribes or brigands will be hard on their heels, if they haven't gotten there already. They know where we are within a radius of ten miles. Scouts will be out everywhere. The enemy's aim can be nothing other than to cut us off between the inner desert and that impassable range that runs parallel to the sea. Arab raiders and Pharisaical and Saduceean shomrim, not to mention further parties of Zealots from Jerusalem, will be ringing us to the south, while other detachments from Alexandria, seeking Roman bounty, will be pressing in from the north and west. Our pursuers' aim is to stopper the only pass through the seacoast range. We are caught between them and the parties closing upon us from the south.

"Mark that ridgeline ahead," he continued. "We must mount to the summit by dawn and be snugged down under cover so that we cannot be seen from below. From the peak we can scan the basin that stands between us and the sea and discover what enemy awaits us there. If daylight overtakes us on the face," he said, "no question remains except whether our end comes within hours or minutes."

The mercenary shared out to the others and the animals what little refreshment the Zealots' horses carried in their water skins, sparing only a ration for what emergency must come with the morrow. He gave the party ten minutes to allay their hunger, if they could scrounge up enough to do so. He himself did without, attending instead to Michael's still-flagrant infirmities and to the continuing distress the Nazarene suffered with his eye.

Michael accepted these ministrations with gratitude. Throughout, however, he studied the mercenary, as he had from his first conscious moment in the aftermath of the clash at the anchorage of Rhinococura.

"If you knew about the girl since the Anthill, why did you save me on the strand at Cut-off Noses? The Roman lieutenant stood before you. You could have handed me over and kept the girl to sell later. The officer commanded you to do so. He would've loaded you down with gold."

Telamon continued to attend to Michael's mutilated eye.

"The lieutenant knew then too, didn't he? From whom? Some other jailhouse informer? Severus surely knew as well. Then why have you kept me? I'm worthless to you, yet you have endured grave and parlous pains to preserve me. Why?"

"Perhaps," said Telamon, "I have grown fond of you."

The witch cackled at this. She fixed the Nazarene with a bony finger.

"You dream in daylight, Christian! Can you imagine this villain has tempered his intentions toward you and the child? Why? Because, before, he had only to turn in a letter, setting you and the girl free . . . while now he must deliver up the child herself, knowing she will face torture, crucifixion, and death? Can you dream that this has moved his stony heart?"

David and the girl pressed close to attend this disputation. The sorceress's glance swung toward the child. The woman gestured to Telamon.

"Regard him—this killer-for-hire who scorns mercy and murders with the heartlessness of a machine. Listen to me, brat! Can you believe he cares for you?" She indicated the x dagger that the girl wore in her belt. "Why? Because he has set that harlot's hatpin in your fist? Look at him! For a fortnight the lot of us have endured trials of death together in this wilderness, yet not once has he even asked your name, or mine."

The sorceress turned to the boy and to Michael.

"He only knows yours because the Romans told him. He will not even name these horses and pack mules, or that pair he led before the chasm.

Why? Because he cares for nothing but himself. His god is money . . . and before this idol he abases himself without shame."

The first glimmers of dawn fell now upon the ridge to the north. The witch's claw indicated its summit.

"Do not deceive yourselves that this champion seeks a way to preserve you from Rome or from the tribes and brigands. His aim is to make away to the west. He will take you to Alexandria, that's his plan! To sell you to the governor or to the Jews, whichever will bid higher!"

Michael had remained silent throughout the sorceress's harangue. "I don't believe you, sister," he said now.

Telamon finished dressing Michael's eye.

"Shut up, the mess of you! Get something into your bellies. We move out in the count of a hundred."

Michael stood now.

Again he thanked the mercenary for his care. It was clear, however, that the Nazarene had no intention of obeying the man's order to pack out. He must speak. Even the horses seemed to sense this.

"How long, my friend," said Michael, addressing Telamon, "did you serve in the legions?"

"I can't remember."

The Nazarene smiled. "Ten years? Twenty?"

Telamon again commanded the party to make ready to move out. "Twenty-two," he answered grudgingly.

The Nazarene considered this. The figure clearly did not surprise him.

"Nor were you, I'll wager, a common foot-slogger. What rank did you hold? Captain of ten? Fifty? Centurion?"

The mercenary shouldered his kit. He would not answer.

Michael continued. "A soldier of rank serving all those years would tot up a tidy bundle, wouldn't he? Further, a legionary's discharge bonus comes to, what . . . fourteen years' pay? Throw in reenlistment incentives over the course of service, prizes of conquest, loot and booty . . . such a man could retire and live like a lord. Buy a farm, take a wife, raise a family. Many have. Why not you?"

"Because," said the witch, "he sprees his loot. Throws it away on gambling and whores, as they all do."

"No," said Michael. "I don't believe that either."

David and the girl had pressed close now, attending upon every word. The Nazarene addressed Telamon.

"Our friend the witch declares that you worship naught but treasure. And so it would seem, from your own speech. Yet you trek with as little resource, if I may say so, as a holy man or a renunciant."

"Indeed," said Telamon. "These are my vocations."

Michael smiled.

"Why have you no money, Telamon . . . if I may address you by name? You cannot deflect this with a jest or dismiss it with silence—you who have surely amassed fortunes serving the eagle of Rome."

It was the man-at-arms' turn now to smile. He grasped the halter of Michael's mule, along with that of his own, and stepped off toward the distant ridge.

The Nazarene with two unsteady strides overtook him. He seized the leather and compelled the mercenary to draw up.

"Let me guess," said Michael, facing the man-at-arms directly. "You have donated every copper you've earned—and to those as could neither make return or care to."

Telamon again made no answer, only tugged his animal by the halter apart from the Nazarene.

"Clearly you are not the brute you pretend to be," Michael observed, speaking with emphasis for the benefit of David and the girl. "What, then, are you? I have studied you, brother, more than you know. You claim to believe in nothing. Your actions belie this. I believe you possess, if I may say so, a profound and highly developed philosophy, whether you will admit it or not, or acknowledge this, even to yourself.

"I have watched you kill," said Michael. "You perform the act not like a butcher but like a monk. I witness no rage within you toward the foe. You take no joy in the slaughter. Stop me if I speak aught but truth. I have watched your face as you take station in readiness to face a mortal foe. You step into that moment—'beneath extinction's scythe,' as the poet says—having accepted, even embraced, your own death in advance and willingly offering this up. This is what makes you unkillable. Call me out if I speak false."

Telamon responded nothing.

David attended intently, as did the girl, and indeed the witch.

"This is an act of profound self-abnegation," continued Michael. "Worthy of him who offered the same upon the cross. But let me press this proposition further, Telamon. To whom do you offer your life? To money? To randomness? To nothing? Shall I tell you what I think, my friend?"

"I'm sure," said Telamon, "that I could not stop you."

"Brother, I believe that you, in battle, offer your life to the one who stands unseen and unborn within you. I mean that self you will become. You want to die. Tell the truth. Only then may you become that which, within you, yearns desperately to be born."

Telamon smiled. "You will not convert me, brother."

Michael responded with his own smile. "On the contrary, it is you, mercenary, who are converting me. You have given me my life and preserved it when others would strip it from me. You have given me my life when you yourself had every incentive to take it, and for that prize—money—which you claim to value beyond all others. You are a model and paragon for me. You are he, in part, whom I wish to become."

THE SUMMIT

THE GIRL'S NAME WAS RUTH.

The man-at-arms inquired of Michael as the party raced the dawn toward the track that ascended the ridgeline.

The girl heard and turned in her saddle.

The mercenary, afoot, faced toward her as they trekked.

"I am Telamon," he declared, "of Arcadia, in Greece." He extended his hand. The child took it.

The sorceress, trailing, observed this communion. She spoke:

"And Ruth said, 'Entreat me not to leave thee, or to return from following after thee. For whither thou goest, I will go. Where thou lodgest, I will lodge. Thy people shall be my people, and thy God my God.'"

The others turned back toward the woman. Their expressions seemed to inquire, *Does the witch mock?* But the woman's tone seemed indeed sober, even solemn. She intoned as if proffering a prediction.

"Where thou diest, I will die, and there shall I be buried. The Lord do so to me, and more also, if aught but death part thee and me."

Now on the summit, the party, absent the sorceress, whom Telamon had bound to a granite shelf beside the animals in a notch a quarter mile below, strained beneath the noon glare, scouring the ten-mile plain to the north. The company lay prone, four abreast, at the pinnacle—Telamon on the left, the girl Ruth beside him, then Michael and David.

The pan beneath was of firm level sand, cut by dune lines at intervals of about a mile. A forbidding granite ridgeline sealed the basin along its northern rim.

A fierce gale ripped across the pan from south to north, raising great clouds of alkali and loess that ascended as cyclones and storm funnels.

The child's vision now, as earlier, proved the keenest. After an interval scanning tediously across the deep distance, she pointed to a crease or canyon-head, barely perceptible, at the base of the ridge ten miles distant—a notch that appeared to be some kind of pass, or to lead to a way across the range to the sea.

It took Telamon long moments before his focus settled and permitted him to see, barely, what the child indicated.

The girl pointed out three mounted columns, miles apart, advancing across the flat from the east, toward this notch. The leading column included wagons.

"Severus," pronounced Telamon gravely. "Only Romans use wheeled transport in this desert to pack their impedimenta. Our friend the tribune has caught up by sea, summoned by his nephew, the young lieutenant, as this officer said."

Michael reacted. "Severus? How do you know? How can you be sure?"

The man-at-arms smiled. "You're more important than you realize, Michael. You and the Apostle's letter."

At that moment Telamon's attention was caught by what he feared was an additional, and new, mounted column. He turned to the child. "What's that line of dust?" He pointed to a squall of sand-colored billows, scudding erratically across the plain.

The girl answered in sign, dismissing this.

"What is she saying?"

"Tumbleweeds," said Michael. "Like the storm of diaspores that trapped us last night."

Telamon peered intently, shielding his eyes from the sun, until he had satisfied himself that the child's determination was correct.

The party remained on the summit for most of an hour. During that time the three additional columns converged upon a single point at the foot of the mountains. The girl spotted another—horseback- or camel-mounted, it was too far to tell—then a sixth. All were coming together at the same notch at the base of the range.

"Give me a horse," said Michael to Telamon. "Let me draw them off. The rest of you may see a chance to get through."

The mercenary rejected this.

"Every party down there knows about the girl," he said, "or suspects. They'd let you run. Even if they did chase you, the Arabs or the Black Hoods would run you down in minutes with three men or fewer. That notch will stay as stoppered as it is now."

Telamon led the company back down the mountain to the hollow where the mules and horses waited. He unbound the sorceress from the boulder to which he had secured her.

"So you didn't steal the animals and run," said the mercenary.

"I have become attached to you."

The company descended the mountain to its base.

Telamon permitted the party one cupful of water and whatever bread each yet carried.

They sat in a circle and considered their predicament.

"The mountains block the way to the sea for more miles than we dare cross in the open. I saw only one way through—that notch where the columns had converged."

"Meaning what?" said Michael.

"Meaning they've got us in a bottle. The Arabs from the Anthill and Cut-Off Noses, allied with our young lieutenant and the equites legionis who chased us to the chasm, joined, I'm certain, by further parties of Zealots or shomrim from Alexandria or Pelusium, plus whatever bandits and clan raiders have cut themselves in on the main chance. Not to mention

Severus, with half a cohort of cavalry—and his career and hope for the future on the line. They know there's only one way through those mountains to the sea, and they're waiting for us there."

David suggested a dash, after dark, west toward Alexandria.

Telamon shook his head. "If Severus is here with a heavy column, he has surely sent subordinates ahead by sea to summon even more resources from Egypt, from the west. The Third Cyrenaica and the Fifteenth Apollinaris are at Alexandria. What forces they send will be their finest horsemen mounted on their fastest and sturdiest stock, supplied with abundant water and fodder to pursue us deep into the desert—deeper than we dare go."

Sundry alternatives were proposed and rejected.

At last Telamon stood. The mercenary stretched and scratched at his beard. For long moments he said nothing. Clearly he continued to puzzle over what course of escape, if any, lay open to them.

The others were exhausted and wished only to shut their eyes.

"Go ahead," said the man-at-arms. "Grab what sleep you can."

Telamon began slowly to move off.

The girl's glance tracked him.

After an interval, she rose as well.

David's eyes followed her.

Telamon moved away along a narrow trail.

He seemed unaware of the child Ruth shadowing him.

The mercenary halted once, knelt, and scraped a design in the dirt with a stick. The girl stopped too, maintaining a distance. Telamon stood again and, still ruminating, resumed his ramble.

The ground lay flat and unbroken between the camp and the trace upon which Telamon trod. David watched from a distance. He remained beside Michael and the sorceress with the animals.

The girl Ruth continued to trail Telamon as he drifted, deep in thought. She kept behind him, deliberately it seemed, remaining wide of his line of vision.

When he stopped, she stopped.

Each time she remained perfectly still, observing him.

At length the mercenary came to a likely spot and sat.

The girl took up a seated position as well, yet behind him, at a distance, out of his line of sight.

The mercenary remained upon his station.

After an interval, the child stood and advanced, one step at a time, into the periphery of the man-at-arms' vision. She sat. Clearly Telamon was aware of her now.

He did not react.

The girl got up and moved closer.

Finally she sat directly across from him.

David could not contain his curiosity. He rose from the camp and, advancing with no small stealth, made his way to a stony rise from which he had a prospect of the man-at-arms and the girl.

The man did not speak.

He did not look at the child or acknowledge her presence.

But he made no attempt to send or drive her away.

The girl for her part offered neither sign nor signal.

She made no grunt or gesture.

She did not scribe in the dirt.

David watched.

What were they doing, the child and the man-at-arms?

The boy could come to no conclusion.

All he knew was he felt a keen pang of envy.

25

THE NOTCH

THE ROMANS HAD SET UP a windbreak to protect their camp from the gale out of the south. Two canvas sheets, the halves of an eight-man tent, had been lapped together, with the center line held down by the fore and aft wheels of one side of an impedimenta wagon—holding the baggage, water, and food—and the two halves of the sheet spread at a right angle, one flat on the ground for the men to sit upon, the other lashed upright to one side of the wagon to break the wind. In this tidy pocket, four cavalrymen were taking their evening meal, or trying to, amid the snapping and booming of the tent sheet in the wind and the buffeting that jostled and jangled even the heavy equipment wagon.

The cavalrymen failed to take note of, or perhaps didn't see at first, the odd, rolling lights approaching from the fairway of the plain.

One of the equites, the youngest, heard a cry from a hinter section of the camp but thought it only a trick of the wind.

Then they saw the fireballs.

Vaulting and bounding out of the darkness, driven by the gale, came first a half dozen, then a second wave twice that number, of sizzling, flaming *Amaranthus diaspores*—tumbleweeds. Half the height of a man and blazing with the resiny pitch of their cores, these incendiaries walloped into the gear wagon and bowled against the windbreak. In moments the canvas was ablaze. The cavalrymen stumbled to their feet, grasping for their weapons, cursing and bawling to one another.

They heard cries now from the adjacent camp, that of the Nabatean Arabs, and from another beyond it, of tribal brigands. Flames leapt from these sites too.

Horses bolted past the Romans.

Their own horses.

The cavalrymen spotted a youth and a wild young girl, mounted on a pair of the stolen animals, stampeding the others—a drove of at least two dozen, bearing only their halters and sheared picket lines—before them into the desert.

The youngest of the cavalrymen was on his feet now, clutching his lance and *spatha* broadsword. He saw officers and other troopers dashing forward. Fireballs continued to barrel in upon them from the darkness. One struck the young dragoon head-on. He batted it aside, swatting at the blazing spines that adhered to his flesh and his tunic.

The young horseman saw Severus, his commander, sprint onto the scene. The tribune was unarmored, bareheaded, and disheveled, clutching his gladius and shouting to the trooper to tell him what was going on. The cavalry lieutenant raced into view as well, trailed by a score of mixed composition—legionary equites and auxiliaries of Syria and Samaria—also afoot, disordered, and bewildered.

The young cavalryman tried to speak but his lungs refused to work. He had felt, a moment earlier, a jarring shock in the equator of his belly, just below the solar plexus, but had thought the blow only a buffeting of the gale.

He looked down now and saw the vanes of an arrow shaft protruding from the pit of his breast. The warhead had breached the cage of his ribs and stuck out now from the center of his back, along with two more handsbreadths of shaft. The horseman felt more embarrassed than hurt. He could see his commander staring with an expression of distress and disbelief. The youth bent at the knees, seeking the sand at his feet. He thought, *Let me rest just for a moment, then I'll get up.*

Instead the earth rushed up to meet him, smacking him full in the face. He could sense the lieutenant hurrying toward him to help.

"Leave him!" the young trooper heard Severus cry. "He's caught it."

The cavalryman rolled to one side, feeling the shaft that impaled him snap inside his rib cage, directly below the solar plexus. He clung to consciousness long enough to see, above him, a mounted, bearded banshee break out of the darkness, behind the next wave of fireballs. He witnessed this man, wearing a cap of fox skin with agate eyes and teeth of marble riding his own fiery brow, gallop dead-on at Severus and fling from less than twenty feet a pilum, aiming dead-center at the commander's chest.

From his berth in the dirt the young cavalryman saw this officer dive sidelong in the evolution called by the legions "beetling," dodging the missile and springing nimbly to his feet, sword in hand, to confront the onrushing phantom.

The young rider saw the look of murder that passed between his commander Severus and the man in the fox-skin cap as each slashed furiously at the other—one on horseback, the other on the ground. Legionaries and Arabs pounded onto the scene then, hurling darts and slinging lances at the fox-skin man, who braved these for long, long moments, seeking passionately to get at the commander and kill him, before accepting that the fusillade of missiles must overwhelm him. He wheeled his mount and spurred hard away.

Hooves pounded past the young cavalryman's ears. He heard more shouts and cries and felt yet more fireballs bound past him.

Then the attackers—driving away what seemed to him like half the detachment's mounts—bolted back the way they came, into the wasteland.

26

THE PELUSIUM ROAD

FOR TWO DAYS THE PARTY pushed west toward the Nile, riding the strongest of the Romans' horses and leading their own and as many of the legionary cavalry's and the Nabateans' as they could handle. On the third day they released all save what they needed for pack and saddle mounts. The company did not attempt to cross the range that separated them from the coast road and the sea, which course Telamon adjudged too hazardous, but pressed forward across a seemingly endless gravel-carpeted plain.

Their object was the Pelusium road, which traced the course of the easternmost mouth of the Nile from Heliopolis to the sea.

Following the storms, the wilderness turned sere and brutal again. The party trekked beside their animals, muffled not only against the sun blast from above but the furnace radiating off the surface of serir over which they picked their way as if treading upon an iron skillet.

Telamon unbound the sorceress's wrists. He permitted her to trek alongside the main of the party.

Against all expectation, the witch had moderated her demeanor. She no longer plagued Telamon and the others with her harangues and diatribes. She made her collections of herbs and roots with dispatch. She produced poultices that seemed to ease the Nazarene's suffering.

"Here," she said on the second morning. "Chew this."

She gave Telamon and the others each a bitter leaf, bluish green, which she identified as *era gibla*, "bridal kiss," with instructions to fold it in quarters and chew it with deliberation, not swallowing but letting the juice sit beneath the tongue until it was absorbed.

"What will this do? Kill us?"

"It will keep you awake."

In camp at night the witch produced a brew of *zahram*—desert hawthorn—and *bardagoosh*, a type of sage. Ingesting this, even without food, she said, the party could travel half a day without fatigue or hunger.

Telamon called the party together.

"I know it is difficult," he declared. "But we must press on with all possible speed. Severus will have sent fast riders through the notch to the sea, summoning even more assistance to intercept us from the west. Our party must slog across raw wilderness, while his couriers have the luxury of the coast road. By boat his dispatches have probably reached Pelusium and Alexandria already."

Our object, Telamon repeated, is the Pelusium road.

"I have labored in its construction. I know it well. It runs north-south, paralleling the easternmost mouth of the Nile. We need only to press on toward the setting sun to strike it."

That night Telamon permitted a fire, satisfied that his band of fugitives had for the moment outdistanced its pursuers. With entrenching tools they hacked out, within the channel of a dry wadi, what became a silty but drinkable pool, a spade's-width across and a meter deep. For a meal they shared *kishar*—dried goat meat—and parched barley from a saddle pack discovered on one of the Arabs' horses. The sorceress made a bark tea that refreshed them and restored their spirits. For the first time since before the pastel canyon, David felt secure enough to let his shoulders fall.

The youth regarded his companions about the fire. What was the witch thinking? She could not flee, however much she might wish to. Nor could Michael and the girl Ruth. Without Telamon they would be carrion within days, if not hours. Each, it seemed, had accepted for the moment his or her station as dependent upon the mercenary.

Yet at the same time, David thought, the company's collective ordeal, and the fact that each individual had endured it with a measure of fortitude, even honor, had fashioned a species of bond between and among them. When the witch poured tea for Telamon she did so, it seemed, without rancor. The child Ruth, for her part, had settled onto a stone shelf between the mercenary and the Nazarene as if each were her blood kin. Even the horses seemed to have relented their instinct of flight. The mercenary did not hobble them. Like their human counterparts, they had nowhere to run.

The company devoured their dinner in silence, peering into the fire and listening, as all will at night in a wilderness, to the animal noises and sounds of wind and weather beyond the fall of firelight.

It was the Nazarene, at length, who broke the silence.

"May I ask you a question, mercenary?"

"If you wish," replied Telamon. "I make no pledge to answer."

Michael, in the days since the attack of the Zealots, had begun to regain his strength. He could ride now. Afoot his endurance remained uncertain, but, given sufficient intervals of rest, he could be counted upon. He could keep up.

"Do you believe in God?" he asked now.

"Not yours," said Telamon.

Michael smiled. "Then you believe in *something*?"

"Perhaps."

The Nazarene regarded his counterpart.

"Do you really despise me as thoroughly as you seem to?"

"On the contrary," Telamon replied, "I admire you. You are a warrior and a man. I have nothing but respect for you."

"Then what is it you hold so in contempt? My faith? My belief?"

The girl Ruth sat between Michael and Telamon, turning first to one, then the other as they spoke.

"On the trek through Gaza," Telamon said, "the boy and I stopped at the stock pens just east of the entry to the wilderness. The horse that you and the girl escaped from the Narrows on had been found and brought there. I had a yarn with the stock master. He asked me what I knew of the 'new religion.'"

"Meaning mine?"

"I told him I knew nothing of it, yet could limn its contours without laboring for a breath. This new faith would be, I told him, based upon an event or events that never happened . . . in fact *could not have* happened. And that it would promise a future that could never be. Oh yes, I forgot," added the man-at-arms. "All without proof."

Again Michael smiled.

"Can you really believe in nothing, mercenary?"

The children, David and Ruth, listened with rapt attention. Even the sorceress had, for once, shut up.

"What is belief, Michael? Does one 'believe in' the sun? The seasons? Even this flesh we inhabit? Belief is not necessary for these. Their reality is self-evident. Belief is only needed for *that which does not exist*."

"Does God exist?"

"Which God? The emperor at Rome? The peacock of the Yazdani? What if 'God' indeed is naught except the reflected and magnified image of the worshippers who have raised Him up? He is vanity. His adherents worship nothing grander than a reflection of themselves—and a vain one at that. And what is the produce of this vanity, save cruelty and brutality, to themselves and to others?"

"You sound bitter, my friend."

"This world is the only one that exists, brother. Learn its laws and obey them. This is true philosophy."

For long moments Michael remained silent, as if waiting for the man-at-arms to speak further. When he did not, the Nazarene cleared his throat. "And what of worlds beyond this?"

"There are no worlds beyond this."

Telamon poked at the fire, scattering embers and setting sparks ascending. David looked on with fascination. He had never seen his master speak at such length on any subject—and certainly not with such vehemence.

Telamon reckoned this. He was angry, clearly, with himself and with the course of this conversation.

"You asked," the mercenary said to the Nazarene, "what god I worshipped. She is a goddess. The oldest and most primordial of all, called by my countrymen Eris."

"Eris?"

"Strife. All things are born in strife, even the earth itself, and all are extinguished in strife."

The Nazarene absorbed this thoughtfully. "So you have made yourself a warrior?"

"Yes."

"And has that answered your riddle?"

"What riddle?"

"The riddle of your life. Of yourself."

Telamon stood. The girl Ruth's eyes tracked him, as did those of David and the sorceress.

"Have I upset you, brother?"

"You could not."

"Sit. Please. This is our hour to speak truth to one another."

With grave reluctance, Telamon assented. He resumed his place beside the fire.

Michael dipped a cup of the witch's warming tea. He passed it to Telamon. The mercenary took it.

"Of course, you know," the Nazarene said, "that my faith rejects every 'truth' you espouse. In fact, I believe the categorical opposite."

Now it was Telamon who smiled.

"What you call 'real,'" said Michael, "I call illusion. Self-delusion. Only that is real which cannot be touched or seen, save by the eyes of the heart. If I believed as you do, mercenary, that this world and its laws were all there were, I would cut my throat now and save you and the Romans the trouble."

Michael indicated the pack and saddle mounts hobbled just outside the circle of firelight.

"If we cannot believe in things beyond what our senses deliver, then we're no better than these animals and there is no hope for any of us. That is the difference between a man and a beast: we can perceive *that which is not*, and strive, if not to bring it forth into reality, then to enter it as spirit. I pity you, brother. You have yourself and nothing more."

For long moments none spoke.

It was Michael, at last, who shifted upon his seat and turned to face Telamon directly.

"There is another world," he said, "not 'above' this one but *within it*. In this world, all souls are linked by the commonality of their identity as children of God. In this world, care for others, even the humblest—especially the humblest—is the medium by which one may transcend that philosophy of isolation and despair which you so eloquently espouse."

The mercenary's glance remained downcast, held by the fire. "I would like to see this world."

"In the world you inhabit," said Michael, "nothing changes. Nothing can change. This is your truth. But if there ever was a truth that all may accept, it is that *everything changes*. You are a believer too, my friend. You just don't know it."

Despite himself Telamon glanced to the girl Ruth. She watched him with a keen and scrupulous attendance.

Michael's eyes sought Telamon's. The Nazarene held his speech until the mercenary's gaze had met his own with full attention.

"Twenty-two years ago in Jerusalem, I stood present on Skull Hill when Jesus of Nazareth met his destiny."

Telamon's lips declined into an expression of skepticism and dubiety.

"I saw not God that day," said Michael, "but a man. A mortal man. I watched him suffer and die and I departed broken in spirit and soul. Then, three days later, my uncle Stephen hastened to me. 'Come at once,' he commanded.

"I obeyed.

"That day," Michael said, "I encountered him who had perished, whom the Romans had crucified, whom his own devotees had enshrouded and entombed. I saw him again, in form as flesh and blood. His eyes held mine, his voice spoke to me, his hands held mine. He was alive. I saw it."

"And what holy *pharmakon*," Telamon asked, "or 'aid to prayer' had you imbibed or ingested first?"

Michael's expression responded for him.

"Your imagination fed only, then," said the mercenary, "upon grief and anguish and the desperate wish to believe."

"What I saw, I saw. He who touched me, touched me."

"My friend," the mercenary said, "I have served in campaigns from Britannia to Spain and Gaul, and now in Africa and Judea. I have seen men slain by the sword and the spear, the lance and the battleaxe. But one thing I have never seen is a dead man stand up again and live."

"This one did."

The Nazarene searched the mercenary's eyes.

"Let me grant you your skepticism, brother . . . your disbelief, even your scorn. Say you are right. Indeed it may be more than possible that in my grief and sorrow I experienced a vision, a phantasm of the rabbi from Nazareth. Say that's true. Does that make his life and suffering meaning-less? If he were simply a man like you or me and he chose to die rather than betray himself and the meaning he perceived his life was dedicated to . . . isn't that sacrifice a compelling narrative for the rest of us? Even if, *especially* if, he was not the supernatural incarnation of the son of God? A man such as this would be someone to look up to and aspire to emulate, would he not?"

Michael held Telamon's eyes for long moments, then lowered his gaze and sat back within the envelope of the firelight.

Telamon glanced to the child Ruth, then to David, and finally to the sorceress. In all their eyes, the witch's included, glowed the disposition, even the eagerness, to embrace that contention of Michael's that to him, the mercenary, could be nothing but preposterous.

The man-at-arms turned at last to the Nazarene, with a smile.

"I see now," Telamon said, "why the garrison commander of Jeru-salem has trekked into this wilderness to hunt you . . . and why he, and Rome herself, consider you the most dangerous man in Palestine."

BOOK EIGHT

THE MINISTRATIONS OF EMPIRE

27

THE CISTERN

SUNLIGHT DANCED GAILY OFF THE surface of the pool. The water was so clear you could see twenty feet down to the bottom.

Into this, Telamon flung the fully clothed child.

The girl howled as if she'd been tossed into vinegar.

Thirty-six hours had passed since the night beside the fire. For this interval entire, save two brief halts to rest and water the horses, the party had trekked west paralleling a trace that Telamon identified as the "Sledge Road." Along this course, the mercenary declared, two legions of Rome had toiled for nearly three years, transporting massive stone blocks and other construction materials for what would become, when completed, the longest and most ambitious aqueduct ever built outside the Italian peninsula.

Michael, tramping at the mercenary's side, asked him how he knew this.

"I built it."

The Tenth Fretensis labored for thirty-four months upon this enterprise, Telamon said. "I can show you the quarries in the mountains sixty miles south and the skid roads down which the cut blocks were hauled on sledges drawn by teams of a hundred mules."

At one site along the way Telamon drew up and indicated a chiseled-stone marker, half buried by drifting sand, called by the Romans *memento,*

"I remember,"

LEG X FRE ET LEG VI FER

signalizing, he said, the labor of the Tenth Fretensis and the Sixth Ferrata.

"This work is what the legions call *penitentiae*, 'penance.' Its object was to whip a corps gone sour into shape for an upcoming campaign in Armenia. No women were permitted, no wine, no camp slaves, nothing."

"Did it work?" Michael asked.

"Everything Rome does works."

The party had trekked now to within sight of the aqueduct itself. Latin ambition had intended these works, upon completion, to supply an as-yet-to-be-built harborage and watering stop along the Gaza-Alexandria highway. The aqueduct's source and terminus to the west and south, Telamon said, was a great cataract of the upper Nile. Roman engineers had here completed construction on a stairstep ascender powered by screw propellers buried in the current and pumping river water to a reservoir basin the size of a lake. Give these bastards credit, the mercenary said. With a declining slope as slender as one foot per mile they could make water flow.

Construction of the aqueduct had begun in the seventh year of the reign of Claudius—nearly two decades after the crucifixion of Jesus of Nazareth—and had been abandoned after three years of labor with the outbreak of what would become, in Galilee and Jerusalem, the precursor of the First Jewish Revolt. The road remained unfinished still, four years later, in the second year of the imperatorship of Nero.

A spectacular double-tiered waterway ran for eight miles west-by-north toward the sea. It ended in the middle of a basalt wilderness, abandoned thirty-one miles short of its intended terminus, the projected seaport of Aquila Agrippina, a day's trek east of the Pelusium mouth of the Nile, whose fortress is called in Hebrew Sin, at a coastal village called Firdana.

Twice on that morning and three times during the postnoon, the party was nearly discovered by mounted companies patrolling the aqueduct road. The third time, they found themselves exposed in a featureless basin. They had to lay their horses flat on the earth, holding them by their own weight on the animals' necks. David was certain the party's luck had at last run out. But the midday glare was so dazzling that the foe passed by, a hundred paces distant, and did not see them.

The company arose from this escape gravely shaken. When he had gotten them off the pan and under cover, Telamon called the party together. He sat. So did the others.

"Patrol activity will increase in intensity the closer we get to the Nile. One of them is certain to spot us, if not now, then after we have struck the river. Here is what we will do," he said, indicating himself, Michael, and the sorceress.

"We three, upon first pursuit by a foe we cannot slip free of, will make a demonstration of flight. We'll mount and ride, as fast as we can, leading the enemy after us."

The sorceress glared. "What ruse is this?" She confronted the mercenary. "You will turn about and snatch the child yourself!"

"Shut up," said Telamon.

"Is this," said the witch, "what scheme you have been plotting all along?"

The man-at-arms motioned David and the girl to his side.

Into the palms of each he set a golden eagle.

"When Michael and the woman and I have drawn the enemy off, you will make for Pelusium, hire a boat, and cross to Corinth."

At this, even the Nazarene drew up.

"Do you mean—" he began.

"By God," declared the witch, "the sun has reversed his course in the sky!"

She turned to the child and to the youth, to mark their reactions.

David's fingers closed about the heavy coin.

The girl pressed hers back at once into the mercenary's palm. She shook her head adamantly. The child threw her arms about Michael's waist and would not release him.

"A girl loves her father," said the sorceress.

Michael stroked the child's tangled hair. "Oh, I'm not her father," he said, as casually as if this fact were, and had always been, self-evident.

The mercenary, and the sorceress as well, reacted with surprise.

"I don't know who her father is," said the Nazarene. "I encountered the child in prison, alone and made bereft by the death of her mother. I assumed responsibility for her. But I am not her father."

Telamon studied Michael for long moments. *Indeed,* the mercenary's expression seemed to say, *I believe you.* "The plan remains," he said. "You, the witch, and I will draw the first patrol off. David and Ruth will flee on their own."

"Let me be the one to ride," said David at once. "Take Michael. You can protect him and the girl. I can't."

Telamon rejected this. "The pursuers, if they're Romans, will believe I have the letter or the girl. They will think me too greedy to part with such a prize. Zealots or Nabateans will believe the same. If I know the hearts of these villains—and I do—their thirst for my blood will be even greater than their lust for gold."

The month was now November. The day lacked but five or six hours till sunset. "We will press ahead to a safe site by the aqueduct itself," said Telamon. "We'll rest and water the animals there."

He charged the sorceress with decocting some brew or chew that would keep the company alert through the hours of darkness. "We'll rest and refresh ourselves and the animals at the aqueduct. The Nile lies less than five miles beyond. We can't stop. We must get to the river and be under cover by dawn."

David had never heard the mercenary's voice so grave or so charged with fatal purpose.

"What I say next, take to heart, each of you," Telamon said, "as if your lives depended on it."

He paused to make sure he had every soul's attention.

"If you are taken, remember this: break away at once."

He spoke now directly to Ruth.

"At once. In the first instant. Every minute that passes once you are captured makes it more difficult to escape. The foe will bind you, incapacitate you, break your arm or leg, blind you. Escape *in the first moment.* Do anything—anything—to get away."

He passed a Roman cavalry saber to Michael, checked that David had his dolabra ready, and returned to the witch her pair of throwing knives. He made sure that Ruth had her **X** dagger.

The mercenary addressed the sorceress directly. "These roots and herbs you gather. What medicines can you make from them?"

"I can remedy anything short of your black heart."

The man-at-arms considered this.

"Can you make soap?"

The party reached the aqueduct an hour before sunset. Setting himself and David as sentries, Telamon pointed the others to a stone-founded pool at the base of an archway, the produce of the Romans' love of baths and bathing. "Five minutes, no more. Scour the grime off. It will keep us awake for an all-night march."

The witch performed a quick collection.

The plant she gathered for soap was called Adam's needle. The sorceress cut palm-sized cubes from its spines and pounded these until the pulpy insides, which she identified as *saponica,* produced a thin lather that released a scent like lavender, only stronger and more bitter. The witch bound these with stalks of the same plant into bundles the size of a man's hand. "Keep these away from the eyes. The oil will sting. Otherwise they are as good as anything you will find in the finest perfumer's shop."

It was then that the mercenary caught up the child Ruth and, with a laugh, flung her bodily into the pool.

"Let's see what's under all those layers of dirt!"

The child rebelled at once and sought to scamper clear. Telamon snatched her up by both wrists. He had a bundle of the soap and made to scrub her. Michael too was laughing now, as was David. The sorceress intervened in outrage, declaring it unseemly for a grown man to bathe a female child.

The witch took over.

Into the pool she went after Ruth, with the girl kicking and punching to squirt free. By now the child's tangled mane was soaked and her robe and tunic plastered to her body.

The witch tugged at the child's garments. "Get these filthy rags off! How else can I scrub you?"

A brawl ensued, with much splashing and thrashing, to the amusement of the others. In the end the sorceress simply overpowered the child. She hauled her clothes off.

Naked now, the girl punched the witch furiously, full in the face. The child snatched at her shorn robe and tunic. The witch would not let the garments go.

Ruth scrambled from the pool, scarlet with shame. She dashed straight to Michael and flung herself into his arms. The onlookers recommenced their laughter, believing the girl's frenzy to be provoked by feelings only of modesty.

All merriment ceased at the sight of the child's back.

Lurid welts and stripes plaited the girl's flesh from her waist to her shoulders. Even the witch gasped to behold these. But this was not the whole of it. Interspersed among these marks could be seen the spatula-shaped scars made by a branding iron. David covered his eyes and turned away. *What species of monster*, he thought, *inflicts such horrors on an innocent child?*

The girl wept now. Michael wrapped his robe about her.

"Who did this to you?" David blurted. "What kind of—"

"Shut up!" commanded the sorceress. The woman moved swiftly to the child's side, covering her with her own garments.

The girl clung to Michael, burying her face in the folds of his robe.

All eyes turned to Telamon for his reaction.

For long moments the man-at-arms remained silent.

He waited, motionless, until he saw the child Ruth turn and peek from the wrapper of Michael's robe.

Then, setting his weapons aside, he stepped out of his caligas and crossed, barefoot, to stand before the girl.

"Hold these for me, will you?"

The man-at-arms stripped his own garments and handed them to the child. He turned and stepped, naked now, into the pool.

The girl's eyes tracked every step.

Across the mercenary's back and shoulders could be seen the same species of welts and scars as those upon the flesh of the child.

The others reacted as they had to the original exposure.

Telamon scrubbed quickly and climbed from the pool.

He crossed back to Ruth.

Such a look passed between the girl and the man-at-arms as David, recalling the moment later, had never seen.

The child handed the mercenary his robe and tunic.

Telamon tugged these on.

He turned toward the setting sun.

"Get your heads down, all of you. We'll rest till an hour before dawn, then set forth. I'll take first watch and last."

28

THE AQUEDUCT

D AVID AWOKE TO A TRACE chain around his neck and the point of a sword at his throat. It was still night. Horses and men raced across the camp. The youth felt himself hauled violently upright by warriors in armor. He glimpsed a burning-down bonfire on a rise to the west. He tried to move but his limbs felt like lead.

The boy reckoned at once what had happened.

He had fallen asleep on watch. The witch had drugged him. Somehow she had switched out the brew she regularly left him to augment his alertness for his hours on guard.

She had set the bonfire to lead the Romans in.

The youth glimpsed his master. Two legionaries held him, pinning his arms behind him, while a third smashed him full in the face with an iron helmet. Another, wielding a quarterstaff, took the mercenary's legs from under him. Two thunderous blows seemed to shatter the man-at-arms' shins. He dropped deadweight within the grasp of his former comrades.

David heard himself screaming. He twisted in the grip of the soldiers who held him, seeking sight of the girl, of Ruth.

The boy was calling, "Run! Run!"

He saw the sorceress. The witch dashed across the camp in a state of frenzy, this way and that, bawling something David could not comprehend. Torches and firebrands split the darkness.

A blow from a club drilled David senseless. Hands dumped him to the earth. He fell upon Michael. The Nazarene was bound with heavy rope. Both arms were bent at unnatural angles.

He saw the lieutenant.

He saw Severus.

He saw the girl dash past in the torch flare. She was barefoot, clutching the **x** dagger.

"Her! Her!" the witch was shouting.

The child stumbled and spilled. A corporal in a cloak and heavy hobnails leapt upon her. She plunged the blade into his thigh. He swung a fist. The girl ducked. Others sought in vain to collar her.

Somehow Telamon, bound in chains, had gotten to his knees. "Run!" he cried.

Ruth did.

"Seize her, you idiots!" the witch was bawling in Aramaic and pidgin-Latin as she scampered furiously across the camp. "She's the one! The one you want!"

The girl darted like a hare, speedy and low to the ground, jinking in odd directions as she flew.

"Don't kill her!"

This from Severus.

David saw the commander now, in armor, striding across the melee, swatting at men with his riding crop as they sought to overtake the girl. As she sprinted past the two troopers who had pinioned David, one of them grabbed at her. David's right arm came free. He heard in his head Telamon's injunction:

IF YOU ARE TAKEN, ESCAPE AT ONCE.

The boy jerked free.

The witch's brew still unstrung him.

The youth could not feel his feet. His calves seemed made of stone.

Somehow he ran.

The camp beneath the aqueduct had become a free-for-all of Romans and Nabateans, afoot and on horseback, all, it seemed, scurrying at once in pursuit of the boy and the girl.

"Her!" The witch howled. "Catch the brat!"

The child vaulted up a great pile of foundation stones. Her bare feet sprang from one cut block to another.

David followed.

He could hear the curses of the men behind them, pursuing in thirty pounds of armor.

Flung stones whizzed past their ears.

Somehow David and Ruth were on top of the aqueduct, in the channel of the watercourse. Ahead the sluiceway ran as far as he could see—a quarter mile, a half mile, more.

Along this, girl and boy fled as fast as their feet would bear them.

Riders and men afoot pursued below.

The children covered a hundred feet. Two hundred. Three.

Beneath the aqueduct the ground dropped away. A plunging ravine, three furlongs across, had been bridged by the span of arched stone. Oaths ascended from the riders and foot-pursuers below as they found themselves brought up short by the drop-off. Ahead atop the aqueduct, the girl Ruth flew like a swallow. David caught a second wind. He galloped in her train.

Back at the site of capture, Severus clutched his nephew, Quintus Flavius Publicus, by the shoulder of his cloak. The lieutenant acknowledged his orders. With a cry, he sent a second round of horsemen in pursuit, Nabateans as well as Romans. "A golden eagle for him who brings in that child!"

What took place now at the camp neither David nor Ruth in their flight could know, nor would they reckon even later, save by glimpses at a distance and snatches of speech carried on the wind.

Telamon, half strangled by a chain around his neck, had been lashed by cords to the flank of an impedimenta wagon. Severus, standing before him, demanded that he call the girl back.

"Round her in! She'll obey you!"

"I will not."

Severus backhanded Telamon across the face. The legionaries holding the mercenary jerked the captive's bonds tighter.

"Call her or I'll gut you where you stand."

The commander plunged his right hand into Telamon's left caliga. He snatched forth the second x dagger that the mercenary concealed there.

"Keen as ever, is it, peregrine?"

So swiftly that the eye could barely follow it, the tribune's fist slashed three strokes—backhand, forehand, backhand—across the mercenary's bare chest.

"Call her back."

"I can't."

"You mean you won't."

At this, the sorceress thrust herself forward. "Make *him* call," she cried, indicating Michael.

Two soldiers held the Nazarene, bound, on his knees, in the dirt at Telamon's feet. The sorceress pressed truculently before Severus, cursing him and his men for letting the child escape. The commander needed neither Hebrew nor Aramaic to appreciate the tenor of her harangue or to feel the lash of its contempt.

"Get this harridan off me!"

The witch now set hands upon the lieutenant himself. He recoiled and cast her apart from him. The woman seized the officer again, propelling him back toward the Nazarene.

"Make *him* call! The child will answer him!"

Dawn glimmered.

In the darkness within the great ravine, the girl and boy skimmed barefoot from bush to trench to cutbank, flying within the shadows back toward the capture site.

Great mounds of stone blocks, abandoned with the aqueduct, lay at intervals along its derelict course. The boy and girl dashed from one to another. They could see the torches and hear the cries of the soldiers and cavalrymen who scurried this way and that, seeking to find them.

Severus, at the site of capture, stood now above the bound and hobbled Michael. The tribune commanded his prisoner, as the witch had urged, to rise and call the child in.

The Nazarene would not so much as answer.

"Take his other eye," spoke the commander.

The hobnail corporal obeyed.

Michael plunged to the earth pressing both palms to his face. Blood in shallow gushes leaked through his fingers.

"Stand and call, may the gods damn you!"

The witch stood.

Telamon glared at her.

She seemed to take a perverse pride in Michael's defiance of the might of Rome. She addressed the commander. "Open his guts." Though the girl had escaped for the moment, the woman declared, this man's bowels yet concealed a second copy of the Apostle's letter.

By dash and scurry, David and Ruth had worked their way back from the aqueduct runway to a vantage behind and atop a pyramid of stone blocks some two hundred paces south of the capture site. Full dawn was upon them now. Wriggling into the interstices between the stones and down into the core of the pile, they reached a covert from which they could not be seen, yet they themselves, peeking between the blocks of stone, could command the full field below.

The children could not hear the full exchange between the Romans and the witch. They caught snatches on the wind. "So you have come over to the side of the emperor," the lieutenant seemed to say.

The sorceress spat.

She thrust a bony arm at Michael, apparently urging his captors to do their worst.

Severus would not have it so simply.

The boy and girl could see the tribune order two of his men to seize the sorceress. Into her right hand the soldiers thrust a blade of some kind, not a military weapon, but a tool, it seemed, of the slaughterhouse or the *macello*, the butcher shop.

"You want it so bad, witch. *You* slice him."

A second round of oaths and imprecations succeeded, with the sorceress violently refusing and cursing the Romans as cowards. The legionaries compelled her onto her knees before the Nazarene.

"What, you've suddenly become delicate?" bawled the hobnail corporal into the sorceress's ear. "One thrust, sweetheart. It's called 'spilling the groceries.' Do it, darling! You're the one who wants it!"

From their hiding place within the pile of building stones, David and Ruth could not see Michael's face or hear his speech, if in fact he offered any. They reckoned only his posture. The Nazarene neither shrunk nor quailed, but held himself upright upon his knees.

David heard the witch's cry and saw her execute a tentative stabbing motion. Hoots of derision ascended from the soldiers. The corporal with the hobnails lowered himself behind the sorceress so that his knees imprisoned her hips and his shoulders and arms wrapped about her from the rear.

"Here, my pretty. Let me help you."

And, clamping the blade in her fist with his left hand and seizing her forearm with his right, he drove them by his own exertion again and again into the flesh of Michael's belly. Two other legionaries held the Nazarene upright with his loins exposed.

The witch bayed and howled.

Telamon looked on helplessly.

The child Ruth, watching from among the blocks of stone, doubled upon herself in agony. David had to hold her with both arms and all his strength. No cries escaped her, yet she writhed as thrust upon thrust further opened the Nazarene's belly.

The Romans now forced the witch to dig into Michael's entrails with her fingers. The sorceress shrieked like a wounded beast. Cuffs and blows held her from squirming free.

The Nazarene's limbs kicked in agony beneath him; his body writhed and convulsed. Yet he made no sound. Then at once his spirit fled. He crumpled from the waist.

With a cry of woe, the sorceress sprang free of her captors. Her arms to the elbow and the entire front of her smock were slathered in sputum and tissue. Her face and neck, even her tangled mane, glistened with the blood of the Nazarene.

Michael had fallen now, life-fled, released by the two who held him. His head lolled grotesquely from his unstrung neck.

At a sign from Severus, the legionaries and even the Arabs let the witch flee through their cordon. David saw her sprint, like a mad thing, away into the desert.

Above and around the children's hiding place, Nabateans and Romans redoubled the intensity of their search.

Now Severus and his men turned to Telamon.

29

THE MINISTRATIONS OF EMPIRE

"UPEND HIM!" THE HOBNAIL CORPORAL CRIED.

In moments the Romans had rifled the mercenary's cloak and kit. From his distant vantage, David could see a runt sergeant with orange curls dig Telamon's remaining golden eagles from a packet of his kit. The man displayed these triumphantly.

"Haul him up!" the sergeant bawled. A chain was secured about Telamon's neck. As the iron ran tight, it seemed nearly to snap the mercenary's spine. David strained to see. The chain ascended to some kind of elevated tackle. The man-at-arms, half strangled, was lashed by cords to stone projections in the face of the aqueduct wall.

A heavy rope was looped around his chest, beneath both arms, and drawn tight from behind. When he struggled against this, the corporal with the hobnails swatted him below the eye as hard as he could with the butt of his gladius. A second cord was wound around both the mercenary's ankles, double-lashing them together.

"Secure the wrist bindings," ordered Severus. "One line around each. Lash them tight. I want nothing slipping."

Telamon was jerked upright by the heavy rope beneath his armpits. Two Arabs, one after the other, spat in his face. A third seized him with one hand by the testicles. Looking directly into the mercenary's eyes, he made an obscene gesture while spewing some curse in the Nabatean dialect.

A cluster of legionaries drove the tribesmen back. The soldiers came forward, collecting about Telamon. Each searched the man-at-arms' face, as if seeking a mark of fear or any indication that the captive would now plead for his life. Several of the men appeared to know Telamon. These peered with even keener intensity. "Are you sure," said one, "this is him?"

"This is the man."

This from Severus, stepping forward. With a gesture he dispersed the others, Romans and Arabs, apart from the man-at-arms. The commander alone, save his lieutenant, stood now before his captive.

"We'll catch the girl—you know that, peregrine. How far can she run? There's not a blade of grass to hide behind for forty miles."

The tribune indicated the mounds of building blocks—a score and more, extending in a line from the capture site for a mile along the path of the abandoned aqueduct.

"She's hiding in one of those—wriggled down beneath the stones," Severus declared. "Where else can she be?"

Telamon could turn just far enough to track the line of mounds. Already Severus's men, assisted by their Arab confederates, were cutting and collecting boughs of flammable sumac and terebinth.

"I'll smoke her out or roast her in place where she hides," said Severus. "Unless you see sense and call her forth."

"I don't control her," the mercenary responded.

"I warn you I'm not playing!"

"Nor am I."

At Telamon's feet lay the physical remains of Michael. The mercenary's glance declined now toward the Nazarene's corpse.

Severus remarked this.

"Has Rome acted too harshly here?" the tribune said. "I've seen you, peregrine, perform far worse in her service. I hired you expecting just that. Or perhaps you think this subversive or Messianic or whatever he calls himself didn't deserve such a grisly end, that the letter he carries, or that the girl bears if the witch speaks true, is not worth such extravagant measures to intercept and destroy." Severus used the Latin *exstirpare*, meaning to root out and destroy utterly.

"The emperor," said Severus, "fears no power on earth. Armies cannot overawe him. Insurrection cannot drag him down. Only one force unsettles Rome's slumber—that which this missionary bears in words and speech."

The commander paused and glanced about at the legionaries and their officers attending every word.

"Faith," said he. "A dream of deliverance—not only in the next life but in this one here and now. The 'kingdom of heaven'!"

Severus turned back to Telamon.

"The most dangerous thing in the world is faith. That is why I selected you, peregrine—you and no other—for this assignment. A man who believes in nothing . . . who takes pride in believing in nothing.

"Yet you have failed me. Indeed, you have, it seems, gone over to the foe—and at a toll to you of a considerable fortune! Why? What has turned you? What made you change your mind?"

Three legionaries scurried into view, signing for the lieutenant's attention. This officer, it seemed, had commanded them to fetch a certain item. They saluted now, indicating they had done so.

The soldiers bore a stout wooden beam, collected apparently from the construction materials lying about the site.

"Good," said the lieutenant.

With a gesture he directed the soldiers to rig the beam horizontally and secure it to the tackle already mounted above Telamon on the face of the aqueduct. The three, assisted by others, took the timber in hand and elevated it behind the mercenary. The hobnail corporal and two others seized the man-at-arms and manhandled him rearward until he stood directly beneath this instrument.

Severus signed for his men to hold.

He regarded Telamon, it seemed, with genuine mystification.

"What is it?" he asked. "Is it me? Do you hate me that much? Is it Rome? Has your heart turned so fervently against the comrades with whom you once served?"

The tribune indicated the beam rigged above Telamon's shoulders.

"You would drain your life in agony . . . for what? Some vain and empty gesture against the emperor? Against the supreme and unshakable power of the world?"

With a blow of his hand the commander struck the horizontal spar.

"Do you see what you compel Rome to do? Do you understand the end you call down upon yourself? We were brothers once! The way I sheathe my sword, the very manner in which I buckle my armor I learned from you! What has become of you?"

The man-at-arms responded evenly, absent rancor. "I might ask, brother," he said, "the same of you."

The tribune took half a step back.

"Bind him to the instrument."

At their commander's signal, the legionaries cut the rawhide thongs that yoked Telamon's wrists. They spread the mercenary's arms wide, each to one side, and lashed them to the wooden beam.

"Spike him, sir?" inquired the sergeant.

Severus shook his head.

He stepped again toward Telamon.

"It's something else, isn't it? What?" The commander indicated the corpse of the Nazarene in the dirt. "Friendship for this man? Respect for his courage?"

"He was a man," said Telamon. "A better man than me."

Severus took a single step back.

He glanced to the lieutenant.

This officer advanced to the fore.

"Hoist him!" he commanded.

With a triple winding, the soldiers secured Telamon's wrists to the extremities of the timber. A second binding lashed him at the elbows. At a nod from Severus, the legionaries hauled upon the lines securing the beam to the tackle. The spar rose. Telamon felt his weight being lifted.

Throughout this process, the tribune's eyes never left the mercenary's.

"Or is it admiration for the Apostle, for Paul himself? Consider this, then. Pursuit parties of Rome have intercepted *two other copies* of this same letter you bear . . . and were close to capturing a third when I departed Jerusalem. Yes, he is canny, this Christian! Your letter may be only a decoy. Have you thought of this, peregrine? It might not even be a letter at all."

The commander searched Telamon's eyes to see if the man-at-arms had in fact considered such possibilities—or if their introduction now discommoded him in any measure.

"You haven't seen the letter, have you, peregrine? It's all in the girl's head. What if it's gibberish? What if it's nonsense? Can she tell, this urchin of the street and the prison yard? You suffer, my friend . . . you die, in fact . . . for nothing!"

"If you believe this, tribune," Telamon answered, "why are you here?"

A light went out of the commander's eyes.

"String him up," he cried. "High! Raise him! I want him visible for miles."

The legionaries hauled on the two ropes, one affixed to each extremity of the spar.

The man-at-arms felt his feet leaving the ground.

"Together, both lines!" shouted the lieutenant. "Keep the beam level!"

A legionary stepped up before Telamon, tugging his gladius from its sheath. Plainly he intended to deliver what the Romans call *ictu misericordiae*, a "stroke of mercy," to hasten the captive's passage from this life.

"Hold, fool!" bawled the orange-haired sergeant. He caught the fellow's arm and thrust him roughly aside. "Would you cheat us of our spectacle?"

From their distant vantage concealed within the mound of stones, Ruth and David could catch only snatches of the commander's words borne on the wind—and none of the mercenary's responses, if indeed he made any. They saw only, through chinks in the front of stone that concealed them, the tribune, and on the instant the lieutenant, continue to address their prisoner as they did, absent haste and seemingly void of malice.

As Telamon's body rose, the apparatus swung rearward several feet, banging roughly against the stone face of the aqueduct. Severus moved with this motion, keeping close to the mercenary's side as his figure was hoisted.

"Hold! Stop!" yelled the orange-haired sergeant. Telamon hung suspended half a body-length off the ground. The sergeant and three others seized him, two by two, by the legs and ankles. At a command from the sergeant, all four jerked down as hard as they could.

Telamon felt both his shoulders wrenched from their sockets.

His gut convulsed. The contents of his belly, what little there was, spewed as liquid from his gorge. Both eyes rolled. The mercenary's gut spasmed and contracted. Both legs flailed.

"Higher!" ordered the sergeant.

The ropes went taut.

"Make him a stand," Severus commanded.

The legionaries scurried to erect a cairn of stones beneath Telamon's dangling feet.

"Give him just enough to reach at a stretch but not enough to bear his weight."

The first company of search riders now came galloping back. They reported that they had not, yet, found the girl and boy.

Severus sent the party back out immediately, adding all the Arabs and most of the Bedouin raiders who had attached themselves to his company. "No one eats or drinks till you bring me those brats!"

Turning again to the mercenary, the tribune directed his legionaries to stabilize the beam upon which Telamon hung. A ladder was found among the site debris. With this, elevated and manipulated, supplemented by rough heaves upon the lines and tackle, the soldiers succeeded in steadying the captive. His soles hung six or seven feet off the ground. His back, beneath the crosswise beam, beat lightly against the stone face of the aqueduct.

"You steel yourself, mercenary. I see it in your eyes. You have set your will to endure." The commander's tone was private, even confidential, yet his words were spoken with sufficient force for the most proximate legionaries, and even those not so near, to hear. "Do you think it cannot get worse? Believe me, it will."

The tribune motioned two soldiers forward, directing them to halt immediately beneath the crucified man.

"Show him what you have brought for him."

The taller of the two soldiers extended his right hand, protected by a farrier's glove, toward Telamon.

In this was a cloth sack. Its mouth was ample enough to be tugged over a man's head.

In the sack writhed a swarm of living scorpions.

"Am I a monster? You know me, Telamon. I am no such thing. So I will extend one final proposition of clemency. Can you hear me? Move your head if you can."

The mercenary turned toward his tormentor.

"Call the girl in," said Severus. "I will set you and her free . . . and the boy too . . . upon your pledge that you will not see the Apostle's letter through to its destination. Flee. Live your life. The golden eagles I promised, I shall give to you. Take them. On my honor as a Roman, I will not pursue you, nor permit others to do so. See reason, for the sake of heaven! Take my offer and go free!"

Telamon answered at once.

"The child," he said, "will never accede to this."

Severus turned to his men, speaking now with force and projection for all to hear.

"You are my witnesses, brothers and comrades! I have proffered to this man such clemency as no other would have. Yet he spurns me. You have heard him. He spurns us all. He spurns Rome. He has left the empire no choice but to do what justice demands!"

The lieutenant motioned to the tall soldier.

The man came forward.

Severus peered up to Telamon. "We'll smoke the girl out before sunset. By then you will be unable to speak. Have you any final message for us to impart to her?"

The man-at-arms spit toward his tormentor. The spittle, lacking all moisture, spilled over the mercenary's lower lip and dribbled impotently down his chin.

Severus nodded to the tall soldier.

This legionary, aided by his fellow, mounted to the peak of the cairn.

He carried the bag of scorpions in one gloved hand, using Telamon's suspended body as a handhold to haul himself up with the other. "Keep back," the trooper called to his companion below. "One of these might spill."

The soldier pulled himself up to the same height as Telamon. He displayed the sack directly before the mercenary's face.

"Get on with it!" called Severus from below.

The soldier worked his way to one side of Telamon, using the man-at-arms' racked limbs to steady himself. From this angle, he tugged the sack over the prisoner's head and cinched it tight.

"Thank me, brother," the soldier addressed Telamon as he performed this. "I'm doing you a favor."

30

A SEPULCHER OF STONE

THE FIRST NIGHT PASSED, AND the following day.

The Romans and Nabateans scoured the site and the surrounding desert in every direction. Their exertions concentrated upon the great mounds of building stones. These they probed in sequence, advancing from the nearest extremity of the line to the farthest. At their commander's direction, the legionaries and their allies dispatched the slightest and slenderest of their number to wriggle into the interstices between the blocks. When this technique failed to discover the children, the searchers compressed great bundles of brush and tinder between the stones and tamped these with long rods deep into the cores of the mounds. They set these alight, adjoining fascines of resinous elah and sumac and ramming these likewise into the bowels of the rock piles. Their object was to produce the densest smoke and most noxious fumes possible, to drive the children forth, if indeed they had hidden themselves in these spaces.

David and Ruth burrowed to the bottom of their pyramid, fleeing the smoke and the dripping, flaming oil. Each sheathed the other's shoulders and back beneath double- and triple-folds of their robes. They covered their noses, mouths, and eyes with head wraps. Still the fumes scorched their lungs to such poisonous effect that each, at moments, lost the will to endure and had to be silenced and held down by the other.

The expedient the children found was to fill their mouths with sand and, sealing the airway of their noses between two fingers, breathe only through this medium.

So they lay, David and Ruth, clinging to each other with their eyes squeezed shut against the choking, toxic vapors that suffused their sanctuary.

For thirty-six hours the girl and boy remained immured within their sepulcher of stone. The weight of sand and the mass of ash above them deadened all sound, filling both with dread that those who hunted them could be close but that they, the children, had no means of hearing or feeling their approach.

The sensation of being entombed, of being blinded and straitened within their narrow berths, added to the terror and made the hours pass with interminable slowness. At last, when they could endure their interment no longer, the children, despite the continuing presence of the Romans and Arabs, wriggled their way upward through the voids between the stones and, reaching the surface of the mound, dared to peek about.

The hour was noon. The boy and the girl had grown desperate with thirst. Several times David made signs that he wanted to try for the cistern, from which the Arabs and Romans drew water for themselves and their horses throughout the day and night. Each time Ruth gripped him hard. She would not let him.

All day the Romans continued dispatching mounted parties of their own and their Arab and Bedouin confederates to the north and east, apparently to account for the possibility that the boy and girl had made good their escape somehow and were hastening toward the sea. Other search parties, mounted and afoot, continued to scour the area immediately around the camp and in the dunes to the south and west.

For hours the girl and boy remained motionless within their covert. They could see the tents, the impedimenta wagons, and the rope hitching lines of the Roman, Arab, and Bedouin camps. They could see Michael's body, on its back, unburied yet. And they could see Telamon.

The sack of scorpions remained in place over the mercenary's head. Could the creatures still be alive? Could Telamon? The man-at-arms' head hung slack at the neck. His jaw had fallen flush against his chest.

He did not move.

Search parties continued to be sent out by Severus. The boy and girl could see the Roman commander pacing between the canvas fly that provided a triangle of shade over his bedding site and the stone drinking pool at the base of the cistern. They could see him conferring impatiently with the chieftains of the Nabateans and the tribal brigands. Altercations broke out. Three hours into the postnoon the main party of Bedouins, twenty in all, mounted in a fit and spurred off.

From time to time Severus crossed to the crucified figure of Telamon and spoke alone to him. The mercenary's head made no motion. His face did not turn toward Severus, nor did any part of his body respond. He hung, inert. The boy and girl were too far away to hear what the Roman was saying.

Did the fact of such "conversations" mean Telamon was still alive? Or was the tribune speaking, as if upon some perverse impulse, with his corpse? Was Severus's speech intended to torment his former legion-mate? It seemed to the girl and boy more like the commander was conferring with, even confiding in the mercenary. He addressed the motionless figure in such a manner as he employed with no other among the camp, including his nephew the lieutenant.

That night, in the second watch, wolves came.

The Romans drove the beasts off initially with stones and curses, then again, and a third time after that. But hours later, David and Ruth could see the pack's yellow eyes glittering in the dark.

Sometime during the third watch the creatures infiltrated in earnest. The Roman and Arab pickets faced the leaders back with firebrands and leveled lances. But the pack was not after the living men.

The wolves went after Telamon.

The boy and girl watched helplessly as the beasts circled the mercenary's suspended form—at a distance first, in skimming rushes, with their ears flat and the fur up on their backs; then closer, in darting-and-withdrawing approaches, growing bolder with each advance. The wolves neither growled nor barked. The pads of their paws made no sound on the sand. The Roman and Nabatean sentries had withdrawn from the crucified man. Their lowered their lances. They were summoning their comrades to watch the show.

Telamon's bound feet moved.

Ruth's hand clutched David's.

He was alive!

The mercenary's soles swung beneath his suspended torso. His toes found the rock cairn below him. He pushed up from the stone, straightening and lengthening to keep his flesh as high off the ground as he could get it.

The wolves began making passes.

The bolder ones went first, rushing at speed, then leaping with a capering, twisting motion, snapping in midair with their jaws. The cannier creatures followed. They began using the face of the rock pile as a surface from which to launch themselves. A wolf would trot toward the cairn, gaining speed as she approached, then vault onto the vertical face, propelling herself upward with first her fore, then her hind legs.

To the Romans and Arabs this was a grand spectacle. They were placing bets on which wolf would draw first blood. "Cut him down!" one soldier cried. "Let the dogs get at him!"

The fellow was shouted down by the others.

This sport was more fun.

A wolf's jaws reached Telamon's feet. They snapped together with a sound like a catapult stone smashing into a city wall. Blood sprayed. The smell made the beasts frantic. One after another took wild, snapping leaps at Telamon's dangling feet. So many came at once that the creatures began brawling with one another.

The soldiers and Arabs cheered them on.

At length the beasts wearied.

Even the Romans grew bored.

The wolves retired.

Telamon's form hung again, lifeless and unmoving.

Finally with the morning the Romans and Arabs packed up and left.

— 31 —

SCORPIONS

DAVID AND RUTH WATCHED THE last rider vanish around the terminal dune west of the aqueduct. The children waited for the count of a hundred. They held in place for a second hundred, and a third. At last they scrambled from their hiding hole and dashed toward Telamon.

The girl ran ahead, barefoot. David found himself holding back. His heart hammered. The youth glanced in the direction that the departing Romans and Arabs had taken. He peered again, and a third time after that.

"What," David called to the girl, "do you mean to do?"

The child stood now at the base of the cairn. The stones were piled higher than her head. Atop these, Telamon's bare feet, which to David's eyes appeared unrecognizable as extremities, swung, yet suspended, with only their toes, or those gorged appendages that had once been toes, grazing the surface. The girl set her fingers into cracks above her on the rock pile. She began to pull herself up.

"What are you doing? You can't take him down!"

David knew he should approach. The man-at-arms had been his mentor. He, the youth, had worshipped him. He must help the girl. He must assist her in rendering succor.

But he could not.

"He's dead!" David called. "Leave him."

The girl stamped her foot. She motioned to David to hurry.

David pointed in the direction the Romans and Nabateans had taken. "They'll be back! They know we'll come out of hiding. We can't stay here!"

The boy darted forward, seeking to catch the child's arm and drag her away. She evaded his grasp and stamped again, more impatiently.

David refused to come forward. Backing away, he tripped over something.

Michael's body.

The Nazarene's remains lay in a tangled heap, unburied. The Romans had left him where he had fallen. David recoiled at this sight as well.

He glanced again toward Telamon. The scorpion sack remained in place over the mercenary's head.

"He's dead! Leave him! We have to get out of here!"

Three times David threatened to leave the child.

Three times he commanded her to come away.

She would not.

Telamon's weight hung from a pair of ropes, each lapped three times about his upper limbs. The first binding secured his wrists to the extremities of the beam from which he hung. The second bound his arms at a point above the elbows. Each line was anchored to projecting spurs in the facing of the aqueduct.

"Come away!" David called. "Help me bury Michael!"

The girl signed that that chore must wait. *We must save this living man!*

She set stones and brush to make a heap against the base of the wall from which Telamon hung. Mounting upon this, she sought purchase for her bare toes within the crannies between the stones of the facing. Hauling herself up by finger-holds, she climbed first to the height of the man-at-arms' feet, then to his knees. She held her **x** dagger clamped between her teeth.

"Stop!" David paced below in agitation. "He'll plunge deadweight!"

The youth at last was compelled to come forward. He averted his eyes from the sight of the bag over Telamon's face and head.

He climbed too, with his own dagger.

"The Romans will crucify us too. Or worse."

The girl signed to him, *Cut through your rope when I cut through mine.*

"He's going to plunge. We can't handle his weight."

The girl cut.

David had to as well.

The man-at-arms did plunge, reeling free first on the girl's side as her blade severed the line, swinging violently toward David and in fact onto him as he clung to his own toe- and finger-holds. The boy cried out in horror as the sack of scorpions swung into his own face. He sawed desperately at the rope from which Telamon's left wrist hung.

The mercenary's body folded from the top, knees and ankles collapsing beneath the weight of the torso as it fell. His arms dropped like a puppet's when the strings are cut. The man-at-arms crashed onto his breast and face, which was still bagged inside the scorpion sack, at the base of the pile of stones.

The girl leapt from her perch and sprang to the mercenary's side.

"He's gone!" cried David. "Scoop sand over him and let's go!"

The child would not listen.

Seizing Telamon by both wrists, she tugged and hauled until she had straightened his torso upon the sand. She took hold of his ankles and did the same.

David lowered himself tentatively from the aqueduct face. He kept peering about for any sight of returning riders. He strained to hear voices or hoof strikes approaching.

The girl wrestled Telamon's body into a posture face-up on the sand.

"Leave the bag! Don't touch it."

The child tugged at the tie that held the sack in place.

"Watch out! Those little bastards are still in there!"

The child jerked the sack off in one violent tug.

The bag came away empty.

David saw Telamon's face.

"Oh God!"

His knees gave way beneath him. He felt his palms strike the sand. He could hear himself retching and feel the convulsive heaving of his belly.

Telamon's face was purple and swollen to half again its size. Where his eyes had been appeared now only a surface of glossy, distended tissue. He looked like a bladder, the type that children paint faces upon for the festival of the Dionysia and inflate by blowing into one end. Only there was no face on Telamon's face.

The girl never looked away.

She knelt over Telamon, pressing her ear to the center of his chest.

David continued to puke up the meager contents of his belly.

The girl was dragging Telamon by the heels, with monumental effort, toward the rim of the cistern. David could hear her drawing water, first with her cupped palms, then with the weave of her own garment, which she plunged like a sponge into the pool and wrung over Telamon's face.

The child crossed to David, kicking sand at him. David felt her seize him under one arm. She pulled him upright, gesturing urgently to the circle of stones that held the ashes of one of the Romans' fires.

"What? What do you want?"

She wanted him to make a fire.

"Is he alive?"

The girl kicked David in the ribs. She pulled him hard toward the circle of stones.

David resisted. "A flame gives us away!" The girl kicked him harder. She punched at his face with her fists.

"All right! Stop, damn you!"

David scraped together brush and camel thorn. He struck a spark into a nest of tinder. The girl came over and kicked him again. She thrust a cracked clay basin into his fist.

When he had the blaze going and had heated water for the girl, David withdrew. For minutes he struggled to gouge out a pit in which to bury Michael's remains. But the ground was so hard and stony that without tools he could scrape only a shallow trench. David dragged the Nazarene's corpse into this depression and piled stones upon it. He thought, *This at least will keep the wolves from Michael's bones.*

David retreated up the carved steps in the facing of the aqueduct to the sanctuary of the summit channel. From this height the youth peered in all directions, listening intently into the deep distance.

He could see the girl below him in the shadow of the earthwork. In one hand she held the coin-sized whetstone that she normally wore on a rawhide thong around her neck. She was sharpening the point of her dagger.

David peered with dread and horror.

Kneeling over the motionless Telamon, the child seemed to pause as if calling upon heaven for assistance. Then, with excruciating tenderness, she lanced the flesh beside Telamon's left eye. David could not see the gush of whitish yellow fluid that first leaked, then spurted from this puncture; his vantage was too distant to reckon much more, nor did he wish to. He saw the girl recoil and even for a moment seem to back away in revulsion. She recovered at once.

The man-at-arms had neither moved nor made a sound. *He's dead,* David thought. *The girl is crazy. She's tending to a corpse.*

The child had brought a basin of steaming water from the fire. Into this she dipped the weave of her garment. She daubed tenderly with the fabric at Telamon's wound.

At length David climbed down.

He felt keen anguish and self-reproach but could not make himself come near his master's body.

For hours the child Ruth tended to the mercenary.

How many perforations did she assay in the purple flesh of the man-at-arms' face?

How many times did she bathe him and cleanse his wounds?

David settled at last upon the sand beside her.

Through the midday blaze and into the even more brutal fever of the postnoon David watched the child bend forward, pressing her lips to the suppurated flesh of Telamon's face to suck out such portion of the poison as she could take in between her lips. She spat the venomous stuff into the sand, then flushed her mouth with water from the cistern.

Again and again the child performed this service.

The man-at-arms never moved.

32

THE LIVING AND THE DEAD

ALL NIGHT THE CHILDREN HAULED the pole litter. Each took one side. They traded when their backs and hams became too weary to carry on.

The man-at-arms' breath could be discerned now—drafts so shallow the boy and girl must set an ear directly above the mercenary's mouth to feel, more than hear, the exhalation.

The children had fashioned shoulder straps, woven of tamarisk boughs, and rigged tumplines made from shreds of their garments. The toes of the litter poles scoured deep gouges in the sand and shingle, which the girl and boy at intervals obscured as best they could, setting the litter down and dashing back along its traces, abrading the track with sweeps of acacia and camel thorn.

When the first glimmers of dawn appeared, the children wrested the litter off the ground and, bearing Telamon's weight as soldiers carry a wounded comrade upon a stretcher, sought a covert for the day's lie-up.

The pair made no more than a half mile the first night, and little beyond that on the second.

Patrols and search parties passed without cessation.

At intervals the girl resumed her ministrations of Telamon's wounds. The heads of both upper-arm bones, it was clear, had been wrenched from their sockets. The mercenary's arms flopped, unstrung as a doll's; they must be lashed to the rails of the litter or they would trail in the sand. The man-at-arms groaned with each jar and jostle. Lurid abscesses had formed in the flesh about his shoulder joints. Beyond moans of pain, the man-at-arms could produce neither sign nor speech.

His flesh felt on fire with fever.

The child Ruth lanced the abscesses about the mercenary's face and cauterized the incisions with the flat of her dagger seared in the coals of such pit fires as the children dared make at the sun's zenith when flame or smoke offered the least chance of giving them away. The girl gathered such medicinal plants as she had observed the sorceress collect. She treated the rents in Telamon's flesh with the seeds of devil's pocket ground into a paste and sealed them with the juice of blue-jacket petals crushed between her fingers. Telamon moaned with each extension or protraction of his limbs. His eyes remained sealed within the distension of tissue that was his face.

"Is he better? Can you reckon any improvement?"

The man-at-arms had not moved so much as a toe. He could not see or speak. Breath came, when it could be felt, weakly and in shallow, labored drafts.

Noon of the second day, Ruth motioned David to cross to her beside Telamon's prone form. A crude but effective language of sign had evolved between the children. *Make ready,* the girl communicated to the boy.

"For what?"

The child positioned David at Telamon's left shoulder. The mercenary lay unconscious, on his back on the litter, which itself rested upon the ground concealed in a wash beneath mounds of acacia. Could the man-at-arms hear? Was he aware of the children's presence?

The girl took hold of Telamon's left wrist and forearm. With scrupulous care she extended this limb alongside his ear so that it stretched above his head parallel to his spine. She clutched the wrist with one hand and the elbow with the other. She braced both her soles upon the earth. The girl indicated to David that, on her signal, he was to punch Telamon with both fists as hard as he could in the center of the chest.

David did.

As the man-at-arms convulsed, the girl jerked the bone of his upper arm out and away from the socket of his shoulder till she felt a scraping and then a void. Into this she thrust the bone-head.

The mercenary's body convulsed from sole to crown. David leapt upon him, full-weight, to hold him steady. Spittle slung in great gobs from the grotesque vent that was the man-at-arms' mouth. David thought he saw Telamon's eyes open, for an instant only, before shutting and sealing again in agony.

The girl sprang backward. The mercenary's arm had dropped from her grip. She stood wide-eyed and paralyzed for what seemed to David interminable moments. Then, with a breath, she stepped again to Telamon's side. With the tips of her fingers she gently probed the tissue of his shoulder. The man writhed in torment.

"Is it in?" demanded David.

The child only shrugged.

Long moments passed. Again the girl's fingertips tested the spot.

"Is the bone in? Damn you! Can't you tell?"

The girl snarled furiously.

The youth cursed her again. "Is it in or not? Do you have any idea what you're doing?"

Twenty minutes later the children did the other shoulder.

On the third evening they reached the reed country that marked the eastern verges of the Great Bitter Lake.

"The Sea of the Exodus," said David.

Telamon could produce sound now, but only in episodic throes, void of all sense, which were succeeded by states of insensibility so profound they appeared to the children to stand only a handsbreadth from death. The man's fever continued to rage. Snapping from it upon one instant, he sought to rise, only to shudder with agony the instant he set a hand upon the earth to push himself up.

His eyes would not open.

His mouth could not take food.

It took both children working together to prize his lips apart and drizzle between them a quarter cup of water. The exercise took the better part of an hour and produced not satiation or even amelioration but only spasms of torment and convulsions of distress. When the child Ruth sought to swab Telamon's brow with a cool cloth, he raved incoherently and writhed like one wracked upon the torturer's table.

After dark of this third night, David ventured abroad, seeking any sign that might tell the children where they were. Their camp sat, though neither knew it, within a day's march of Memphis and forty miles from the port city of Pelusium and the easternmost mouth of the Nile.

The country was populated.

From a shallow rise a quarter mile from their hiding place (the desert ran right up to the salt waterline below), David could see fires—a dozen scattered to the south and more in clusters along the shore to the north.

"A village," he reported back at camp. "People."

By sign the girl communicated, *We must go back. Into the desert. We will be found here.*

"Are you crazy?" said David.

Both children had become so burned by the sun and so desiccated from want of water that their mouths would not close. The ducts of their eyes could no longer produce tears. Desert sores ravaged their faces, hands, and feet, producing open cracks and fissures that grew wider each day and sent the pain of rending flesh through them with the slightest bump or jostle. Their lips were so blistered that even the few swallows of water they dripped down their throats each evening produced a sensation like fire.

The inside of David's skull felt like it was roasting, as if the brain in its pan were being cooked—even at night, even out of the sun.

David realized he could no longer tell reality from vision.

"We must risk approaching one of the villages," he told Ruth. "For help. For water. We can't continue like this."

Twice in that night patrols passed—one mounted, one afoot—so close that the children could hear the speech of the searchers and smell the palm-grease stink of their torches.

David almost cried out.

Recalling later, he believed he had.

The patrols passed on.

Later that night—or maybe, David thought, it was the following night—the youth sat watching Ruth minister to Telamon's wounds and abscesses. What water they could find during the day went to this tendance, not to quench their own thirst.

David considered killing Telamon.

A thrust with his dagger . . . even a feeble blow to the head from a stone would suffice.

The boy would have water then.

He might survive.

He debated murdering Ruth.

The youth weighed a number of options. *I must be canny*, he thought. *The girl is clever. And she fights like a wildcat.*

The boy was debating between strangling her in her sleep or suffocating her by burying her face in the sand, when he noticed the child react to something.

He looked and saw what it was.

One of the slits that were Telamon's eyes had opened partially.

The sight struck David with horror. He peered. The mercenary's eye reminded him of orbs he'd seen in the shore market on dead, or nearly dead, fish. The pupil had that same flat, affectless stare. This was, to David, the most grotesque apparition he had ever seen.

Ruth's reaction was the opposite. She sat up at once in an aspect of sudden and soaring hope.

Telamon managed somehow to turn his head toward the girl and open his eye a tiny jot wider.

The mercenary's right hand, which had been lying palm-down on the ground cloth beneath him, turned over, becoming palm-up.

Ruth set at once her child's hand within the bowl of the man-at-arms' palm. Telamon's eye fell shut, as if he lacked the strength to hold it open even a moment longer.

But his fingers closed about Ruth's hand.

When David's glance rose to the girl's face, he saw a single tear tracing a trail down the grime of her cheek.

33

PURSUERS

DAVID SAW THE DUST FIRST, at noon in the blue distance, advancing out of the north, the direction from which the main of the parties seeking them had emerged during the trek from the aqueduct. The youth at first took the cloud for a squall of wind or *migdal*, "dust tower." Such whirlwinds appeared in this wilderness by the hundreds during the heat of the day.

Then the *migdal* parted and became two.

The pair of towers continued advancing, one along the margin of the reed lands, the other east in open desert.

David stood.

The girl held for a count of thirty. Then she rose too.

The boy and girl scrambled now, struggling to manhandle Telamon's weight onto the drag litter. "Which way?" David peered about him.

Ruth had become as unstrung as he.

The children simply grabbed the poles of the litter and dragged it, as best they could, away from the approaching horsemen.

The Hebrew language, as has been noted, is bereft of profane expression. David employed Arabic instead. He cursed the child Ruth, and the black heart of heaven, and his own rotten luck.

We will be captured!

Put to the flame!

Crucified!

The boy cursed his own cowardly heart, which would abandon the man-at-arms if only shame and self-outrage would release their grip upon him. How heavy his master had become! How could the man weigh so much still, when every drop of fluid had been wrung from his guts?

The litter gouged deep creases in the earth, leaving tracks that a blind man could follow.

The girl's strength was gone. Her limb of the litter veered and tottered.

"Pull, damn you!"

The verge of a dry wadi stood only half a furlong from where the children labored. A place to hide if they could but lift the stretcher so it would not leave tracks! But their final vigor had fled. David cut the man-at-arms free.

"Drag him by his heels!"

The children did.

With excruciating exertion the boy and girl succeeded in hauling their cargo to the lip of the dry riverbed. They slid him down like a log sledge. The man-at-arms' head dragged in the sand. Nothing on his body moved. He was dead weight. A corpse.

David dropped his master into a trough at the bottom of the cutbank. The boy clambered with what little force he retained back up to the crest.

The two clouds pursuing them had converged.

The youth could see horses now.

He slewed back down the slope. "Bury him!"

With their hands the children scraped sand and gravel over the man-at-arms' prostrate form. From the bank they tore up hyssop and winter broom. They stacked these sedges about and atop the mound of sand, from which half the mercenary's body yet protruded.

Telamon groaned and rolled onto one elbow. "Give me a blade!"

The children stared.

The man-at-arms' features contorted from the pain of trying to lift his own weight.

"My sword! Give it to me!"

The girl obeyed.

The man's fingers could not close.

The gladius spilled from his hand.

David could hear the horses now. The earth in the wadi trembled.

The girl stood, facing in the direction from which the first pursuit party advanced.

She clutched her **x** dagger.

David snatched the man-at-arms' sword from the dirt.

He too stood.

The children could hear men's voices now.

Around one wing of the dry riverbed rode the foremost pursuers.

More emerged around the facing flank.

Not Romans.

Not Black Hoods.

Not Nabateans.

David straightened to his full height, gripping the gladius. He faced toward the horsemen advancing from the left wing.

Ruth with her dagger turned to the column spurring from the right.

The riders came up fast and loud.

Their leaders reined in, ringing the children. Steam jetted from the horses' nostrils; slaver slung from their muzzles. The iron bits of their bridles worked in the beasts' jaws. David could hear the metal scraping against the animals' teeth as they, the horses, sought to bite the iron and keep it from digging into the flesh of their gums.

The lead rider sprang down. He wore thorn boots beneath the baggy *silwar khammous* trousers favored by brigands and long-distance raiders. The weapon in his fist was a Syrian saber with a curved blade and a cross-guard. With this he indicated Telamon, who had managed to rise, some-how, to his knees.

"This is the man!" the leader called to his comrades.

Two more riders dismounted. The first, with a blow of his lance, dis-armed David of his gladius. The second seized the youth by the hair and drove him knees-first into the sand.

"Unarmed," he called to the others.

The lead rider loomed above the girl. "You are the mute," he said.

The child backed before him, clutching her blade.

"And you?" The leader addressed David. "The novice-at-arms."

Telamon struggled to rise. He could not. He lurched, unarmed and barely able to see or speak, to a position on his knees before the leader, as if to defend the children. The girl dashed to his side. David felt himself hauled roughly to his feet by the rider who held him. The boy could sense the fellow's saber at his neck. He thought, *They will take my head now.*

The leader regarded Telamon.

"You don't recognize me, do you?"

The rider extended his right arm before the mercenary. David and Ruth stared. Crawling upon the back of the fellow's hand and wrist, and emerging in twos and threes from beneath the hem of his sleeve, came a tidy cluster of bees.

BOOK NINE

THE NILE

34

THE MAN MADE OF BEES

THE MAN MADE OF BEES' name, David recalled, was Timothy.
He and his comrades had a Greek doctor with them. The physician's name was Eryximachus—Eryx for short. The company called themselves by the Hebrew term *kvutzot*, "young warriors." David recognized a
number from the Anthill.

For nine days Timothy and his companions remained with Telamon
and the children, moving them—sometimes in daylight, more frequently
after dark—from cave to cloistered camp to cave again; then, when such
refuges became untenable on account of the number and frequency
of patrols of Romans and Arabs and Egyptians scouring the region, to
such stilt-founded hamlets and "shy camps" of the riverine tribes as they
deemed safe, at least for a night or part of one. Clearly these fellows knew
the ground and every covert upon it.

For the first time in what seemed like months David had enough
water to drink. "I could guzzle the whole river," he said. The physician
would not let him. He restored the boy, and Ruth, by stages. Their meal
was a gruel made of the stalks of fennel baked in a cone-topped clay oven
called a *tagine* with a type of river bream that the locals ate—head and
all—and assorted root vegetables whose names David could neither pro-
nounce nor remember.

These reed lands, made fertile by the rich silt that descended out of the highlands of Ethiopia and the Sudan each year with the flood, grew flax, rice, wheat, and millet in quantities unimaginable. David marveled at such a landscape of bounty. No hills were found in this quadrant of Egypt. One mounted for a vantage to towers made of woven weeds and transited from place to place not by foot but by raft or reed boat. A traveler went "down to" Alexandria, though the direction by the stars was north.

The villages along this section of the Nile were not independent but for millennia had been ruled as precincts of the fiefdoms of the Twenty-Seven Great Families of Egypt. The fellahs of these colonies had survived twenty-two centuries of bondage under the pharaohs, as well as conquest by Alexander, subsequent rule of the Ptolemies, and, since the days of Caesar and Mark Antony, of incorporation into the empire of Rome.

A hard, proud poverty illumined these riparian races. Faces shone as charcoal, burned by the sun. Hair was worn short by the women and long by the men, wound and wrapped within white cowls called *toctinai*, or "tocks." At dusk the tillers bathed, not in the river, which was too thick with sediment, but in elevated side channels called *mantera*, to which the water had been lifted by weighted cranes and sluiced till it was clear as sunlight. Here, at this hour only, the men unbound their hair. They sang as they bathed (and their wives and daughters serenaded them as well), flinging their jet tresses over their heads to float before them in the current, while each man wrung his own with arms outstretched.

To David this was a sight of unwonted charm and delight. With such toil these fellows labored, and for such slender compensation! Yet how contented they seemed. Men of the Reed Lands wore neither tunics nor trousers but short wrapped skirts called *pteratai*, "waders," made of linen. Foremen wore a skirt of longer length to show that they didn't have to tread so deeply into the mud.

Dwellings were built on stilts in this country. One passed between these upon plank walkways that had been laid out, not above the water's surface in plain sight, but tucked below at ankle- and even calf-depth to confuse and frustrate an invader. Toddlers and grandmothers knew these tracks by heart. They glided upon them as swiftly as darting carp. Those of

Timothy's party, on the other hand, as intimate as they were with the villagers and their ways, plunged to their hocks in the muck when they dared these covert walkways, much to the amusement of the river dwellers.

The Nile dominated everything in this land of reeds. Tillers harvested in the manner of their ancestors. The gods here were the sun and the river. Such affairs of state as dominated discourse in Alexandria or Pelusium seemed in this quarter so remote they might as well be proceedings upon the moon. In fact, this orb, called here by her Greek names Phoebe, "Bright," and Europa, "Broad Face," was closer, as she ruled over the night with gentle benediction, bringing surcease from toil.

By the fourth day, Telamon could speak. He could sit up and take food, even rise to his feet, though only with extreme difficulty and incapacitating pain. To take a step, or even stand for more than a moment, was out of the question. The girl and boy attended upon him, never straying more than a few paces from his side.

"Why," Telamon asked Timothy that evening, "did you come after me?"

"To kill you," said the man made of bees. "Or save you, whichever course you permitted."

Telamon sat this evening in a near-upright position, supported against a saddle with its blanket rolled for a bolster. The company, including several of the kvutzot, roosted around a pit fire of acacia upon a small, dry island, called a "traveler," adjacent to a village of the Reed Lands.

"News of the calamity at the Anthill reached us in the Lavender Valley within thirty-six hours. Another day, and Roman cavalry from Jerusalem appeared in force. They were searching for the letter—the epistle written by Paul the Apostle and intended for the *polis mysteriodis*, the hidden community in Corinth, Greece.

"The Romans had learned that the Nazarene Michael and the girl-child had stopped with us for a night in their flight. The soldiers believed that Michael carried the letter, or that he knew where it was, and hastened now to acquire it. They had no idea, then, that the girl herself was the letter, that she bore its contents within her memory."

"How did *you* know?" Telamon asked.

The man made of bees made no answer.

"We in the valley feared that you had worked this out somehow on your own and would overhaul Michael and the girl, take them captive, and return them to the Romans, as was your commission from the tribune Severus."

"When did you learn that the girl was the letter? Did you know it when you welcomed me and the boy?"

Again Timothy simply smiled.

"The Romans believed that we in the valley possessed intelligence of Michael's route. They commanded us to guide them in pursuit. When we refused, they beat and then murdered the officials of the settlement. They devastated the crop in the fields and ravaged what stores of oil and essence we had set aside for future trade."

Telamon absorbed this gravely. He asked if the Romans had known of his own passage through the valley. Did they, he inquired of Timothy, interrogate you or others about this, or attempt to learn from you our intended route? "Did they ask if you had seen or spoken with me and the boy?"

"The Romans knew your route, or guessed its contours, from your earlier stop at the stock pens in Gaza. And they knew that your path would follow that of Michael and the child."

The man made of bees volunteered nothing about his own treatment at the hands of the equites legionis. It was not hard to deduce from his silence, however, that the horse troopers of the Tenth Legion had scourged the fellow with their customary thoroughness.

"We followed your trail from the Anthill to the strand at Cut-off Noses," said Timothy. "Then from well to well to the site of the Black Hoods' attack, and finally to the aqueduct."

Timothy said that he and the kvutzot had found the cairn that sheltered Michael's bones. They discovered signs of Telamon's crucifixion and of the children's labors to succor and resuscitate him.

Twice during the next three days the company had to move, displaced by the proximity and frequency of patrols. The riverine villagers, declared the man made of bees, could be counted upon to shield the fugitives for only so long. They were poor, and fortunes were being offered for information leading to the fugitives' apprehension.

The gravest danger to Telamon and the children, Timothy said, would come not from the Romans or the Arabs but from the Hebrew communities in Pelusium and especially Alexandria. This city, the greatest not only in Egypt but in all the East, held the most prosperous and prestigious population of Jews in the world, second only to Jerusalem. These were merchants and magistrates, sea traders, army officers, scholars, patrons of the arts. The Great Library had been funded since Ptolemaic times by this community's largesse.

The Romans may control Egypt militarily and administratively, Timothy declared, but the Jews owned it financially, culturally, and philosophically. The prosperity of their community and indeed its very existence, they believed, was as threatened as the Romans', though for different reasons, by these missives of the Apostle Paul.

"The emperor blames them, the Jews, for the rise and spread of this Messianic cult, as it has taken root and expanded so spectacularly almost entirely within the Hebrew community." Indeed the so-called "good news" of the Kingdom of Heaven was intended, Timothy said, at least so far, exclusively for the children of Israel. "The Zealots and the Judaic establishment fear this new cult as it aims, they believe, to supplant and even replace the religion of Moses and the prophets. The secular masses are more afraid of Rome, which may, and already has, struck at the Hebrew community as accomplices to political sedition."

Such bounties as the emperor had published, Timothy continued, would seem a pittance alongside that which the Pharisaical and Saduceean establishments would put abroad and no doubt already had. "And those who hunt you will be no ragged bands of vigilantes or freebooters, but crack professionals—contract man-hunters, militia, or other organized companies, funded for profit and centrally coordinated, so that if you should elude one such band, allied forces will learn immediately your direction of flight and converge to overhaul you."

Throughout these initial days, the physician Eryx labored to restore Telamon's limbs to sensation and mobility. Assisted by others of the party, the surgeon re-dislocated the mercenary's shoulders. He set the bones again within their sheaths, splinted them, and sucked the inflammation out with compresses of honey, hyssop, and vinegar.

The party had brought gallons of honey in clay jars.

"A man expires on the cross," the doctor said, "not from loss of blood or trauma to the sinews but from ravagement of the nerves and the internal organs, caused by the drainage of fluids into the lower extremities and the deprivation of the more elevated ones. A man goes blind and deaf. He cannot breathe. The heart cannot support such distress. It gives up."

The physician explained Telamon's state in detail to David and to Ruth, who attended, rapt, to his discourse.

"Your friend's upper limbs will recover. They are coming around already. What concerns me is the trauma sustained by his lower extremities—his legs and feet. They are gangrenous. It is a miracle he has not lost them. The pooled blood over days has ravaged the lower joints and tissues. He must not stand or walk."

From locals, the kvutzot acquired contemporaneous intelligence of the imperial dragnet. Roman patrols out of Pelusium and Herodopolis ranged along both shores of the Great Bitter Lake. Others, including pursuit parties of Nabatean and Senussi raiders, as well as Black Hoods from Alexandria and Saduceean and Pharisaical shomrim out of Memphis and Heliopolis, prowled the Nile as far upriver as Cene and Aphroditopolis. These place names meant nothing to the boy and girl at first, but with the assistance of maps scratched by Timothy and others in the earth, they came quickly to grasp their position in relation to the desert out of which they had come, the Nile and Alexandria that awaited to the west, and the Roman Sea to the north.

A bounty had been offered by the legate of Alexandria, Tiberius Claudius Modestus, for information leading to the capture of Telamon and the children. The reward was sixty thousand denarii—five years' pay for a centurion, twenty years' for a legionary infantryman. Entire downriver tribes including their women and children, Timothy said, had vacated their villages to comb the wastes between the Pelusian Nile and the Reed Lands seeking this prize.

Evening was the time when Telamon suffered most. Heat seemed to leave his body with the retiring sun. He quaked and shivered. Fits of palsy seized him, accompanied by a terror whose source appeared to be possession by spirits or demons. These bouts could not be quelled except by the child Ruth clamping his hands in both of hers and crooning to him as a mother sings for a babe.

Timothy too sat with Telamon through these hours. He fed him honey, dipped upon a wooden spoon and slipped between the mercenary's lips. Timothy spoke to the man-at-arms in Latin and Greek, though he said he could not tell if the mercenary heard in these hours or, if he did, if he could comprehend.

David attended these sessions as well. It seemed to him that the man made of bees spoke not so much for Telamon's benefit as to instruct the children in a philosophy, even a faith, that was neither Nazarene nor Roman but derived of his own private suffering and occult thought.

He spoke as if to the man-at-arms:

"All your life you have striven, my friend, to be superior to adversity, to endure heat and cold, hunger and fatigue. You have trained yourself in the academy of privation to want nothing and no one, to need nothing and no one. Now look at you. You are helpless. Dependent utterly upon the charity of others."

David studied the mercenary's expression in these moments. Did he hear? How would he answer if he could? The youth too regarded the girl. What did Ruth hope for Telamon? For herself?

"So was I," continued Timothy, "when I was brought, as little more than a boy, before the magistrates and charged as a habitual thief and cutpurse. So was I upon the cross. So was I when the Nazarene Michael took me down and bore me, himself, and others to safety in the Lavender Valley."

David remarked Telamon's lids fluttering in moments such as these. The child Ruth would rise to her feet then and take station between the mercenary and the man made of bees—her way of communicating that such converse must for the moment cease.

Timothy made clear to the children his intent to transport Telamon, as soon as the man-at-arms could travel, to sanctuary in the Lavender Valley. There the mercenary could be protected. There he could heal.

"How long will such healing take?" David asked.

"With no setbacks, eighteen months."

The youth found himself glancing to Ruth.

"What, then, about the Apostle's letter?"

"The letter," said Timothy, "will find its own way to Corinth. Or it won't. In any event, its further transmission, by any means and all, has become impossible now."

35

A FACE BEHELD IN DARKNESS

THE MERCENARY BEGAN, BEFORE HE could even stand fully to his feet, to instruct the boy and girl, in earnest and with great urgency, in the practice of arms.

The physician Eryximachus commanded Telamon to discontinue this exercise at once. He forbade the mercenary to rise from his bed. He proscribed all toil, mental as well as physical, but specifically and with vehemence such exertion as instruction in combat.

Telamon would not hear this.

Timothy and the others of the party looked on in consternation as the man-at-arms, on his feet at the commencement of these sessions, then upon his knees when he could no longer sustain such exertion, led the girl and boy apart from the company into a site at the margins of the Reed Lands. The mercenary had located a copse of runt tamarisks whose boles would serve as Roman-style posts upon which the boy and girl could train.

Timothy confronted Telamon. "Have you gone mad? What can you intend by these preposterous exercises? You will cross the sea to Corinth? Take on the Romans?"

Telamon hobbled past Timothy to the site of instruction. The man made of bees stalked after him in exasperation.

"Two things you must hear and understand," he said. "The Apostle,

I have told you—and the Romans know this as well—has not dispatched only one transcription of the letter. His scribes have produced a dozen duplicates, perhaps more! For all we know, one, two, or ten have already reached the underground community in Corinth. Cease these exertions at arms! You will kill yourself, and these children, to no purpose.

"Nor is your proprietor Severus any less clever than his adversary. The villagers along the river report that he too has fashioned a ruse. The Romans have outfitted sham parties, costumed and accoutered to look like you and the girl and boy. He has put these counterfeits abroad in Pelusium, in Alexandria, and in every embarkation port in Egypt, seeking to draw into his snare any who would abet the Apostle in his errand. What chance do you have? Look at you. You can't fight, and certainly these children cannot. Cease this madness. We will leave you if you don't."

The mercenary refused to listen.

He rehearsed the children over and over in the close-quarters assault of adversaries taller and stronger than they. He taught them to fight with the dolabra, with the dagger, and with weighted darts. Blows of the former and thrusts and volleys of the latter two, the man-at-arms instructed, were to be delivered upon the opponents' lower extremities. He taught the children to attack in tandem. Boy and girl drilled to make rushes upon the foe's thighs and calves and even his feet. The pair scurried again and again in patterns of "X" and "S," as called out by the mercenary, all the while maintaining a ground-skimming crouch.

On the instance when one of the children—almost always the boy—disregarded or failed to follow the mercenary's instructions and rushed in an upright or half-upright position, Telamon had him repeat the exercise with a heavy stone in his off-hand and, should this not succeed in achieving the desired end, he fashioned a rucksack for the boy and loaded it with rocks and sand. "Stay low! Go for the Achilles! Believe me," the man-at-arms assured the children, "if you slice a man anywhere below the calf, you will get his full attention."

Telamon blindfolded the children and made them dash repeatedly at the post from short range, slashing with the dolabra as they passed. He taught them to tumble and rise again. He made them parry blows in a shuffle side to side.

Timothy and the others observed these sessions with mounting alarm, as the mercenary, after each, discovered himself so unstrung with exertion that he could not even crawl back to camp but must be physically borne.

Again the doctor demanded that Telamon desist.

Again Telamon refused.

Eryx pleaded with the children. Boy and girl simply faced him, responding nothing.

"Do you want your man to die? Do you wish, yourselves, to be the engine of his end?"

After the meal that evening, Timothy sought the mercenary's attendance man-to-man. "Sit with me, please." He included the children. "All of you. Let me tell you a story."

Telamon relented. The children took seats on either hand. The site was a fireless circle, at the hour approaching sunset, on a bank beside the steaming, silt-heavy river. The physician attended as well, along with two of the kvutzot.

"In my youth in Jerusalem," Timothy began, "I made my way as a petty thief and cutpurse. My prey were pilgrims and other innocents freshly arrived in the holy city. This you know. Michael has told you, and I have made reference to it myself.

"The temple constables caught me many times. I could not, or would not, reform my ways. Finally the officers turned me over to the Romans. I was convicted and sentenced to death by crucifixion. This was some weeks before the rabbi from Nazareth met his end in this same fashion.

"My execution was to take place not upon Skull Hill as was his, but behind the ossuary on the slope beneath the Dung Gate, where the city's garbage is burned each night. Four others, all guttersnipe criminals like me, were hung on crosses that dawn. Our perches were so close together we could talk to one another. None of us had families or, if we did, these kept apart from the site of our mortification out of shame or fear of further persecution. We hung in the sun all day. Three died.

"When the soldiers watching over the last two lost interest in our ordeal, Michael and several of his mates slipped in and cut me and the other fellow down. I did not know Michael. I had never met him. Nor was he acquainted with me or the other youth. Michael risked everything to rescue us, for, had he and his friends been apprehended, their fate would have been the same as ours. The other boy expired. But Michael saved me. He smuggled me out of Jerusalem in an oxcart, concealed beneath false flooring, to the Lavender Valley. He himself returned to the city."

Telamon and the children listened with keen interest.

"In the valley I recovered," said Timothy. "There I healed. There I have remained. I have made this site my home and husbandry of the bees my vocation."

Timothy paused for a long moment, regarding the man-at-arms and the boy and girl to be sure he retained their full attention.

"One day, a year or longer after I had been settled in the valley, two strangers appeared at my gate. They introduced themselves as mates of Michael who had saved me. The pair begged of me a kindness. They wished, they said, to abide in the valley for a period. They could neither compensate me for their lodging nor pay even their own board. Clearly these men were on the run. I set at once my home and all I possessed at their service.

"From me these men entreated one commodity only: materials with which to write.

"I provided these. Weeks passed. I never inquired what works these two were composing, or even if that was the exercise upon which they endeavored. I never asked their names, nor did they offer them.

"The pair kept entirely to themselves, never venturing even into the gardens or the beekeeping yards.

"At this time I began experiencing alarming sensations. Visions oppressed me. I heard voices of men crying out in agony. I saw faces of those whose lives had ended upon the cross. Some of these men I knew. Most, I had never seen. Their features seared themselves into my memory. I experienced profound terror at this. What was happening to me? Was I losing my mind? I sensed that somehow these two strangers were the cause of this possession that was afflicting me.

"I determined to send them away. I rehearsed how I would put this to them. The night came upon which I had set myself to do so. I was crossing in darkness to the hut the two men shared, when I saw a third figure step forth from the gate. Clearly this was an individual unknown to me—not either of the original two.

"The man saw me and greeted me by name. This was odd, not to say uncanny, as I had never encountered the fellow before and was certain he could not possibly own acquaintance of me. The man crossed toward me. I found myself seized by terror. I knew at once that this was no man but something other.

"'Who are you?' I demanded, seeking to conceal my perturbation. "How do you know my name?'

"'I am a friend,' the man said, 'of those to whom you have tendered refuge. I wish to thank you, Timothy, on their behalf, for your courage and your kindness.'

"The man came up directly before me. His eyes were dark and filled with such compassion as I have never seen before or since. 'Do not fear,' the man said. I knew without speech that he, like me and those of my vision, had experienced crucifixion and had been transformed by it.

"The man did nothing but look into my eyes, yet such a force of love coursed from him to me that I staggered and could not keep my feet. I fell to my knees before the man. I perceived, again without words, that I was bound not only to him and to the others who had suffered upon the cross, but to all mankind, and that the remainder of my days must be spent in service to them all.

"At that moment, my two lodgers emerged from their shelter. When they saw me with the man, they dashed forward in consternation. They helped me to my feet. 'Are you all right? Timothy, can you speak?'

"I peered in all directions. The third man had vanished. I inquired in agitation of the other two, 'Where has the man gone? Who was he? What just happened to me?'

"My lodgers said only, 'Now you too have beheld him.'

"The next morning the strangers departed. I never saw them again, or their companion. Nor have I in the intervening years heard from them or of them. Yet that encounter remains the consummate and defining hour of my life."

Telamon absorbed this tale with sober abstraction. His expression showed that he knew neither what to make of it nor what message the man Timothy intended to impart.

Timothy saw this.

He smiled.

He addressed Telamon directly.

"The man who rescued me from the cross was Michael, as I said, whom the Romans under Severus slew, as you witnessed at the aqueduct, and whose remains these children interred and which I and my comrades came upon in our search for you. This man Michael was nephew to Stephen, a follower of Jesus, who himself met his end by a sentence of stoning pronounced upon him by a Roman magistrate, a Jew and great persecutor of Christians, who called himself Saul of Tarsus.

"This Saul, as all men now know, experienced upon the road to Damascus a miraculous visitation of divine origin. He turned apart from the service of Rome, reconstituting himself not as a persecutor of those who followed this new faith, but as its most canny and passionate champion. He took the name 'Paul the Apostle.' Yes, *that* Paul—the very man who composed the letter which this girl-child, Ruth, and the Nazarene Michael were carrying and which you, Telamon, were charged by Severus, the garrison commander of Jerusalem, to retrieve and deliver back to him."

The man Timothy sought Telamon's eyes.

"The visions I experienced in my terror . . . the faces of men I beheld? One of them was yours."

Telamon's glance remained hooded.

"I recognized you the moment you entered the Lavender Valley. Do you remember when the bees swarmed about you without alighting upon your flesh? They had never done that with anyone other than me, ever.

"Yet your apparition in such a manner cast me into confusion. Those who have ridden the cross and survived possess a certain 'look.' This is unmistakable. You," said Timothy, "did not have this look."

David's glance swung from the man made of bees to the mercenary.

In the eyes of both resided a sorrow, and a compassion, that he, the youth, had neither apprehended nor appreciated before.

"You have it now," said Timothy to Telamon.

To David's astonishment, the man-at-arms did not deflect or dispute this.

Ruth perceived this as well. She glanced to David. Both their expressions confirmed this understanding.

"You cannot stay here, Telamon. The Romans or the Arabs will find us soon. It is a miracle we have not been discovered already. You must be conducted to safety. You must rest, you must heal. Come back with us! We can protect you. Our guides will see you past any parties sent to pursue or intercept you.

"It would be madness," Timothy said, "to attempt to cross to Corinth. The Romans have probably wiped out the hidden community already. How will you get through the cordon of legions that has no doubt been thrown up about the city? With what forces? These children? Even if you did get through, what can you hope to accomplish? Reports have been abroad for months that the Christian communes are breaking apart beneath Rome's campaign of terror. A man betrays his own brother; another is taken and informs upon his mates to save his own neck. How will such affrighted souls react to you, about whom the Romans have spared no measure to sow suspicion? Come back with us! You have done all a man must and endured everything a man can. My comrades and I have come to save you! This is the meaning of my vision! This is why I am here!"

Telamon considered this gravely.

"With respect, Timothy, I must take issue with your interpretation. Your vision, if one were to believe in such things, may mean the exact opposite—not that you were called to bring me back to safety, but that you were sent to succor me so that I might go forward.

"I have survived the cross," the man-at-arms said, "not to abandon my mission but to see it through."

For long moments Timothy offered no answer.

"You understand," he said at last, "that I and my men cannot go forward with you."

Telamon's expression acknowledged this.

"The sea crossing to Greece will be perilous in the extreme," Timothy said. "The sailing season has ended. Already winter gales blow. The Romans themselves will not risk a crossing in any vessel smaller than a four-banker." He paused and smiled. "Yet, for enough gold, I imagine you will find in the port of Pelusium some small-craft skipper reckless enough, or greedy enough, to try."

Telamon did not contest this.

He extended his hand.

"Thank you, my friend."

The man made of bees clasped Telamon's hand in his. "What will you do," he asked, "when you reach Corinth?"

The man-at-arms turned toward Ruth.

His eyes met hers and held them.

"That which this child commands," he said, "I shall perform."

BOOK TEN

ARCADIA

36

THE SEA IN WINTER

THE GIRL STRODE AHEAD, BAREFOOT, treading over spiny leaves of oak and sharp stones as if upon a carpet of wool. She waved back to the man and boy. *Come! Follow! Why do you tarry?*

The country called Hellas is constituted of two distinct regions—a northern and a southern—conjoined by an isthmus.

Upon this neck of land sits the city of Corinth. She is one of the great *poleis* of Greece, a mighty port of commerce and seat of power on a par, or nearly so, with Thebes and Argos, Athens and Sparta.

The High City, the Acrocorinth, rises upon an eminence overlooking the arms of the Gulf of Corinth and the Saronic Bay. From the headland northwest of the city one can see on clement days across to Iteas Bay and the bluffs beyond which the Priestess's Road ascends to Delphi and the great sanctuary of Apollo.

To the east of Corinth twenty-two miles lies the city of Megara, a sea and land power and rival in ancient days to Athens. Trek farther and you enter Attica herself, whose principal *polis*, Athens, lies but twenty-five more miles down the shoreline road. This had been little more than a cart path when the Romans acquired dominion over Hellas. They built it up into a legitimate highway.

South of Corinth lies the Peloponnese, the mountainous spine of

southern Greece. Argos, capital of ancient Mycenae and seat of Aga-
memnon of old, is situated but two days' tramp away, forty miles. South
of these lies the region of Lakedaemon, whose principal polities are Sparta
and her tributaries, Pellana and Selassia, as well as Geronthrai and the
port of Kythera. The inhabitants of these cities and of others in neighboring Messenia are called *perioikoi*, the "dwellers around." Their armies are
compelled by ancient treaty to follow the Spartans "whithersoever they
shall lead."

All these states of southern and northern Greece as well as their
hinter villages lay now under the heel of Rome. Intercity and over-
seas commerce were conducted using Roman coin and currency and
accounted by Roman weights and measures. Disputes at law were adju-
dicated in Roman courts, presided over by Roman magistrates. Days of
the week and months of the year were Roman on all official documents
and correspondence, though the cities and towns of Hellas retained for
domestic usage their ancient calendars.

The navies of the Greek city-states trained and sailed under ensigns
bearing the eagle of the emperor. Their oarsmen were paid in Roman spe-
cie and rowed under Roman command.

North of Lakedaemon, dominating the mountainous woodlands that
transect the Peloponnese, sprawls the region of Arcadia, the largest in
Greece and, save the wild northernmost provinces abutting Macedonia
and Illyria, the least domesticated.

Across this region Telamon and the children advanced, bound for
Corinth.

Timothy had remained with the mercenary four days beyond that
terminal evening. The main of his company, seven men mounted, with
four pack mules, set off at once on the recrossing of Sinai to the Lavender
Valley. Three men, including Timothy, remained with Telamon and the
children.

These were joined on the third day by a river barge captain from the
port of Pelusium, an Egyptian Jew named Tomer ("Upright"), a cousin of
one of Timothy's comrades, and his son, a youth of fourteen years serving as mate and steersman. Their vessel was a raft constructed entirely of

reeds. The craft looked as if it would sink under the weight of two men, but, upon the stream, its skipper declared, it could bear 220 sacks of grain, enough fodder to feed a cohort of cavalry for seven days, or forty hundred-weight casks of oil or wine. The barge's draft was so shallow that it could glide, propelled by a single stern sweep, across a plain of reeds no deeper than a man's ankles.

Father and son transported the fugitives down the Nile not to Pelusium, which they adjudged too dangerous, but—transiting west via canals and tributary channels known, it seemed, only to them—to Alexandria herself. These would accept no remuneration, neither sire nor scion, but had embarked upon the journey, they declared, for the adventure only.

With gleeful satisfaction the barge skipper reported that the pursuit of Telamon and the girl Ruth had become a worldwide sensation.

"Songs are being written about you, my lass. You are more famous in Egypt than the first Cleopatra! Tales of your trials and hairbreadth escapes have crossed the sea even to Rome. The emperor himself clamors for your head!"

The final proposition urged upon Telamon by Timothy (which he declared of critical importance now, in light of the scale and intensity of the dragnet seeking the party's capture) was that Ruth commit to paper the contents of the Apostle Paul's letter. To this end he produced the necessary implements and pressed these into the man-at-arms' keeping. "God forbid something should happen to this child. You must have the epistle in some form that may survive."

Timothy would not release Telamon until he, the mercenary, had pledged on his honor to effect this.

It was the bargeman Tomer who saw Telamon and the children safely down the Nile to Alexandria, to the harbor precinct of Posidium, and into the tavern-based company of "those who know how to keep their cheese-holes shut."

The westernmost embarkation quay of Alexandria—and the most likely to escape imperial observation—is called the Portus Eunostos, the Old Port. Posidium perches upon its extremity. The Great Harbor itself, lying immediately to the east, is called the Pschent, the "Double Crown," because its arms, sixteen stades tip to tip, flank the Pharos lighthouse, setting it off like a jewel within a royal tiara. The Great Causeway, the Heptastadion, links the mainland to Pharos Island. Within these precincts and other neighboring quarters, declared the barge skipper, reside seamen of such intrepidity as would challenge the Hyperborean maelstrom in January.

In the event, Telamon and the children discovered, none would consent to put forth. David could see why. Stationing himself that first morning upon the strand between the seawall called the Pteron, "the Wing," and the causeway that led to the Lighthouse, he experienced such a blow, ripping across even the protected precinct of the harbor, called the Goblet, that he must plant his feet wider than shoulder width and sink his soles mightily into the sand to keep from being blown over. Not a solitary craft dared the offing. Skiffs and bumboats were beached keels-up, with lines lashed to great stones to hold them from bowling. Whitecaps coursed across an arena of savage chop, their crests whipped clean by a hard, spumy gale. And this was within the harbor.

Worse, David could see, the interval of chop, crest to crest, was between ten and twenty feet. In other words, such a sea as would hammer a great boat to break its back and would turn a small craft into a bobbing top. No sail could beat into a gale like this, and a following wind would tear the linen to scraps if it didn't snap the mast or masts entire.

A coaster captain, whose name Telamon did not ask and who did not himself volunteer it, explained the rigors of navigation in such season. Sailing months, he declared, ran from the rising of the Pleiades, around the calends of May in most years, to the setting of Arcturus in mid-October. Beyond that date no one except skilled coasters ventured from any harbor, and these only into waters they knew intimately—and certainly never out of sight of land.

"Look about the harbor, brother. You see craft careened for refitting, replanking, and repainting. In shops you see sails being mended, rigging being rewoven, hanging tackle being refurbished and replaced. The sailing year is over! Not even a madman will put to sea at this season!"

Telamon listened patiently.

"There is a tale of old," he spoke at last, "of King Philip of Macedonia, Alexander's father. The king had got it into his head to besiege a certain city, whose citadel was sited at the summit of an eminence of such precipitous ascent, his generals assured him, that no attacking force could scale it in numbers sufficient to storm the battlements and overthrow the fortress. The track was so steep, his commanders told Philip, that it simply could not be mounted. The king only smiled. 'Not even,' he asked, 'by an ass laden with gold?'"

Telamon set his last two golden eagles—the ones he had given earlier to David and Ruth—upon the tavern table.

Thirty-six hours later the party had acquired a captain and a vessel and, seven days following, had seen themselves deposited ashore, at midnight, within a nameless, mooringless inlet half a league south of the Lakedaemonian port of Gytheion.

They had reached Greece.

37

PELOPONNESUS

HELLAS HERSELF, THAT IS, THE land-bound territory as opposed to the island nations of the Aegean and Ionian Seas, is constituted of three types of principalities. First are the maritime states, sited upon ports or harbors, such as Athens or Corinth, which depend for their prosperity upon trade and seafaring. Second are the inland agricultural dominions, as Argos or Thebes. One may add such horse-pasturing kingdoms as Thessaly and Phthia.

The third type of province is the hill country. Cities are rare in these highlands. The population clusters, when it does, within villages, hamlets, and isolated outposts, some no grander than fortified strongholds. Such uplands are hospitable neither to the cultivation of grain or fodder upon any scale greater than that of subsistence, nor to the husbandry of cattle or swine. Olives fare poorly here. Even sheep and goats struggle for pasturage and must be protected at all times from thieves and predators.

These are the poverty-bound parts of Greece, the backwaters. The clans that inhabit these highlands, at least those of the Peloponnese, are of such antiquity that they speak a dialect neither Dorian nor Ionian, but Pelasgian. Here are clefts and hollows that neither the Spartans of yore nor the contemporary Romans dare enter, save under truce negotiated in advance with the hill chieftains and paid for, not in gold, which the highlanders scorn, but livestock and oil. Here a kin-group's livelihood consists of hunting and fishing, and, for no few, banditry.

This, the girl signed, *is my mother's country.*

No highways cross these eminences. Few are the throughways that merit even the name of road. One transits these wildlands by footpaths, most broad enough for a single man only, or "traces," which are little more than game trails. Such regions are a jumble of valleys and peaks, many without a name, populated by wolf and hind, boar and eagle, and the type of grayish red fox called by the Romans *vulpinos.* Game of all kinds abounds in these uplands. Paths are level only when they track creeks and tributaries. Clearings are rare and small. One recognizes a native of such a region by his garb, which is frequently of animal hides, and his cap, which is often of fox-skin or wolf.

"How do you know this country," David asked, "if you have never seen it?"

By sign the child made known that her mother had taught her, reciting tales upon many an evening. She knew, the girl communicated, every crease and run. *Three ways meet*, she signed, *beneath two oaks. My mother's village lies upon the overhill trace.*

Both David and Telamon could by this time interpret the child's language as clearly and immediately as speech.

"How far?" David asked.

But the girl only kept trekking.

Telamon's physical state, which had been improving steadily since the Reed Lands, at this point took a turn for the worse. He had been able since Alexandria to make his way upon a pair of crooks. The accumulated impairment to his arms and shoulders now made this impossible. Worse, a form of paralysis had begun to afflict his upper extremities. His fingers would not close about a sword or dagger. He could no longer grip even a stone.

The month was now December. Storms descended from cloud-shrouded peaks. Hail and gale-driven sleet rendered the stony heights slick and treacherous. A type of frigid fog called in Greek *amike* fell upon the vales and glens with the descent of night, rendering even the most compact covert dank and wretched. Nights grew bitter and the hollows in shadow remained frost-bound till noon.

Telamon refused to slow down. He hobbled, clutching at branches and limbs for support. The boy and girl would tramp ahead, then hold in place until the man-at-arms caught up.

When they rested, the mercenary continued his instruction in the practice of arms.

The fourth noon they waded across a river.

"I know this place," Telamon said. "Its name is Alms Ford."

The watercourse was little more than a creek but one that from mid-crossing gave out onto a prospect of a furlong in either direction. The far bank held a wide strand, bright in the sun, with clean gravel underfoot.

"This was a mustering site," said Telamon, "and may still be, for the clans of the creases that lie above this stream and whose tributaries feed into it."

Girl and boy regarded the man-at-arms. "How do you know this?" David said.

"This is Arcadia. It is my country."

The man-at-arms addressed the girl. "Your mother's village of the three ways. I know it."

The child Ruth made no pointed response. David found himself struck by this. *Would not this girl*, he thought, *whose kin have no doubt inhabited these hills going back centuries, wish to query Telamon about this state-ment, which links his own origins to hers?*

Yet Ruth put forth no sign. If anything, her glance seemed to turn away from, and even deliberately avoid, Telamon's.

The mercenary himself looked away.

He addressed David.

"You're wondering what crops grow in such country. I'll tell you. Men. Soldiers. A youth coming of age in this place dreams of escape only. I swam out at fifteen. With what aim? To fight."

Now Ruth did turn back. Both children attended intently. But Tel-amon offered nothing further on this subject.

Only at day's end when the party had settled upon a defensible eminence and thrown together a supper of wild cresses and mountain trout hand-splashed from a brook, with a trench fire and a lean-to crafted snug against the night frost, did he relent.

Leaning back against the bole of an oak, with his feet swathed in skins and his paenula fastened closely about his shoulders, he told them how as a lad little older than David he had set out from his village, perhaps along this very path (he could no longer recall), made his way to the embarkation port of Kythera, and from there took ship to Sicily, to seek entrance into the profession of arms. Like all who could not claim Roman citizenship, Telamon was not permitted to enter Italy, nor in fact to apply directly for the legions.

He enlisted as an auxiliary, a light-armed skirmisher, and fought in Dacia, Moesia, Gaul, and Britannia before traveling on his own to Hispania Citerior—"Nearer Spain"—and undergoing the legionary trials at Cartago Nova. He was accepted there into the Tenth Fretensis. He served, the man-at-arms said, for twenty-two years of his twenty-five-year enlistment before being granted early discharge for valor at the Battle of Komana in Cappadocia.

"Yet now, returning, I cannot tell you which road goes to my ancestral home or even if any of my clan are still alive."

Telamon paused. David and Ruth glanced to each other. Neither had ever heard the man-at-arms speak at such length on any subject, and certainly not on one that touched upon him so personally.

The mercenary remarked the children's expressions. He smiled.

"I was a boy like any other in these hills. I hunted. I tramped. I dreamed of getting out.

"One day a man fled to our house—a lone soldier, hunted by enemies in the after course of defeat in some battle. My father was absent, away on campaign himself. My mother and sisters vacated our homestead, fearing this man's wrath, or that of those who pursued him, should they find that our farm had provided him refuge.

"I stayed. I took the man in. I was nine or ten. I hid him in the underground 'fort' I had built and played in during children's games. I brought him barley loaves and wine. I made dressings for his wounds and burned the bloody rags when he was done with them. He never spoke a word to me, this dirty hunted fellow, nor I to him. I did not ask his name, nor did he inquire of mine.

"Twice gangs of his enemies came searching for this man. I stood before the entrance to the lair where he lay hidden and lied to their faces. I convinced them. I could smell the soldier in his covert at my feet, but somehow those who hunted him did not.

"On the seventh evening he made preparation to leave. His wounds were too severe to survive. He knew it. He wished to save me the trouble of disposing of his corpse and of explaining its existence to the authorities, should they come to learn of it. I understood this without speech. I pointed him up the hill. There were dens in the rocks. He could settle himself and die there. He had one spear, an eight-footer with a butt spike, which he leaned upon like a staff, and a shortsword that he carried by a baldric over his shoulder. I gave him a stew of goat meat wrapped in grape leaves and a carry-skin of wine. 'Is there a god,' I asked (my first and only words to him), 'to whom you wish me to make an offering upon your death?'

"'Eris,' he said.

"Strife.

"The soldier, I believe now, spoke in bitter jest. But I took his speech in full earnest. I knew in that instant that I would be a warrior. Not like him. Not a farmer conscripted into his city's service and abandoned in need by his own countrymen.

"I would fight for no flag and no cause.

"I would fight for the fight alone.

"I would fight in the name of the goddess and the bitter but incontrovertible truth she embodied."

The man-at-arms turned now toward Ruth.

"To this pledge I have held true," he said, "until the night I met you."

38

THE VILLAGE

THEY WOKE TO THE CRIES of hounds bursting from the brush at their feet. Men brawny as bears loomed over them with clubs and huge hardwood war mallets. David's hand flew to his dolabra, to find it snatched away and turned against him in the fist of a grinning, oafish brute his own age.

Two bear-men had hauled Telamon upright and were cuffing him violently. Questions, stinging with hostility, were being hurled at the man-at-arms in a language David did not recognize and could not comprehend.

The girl had squirted free of whatever lout had collared her and was kicking him furiously in the shins. Spittle spewed from her lips. David heard the word *snyrem*, which he would learn later meant in the Pelasgian tongue "hellcat."

Telamon struggled to free his arms from the two mountain men who held him. He had no strength to move. His captors reckoned this. One, the leader apparently, grunted something to his companion.

They released Telamon.

The mercenary dropped to the earth on his knees.

Ruth sprang to his side with her dagger in her fist.

The bear-men ringed the three in. A query, and another and another, was bawled at Telamon in the savage, incomprehensible tongue.

He answered.

The men understood him.

David had never heard this dialect before. It was not Greek, rather a tongue from another world, another time.

Telamon was indicating himself, David, and Ruth, and declaring something to the mountain men. These turned to the children. One fellow reached under David's robe and groped him roughly. A second searched the crease of David's buttocks. He jammed two fingers into each of the youth's ears, then forced David's mouth open and stuck half his hand in. David writhed and spit. The man walloped him across the temple, knocking him nearly senseless. Ruth was disarmed and searched. The bear-men seemed satisfied. They grunted something to the others, which seemed to quell the main freight of their belligerence.

The leader had discovered Telamon's tattoo.

LEGIO X

He seized the mercenary's arm and twisted it so the others could see.

"You!" he demanded. "You savvy Roman?"

"And Greek too," answered Telamon. "Do you?"

An hour later, or perhaps three or four, the captives (for that was what they had become) had been driven across two peaks and three watersheds to a site deep within a mountain fastness. Though David had witnessed neither horn sounded nor courier dispatched, a congeries of no fewer than three dozen—women and children as well as men—awaited their arrival. Runt ponies, ducks, geese, and hunting dogs, above two score of the mangiest, ugliest curs David had ever seen, surrounded the newcomers. Telamon's armor and weapons were dumped in the center of the ring.

His **x** tattoo was again displayed.

Cries of outrage greeted this. A dame stepped before Telamon, lifted her skirt, and turned about to display her dirty buttocks, then wheeled and kicked the man-at-arms furiously in the privates. Hoots of derision and delight saluted this.

David heard the same phrase shouted repeatedly from two score throats, accompanied by gestures that seemed to indicate the act of evisceration and disembowelment. The girl Ruth had taken station before Telamon.

She faced the bear-men.

She gestured in sign.

To David's astonishment, the mountaineers and their women seemed to understand.

By degrees their fury and suspicion abated, replaced by wariness, then curiosity, even interest.

What was the girl communicating?

David saw her mime the act of crucifixion. She indicated Telamon. This produced a profound impression. The leader of the mountain men probed the mercenary's shoulder joints. He exposed Telamon's feet, still purplish and swollen. The chief's fingers pressed Telamon's palms, apparently seeking a response of muscle contraction. When this did not come, the fellow produced a great expulsion of breath and turned to his compatriots with an expression that seemed to accept and confirm all that the girl Ruth had imparted.

In dialect, Telamon asked if the men knew of a village where three ways met beneath a pair of oaks.

The bear-men responded at once.

"Gone," said one in rude but comprehensible Greek. "And all who dwelt there."

Ruth reacted with anguish.

"Murdered by Rome," said the fellow. "Three days past."

39

THE TRIAL

A FORUM OF JUSTICE WAS CONVENED, constituted of a council of seven men, apparently tribal leaders of the district and kinsmen of the slaughtered habitants of the village of the Three Ways. Telamon, David, and Ruth were charged as accessories to, or agents of, the imperial troops who had carried out the massacre. Deliberations lasted for a night and a morning.

The accused were found guilty and sentenced as follows:

The mercenary and both children were to be put to death. A single grave would be dug in a precinct of the watershed reserved for disposal of the bones of murderers, traitors, and outcasts. Over this pit the trio's throats would be slit. When the life had been bled out of them, their heads would be severed from their bodies and their hands and feet cut off. They would be buried naked, facedown, without arms or any identifying talismans or amulets. No marker would signalize the site of their interment.

This was to ensure that their spirits wandered havenless for eternity.

As punishment was being pronounced, David, to his consternation, found himself weeping. Tears sheeted. He experienced a burning shame at this, yet could not call his despair under control.

The child Ruth stood immediately upon his left, between him and Telamon. Neither she nor the man-at-arms reacted. Both stood unblinking.

The three were ordered remanded to a site of detention, where they would await execution. As the keepers—four warriors of the canton—took hold of the prisoners to remove them to this location, Telamon requested leave to speak.

Could the child, he asked of the council, at least be permitted to visit the devastated village? This was the birthplace of her mother, the mercenary said, and the site to which she had been faring over sea and land from Jerusalem, seeking her kin, whom she had never known. Might she at least see her home, the village of her origin, before the sentence of death was carried out?

This plea was denied.

The issue—as nearly as David could grasp it, delivered as it was by the council chief partly in the Pelasgian tongue and partly in legion-crude Latin—was one of piety and reverence for heaven.

Arcadia herself, the tribunal chief declared, and this region in particular—the canton of the Aleuadai—had in ages past been the province not of the Olympian gods but of the generation of Titans that preceded them. Here this race of immortals had reigned in the eons before the ascension of Zeus. From this place the Titans had been expelled to Tartarus. The clefts and vales of Arcadia retained to this day the grief and woe of that extinguished nation.

Within this territory, the chief declared, all crimes involving blood-guilt or ritual pollution—as this massacre enacted by the Romans—must be cleansed and purified according to the Lost Ways, rites of such antiquity and preserved in such secrecy that they could be carried out by none save the elders and priests versed in this ancient lore.

The council principal took pity, however, on the child Ruth. A representative would be dispatched to the site of slaughter, he pledged, to retrieve and to return to such kin as remained those effects of the slain deemed appropriate by the elders.

This proxy was sent forth.

Telamon and the children were led away to an underground barrow—a sort of root cellar excavated into the side of an eminence. Here they would abide until summoned to their fate. Water in a clay pitcher and bread in a wooden bowl were handed in to them, along with a bucket for their physical necessities.

"How soon?" said Telamon to the senior of the warders.

The execution would be carried out, the man replied, immediately upon the return of the priests from the devastated village.

Telamon took a seat against the rear wall of the cell. The girl sat across from him, looking straight ahead.

David took station as far away from the man-at-arms and the child as the constricted interior would permit.

He could not stop himself from sobbing.

A day passed, throughout which, despite all exertions to the contrary, the youth relived, over and over in his mind, the ordeal of the tribunal and its issue.

Telamon and the children had been held for the trial in the central communal lodge of the village—a pit, like the den of a she-bear, half underground, contrived like a fort, with a bare dirt floor, walls of stone, and a roof of massive hardwood timbers that could not, save with monumental effort, be hacked or sawn through or set ablaze. The single entryway was as narrow as that of a crypt, studded with embrasures, and twice left-turning—clearly meant to expose the men of an invading force to attack on their unshielded side.

The man-at-arms and the children were led into this burrow and seated between two rows of mountain men armed with axes and longswords. By this time, thirty-six hours after the party's capture, the men of the district, which apparently included a dozen adjoining watersheds whose inhabitants considered themselves blood kin or relations-by-marriage of the despoiled village, had collected both to grieve and to debate a response to the massacre and to other recent outrages.

Numbers of these fellows, it became clear, had served like Telamon as soldiers-for-hire in the war divisions of Rome. The interrogation, when it began, was conducted in Latin, or such pidgin argot as these former legionaries and auxiliaries yet retained. David reckoned he could make out one word in three. These veterans' wives and children attended as well, along with what seemed like half their livestock. Goats, pigs, stoats, and dogs mingled and settled upon every surface.

The interrogation began at sunset and continued throughout the night.

"Who are you?"

"Where are you from?"

"Why did you come here? Upon what errand?"

The chiefs of the mountain men apparently knew the answers already, or at least so David surmised by their expressions and the interchanges between and among them. They had heard of the imperial dragnet. They knew of the bounties offered by Rome.

Telamon answered for himself and for David and Ruth.

He spoke in dialect and soldier's slang. He kept his responses short. He appealed to no shared lineage or nationality. He did not attempt to extenuate any actions taken by him or the children, nor did he endeavor to mount any elaborate defense. Clearly the tribunal respected this. Here was manly conduct, worthy of a warrior. David dared to indulge a glimmer of hope.

Telamon declared for the council that the child Ruth sought the village of her deceased mother, believing that her kin would welcome her and that she and her companions would be safe there.

The council considered this.

"Where do you go now?"

"Our aim is Corinth."

"To do what?"

Telamon told of the Apostle's letter and the party's intention to deliver it to the underground community in that city.

"Our village, then," declared the chief interrogator, "was burned because of you. Our people were massacred on account of your errand."

Telamon did not contest this.

The chief indicated the child Ruth.

"Because of this girl."

Telamon stood.

"If you want a life, take mine."

The chief and the council studied the man-at-arms. They took in Telamon's many wounds and his state of physical infirmity.

"You are of these hills," said the headman. "Yet in thrice ten years you have never returned."

"I'm here now."

"Not by your own wish. Are you a Christian?"

"No."

"A Roman?"

Telamon shook his head.

"Are you this girl's father?"

"No."

"What relation, then?"

"None."

"Why offer your life for hers?"

"And for the boy's."

The council conducted its deliberations where it sat. The judges debated earnestly and at great length, while the listeners attended with keen interest, following every nuance of the examination.

The prisoners' fate turned, apparently, upon points both subtle and self-contradictory. Was the child truly the cause of the massacre? Indirectly, indeed. Yet the slaughter was carried out by the Romans acting for their own purposes. The child and her comrades had nothing to do with this. In fact, they, the captives, were not only in ignorance of this crime, but their own actions and objectives could not have been in greater opposition to it.

All night the council debated. Few listeners vacated, and those who did were replaced at once by others, all of whom seemed to be fully informed and conversant with the latest twist in the deliberations.

At noon, sentence was handed down.

The day passed, and the night. At dawn a dame appeared with a meal. The keepers unsealed the entry to the barrow—three heavy planks in the chamber's outer facing—and handed her in.

This was the first chance the child Ruth had had to communicate with a woman of the canton. By sign the girl inquired of her mother. Did any in this village or that of the Three Ways remember her? Was she recalled fondly or with kind regard?

"She left to follow the legions," declared the dame. "That will tell you all you need to know."

Ruth blanched to hear this.

The woman took the bucket with the night soil and replaced it with a fresh vessel.

"Forget her," the dame said to the child. "She was a soldier's whore."

All day David and his companions listened to the sounds of men coming and going. Hounds bayed. Horses could be heard, both ridden and led.

"The priests returning?"

Telamon shook his head.

Toward dusk they heard the clinking of armor and weapons and other sounds of horses being saddled. Men's footsteps sounded immediately outside.

Planks were removed again from the barrow's facing.

"Get out!"

Telamon and the children stepped forth into the fading daylight.

Their weapons and baggage were dumped at their feet.

Riders and armed men of the village could be seen hastening in all directions. Women and children followed carrying great bundles, apparently of their and their kin's necessities.

"Go! Get away from here!" Telamon and the children were told again.

"What has happened?

The chief keeper, himself making haste to depart, answered.

During the night an elite reconnaissance element of Roman cavalry had appeared at an overhill hamlet, led by a young lieutenant who claimed to have crossed by sea from Alexandria. His detachment had been dispatched, this officer said, from a march-camp of two cohorts, eight hundred men, established two nights previous at Orchomenos, a day's trek north of the village. Infantry and mounted contingents of this formation would be advancing into the canton within forty-eight hours, said the lieutenant.

This column would advance from village to village.

It would be seeking Telamon and the girl.

The lieutenant identified the mercenary by name and appended a physical description. He himself, the officer said, had clashed with this villain. He warned the leaders of the overhill hamlet that his commanders were in possession of reliable intelligence that they, or others of the adjacent villages, had captured this renegade and the girl-child he protected and that indeed they held these fugitives still.

The lieutenant demanded that the captives be handed over to him at once. He cited a reward of bountiful munificence, then threatened to devastate the entire region if he found that the inhabitants had indeed detained the man and the child but failed to turn them over.

"Where," asked Telamon, "is this lieutenant now?"

"Rode off," the keeper answered. "With nothing."

The mountain people were packing up the whole village, clearly intending to move deeper into the hills, readying to fight.

"And us?" said Telamon. "Why have your people not turned us in?"

Mates of the keeper hastened up, leading horses. The fellow sprang aboard. He indicated the council elders, also mounted, preparing to move out.

"If the Romans want you dead," he said, "our wish is that you live."

The mountain men appeared cheerful, or at the least undaunted, at the prospect of abandoning their homes for the winter fastnesses. The dames' and elders' eyes shone. Even the dogs capered underfoot in hale spirits.

All animosity toward Telamon and the children had fled. The village seemed to regard their late captives as comrades, and even, in some unvoiced way, as family. As the man-at-arms and his charges collected their weapons and kit, the council chief reined in above them. Two youths brought parched meat in a wrapper of straw.

"Where will you go, brother?"

"Where we intended," said Telamon, "before your hospitality intercepted us."

The chief laughed. He offered the older of the youths—his own nephew, he said—as a guide.

A commotion intervened. Torches could be seen, mounting the slope from the watershed valley. "The priests," someone cried. "Returning from the Three Ways."

At once all decampment ceased. The people swarmed toward the arrivals. Telamon and the children swelled this crush.

The envoys were two, an older man and a younger, leading a single mule. Grieving relations surrounded them, eager for their report. How many were slain? Had any survived? What did the envoys find?

The priests distributed bundles from the devastated village—such possessions or personal effects of relatives as had not been lost to fire or pillage. A great number of these were taken in hand by the kin of the massacred. Toward the end, the elder of the priests produced a small parcel "for the child who came."

This was for Ruth.

Few among the villagers took notice of this exchange. The priest himself handed off the bundle with barely a glance.

But the child Ruth received this parcel with grave appreciation.

The bundle was wrapped in a doeskin pouch cinched at its neck with a rawhide thong. David moved beside Ruth to help and to see. Telamon stood at the child's opposite shoulder.

The parcel, the priest was saying, had been put together specifically for Ruth, by her kin, apparently years earlier, in anticipation of her eventual arrival. It held items sent home from foreign lands over a period of a decade or more by her mother.

The girl did not tug excitedly at the wrapper or eagerly tear the bundle open. Her eyes were wide with trepidation. She glanced first to Telamon, then to David.

Roundabout, numbers of the mountain people were undergoing the identical proceeding—taking into their possession the terminal effects of their lost loved ones.

Ruth opened her packet and withdrew its contents—an ebony stylus and a wooden tablet with a beeswax writing surface, along with a sheaf of mismatched documents in Latin and Greek—common army administrative papers, orders, reports, invoices for materiel, many of these dog-eared and torn, with cross-outs and excisions. The papers were apparently scribal stuff thrown away by army secretaries. It was, David thought, the sort of discarded material that an unlettered individual might use to teach herself the alphabet and the shape and sense of the written word.

Ruth could find nothing more. She probed the pouch twice, even turning it inside out to scour its innards.

She glanced to Telamon in what seemed to be despair, then slumped, crestfallen.

David took the child's shoulder to comfort her, but she flung his hand off and turned away.

The youth faced toward Telamon. "What was she looking for?"

"A sign," said the man-at-arms.

"Of what?"

"Of something," he answered, "that would link her and me by blood."

Several of the mountain people, witnessing this exchange, drew up in their preparations of decampment. They turned toward the man and child. No few stepped closer to observe the moment.

Telamon crossed to Ruth and knelt, setting himself at her eye-level. The child remained faced away from him. She did not turn back.

The man-at-arms addressed her with great tenderness.

"You were thinking that I might be your father. That was your hope when you searched through your bundle, wasn't it? To discover some artifact or correspondence that would establish this."

The child offered no response, either by sign or posture.

"Of all the soldiers of all the legions in all the lands," said Telamon, "and all the thousands of women who followed them?"

Ruth remained faced away. Yet her bearing indicated that indeed this was, against all odds, what she had hoped.

Telamon reckoned this.

"Will you hear the truth?" he said. "I wished this too. I have been calculating the years and the months . . ."

At this, the child turned back. Her glance searched Telamon's eyes, as if to confirm for herself that his words were the truth.

"But of the time that your mother and I might have crossed paths and, unknown to me, produced a child of your years . . . I was, for that full interval, on punishment duty in the desert, laboring on the aqueduct that the three of us passed. No furlough. No leave. No women."

One of the council elders, overhearing this exchange, stepped forward. Addressing not alone Telamon and the children, but all who attended upon this proceeding, he declared as follows:

"If the child indeed can identify no father of blood, it seems to me that heaven will take scant offense if she chooses, now, one of her own."

David took to this idea at once. So, apparently, did the main of the others attending. The youth turned to the girl to see if she shared this feeling.

Ruth answered in sign.

"What did she say?" asked the elder.

David replied. "She said, 'I have chosen one already.'"

In that instant, the council chief of the mountain men reined in above Telamon. "Collect your kit," he commanded. "You must move out at once." The chief declared the Roman attack force was marching south even now. He motioned to his nephew, the guide, to take charge of the man-at-arms' party. "My boy will lead you by tracks that those sons-of-whores will never find."

On all sides village families were packing out, on foot as well as mounted, upon different traces and trails heading deeper into the mountains.

The chief, on horseback, gestured in farewell to Telamon. "The Roman lieutenant," the man said, "told one last thing of Corinth."

The mercenary drew up.

David and Ruth turned toward the headman as well.

"They're burning it," he said. "Four legions, called in from as far away as Moesia and Macedonia. The Romans are torching the city, end to end."

BOOK ELEVEN

CORINTH

– 40 –

MENS BELLATOR

L IKE ALL GREEK CITIES, CORINTH is constituted of two distinct municipal entities—"the city," *asty*, and *chora*, "the town." To this in Corinth's case must be added a third division—the two harbors, Lechaeum and Cenchreae.

David ranged through the first two, sent in by Telamon to reconnoiter. A boy alone, the mercenary reckoned, would be the least likely scouting configuration to draw attention to itself. Unarmed and garbed as a common youth of the street, David could roam anywhere and enter any precinct. He could slip in and out of crowds and assemblies, strike up conversations with strangers, and even interrogate, feigning innocent curiosity, legionaries and officers of the constabulary. Pretending to be upon an errand or seeking, say, to deliver a message, a boy could ask directions, inquire of the unit names and dispositions of troops. He could ask about the underground communities.

The topography of Corinth is as follows:

The High City, the Acrocorinth, ascends above the town upon a natural eminence at once awe-inspiring and spectacularly defensible. Walls with five great gates secure the citadel, of which the most famous is the Dipylon, the Double Gate. Behind its battlements, which are thirty meters high at the city's most vulnerable point, the southeast, and ten meters thick at its deepest, the city is banked and uneven, following the rugged shape of the land. Streets are steep, lanes narrow and stepped. The central avenue is so precipitous it is called "the Staircase" and in some places "the Ladder."

The Roman administration of Corinth is headquartered at offices in the South Stoa, the central open space of the High City. Corinth has two markets—the Roman Market and the Greek Market. The grounds and covered stalls of both had been commandeered to make depots and command centers for elements of four legions—the Fifth Macedonica, the Seventh Claudia Pia Fidelis, the Eighth Augusta, and the First Germanica. Troops of these legions were quartered in cantonments about the city and in march-camps they had erected themselves. Cohorts of the first two legions had rotated between Moesia and Dalmatia, their operating bases, and Corinth for the preceding twenty-seven months to maintain order and to hold the restive Greeks in subjection. The latter two had been called forward from Novae in Moesia and Colonia Agrippipensis on the Lower Rhine to reinforce the first two in suppressing the rising unrest produced not only by the underground Christian movement and the reaction to the crackdown upon this, but also by a reinvigorated Corinthian irredentism that sought to restore the autonomy and self-determination of old. The heavier Rome's hand had become, the more bitterly the subject populace resented it and the more violently it resisted.

Below the Acrocorinth sprawls the chora, the town, carpeting the slopes that descend to the north, west, and south of the citadel and spread out from the highways leading to the two ports, Lechaeum to the northwest on the Corinthian Gulf and Cenchreae on the southeast, facing onto the Saronic Bay. These lanes are home to the commons, the secondary marketplaces and gymnasiums, and the suburbs cascading down to the harbors.

From Arcadia, the forty-mile trek to Corinth should have taken two or at most three days for a party hale and in fettle. It took six for Telamon and the children. The mercenary dismissed the guide on the second morning, for the fellow's own sake. The youth was distraught with care for his family back in the mountains.

From the second morning trekking north, though yet more than thirty-five miles from the city, the party began encountering refugees. Families passed on foot, drawing carts and barrows. All were fleeing for the interior.

"Are you Christians? From Corinth?" David asked one particularly ragged congregation. "Tell us, what is the state of the city?" The fugitives hastened past without speech. Others who did stop inquired only the way south. How far to the frontier? Troops ahead? A town with a market?

Telamon's resources had begun seriously to fail. He could not maintain the pace even of an ancient, but must rest at the end of each quarter hour to recover his trim and gird himself for the next section of passage.

A change had occurred in the emotional correspondence between the man-at-arms and the child Ruth. David observed this alteration with bewilderment at first, then a curious and self-reproaching envy. Man and girl no longer communicated by sign or, on Telamon's part, by spoken word. Ruth trekked in the lead; the mercenary struggled to bring up the rear, with David in between.

Was the cause of this embarrassment, on both their parts, the exposure, indeed self-exposure, of the inmost holdings of their hearts? Telamon for his part would no longer accept assistance from the girl, as he had previously, either to mount or descend a troublesome passage of the trail, nor would he permit her to ease his burden in establishing or striking camp. He avoided her gaze, as she ducked his. Yet, despite this surface estrangement, the two seemed to David to have melded in some undeclared manner into a unit, hermetic and indisseverable. Each appeared to ken the other's thoughts without gesture or speech and, in fact, to anticipate the other's intentions and to respond or initiate action in advance. In the lead the girl, coming upon a fork in the trail, of which dozens presented themselves within a day's tramp, retarded her advance only a moment, as if seeking upon the air some sign or indication from the man-at-arms, who trekked, often so far to the rear that he could not possibly reckon that a route decision was even necessary; then, as if sensing some direction from him, she led right or left, and decisively so.

A hundred questions tumbled through David's mind. He wished

desperately to interrogate the girl alone, or Telamon, or the pair of them together. Yet when he approached either, even in silence, each immediately threw up a barrier, invisible but impenetrable.

Only once could David achieve a glimmer of insight. The man-at-arms continued his instruction of both children in the manual of arms. Concluding one such session, in which Ruth had exceeded David not only in assimilation of instruction but in force of application, Telamon took the youth aside. He spoke confidentially, for the boy alone.

"What I have been teaching you and Ruth is called in the legions *mens bellator*, 'warrior mind.' I have known men who fought bravely and well for twenty years but who still had not mastered this. This girl has it already. That's why she's better at exercise of arms than you are. Do not fault yourself on this account. The child simply has the gift. She is a complete warrior already. Do not compete with her. Fight at her side. Be proud of her. Learn from her."

On the sixth morning, the party reached the Hill of the Dolphins, looking out upon the Acrocorinth and the Corinthian Gulf. This eminence, famous throughout Hellas for its wayfarers' shrine and its half-sized bronze of the goddess Mercy, into whose cupped palms travelers deposited coins meant to be taken up by others in need, had been reconfigured into a roadblock and interdiction point manned by imperial troops and cavalry. Access in and out was debarred. Built up on the eastern flank of this complex was a massive and squalid bivouac of refugees and families attempting to flee the city. The highway junction and the environs for acres roundabout had become a legion march-camp, fenced with a palisade and fortified by earthworks including a fifteen-foot ditch with sharpened stakes. Telamon recognized the banners of the Fifth Legion, the Macedonica.

The party snaked around these encampments, finding after an interval of investigation an unfrequented copse of pine with a vantage, around a dogleg, over the harbor of Lechaeum and the northwest suburbs of the city.

They could see smudges of smoke above the port and hear clashes in the distance. To the south, a double line of Roman picket vessels blockaded the bay.

Telamon addressed the children. "It is no easy thing to burn a city. The occupying force advances precinct by precinct. There's a science to it. The Romans know it well."

Telamon told of the razing of Corinth two hundred years previous. The consul Lucius Mummius with two legions—twenty-three thousand infantry and thirty-five hundred cavalry—defeated thirteen thousand infantry of the Greek Achaean League. The males of the city were put to the sword and the women and children sold into slavery. "This was the same year that Carthage fell. The cities' fates were identical, except that Corinth was left to be resettled at the conquerors' whim."

The hour had come for Telamon to dispatch David into the metropolis. He sat the boy and Ruth down, addressing them gravely. "You understand, I would perform this reconnaissance myself—"

"You would be spotted in a moment," said David. "Even in disguise. It must be me."

The man-at-arms made certain that David had gotten food into his belly. He rehearsed the boy in what intelligence he, Telamon, needed; the most likely places to secure this information; and how to conduct himself, should he be stopped by soldiers or officers of the constabulary.

"The leader of the Christian community, we know from Severus, is a man called 'Simon of the Harbor.' But which harbor—Lechaeum or Cenchreae? Is this individual even still alive? Where? If he is fled or murdered, who stands in his place? Failing to ascertain Simon's whereabouts, is the woman named Miriam, his sister, to hand? Or the other, Josepha called Parthenos, 'the Virgin'?"

Telamon briefed David in the descent of the trail from the pine grove and, more critically, the route back, which must be negotiated in darkness. "You cannot carry a weapon. There will be patrols and checkpoints everywhere."

The man-at-arms went over with David proper practices for negotiating the curfew—cut-off times would be different in different quarters and may be amended capriciously at the whim of a precinct commander—with especial emphasis upon the hour by which, at the latest, the youth must make his way out of the city, as well as what sign and countersign he must use and recognize when he returned to the pine copse.

Ruth listened to these instructions intently.

Telamon saw in both children's eyes the recognition that the ultimate trial stood at hand.

"What you two have learned," he stressed to them, "is the mind of battle. Embrace it as you have, and despite your tender years you will be objects of terror, even to the vaunted Romans."

Telamon handed David his own last portion of kishar, dried goat meat, and his carry-skin of wine. He addressed the youth soberly.

"Tell me. What did your father train you to be?"

David's expression showed he did not understand.

"What calling or vocation? What was your father's fondest wish for you?"

The youth answered at once. "A rav. He wanted me to be a rav."

"What is a rav?"

"A teacher. A kind of priest."

The boy felt himself flush to declare this ambition. He glanced on the instant toward Ruth, then turned with an expression of discomposure back to Telamon.

"It is true, I cannot read or write. But I can recite the Books of Moses end to end."

Telamon regarded the youth.

"A teacher," he said, and set a hand warmly upon the boy's shoulder. "This night, perhaps, you will teach me something I have never known."

41

THE CITY AND THE TOWN

D AVID STAYED IN THE CITY fourteen hours. He could have made his way out sooner, having acquired with ease the intelligence Telamon sought. He chose to stay. He was enjoying himself.

The polis of Corinth was being put to the torch, but in a desultory, most un-Roman-like fashion. Elements of four legions, as David confirmed now at firsthand, had concentrated upon the site, each apparently refusing to consult the others or to work in coordination with them. The populace had either vacated or been herded into provisional camps to await the conquerors' pleasure.

Nature herself seemed to conspire in the protracted, agonizing reduction of the city. All morning, storms rolled in off the gulf, retreating briefly—the signal to Roman firebrands to resume their labors—then returning, quenching and frustrating, for an interval anyway, the *incendiarii*'s endeavors.

David ranged the city with impunity. Packs of youths, locals and incomers from the countryside prowled the lanes seeking loot and excitement. David fell in with several of these gangs. Telamon had instructed him to acquire the identities of the legions and their commanders. How many? Where camped? With orders to do what?

From the boys, and later with his own eyes, David learned that a detachment of the Tenth Fretensis was here from Judea. "Commanded by whom? Arrived when?"

An hour of investigation, and David had his answer.

Severus.

Marcus Severus Pertinax, senior tribune and commander of the garrison of Jerusalem, was here with two companies of the Tenth Legion. These had crossed by sea, a sergeant of this very detachment informed David, from Judea via Pelusium in Egypt. Two Moesia-based legions, the Fifth Macedonica and the Eighth Augusta, were the ones doing most of the dirty work. These had made a demonstration of burning the High City, sparing the Greek and Roman markets, the law courts, both Stoas, the imperial administration buildings, the Bouleterion, and the Temple of Apollo. Over sixty thousand inhabitants of the town and the city had been displaced or detained.

"What of the Nazarene communities?" David asked.

"Dead or crucified, save an odd lot or two still at large."

"Where would they be?"

The sergeant touched the leather purse at his hip.

"There's a silver actium in it for you, boy, if you find out and tell none but me."

Like the fortified camp that David, Telamon, and Ruth had encountered on the Hill of the Dolphins, the legions had thrown up campaign-style bivouacs with staked ditches and palisaded walls in a number of locations about the city, including the Ball Fields; both extremities of the Diolkos, the portage road between Lechaeum and Cenchreae; and upon the entry lanes to both harbors.

David found no trouble entering these camps. Though the city was being incinerated precinct by precinct, commerce in day-to-day necessities continued to be conducted with undiminished vigor. David advanced to the portal of a *castrum* just outside the High City. Barefoot in his dirty tunic, displaying only a cast-off dispatch scroll he had picked up as trash in the street, he called out, "Laundry pickup!" He was waved in without so much as a glance.

Camp streets were mud. Within the walls, six great pits of smoldering sulfur had been set up, from which incendiaries—not legionaries only, but contractors of the towns roundabout and even volunteers from the city itself—acquired their firebrands and ignited them. Piles of filthy, tar- and tow-spattered tunics sat outside the *contubernia*, the eight-man tents of the legionaries. David grabbed several and slung them over his shoulder. With these and a brisk stride, he could move with impunity throughout the camp.

One hour in, he spotted Severus.

The commander cantered past at the head of a company of equites. The hour was nearly noon. "Who is that?" David asked a corporal standing beside the mire track that was the camp's *via principalis*. "From Judea," the fellow answered. "Some big auger, come in by sea."

David dumped his bundle and scurried in the outfit's train. Severus's troop exited the camp onto the flat outside the Dipylon Gate, called in pre-Roman days the Ball Fields but now the Campus Martius, the Field of Mars. The column crossed the High Street that lapped the citadel upon the west-facing side, and thundered down the hill called the Street of the Tripods for its lineup of hero shrines. The pavement of cobbles was slick from the ongoing downpour. A horse lost its footing and spilled, slinging its rider and skidding downhill with eyes wild and all four legs thrashing. Half a dozen others tumbled as well, snarled in the pileup.

At the head of the column, Severus saw and heard nothing. The detachment pounded away into the lower quarter toward Lechaeum harbor. Behind the tribune's company came two others, moving as fast and fanning out. In the train of these, apparently from tributary camps, came infantry legionaries in their visorless Gallic helmets with their crests black in the rain and their rear deflectors sluicing the deluge. They wore segmented armor without cloaks. They carried firebrands as well.

David followed on foot. All through the postnoon he ranged across quarters that seemed abandoned when Roman forces transited, only to spring to life in the aftercourse of their passage. He approached and put questions to half a score of freebooting youths and looters, as well as numbers of armed partisans erecting barricades, housedames defending their streets with brooms and cudgels, and elders denouncing the occupiers and urging their compatriots to resistance with fiery harangues. David could locate with certainty neither the seat of local political resistance (apparently no such site existed) nor learn the hiding places of the Nazarene underground.

Yes, the youth determined, the rebel called Simon of the Harbor yet lived and fought, though where and in what manner none could or would say. The "harbor" of his name was Lechaeum. That, half a dozen confirmed.

Night was coming down. A steady downpour continued to sluice off the rooftops of the city. David decided he had acquired enough intelligence to permit Telamon to determine the next step. To linger would risk being cut off by a curfew or cause his master to fear he had been killed or captured—and stir him into hazarding an incursion prematurely.

The boy would go back.

He traversed the potters' quarter, called the Keramicos, and the Roman agora, keeping to shadow, seen, he was certain, by no one. As he climbed the hill to the pine copse David rehearsed what he would report and in what order he would report it. He felt pride in himself. He was eager to impart his intelligence to Telamon. He felt certain that the man-at-arms would approve his work and praise him.

Dropping prone some thirty paces shy of the summit, David hissed the password. He had to do this twice before receiving the countersign.

The youth scurried forward, keeping low to the ground. He entered the grove in a crouch beneath boughs, from the northwest, the quadrant from which he had departed.

The first thing he saw was Telamon, on his feet, arming.

Behind the mercenary and hunkered over a dimly flickering smudge of tow knelt Ruth. David glimpsed an unwound scroll and some kind of stylus. The girl was scribing something.

"What has happened? What's going on?"

Ruth's hand stopped moving.

"Keep going," Telamon commanded the child. He continued cinching the rib straps of his armor.

David's eyes strained in the gloom.

He spotted a third figure.

A woman.

Wild, tangled mane.

Burning eyes.

The hair stood up all over David's body.

"What?" he said. "How?"

The sorceress crabbed forward into the glimmer.

Ruth signed to David: *Telamon has changed his mind. He's going in alone. He won't let us come with him.*

The man-at-arms caught David by the elbow.

"Sit down," he said, "and shut up."

42

AN ARTICLE OF VALUE

DAVID STARED AT THE WITCH. "How did this she-devil get here?" He turned to Telamon. "Is she a ghost?"

The man-at-arms ordered David to sit. The youth was too agitated even to hear. He attempted to impart to his master such intelligence as he had acquired in his reconnaissance of the city. Half or more, it seemed, had flown from his mind. He reported that the Christian leader Simon was apparently alive and in the fight, though he, David, had not verified this by sight, and that the "harbor" of the man's cognomen was the western port of Lechaeum.

Clearly Telamon had divined the essence of the remainder of David's account—from the smoke above the citadel, from the frantic traffic upon the arteries leading out, and from what he knew of the ways of war and the practices of the legions.

The man-at-arms put one word only to David:

"Severus?"

The boy's expression answered.

"You're certain? Absolutely?"

"I saw him, sir. Tracked him for most of an hour."

Ruth rose on her feet now too.

"Keep your seat," Telamon commanded. "Finish your writing."

The girl defied him, signing again to David that the man-at-arms intended to hold them both out of the final action.

He would not let them fight.

David strained to take all this in. He turned again toward the witch.

"How did you get here? How did you cross the sea?"

The sorceress laughed. "I flew."

David felt his temples flush. He advanced on the woman as if to strike her. Telamon caught him by the elbow.

"I was brought by Severus, you nincompoop!" the witch said. "As a captive for the amusement of the legionary scum who serve beneath him."

David glowered at her. "She's lying! She was turned loose by the Romans to find us!" He stalked to the edge of the copse, to a break in the foliage that opened onto a vantage over the slope below. "Where are they, you battleaxe?" Turning to Telamon, he declared, "We must kill her. Kill her now and get away from here!"

Telamon continued to arm himself, absent haste. He addressed the sorceress. "Are you sent by Severus?"

"May his bowels roast in hell."

"Why are you here, then? How did you find us?"

"I have come to help you, peregrine . . ."

The sorceress held out, in both hands, a bundle of herbs—apparently the produce of her most recent collection.

"Ha!" cried David with fiery emphasis. "What fools do you think we are?" He swiped at the offering to beat it from the witch's grasp. "Take your poison away from here, before we split your guts as we should have the first time we saw you!"

The woman plucked the packet back, preserving it. David advanced upon her to strike again.

"What happened to your 'zeal,' witch? Don't tell us you feel shame over your butchery of Michael . . ."

The sorceress blanched at this, but held her ground. "Zeal takes many forms, my young friend, and may be in the service of the Almighty applied in many enterprises."

"Meaning what?" said Telamon. He studied the woman. "What did the Romans do to you on that ship?"

"Nothing they haven't done before to any in their grasp. And as for finding you, this was no chore." The witch indicated David. "Half a dozen witnessed this ragamuffin commence his clamorous hill-climb a quarter hour past. Another score saw him prowling the city."

David again urged Telamon to put a finish to the woman, or permit him to do so. The youth repeated his accusation that the witch had sought the party out at the command and in the service of Severus and the Romans.

"Kill her and let's go!"

Throughout this confrontation, the child Ruth's gaze remained fixed upon Telamon. The mercenary continued his arming with all care and deliberation. He displayed, as far as the girl could reckon, neither ire nor intention to visit harm upon the sorceress.

David stared, wondering too at this restraint.

The very audaciousness of the sorceress's apparition, here before Telamon and the children, after all the treachery she had worked upon them and Michael heretofore, not to mention the daring she displayed by proffering again her wares of drugs, had made the man-at-arms, it seemed, against all conventional consideration, take the woman seriously. The witch read this in his eyes.

"I read the letter," she said.

Telamon glared. "What?"

"The missive of the Apostle. The Romans . . . that runt corporal, accompanied by his lieutenant . . . came down to me in the bilges. I was chained there. They bore a lamp and the letter."

"Don't believe her!" cried David. "This is more treachery!"

The sorceress's voice stayed even.

"They had copies, they said. Four other letters dispatched by the Apostle besides the one you bear. All had been intercepted. Entire cities have been put to the torch, the lieutenant said, to wrest these from those who carried them."

Ruth's eyes remained upon Telamon. The man-at-arms' glance to the witch commanded her to continue.

"He read the letter to me, the lieutenant. He claimed it was to reward me, to show that my wish to interdict the epistle had been fulfilled."

Telamon's expression again commanded the witch to continue.

"But the lieutenant's aim was only to torture me—to demonstrate that no act of revolution, however daring, could hope to succeed against the legions of Rome.

"Take this," the sorceress again urged Telamon, holding out her bundle of herbs.

"What," the man-at-arms asked, "do you care about the letter, beyond stopping it? Why do you even bring it up?"

"I might ask, mercenary, the same of you. You haven't read it, have you? Its contents mean nothing to you. So it was with me."

The witch declared that she had crossed to Corinth from Pelusium in a Roman flotilla transporting Severus and two cohorts assembled from Alexandria and Jerusalem. She confirmed such intelligence of the legions as David had gathered in the city. The emperor, the woman said, has sent the First Germanica from its base on the Rhine. He has had force-marched three cohorts of the Fifth Macedonica and two of the Eighth Augusta from Singidunum in Moesia. The Seventh Claudia in its entirety was already on its way from Dalmatia. What had begun as a punitive exercise aimed at the Messianic communities had enlarged into a campaign against all malcontents and insurgents of a reenergized and renationalized Greece.

The Christian communities, the sorceress said, had broken apart under the pressure of this overwhelming force. Half or more of the communards had fled. The leaders of what was left were a brother and sister, Simon and Miriam, and a prophetess named Josepha, called Parthenos, the Virgin.

Telamon stopped her. "Why," he demanded again, "are you here?"

David faced the witch, clutching his dolabra.

Ruth stood now too, dagger in hand.

The sorceress answered in a voice of such muted sobriety that her listeners had to strain forward to hear.

"Whatever I or others may have thought, or may yet think, of this self-styled 'Apostle,' he is a prophet inspired by heaven. His words will be the finish of Rome. They must reach all who will hear them."

The sorceress turned to David.

"This, boy," she said, "is my zeal."

Telamon regarded her.

He glanced first to David, then to Ruth, then back to the woman.

"What's in the bundle?" he asked.

The sorceress stepped up before him, extending the packet of medicaments.

"For the span of one sentry's watch," she said, "you will fight with the strength of three men."

43

CORINTH

T HE STORM BROKE IN FULL with nightfall.

Telamon could keep neither the boy nor the girl, nor the witch, from dogging his descent into the city. They tracked him at first, maintaining their distance. As darkness and the violence of the downpour enlarged, however, the three pressed closer. At the head of the Street of the Tripods, they caught up completely.

All the man-at-arms' curses could not drive them away.

Where the lanes conjoined, two vendors' carts and a freight wagon had been overturned, apparently by the citizens in revolt, to form a barrier to the quarter that ascended to the west and north of the square. Whatever violent clash between the locals and the occupiers had taken place here was only minutes over. Telamon and the others scurried across a plaza strewn with paving stones, clearly torn up from the street and hurled as missiles. A litter of splintered staves and shivered tool handles squealed underfoot, along with the sodden remains of torn garments and the ripped remnants of boots and shoes. Two bodies, one male and one female, lay across the shattered spine of a door, apparently part of a barrier blocking a lower lane. Both corpses were barefoot and bareheaded. Every meter of the square was carpeted with the jagged shards of roof tiles and clay crockery, no doubt flung from rooftops onto the imperial troops, and strewn at intervals with mounds of ordure—the larger from horses, the smaller from men—leaching to liquid in the downpour.

"They're driving them to the harbor," someone cried.

"Driving who?" David called.

"The Nazarenes!" the fellow answered, and raced away in that direction. Telamon followed at a pace that his strength would permit. David and Ruth flanked him on either side. The witch sprinted ahead.

Everything in Corinth runs downhill from the High City. Storms in winter, like this night's, send torrents coursing down the steep cobbled streets and sluicing along the stairstepped lanes. Great curvilinear storm drains, surmounted by iron grates stout enough to support the passage of a laden wagon and team, bear away the runoff first into a network of underground cisterns and catchment basins, then into overflow tunnels, down which the flood cascades in volume onto the streets of the Lower City and from there, through other drains and runoff channels, into the harbor precinct and the Corinthian Gulf.

The twin ports of Corinth are the greatest in Greece. Lechaeum's northwest-facing waterfront runs for twenty-nine stades—nearly four Roman miles. Every meter of it, excepting the naval base at Posidonia, is yardarm-to-yardarm with docks and repair facilities, commercial wharves and warehouses, trading establishments, chandleries, and the factories and shops of sail-benders, carpenters, and naval architects.

Every lane of the port, when Telamon and the children careered in, was awash with storm runoff and swarming with citizens in flight.

The Gulf-facing lane that front the harbor is called *To Miselino*, "the Crescent." Peering down this, Telamon could see several formations of troops half a mile ahead, driving citizens before them. In the mad distemper of city fighting, other masses of locals, great throngs, flooded onto the waterfront avenue, rushing in the wake of the legionaries.

Telamon and the children hastened after this mob. All three wore hooded cloaks, drenched now and dark with the wet, beneath which they concealed their weapons. Ahead, David could see the witch, catching the arms of various dames and wenches in the street. The sorceress pointed first in one direction, then another. The object of her interrogation would respond, *No, not this way. There.*

David spilled on the roadway. His dolabra sprang free and clattered away across the stones. He could see Telamon turn with a fierce look. The youth scrambled and snatched the weapon up.

The witch came scampering back to the man-at-arms. She was speaking urgently and gesticulated with vehemence toward the harbor alleys, those abutting the Crescent.

The slope from the High City here dropped precipitously to the waterfront. Gutters raged with runoff. David fell and fell again. Sprinting past an open square, some kind of carters' or teamsters' runway, the youth glimpsed numbers of cavalry horses absent their riders, bawling and wild-eyed, being herded frantically by legion grooms. Their dragoons had apparently dismounted to work their havoc on foot. The steep slick lanes clearly were leg-breakers in the downpour.

The sorceress scurried in the lead. She had become the party's navigator. Telamon limped, grabbing at handholds against walls and along fence facings. Ruth darted at his side, never leaving him. The company had reached the water. Skiffs and dinghies bobbed beside wooden docks and within stone and timber berths. People were fleeing, in pairs and clusters that looked like kin groups, into the alleys that made tributaries off the Crescent.

Christians?

David glimpsed, ahead, a line of open-sided, tile-roofed shelters. Broad sloping eaves, a hundred feet and more end-to-end, sheltered berths cut from stone beside wharf-like platforms projecting into the harbor.

"*To Neorion,*" someone said.

Ship sheds.

The naval base.

The witch scurried ahead, past the shelters—twenty, thirty in a row, all but a few vacant.

Suddenly in the party's path: Romans.

A skirmish line of legionaries, in armor, shields braced before them, materialized from the downpour. Their unbroken front blocked the lane completely.

"There!" shouted the sorceress. She pointed toward what looked like a cave complex in the townside slope.

Into this opening, men and women dashed in dozens, many carrying infants and dragging small children.

The witch waved Telamon urgently to follow.

He did.

David and Ruth raced beside.

The caves were warehouses of naval stores—sails and ropes, fixed and hanging tackle, wine in great jars, oil, grain. The fleeing population poured into these catacombs. David heard hobnails ringing on stone behind him. The legionaries thundered into the tunnel. The fugitives were already in near-total darkness.

The throng turned a corner, and another.

They were now in some kind of sewer or overflow channel.

Faint light ahead.

David heard shouts. "This way! Hurry!"

The gasping, ragged mob emerged from the tunnel into a broad domed chamber sluicing with storm runoff from above. Faint light came from overhead through an iron drainage grate. People were running across this in the lane topside. Floodwater cascaded in torrents onto the fugitives below.

Ahead down a passageway David could see armed men. Not Romans. The men were waving the fugitives forward, shunting them up an adjacent stone stairway.

These guardsmen—shomrim Jews, apparently, of the Nazarene sect—formed a checkpoint, through which the refugees in flight must pass.

The men were checking faces, waving forward those they knew, rejecting all others.

David could see one kin group, including babes and ancients, being turned forcefully back. The rebuff was vigorous and violent. Even at a distance David could make out the whites of the guardsmen's eyes above their masked and muffled faces. Shouts and footfalls of the pursuing legionaries echoed within the catacomb. The guardsmen appeared nearly as terror-stricken as the runaways who streamed past them.

The sorceress raced ahead to this chokepoint. She was shouting something in Aramaic to the guards. They were rebuffing her.

Telamon could only hobble, aided by Ruth as best she could.

David bolted ahead.

A second line of guards, behind the first and farther up the stairway, were dragging some kind of wood-and-iron barricade into place. The last of the fugitive families streamed past this.

"Get back!" one guardsman bawled at the sorceress. He struck at her with the butt-end of his staff.

David raced up to the guard. He indicated Telamon behind, and the girl. "These are the ones! They bring the letter from the Apostle!"

The same guard struck at David.

Two others blocked the boy and the witch. Both carried cudgels and raised them to strike.

"Betrayers!" the first guardsman shouted. "Do you think we are fools?"

From the tunnel behind came the Romans.

David felt Ruth tug his elbow. The family with the infants and elders was wriggling by turns into a pinched side channel with an iron grate door—a tributary storm drain of some kind. The entry was so narrow that only one person at a time could squeeze though.

"There!" cried the sorceress.

She propelled David in that direction. Telamon and Ruth plunged forward too. They had to hold up until the family with the little ones and the elders could be handed through.

David turned to Telamon. The man-at-arms appeared to be recovering his strength. Here came the Romans.

David and Ruth pushed through the tunnel entry. A torrent, icy and slick, struck them at thigh-height.

Against this they surged for half a dozen strides. David clutched at Ruth's arm. "Where's the witch?"

Both twisted rearward.

Through the slit entry partially blocked by the iron grate door the children could see Telamon and the sorceress—the final two figures still out in the main tunnel.

Upon these, bearing torches and swords, rushed the forwardmost element of the legionaries.

David could see Telamon clasp his gladius and turn to face the pursuers.

The sorceress seized his arm.

The mercenary jerked free and, raising his sword, made to turn upon the witch. Clearly he believed the woman was working treachery. The sorceress shouted something directly into Telamon's ear. David and Ruth could hear nothing over the echoing din of the tunnel and the floodwaters raging around them.

The Romans were within fifty feet now.

The witch was pointing toward the slit entry and the iron grate door. With both hands she sought to propel Telamon in this direction.

The mercenary resisted.

The sorceress pushed with greater impetus.

Suddenly she cackled—a great, gleeful croak that carried above the cacophony, even to David and Ruth's ears.

They saw Telamon turn from the witch and duck through the gratework door. He heaved against it from the inside and sealed it.

The last thing the children saw from their vantage within the tunnel was the sorceress, thrashing toward the Romans through the calf-deep flood and flinging herself, bare-handed, onto the shields and sword points of the onrushing legionaries.

The witch fell.

The Romans trampled over her.

David saw Telamon appear directly before him.

The mercenary turned him by the shoulder.

"Go! Now!"

Somehow they were outside.

Telamon sprinted before the children. He led them across a square.

They raced down a lane between shops, and another. The same fugitives and guardsmen fled ahead.

David's lungs felt on fire. His thighs seized like knots of wood. He had shucked his shoes. The soles of both his feet now bled. The throng ahead sprinted around a dark corner into a square under oaks.

Imperial cavalry waited.

Severus.

The lieutenant.

Someone shouted that "the Virgin" fled now among them. The name coursed the length of the column. It seemed to fire the partisans with courage.

David peered about him. The square appeared to be some sort of commercial enclosure—a broad rhomboid with stone walls on three sides.

A slave market.

The youth could see heavy iron rings mounted along the rearmost wall. To these would be chained the chattel, mustered in gangs of eight, called by the Romans *servorum* and by the Greeks *andropodoi* ("things with feet like a man") before each individual was unshackled and borne forward to the stand for auction.

The boy saw the stalls into which children for sale were herded and the covered pens where the purchased bondsmen were held for delivery to their new owners. The enclosure was in breadth half a furlong, a quarter that in depth.

Roman cavalry filled this open side end-to-end.

The fugitives jammed up at the narrow end, trapped within the walls like wild beasts at the gladiatorial games.

David thought, *What a place to die.*

At once a lone female—young, barefoot, dressed in white, with long, dark hair spilling from beneath a cowl that obscured her face—broke from the throng and sprinted forward into the open, toward the Romans. The woman tugged at several others, urging them to follow. All failed of courage. David saw several jerk free and flee back into the multitude.

The woman advanced alone. She was unarmed. She took up a position midway between the Romans and her own people, facing the foe. With a swipe of her hand she flung back the hood that concealed her face. David glimpsed a strong jaw and eyes of fire. The woman was shouting something the boy could not hear amid the storm and the cries of the fugitives calling her back.

The youth could see, behind him, ranks of insurgents forming into a mass. These were arming themselves with paving stones and roof tiles and loose timbers wielded as cudgels.

David heard a trumpet.

The line of horses charged.

In seconds the woman in white was overwhelmed.

Telamon's gladius sprang into his fist.

David saw Ruth clutch her dagger and her weighted darts.

The youth had barely drawn a breath before the equites were on him. He could not believe how quickly the cavalry covered the hundred paces between their skirmish line and that of the rebels. The riders came on "boot-to-boot." Their horses' breasts, striking the front ranks of the insurgents, seemed a wall of solid muscle. Their driving knees and booming hooves drove into the defenders like some great churning engine of harvest.

The guardsmen of the Nazarenes resisted like souls possessed. As the first and then second ranks of horses piled up against the sheer mass of the dissidents, the mounts' momentum slowed and then stalled.

David saw Telamon brace himself in the stance he called "castling." The blade of a cavalryman's swung saber missed the man-at-arms' skull by fractions. David saw Telamon's gladius drive forward and up, into the thigh of the rider above him. Horses are instinctively terrified of anything moving on the ground beneath their bellies. David saw one beast rear with panic in its eyes. Another followed, striking out blindly with its forehooves.

The Romans' mounts began balking. Before and beneath the animals, defenders struck with staves and timbers. Many wielded pitchforks and quarterstaffs. Apparently the rebels had experience dealing with mounted troops in confined spaces.

Reinforcements of the insurrectionists began arriving, or perhaps these were simply the rearmost ranks swelling forward. In the crush David could glimpse only shadows. He saw rooftops swarming with resisters. From these elevated vantages men and women, and children as well, were slinging bricks and tiles onto the bunched-up horsemen. Cavalry's worth, David knew, was in its speed and mobility on the open field and in the emotional terror produced by its seemingly irresistible rush. When such mounted forces are penned within a straitened compass, however, the mass becomes immobilized and its virtues of size and scale become liabilities.

From crouched positions beneath the horses' bellies the defenders poked and thrust with spears and daggers. They struck even with bare hands. The beasts above them reared and bellowed. David could see the lieutenant bawling to his troopers to dismount and fight on foot. The cavalrymen's down-slashes with their spathas were not only worthless against the crouched mass of insurrectionists but actively exposed each trooper, as his striking arm fell, to the fate of being seized from below and hauled from his saddle.

What had happened to the woman in white?

David, penned in the press beneath the horses, glimpsed for an instant this vision of a deliverer. She was alive! Defenders on the rooftops were hauling her clear of the fray. Somehow she had avoided being trampled.

Now further subversives appeared. These hurled themselves forward with the fury of desperation. They had broken out doors from the buildings of the slave market to use as shields and barricades. In pairs they bore heavy tables before them while hurling stones and pots and jars from behind these bulwarks. From the eaves of the slave pens, more rebels flung bricks and paving stones. David glimpsed one champion, bald as a goose egg, sending three sling bullets in a row ringing off the helmets of the horse troopers below.

"Simon!" someone cried exultantly.

David thought, *The leader!*

The boy turned back toward the center of the square. He saw the cavalry lieutenant, mounted above the crush, peer in the direction of this cry. The young officer's glance fixed upon the man Simon. Plainly his intention was to rush upon him. The lieutenant could not advance, however, not even a single stride, amid the teeming press.

David saw Telamon wade into the melee. The witch's medicaments had produced their miracle. As she had promised, the man-at-arms fought with the strength of three.

David saw him unhorse one dragoon with a hooking blow from the flank, then another and another. The mercenary did not loiter even to disable the men on the ground. Others of the rebels fell upon these. David himself swung his dolabra at the Romans' horses' knees. In such close quarters the weapon was miraculously effective. The beasts did not go down, but they reeled and reared in terror, lashing out with their forelegs.

Riders were tumbling everywhere. The technique of crab-walking that Telamon had taught Ruth and David proved spectacularly effective. Ruth slung her weighted darts from so close beneath the horse troopers that these missiles could not miss. The riders never even saw her. The girl hurled her darts point-blank into calves and thighs. With her dagger, she stabbed directly.

Again David spotted the Roman lieutenant. He was spurring his mount furiously, driving the animal within the crush, one stride at a time, toward the eave upon which the leader Simon stood. David thought, *If he keeps this course, I can reach him! I will burst my heart to land a blow.*

The youth waded forward, tucking his dolabra tight to his breast so it would not snag in the press. He thought only, *Let me get near the lieutenant! Lord of Hosts, let me get close enough to strike!*

But horses and grappling men intervened.

David pushed harder.

Through a screen of men on foot, the youth glimpsed the mounted officer. He was close, barely two sword-lengths away, driving toward the rebel leader Simon. The Nazarene champion, at the brink of a roof eave, was fending off another Roman, a foot soldier, who was thrusting a spear up at him from the square below. Simon's back was turned. He could not see the mounted officer coming.

David shoved forward with all his strength, crying out the Christian's name. But in the bedlam no sound could carry. The boy saw the lieutenant's saber elevate to strike a blow.

David raised his dolabra to intercept this. The lieutenant's blade drove downward upon the youth's with the multiplied force of a mounted man striking from above with a weapon that weighed twice that of the instrument that sought to interdict it. A dolabra is an entrenching tool. A pickaxe. Its soft untempered iron tore apart at the haft. David felt himself driven to his knees. In his fists he held a wooden shaft and nothing more.

Above him the lieutenant raised his blade again to strike.

At that instant a man leapt from an adjacent wall—one of the slave enclosures—headlong onto the Roman, hauling him rearward over his horse's crupper.

It was Telamon.

The man-at-arms and the lieutenant crashed together onto the ground beside David.

The youth sought to rise, but the cavalryman, with all the weight of his sodden cloak and armor, had pitched backward into him. David clutched at the officer's arms, to pinion him from behind.

Telamon saw this. With a single blow, delivered with such speed and force that the boy could barely see it, the man-at-arms struck the lieutenant between the eyes with the butt-end of his gladius. David heard the sickening sound of bone giving way. He saw the horrible sheet of red-black ooze gush from the cavity beneath the officer's brow and spill over the bridge of his nose to soak, augmented by heaven's deluge, into the void that was his mouth.

David felt his knees beneath him shudder, as the Roman's dead weight crashed full upon him. He felt the lieutenant's life rush forth with a burst that was almost a sigh.

"Get up!" Telamon bawled, extending his left hand toward David.

For an instant that seemed to the youth interminable, the space within the melee became still and inviolate.

All sound ceased.

No motion intruded.

The moment was like that at the Narrows, when David saw Telamon's arrow pass before his eyes within such a cone of heightened perception that he, the youth, could see the individual feathers of its vanes and the flex of its shaft as it flew.

David felt Telamon haul him to his feet. He sensed the mercenary pressing the grip of the lieutenant's fallen spatha into his fist. David saw Simon, the Christian leader, materialize beside Telamon. He saw him clap the man-at-arms upon the shoulder—a gesture, man to man, of gratitude and respect.

At that instant a second mounted officer burst forward into the circle of stillness. At once all sound and frenzy returned. David turned toward the intruder.

Severus.

The commander saw Telamon.

"You!" he cried.

The tribune's arms to the elbow were slick with gore and tissue. The steel of his saber was deformed and misshapen from the blows it had struck. Blood ran from his mount's jaw, sawn by the iron of the bit.

The commander's heels drove into his horse's flanks. The animal lurched forward. Its breast bowled into Telamon.

Severus's eyes within the frame of his helmet seemed to David like those of a wild beast.

Telamon struggled to sidestep the massive form driving into him, but the horse's churning knees and hooves overwhelmed him. The man-at-arms began to spill. David grabbed him to haul him clear. The youth felt Severus's spatha pass with a furious swish fractions from his left ear.

At this instant the child Ruth appeared directly before the Roman. She was standing at the brink of the eave of the slave pens, eye-to-eye with the tribune. In her fist she clutched a heavy clay roof tile.

The girl slung this with all her strength into Severus's face.

The tile struck the commander full in the teeth, shattering into shards against the cheek-pieces of his helmet. Severus's head rocked violently back. His left hand hauled rearward on the reins as his thighs, calves, heels, and knees clamped hard about his horse's rib cage.

A Roman cavalry mount—any mount, including this charger, which surely was not Severus's own but acquired here in Corinth from the cream of the on-site units—is trained from a colt to back clear of a press when it feels its rider reeling. This the tribune's horse did now.

In that instant, a great cry ascended from legionary reinforcements swarming into the square. They saw their commander struck. They marked his mount's withdrawal. The detachment, foot troops all, now flooded into the square. The mass of legionaries, above a hundred, did not charge blindly across the open center but divided into two flanking forces. Each wing took one wall of the slave pens, right and left, and surged along it with a front of four, in ranks a dozen deep. The insurgents, including Simon, fled before this irresistible advance.

David struggled to his feet. As earlier with the cavalry charge, his eyes could not believe the speed and violence with which the imperial troops had executed this evolution, which would have been difficult even on the parade ground. The youth turned to Telamon.

What he saw froze his blood.

The man-at-arms' face had turned the color of ash. His knees faltered.

Were the sorceress's drugs wearing off?

Legionaries at impossible speeds were rushing from both flanks toward Telamon.

The mercenary's glance to David said, *Flee!*

The boy could not.

Blows rained upon him. Again he went down. He saw Telamon battered by shield-strikes pummeling him from both sides.

The rebels bawled and howled from the slave pen rooftops.

Above the din, David heard Severus's voice.

"Leave him! He's mine!"

Two of the troopers had somehow gotten a rope about Telamon's shield arm. With this they lashed him to the slaver's post, using the very iron ring for which this upright had been planted. The man-at-arms strained but could not free himself.

"Back away! The man belongs to me!"

Severus had dismounted now.

His horse, superbly trained, did not balk or shy, but maintained its station, precisely where the tribune had stepped down.

The ring of legionaries withdrew, leaving the central space of the arena clear. Above on two sides, the insurrectionists hurled oaths and tiles. The foot troops below cleared them with volleys of arrows and javelins.

Severus advanced at a pace toward Telamon.

"Will you castle now, peregrine? Teach me, as once you did."

Telamon's strength seemed to have failed him utterly. He hung, exhausted, from the line that bound him to the slavers' post.

Severus pounded him backhanded upon the mercenary's sword side.

Somehow Telamon's gladius deflected the blow.

David cried and thrashed wildly to free himself from the grasp of the legionaries who held him.

The tribune remarked the boy for the first time. A dark glint lit his sockets.

"Your apprentice would preserve you." He spoke toward Telamon.

The mercenary hacked with all his strength at the bonds that lashed him to the slavers' post.

He could see Severus stepping toward David.

The tribune turned his speech now to the youth. "You and I are students of the same master," he said. "Show me what you have learned."

With a nod he commanded his troopers to release the boy. They did.

David hurled himself upon the tribune.

Severus's heavy spatha took the youth full in the belly. The boy ran onto the steel, bare hands stretching to claw at the commander's eyes.

A cry of agony broke from Telamon.

This wail echoed and resounded from the throats of hundreds.

With a final blow, the man-at-arms cut himself free.

In two strides he had reached Severus.

The commander had turned back toward his foe, eager to direct the same fate upon him that he had visited upon David.

But the youth would not let go of the tribune's spatha.

Impaled as he was, David's hands, both slashed open to the bone, grasped the commander's blade and held on.

Telamon's gladius entered the tribune's abdomen at a point below the nexus of the rib cage and drove upward in one practiced motion between the lungs and into the heart.

Cries of woe and exultation erupted from both witnessing sides.

With his last impulse of consciousness, David beheld Telamon's eyes. In them was rage and grief, but both were superseded by the cold, professional mask of predation.

In one motion Telamon slid his blade free of Marcus Severus Pertinax. The man-at-arms sheathed this weapon, and, lowering himself to one knee upon the rain- and blood-slick stones of the slave market square, seized with both arms David's life-fled form. The legionaries who had pinned the boy backed away before him. Telamon stood, lifting the youth onto his right shoulder. He bore him from the arena, as one comrade will for another fallen in battle.

44

OF MEN AND OF ANGELS

IT SEEMED EACH PERSON THEY chanced upon offered aid.
Guides materialized at each farmstead and crossroads. Tracks and footpaths were pointed out in the dark. Three times the parties in flight were led by strangers to gates in walls or pathways bypassing roadblocks— getaway routes that no person not intimate with the country would even know about, let alone be able to find.

Telamon yet bore David's body. Ruth hastened at the mercenary's shoulder. Twice, when he stumbled, she attempted to take the youth's weight upon herself. Her strength, however, was not equal to this; each time Telamon took the burden back. Clearly the man-at-arms' reserves had reached their limit. Ruth recalled the doctor Eryximachus's warning— that the mercenary's vulnerability would be in his lower extremities. The child watched Telamon lose his footing again and again.

Others among the refugees sought to assist him, to take the weight off his shoulders. The mercenary rebuffed this fiercely. He would permit no one to touch David's body, nor would he allow any to aid him in bearing it.

Ruth, in the moments when she could collect her thoughts, marveled at the fortuitousness by which the insurrectionists had escaped the slavers' impound. At Severus's end, the ring of legionaries, loosing a great cry of woe, had concentrated about their commander, retrieving his corpse behind a wall of their body-length shields. Cavalry closed in to protect the wings. This phalanx retreated, step by step, pelted from the eaves by salvo after salvo of stones and arrows and bricks.

The resisters clambered over the enclosure wall, making their escape across the roof beams and gables of the slave pens. Though numbers of these assisted in clearing a passage for Telamon and Ruth and indeed guided them in their flight, it was clear to the child that few, if any, knew who these strangers were or how they had come to be among their number.

Plainly none, including those who seemed to be leaders, were aware that they bore the letter of the Apostle.

Ruth clutched the scroll she had scribed in the pine copse. She did not know what to do with it.

About her the throng, which had numbered in the hundreds in its initial flight from the city, began to peel off into cells and groups, dispersing into the darkness upon tributary tracks and traces. Some fled east toward Attica and Athens, others took flight west along paths leading to Sicyon and Achaea and the islands of the Ionian Sea.

The main made off south into the Peloponnese.

Twice, when the companies rested, Ruth sought to press the Apostle's scroll into Telamon's hands. By sign she urged him to make himself and their errand known to one in authority.

The man-at-arms either would not or could not hear her. His eyes had gone the color of stone. His limbs seemed to have lost all sensation. He would not let go of David, nor would he permit the girl to aid him, even for a moment.

For what seemed like hours the parties in flight pressed on. Factions integrated, trekked in concert for an interval, then melted away into the dark. Ruth found herself trudging alongside one fellow or lass, only to discover each vanished with a quick clasp of the hand or a hasty farewell.

The storm had passed. At one lightless crossroads—the frontier to the Argolid, someone said—the child found herself in a group led by the woman in white from the slave market square.

This was, she learned, Josepha, called Parthenos, the Virgin. The lady's party at this juncture numbered less than two dozen, though other companies in greater numbers continued to stream through the intersection.

Ruth made a decision. Deliberately stepping apart from Telamon, and with premeditation electing not to inform him of her intention, she made her way to the Virgin. Others of the lady's company surrounded her. By sign the child sought to communicate that she and Telamon, along with the youth whose remains the mercenary carried, had made their way here from Jerusalem, bearing, for the Virgin herself and for the other community leaders, a letter from Paul the Apostle.

Ruth produced the scroll itself. She extended this in both hands to the lady.

To the child's astonishment, the Virgin rejected her. Her acolytes recoiled with even greater vehemence. The lady refused to speak with Telamon or even to permit him to be brought forward. She would not examine the letter, even to assess it for authenticity, nor would she countenance any of her attendants to do so.

Ruth could not understand. The child felt confusion, exasperation, even outrage.

The Virgin's reaction to her approach was one neither of anger nor hostility but rather of anguish and despair.

"For your own safety, leave this company!" the lady commanded Ruth, first in Greek, then in Aramaic and Hebrew. "If you follow, I cannot protect you."

Ruth reported nothing of this to Telamon. She struggled to make sense of it on her own.

Clearly, the girl apprehended, the Christian community of Corinth was riven. At least two factions—and apparently numerous splinter elements—contended for supremacy.

As night wore on and the elements of the community came together briefly in their flight, then parted to independent ways, Ruth sought to overhear such converse as might illuminate or dispel her state of consternation. Two men she tramped beside spoke of the Virgin and her faction. The hearts of these had been broken by the night's "victory" against their Roman persecutors.

"Why?" one asked the other.

"Because the act was accomplished through the employment of arms. We fought. We gave in to hatred. We took lives."

A matron, trekking at Ruth's shoulder for a quarter hour, spoke of Simon and his sister Miriam. The partisans of this faction reveled in the night's resistance and the coming together in action of the mass of the community. "This is how we will survive! There can be no other way."

As for the letter of the Apostle, its apparition at this hour—if indeed the epistle was genuine—was a matter of inconsequence to both camps. To followers of the Virgin, the Apostle's sacramental words could appear only as a bitter reproach and a measure of how far short the community had fallen of the ideals of faith and love to which it aspired. To adherents of Simon and Miriam, on the other hand, the letter, or that counterfeit peddled by knaves and double-dealers, could be regarded as nothing other than a ruse of Rome, meant to expose the community to murder and destruction.

By midnight, fear, fatigue, and exertion had exhausted the congregations in flight. Halts became dismayingly frequent. Companies with elders and minors began to fall out. Telamon himself could barely hobble. His kit and weapons must be borne by Ruth, who herself began to flag severely.

At last a peopled settlement came into view. Word coursed along the column.

Water!

Shelter!

Rest!

The factions came up one by one. The settlement was not even a hamlet but three freehold compounds within sight of one another along a narrow valley. The companies found a welcome. A springhouse with troughs relieved the fugitives' thirst. The column, which had become strung out for miles, now trudged in, element by weary element, to this site of refuge.

With a sign only to Ruth, Telamon bore David's body apart toward the loftiest and most remote redoubt immediately apparent—a notch beneath crags, some hundred feet above the first of the three compounds.

At the man-at-arms' direction the girl remained momentarily below, to fill her water skins and to make certain none of either faction followed up the hillside. Indeed, youths of both divisions, Simon's and the Virgin's, watched her every step. The child was careful to bespeak no one and to draw as little attention to herself as possible as she worked her way up the lines to the springhouse. She filled the skins and hastened, with vigorous strides despite her fatigue, back up the hill to Telamon.

The man-at-arms had scraped a trench, narrow but deep, at the eastern limit of the promontory. The site looked out over a pretty vantage beneath the moon. Ruth scurried up. Telamon had just finished winding David in his own campaign cloak. Together the man and the child lowered the youth's remains. Ruth looked on as the man-at-arms scooped and drove a fall of dirt and stone into the void that remained over their friend.

She thought, *How many times across decades has Telamon performed this dolorous service? And yet,* the child felt certain, *never heretofore has he enacted it in grief this profound.*

The mercenary stood. A glance told Ruth where she must take station.

The man-at-arms spoke one word only,

"RAV,"

then knelt and pressed, until its hilt had disappeared into the freshly overturned earth, the **x** dagger he had carried in his right boot since his time at the inn called the Foot of the Grade and earlier.

Ruth's concern in the instant was for Telamon. All strength seemed to have fled his limbs. Could he even rise?

As the child stepped forward to help, she heard a branch snap and glimpsed shapes advancing swiftly in shadow. Rough sounds came from the path below. Onto the site scrambled guardsmen and armed youths of the faction of Simon and Miriam.

Telamon and Ruth turned to face these.

The guardsmen surrounded them. The intruders' numbers were six, then eight, then ten. They were armed with drawn bows and quarterstaffs. The leader indicated the pair before him.

"Disarm them," he commanded the others. "Bring them now."

45

SIMON OF THE HARBOR

Despite their advantage of strength and numbers, the guardsmen could seize neither Telamon's gladius nor Ruth's dagger, so fiercely did the man and girl resist. Instead the shomrim beat the two with the butts of their eight-foot staffs. They bowled them off their feet with blows to shins and ankles.

The youths drove Telamon and Ruth downslope beneath a barrage of cuffs and wallops.

Down, down, down the path the pair found themselves driven, until they tumbled at last into the clear at the foot of the slope. A congress of three score or more—Nazarenes of both factions, as well as locals of the valley compounds—had formed up beneath torches in the beaten flat before the springhouse. Others swelled the throng, hastening up in twos and threes. Telamon and Ruth were shoved forward before Simon and Miriam.

In moments the Virgin materialized as well, reinforced by a chorus of her adherents.

The flat had become a ring of faces and bodies, penning the man-at-arms and the girl. The guardsman leader shoved both roughly forward.

Telamon spun and struck the fellow in the face.

Blows of staffs and cudgels rained upon the mercenary. He would not go down. Despite all that had immediately befallen them, child and man still held their weapons. The pair faced off against the mob that surrounded them.

At last the man-at-arms spoke.

"We have the letter of the Apostle! We have carried it for you from Jerusalem!"

Ruth pressed the scroll into Telamon's free hand. He held it out to the ring of Nazarenes.

The epistle was spurned by all.

"What is lacking?" Telamon cried. "Is this not what you have waited for? Is this letter not in fact the cause of all this night's bloodshed? We have lost three lives to bring it to you! Is this not what you seek?"

Telamon held the scroll out in offering.

Simon stepped forward, elevating a torch.

In the light could be seen clearly, despite the dirt and blood upon the mercenary's forearm, the military tattoo

LEGIO X

A murmur of fury swept through the mob.

Simon dashed the scroll from Telamon's grasp.

"How stupid do you think we are, Roman?"

"Kill him!" someone cried.

Ruth stared about. Half a hundred countenances devoid of pity ringed her and Telamon.

The mercenary yet clutched his gladius.

Yet all could see he stood at the limits of his strength.

"He's finished!" another shouted, gesturing to the youngbloods to attack. "Take him down!"

Before any could advance a step, the Virgin strode into the torchlight. Taking station before Telamon, she turned and confronted her compatriots.

"Will you crucify this one too?"

Cries of outrage greeted this. Men, and no few women, shouted the lady down.

"Get quit!"

"Step from the way!"

Simon of the Harbor strode up before the Virgin. His sister Miriam advanced beside him. The Christian leader indicated Telamon and the child.

"These are impostors sent by Rome," he declared for all. "As others who have played us for fools before." To Telamon he said, "Four families we have lost—wives and children as well—gulled by frauds like you. Let me tell you: These other actors were better than you. More convincing."

Miriam spoke. "How many more of our brothers and sisters must die, taken in by such treachery, before we stand up to these cowards?"

More shouts of "Kill them!" ascended.

Some intrepid soul dared speak in opposition. This voice cried that the prisoner before them had slain the Roman commander. And the girl struck that villain a blow in the face. "All have seen this!" the fellow shouted. "Can these be frauds, to perform such feats against Rome?"

"I saw nothing of the sort," responded Simon without hesitation, "but a staged spectacle, enacted with fake blood and sham theatrics, meant to play us for fools. We saw the Roman commander borne from the field to ovations from his men. Who among us will take an oath that Severus breathes no more? Not I, I tell you!"

The Christian pointed back down the road upon which the community had fled to this point.

"For all we know, Severus or others in his name ride now upon our heels, led to us by these pretenders!"

Guardsmen made a sudden rush. Blows of their eight-footers hammered Telamon to his knees. In moments the attackers had stripped him of his sword and Ruth of her dagger.

Miriam loomed over the man-at-arms. She clutched a stone the size of a brick.

"Who sent you? Answer me!"

Telamon glanced to Ruth. The child reached toward the scroll on the earth. Miriam swatted this back into the dirt.

"How close behind us are the Romans?"

"There are no Romans."

Miriam smashed Telamon full in the face.

Ruth sprang at the woman.

Telamon, despite the blow, held the child back.

"How close are they? Speak, you bloody betrayer!"

The Virgin caught at Miriam's arm. Others of her party cried out in indignation. The women grappled. Passionate words flew, in Greek and some fashion of harbor dialect.

The Virgin declared, in a voice so forceful it carried easily to the farthest reaches of the company, that Simon and Miriam's actions this night, and especially in this hour, had broken her heart.

"How can we . . . how can any of us stand before our Savior, having given blood for blood—and taken satisfaction in it?"

The young woman proclaimed of Simon and Miriam that the hatred they had shown this night, even toward these "spies"—she indicated Telamon and the child Ruth—had made her regret every word she had spoken and every act she had taken in the name of faith and love.

"Who are we, sisters and brothers? Look at us. What have we become?"

Someone in the throng shouted, "Then take the letter!"

The Virgin responded without hesitation: "I would not have the letter, even were it real, acquired in this fashion—by bloodshed and by the willful abrogation of every tenet of faith and aspiration to which we have sworn."

With her foot the Virgin flattened the epistle and ground it beneath her heel.

This act produced, for the moment, a stunned and unnerved silence.

"And what should we have done, Parthenos?" demanded Miriam. "Let ourselves be driven down beneath Roman steel like our brothers and sisters of Antioch and Cyrrhus and Epidaurus?"

"Yes!" responded the Virgin. "I would sooner that than betray the faith we have sworn to uphold and for which we have given everything."

Telamon reached to the letter.

Blows of cudgels and staffs propelled him back.

Guardsmen drew Miriam and the Virgin apart from the fracas.

"Kill him!" voices cried.

Telamon rose again, shielding Ruth with his body.

Guardsmen battered him to his knees. Others pinned his arms.

Simon came forward, gripping the man-at-arms' own gladius.

"Open his throat!" someone cried. "What are you waiting for?"

The Virgin cried out, seeking to stay this murder.

The lady saw Telamon's eyes find Ruth's.

Simon elevated the blade to plunge it into Telamon's neck.

A voice broke the silence.

It was neither Telamon's nor Simon's.

Nor that of Miriam or the Virgin.

It was Ruth.

It was the child.

"Paul, called to be an Apostle of Jesus Christ through the will of God, and Sosthenes our brother, unto the church of God which is at Corinth . . . "

Telamon's eyes turned toward the child. The man-at-arms, through the sheeting of blood that obscured his features, reacted with astonishment.

The sword in Simon's hand held for the moment.

" . . . to those sanctified in Christ Jesus and called to be saints . . . grace be unto you, and peace, from God our father and from the lord Jesus Christ . . . "

Every glance had swung now to the child.

A silence, consummate and complete, held the community.

Ruth continued to recite.

With each word and each line, it became more impossible to doubt that the verses she spoke were indeed the true composition of Paul the Apostle. This could be no fraud. The provenance of the text was too apparent.

The gathering had fallen utterly silent. Ruth's voice alone carried. The child's timbre had not by some wonder been transmuted into the voice of a grown woman. It remained the voice of a child, which somehow made its effect, reciting the stanzas of the Apostle, even more forceful and compelling.

The main freight of the letter, as the girl recited it, was a plea from the Apostle for unity within the community, for brotherhood and sisterhood in the face of external adversity and even murderous persecution.

Each word fell like the blow of a lash upon those who had given themselves over to terror and suspicion and anger.

Paul wrote, in the girl's recitation, that he knew the members of the fledgling church were under extraordinary duress. He implored them to be true to the spirit of hope and faith and love that had led them to hazard everything to follow the man they called their savior. For without such transcendent love, nothing else was possible, nor indeed could any other thought or action possess meaning.

"Though I speak with the tongues of men and of angels, and have not charity, I am become as sounding brass, or a tinkling cymbal. And though I have the gift of prophecy, and understand all mysteries, and all knowledge; and though I have all faith, so that I could remove mountains, and have not charity, I am nothing."

A man could be heard sobbing. Others of the community embraced their fellows and implored their pardon. The guardsmen who had seized Telamon now let him go.

Simon himself lowered the Roman sword in his hand. He restored it to Telamon.

"Charity suffereth long, and is kind; charity envieth not; charity vaunteth not itself, is not puffed up. Doth not behave itself unseemly, seeketh not her own, is not easily provoked, thinketh no evil . . .

Charity beareth all things, believeth all things, hopeth all things, endureth all things."

Ruth's words of the Apostle spoke directly to, and addressed specifically, the very conflicts and failings of faith that both factions of the community had so vividly displayed this evening.

All knew they had failed the Father.

All understood they had fallen short of the Son.

"Charity never faileth; but whether there be prophecies, they shall fail; whether there be tongues, they shall cease; whether there be knowledge, it shall vanish away. For we know in part, and we prophesy in part. But when that which is perfect is come, then that which is in part shall be done away."

Ruth stood now. When she spoke, her words came not in halting stammers, nor lacking in self-composure or self-belief, but with might and grace and power. Telamon's expression seemed to say, *How could this child, who clearly could have spoken at any time she wished, have held her tongue through all that she, and we, have endured?*

"When I was a child, I spake as a child, I understood as a child, I thought as a child; but when I became a man, I put away childish things."

Ruth's eyes met Telamon's in this moment, as his met hers.

"For now we see through a glass darkly; but then face to face; now I know in part; but then shall I know even as I am known. And now abideth faith, hope, and charity, these three; but the greatest of these is charity."

46

CROSSROADS

"Remain with us," Simon pleaded.

The leader beseeched Telamon and Ruth's exculpation, imploring them not to take flight into isolation and peril but to abide, here and always, with the company.

Miriam, taking station at Simon's shoulder, seconded this appeal.

"What you have done for this community," she declared, "is beyond our capacity to recompense. Further, the fact that you have performed this service not for the sake of those with whom you owned acquaintance, or who were dear to you, but instead for strangers, and at such grave personal peril . . . please," she said, "stay with us. None will be honored more highly or stand in greater esteem within our hearts."

The party stood now at the final crossroads.

"Will you remain, brother?" said Simon to Telamon.

The man-at-arms' expression answered for him.

He wished the company well, Telamon declared. It had been his privilege to be of service to those who had hazarded, and continued to hazard, so much for that which could be beheld and believed only with the eyes of the heart.

The Virgin came forward then. Taking Telamon's hands in both of hers, she appended her own plea for the mercenary to remain with the community. He silenced her, as he had the others, without speech.

The man-at-arms bent and took up his weapons and armor.

The Virgin turned now to Ruth.

"You, child. None has dared as you have, or acted with greater devotion. Surely you will stay with us. I myself will be mother to you, and sister and friend. You cannot be so foolhardy as to resume your life of the highway, apart from all society."

The girl made answer not in speech, only reached to the earth and lifted the man-at-arms' kit and carrying pole.

These she set upon her shoulders.

At this point, one of the company came forward and addressed the lady in white, privately but within hearing of the others. The man identified himself as one who had chanced to trek beside the child Ruth for most of the night fleeing the city. He informed the lady that the girl, to all who had encountered her, appeared to be a mute.

In fact, the fellow declared, the child had throughout the flight from Corinth communicated with the man-at-arms and her other companion entirely by sign and gesture. This was why, he suggested, the man-at-arms had appeared so taken aback when the child spoke aloud, reciting the Apostle's verses. He, the mercenary, had never heard speech from her lips before.

The Virgin turned to Telamon. "Is this true?"

The mercenary's glance toward Ruth confirmed this.

The lady remained silent for a long moment. Then, stepping forward to address Ruth within hearing of all the others, she touched the girl's shoulder to detain her for one final question.

"Since you spoke aloud earlier to recite the Apostle's verses, I have not heard you speak again. Can you speak now, child . . . or write? Will you?"

The Virgin, inquiring thus, glanced for her answer not to the girl but instead to the mercenary, who stood poised to move out upon the road beside her. The man-at-arms offered no reply, only turned in silent accession to Ruth.

"I can," said she to the Virgin. "And I will."

The girl turned and took her place at the man-at-arms' side.

The last that the lady, or the community entire, beheld of Telamon and Ruth was the pair striking off together with the first glimmers of dawn settling lightly upon their shoulders.

SPECIAL THANKS

To Shawn Coyne, who believed in this story from its earliest embryonic stages and who helped structure and shape it through numerous evolutions. To Sterling Lord, aka Lord of Publishing, who found a home for it with style and with dispatch. And to Star Lawrence, thanks for your immediate and passionate belief in this material and for steering and shielding it through its passage to publication and beyond.